Abou

CW00456074

David Kelzman was bo
three years serving in th
on a varied sales career :
petrol, to cosmetics and ladies' underwear.

Taking a mid-career break David went back-packing around France where he worked on a building site in Rouen, and wine harvests in Lyon and Dijon. A few years later itchy feet landed him in Australia where he lived and worked in Sydney. Returning home, he became a self-employed men's fashion agent marketing a selection of British and continental clothing to retailers in Northern England.

Business, holidays, and a love of travel have taken David all over the world, and the many amusing experiences on route influenced him to retire and concentrate on writing. He is married with one daughter, and now lives in Harrogate. This is his first full length novel.

When opportunity collides with ambition.
Where will it take you?

BLAST OFF

Run with the wolves

By David Kelzman

PUBLISHING RIGHTS

Cover design, Simon Cryer
www.northbankdesign.co.uk

Book formatting, Quantum Dot Press
quantumdotpress.com

This book is dedicated to my wife and daughter. For my daughter's endless patience and editing skill, and for my wife's forbearance whenever things went wrong.

Somewhere beyond right and wrong there is a garden.
I will meet you there.

Jalal and Din Rumi

(Persian philosophers 1207 - 1273)

PROLOGUE

Death In Naples

What stroke of madness persuaded me to show up here? Why was I taking the risk? Coming to Naples would not bring back the man they were burying, but I told myself it was the last token of respect I could offer a man who had given me so much.

They had garrotted him. It had taken his enemies over a year before they caught up with him and then the bastards garrotted him and dumped his body amongst rotting vegetables in a rat-infested yard. His life ended, tossed on one side like some useless piece of garbage. A man I admired. The man who had been my mentor.

I had trouble getting into the church. Two black suited guards barred my way and declared '*privato*'. But I didn't fly from England to allow a couple of stiffs to hustle me. I tensed hard and held my ground, and the black suit who gripped my arm discovered he might finish up at the bottom of the church steps unless he gave way. Intervention came just in time. I recognised the man who intervened from my past dealings with the London connection. I had taxied him to the Airport – the man who always wore a black Fedora to cover a scar which split his head in two. He waved the attendants to one side to allow me inside the church.

'Your presence isn't welcome,' he said. 'You will leave after the service.'

'I came out of respect,' I replied. 'What makes you think I want to stay?'

Inside an unearthly amber light beamed down from the church roof. I joined the procession of mourners as they slowly passed the open coffin each one stopping to make the sign of the cross before moving on. The sight was sickening. The man lying in the coffin was unrecognisable. One side of his face had been half eaten away by rats, and his nose was broken and completely flattened onto what was left of his face. No amount of work by the mortician could even start to repair the damage or remind me that the man lying here in the open casket was the man I once worked with.

I stumbled to a pew on the back row. Scented candles added a sickly odour to the damp chill. I shivered, and cold sweat ran down the back of my neck as I pressed both legs hard together to stop them from shaking. Nothing could have prepared me for the shock of seeing the broken body.

Mourners dressed in a sea of black half-filled the rows of seats in front of me, and I watched as one by one local leaders claimed their reserved places at the very front of the church. Little hawk faced men protected by their tight suited minders. The big-timers who made sure they commanded attention, and everyone was aware of it. Overweight and over confident – flashing gold teeth, gold rings and gold watches. Smiles, hugs, handshakes, and waves across the aisles as they acknowledged each other's presence. Brothers in crime who would stick their knives in each other the moment things went wrong, and things had gone wrong, and they were burying the fall guy who had been singled out to take the blame.

The police called him a gangster. He wasn't a gangster. He was caught between international consortiums profiting from criminality which blew up in their faces.

I couldn't avoid being involved. From the day he disappeared the police and everyone else believed I knew where to find him. I knew nothing – but if I had known I would have protected him in spite of their threats.

The service began and the heavy music washed over me. To me he was one of the straightest men I ever had the pleasure of dealing with. He gave me my first chance.

'Do you always want to walk in someone else's shadow?' he had asked. I took that chance and made a success of it, and I had travelled a long way since.

I sat alone on the back pew recalling the places where we worked together. The glamour, the excitement, the heat of the sun, the threats of violence – a different life.

My eyes closed, and I let the service and church music transport me to another place. Into the past where it all began. Roger Kelly, a man without a job whose wife had left him.

I bowed my head and remembered.

PART ONE

1. Roger's Win

On Tuesday Roger pranged the car, on Thursday he was made redundant, and on Friday his wife left him taking with her half the furniture and the dog. There was just a note 'Roger – I am leaving you. Our marriage isn't going anywhere. Please don't try to contact me. Your dinner is in the fridge. Rosemary.'

Redundancy from Town Planning did not come as a surprise. Roger didn't like the work, and he didn't like being moved sideways, so he politely told the head of planning where to 'stick the job'. But nothing about his marriage had forewarned him that he would come home and find Rosemary gone, and his house a vacated war zone. Roger was devastated. He rang Rosemary's mobile time and time again. He phoned her mother who didn't answer. He then tried his brother-in-law who couldn't help, and his wife's best friend said she hadn't heard from Rosemary in weeks. Finally, Roger accepted defeat. He re-read his wife's note, poured himself a large whisky, and sat down on the only remaining chair with his mind in turmoil.

He didn't eat, he didn't sleep, all night he sat thinking, and turning events over in his mind. Jobless, wifeless, and dog-less, he could not fathom out what he had done wrong to deserve this. By the early hours of the morning there was very little left in the whisky bottle, and Roger drifted off into a troubled sleep. He awoke late to the sound of hammering on the front door. Amazon delivering a parcel (which he hadn't ordered) containing a new dog basket for Scott. Ten minutes later Royal Mail arrived with a letter requiring a signature advising him that his mortgage payments, usually paid by Rosemary, were now three months in arrears.

What next? He made himself a strong coffee and emptied the remains of the whisky bottle into it. This could not be happening to him. He knew his wife wasn't pleased with him after he had clonked that poser Paul at Sally Walker's party – but so what, it had been peacefully resolved in the end. If she had been Howard's wife who caught her husband locked in the toilet with Sally's sister, then she might have had something to make a fuss about. What else could have upset her? Finances were stretched, and Roger's approach to money caused disagreements. Still, that couldn't be a reason for walking out on him, could it?

He binned Rosemary's frozen goodbye dinner, picked up the phone and dialled Rosemary's mother again. This time he caught her at home. Roger usually disappeared to the gym whenever his mother-in-law came to visit. She was a long-suffering horse faced woman – a widow, bravely bearing her adversity and telling her troubles to anyone who would listen.

Yes, she was aware that Rosemary had left him. No, she had no idea why. No, she would not tell him where to contact her, but if Roger would bring the dog basket over, she would give it to Rosemary when she saw her.

'To hell with that,' said Roger. 'If she wants the dog basket she can come and get it.'

'You really are an unpleasant man,' said his mother-in-law. 'You were never my favourite – I shan't miss you.'

'Ditto,' said Roger, 'nor your nasty lunches,' and he put the phone down. That was that. He hadn't expected much help.

It was Roger's football day on a Saturday but today football was the last thing on his mind. He was about to call the club and cancel when Bob, the club captain, beat him to it.

'Roger, it's me,' said Bob. 'Listen, I hate to be the one to tell you this, but you are going to find out anyway. Rosemary has moved in with Jack Fearnley, and I thought you might be a bit embarrassed if you came down to the club today.'

'Jack Fearnley, the manager?' said Roger. 'That's incredible. When did this begin?'

'It's been going on for some time,' said Bob. 'But you know how it is – nobody wants to be the whistle blower.'

So that was the answer. Roger just couldn't believe it. Jack Fearnley, an arrogant little man, loud and full of bullshit. He was twice divorced, always short of money, and at least ten years older than Rosemary – not to mention three inches shorter. So why would she want to leave Roger for him?

Roger's first reaction was to jump in the car and go and knock the stuffing out of Jack Fearnley. However, that was a non-starter since the car was in the garage being repaired, and it was a long walk down to the football club. He had second thoughts. Rosemary must have blown a fuse. They had been married for seven years. She loved their new house. To walk out on him for Jack Fearnley just did not make sense. And then he remembered Jack and Rosemary sitting together on the pavilion steps whenever she came to watch Roger play. Jack, flashing his white teeth, and Rosemary full of charm and tinkling with laughter at Jack's crap jokes. She was always a bit weird afterwards on our way home thought Roger. I have been a fool for not cottoning on. She has made a real idiot out of me, and all my pals in the football team know about it.

Stunned, hurt, and miserable, it took some time before he could pull himself together. But Roger was not a man to be beaten. Something had gone wrong with their marriage, but he could not figure out what. It had been a disastrous week. If the car brakes hadn't failed, he would not have wrapped the car around a lamp post, and if the head of Town Planning had not been such a clever bugger Roger might still have a job. And how had Rosemary found time to have an affair with Jack Fearnley? And for her to walk out without even discussing it with him. Well, this wasn't the end of it. He would show the lot of them. First, he needed a plan of action and against his better judgement he phoned his father.

This was going to be tricky. His father provided them with the deposit on their house, besides which both parents liked Rosemary, and considered her a steadying influence on Roger.

'Now then, what's wrong?' asked his father. 'We

don't often hear from you on Saturday morning.'

'Dad, sorry to ask but I could do with a bit of help. I've lost my job. Planning wanted to transfer me to a scruffy little office on the other side of town and work there on Saturday mornings. Unfortunately, I got a bit shirty about it with old rumble-tummy, and he found an excuse to get rid of me.'

'Of course, that would mean you couldn't play football on a Saturday,' replied his father. 'And football is far more important than keeping the job which you passed all those exams for. So, what does Rosemary say?'

'That's something else. Rosemary has left me along with half the furniture, and we are at least three months behind on our mortgage payments.'

'Say no more,' said his father. 'You and I will talk later. I am going to pass you over to your mother.' There was a lull before his mother came on the phone.

'Your father has told me everything and he is not pleased with you Roger. I think I had better come over tomorrow and help sort things out.'

'No mother, please no!' said Roger. 'It's very kind of you, and I would love to see you, but no!'

'I will only stay one night, and we can have a good talk about everything, and I will sleep on your sofa.'

'What sofa?' said Roger. There was a silence.

'Well, don't go seeking out Rosemary and doing anything silly. Your father and I will talk with you tomorrow.'

When the telephone call ended Roger trailed around the house taking stock. He still had a fridge, a cooker, and a washing machine in the kitchen. His spare room-office was intact, as was their master bedroom. However, the guest bedroom and the lounge had been stripped clean of almost everything except one chair and their old television. He went shopping for food, and then spent the afternoon making a few financial calculations. He had to find a way of managing until he found another job, and he had to find a way of managing without Rosemary's teaching salary. Unfortunately, figures did not add up. He could not rely on much redundancy, and as for money in the holiday savings account, he had to admit that his outing in Dublin celebrating Malcolm's stag weekend had been a disastrous over-spend. But was that a reason for his wife to leave him and take off with somebody else?

Tired and dejected he consumed a Tandoori take-away, watched match of the day, and retired early to bed. During the night he had disturbing dreams of playing club goalkeeper whilst a scantily dressed Rosemary scored goals against him, watched and applauded by her mother and Jack Fearnley.

Next day dawned with April sunshine beaming through the bedroom window. Roger was determined to be positive. Moping around was not going to bring Rosemary back, he told himself. After paying bathroom homage to last night's curry, he performed 50 press ups in the bedroom, followed by ten minutes of shadow boxing in front of the hall mirror. He washed and shaved, doused himself with Armani cologne and carefully considered his attributes. At 27 years old he was at his peak: 5 feet 11 inches with a fine head of hair. Good teeth and a well-trained torso. What he lacked in experience he made up for in athleticism, and after all he was only 20 years old when they got married. Rosemary called him 'the fastest gun in the west.' Well, she hadn't been much help in their martial bed either.

With these thoughts running through his mind Roger made breakfast which was not a success; he burned the toast, nearly set the frying pan on fire, and splattered his clean shirt and trousers with fat. Into the washing machine went the splattered shirt and trousers, and then of course he realized – he had absolutely no idea how to use the washing machine. To hell with everything, he wasn't hungry. He got changed, left the mess, and set off on his usual Sunday morning walk to buy a paper.

It was a fifteen-minute walk to the village store, and he immediately missed the company of Scott straining at the leash beside him. Scott was a lively cocker spaniel which Rosemary had acquired a year ago when she took time off teaching. He and Scott were good pals, but the dog could be snappy at times if he didn't get plenty of walks. With a bit of luck, he will be snappy with Jack and do his stuff on Jack's carpet thought Roger and felt cheered by the idea.

Zorba's Store was run by Alex and his son George. They were open all hours and seemed to stock everything from newspapers to floor polish. Alex also ran a wholesale business importing his own cheap wines from Cyprus, and there was friendly price competition between his shop and the Chained Bull opposite.

When Roger arrived, the shop was busy and space in front of the shop counter was monopolised by the monstrous rear end of a sloppy looking woman in love with her mobile phone. The woman was oblivious to everyone around her, including her noisy son who was seated on his scooter and getting in everybody's way. Roger usually scanned the headlines before buying a paper but today he gave way to a big mean looking man with a cheesy pock marked face. Roger bought The Sunday Mail, and tripped over the boy's scooter.

The woman looked up from her phone 'Billy, will yer shut up and cum 'ere now?'

'No! No!' screamed Billy, and rode the scooter over Roger's toes, out through the door, over the pavement, and into the middle of the busy road. Roger moved out like a flash, and with one swoop lifted the boy and his scooter back safely onto the pavement and was rewarded with a smack in the eye from screaming Billy.

Little Billy's mother hurried out 'Help! Help!' she shrieked 'That man is trying to snatch my child.' The big mean cheese faced man appeared at the door,

'You fucking pervert!' he said, stepped out and swung a whopping right catching Roger full on the jaw and sending him spinning to the pavement.

Roger vaguely remembered being half carried across the road to The Chained Bull where he was spark out for nearly 30 minutes. When he began to recover, he found himself propped up on a settee looking at the magnificent breasts of Betty the landlady as she bent over coaxing him to sip from a glass of brandy. Betty's bosom displayed in low cut dresses was one of the main attractions at The Chained Bull. Roger's jaw ached, his head was splitting, and he felt sorry for himself, yet surprisingly enough, he found himself quite enjoying the sensation of Betty's nipple in his ear.

'My poor boy,' murmured Betty. She tenderly bathed his face and then plied him with a creamy coffee. She had always fancied Roger ever since he called into the pub for a pint dressed in his football shorts. She planted a kiss on his cheek making sure he got a full view of her famous breasts. 'You never know – there was always going to be another time.'

Alex came over from the shop.

'Sorry we missed ze bugger Roger. By the time I got hold of George zat big nasty bastard who hit you was down ze road with ze fat cow and her noisy kid.'

'Not your fault,' Roger assured him 'Just thank George for bringing me over here. I have been well looked after.'

'Safe in ze bosom of ze bull – yes?' and Alex leered at Betty who mentally noted Alex's name on her score card of future possibilities.

The pub was getting busy, and Roger started to rally. Alex's son George came over to give Roger a lift home, so he thanked Betty (who delivered another lingering kiss on his cheek) and as they left, she whispered in his ear 'It's my night off on a Thursday.'

Still mussy, and bemused by the offer, Roger wobbled unsteadily to George's car. They regularly trained together at the gym and George was a pal he could rely on. En route home he opened up and shared his woes with George who had a rather macho point of view on such matters.

'It's got to get better,' assured George. 'Relax and get your feet up; tomorrow will look a whole lot different to today. And after all, a woman is a woman, and we chaps can manage without them – although I wouldn't mind a crack at Betty,' he added.

'Well managing without a women won't happen today,' replied Roger. Parked outside his house was his mother's car with his mother in it. She got out of the car and viewed his face with horror. Roger had a sinking feeling that the rest of the day wouldn't get easier and the thoughts of a post-mortem on his marriage, and a description of the morning's events, filled him with dread.

But no man is an island, and we all need some help at times. His mother's visit turned out to be a blessing. She patched Roger up, she washed his splattered cast offs, and showed him how to use the washing machine. She cooked a roast chicken lunch, and they talked and talked all afternoon and well into the early hours of the evening. There is nobody who can quite compare with one's mother in times of trouble. His mother had brought a fold-up camp bed with her so where to sleep was not a problem. When they retired for the night, they both had the satisfaction of knowing that temporary solutions had been found for some of Roger's problems, and he was able to climb into his bed wounded but resolute, and ready to fight another day.

He awoke well rested – a good start to a Monday morning he thought. By lunchtime his mother had tidied the whole house, packed her case, and was just about ready to leave when the door-bell rang.

'There's a couple come to see you,' she said

dubiously. At the door was yesterday's assailant – big mean looking 'cheese face' dressed immaculately in a dark pin stripe suit, standing hand in hand with Billy's mother who was wearing a spotted red dress guaranteed to stop the traffic, with bright red lipstick and rouged cheeks to match.

'I got yer address from Zorba's,' she said. 'Me and Cyril have come here to say how sorry we are, and we want to thank yer for keeping our Billy safe. Also, we will always be grateful to you,' and she smiled up adoringly at big mean looking Cyril.

'If it wasn't for you Cyril and me would never have met, would we Cyril?'

'Sorry governor. I hope there's no hard feelings,' said Cyril giving Roger's hand a bone crushing shake. 'No need for the rozzers to hear about this is there? Here, I've brought you something to make amends,' and he presented Roger with a bottle wrapped in newspaper, plus a small black box which when opened revealed a golden amulet shaped like a pair of boxing gloves.

'A good luck token,' grinned Cyril (he was missing two front teeth). 'Wear it and it will remind you to duck next time,' and with a roar of laughter he slapped a dumbfounded Roger on the back.

'Thank you for being so understanding,' said Billy's mother. 'We must go now. Cyril is taking me out for lunch,' and with a happy smile, and a wink from Cyril they turned and departed. Roger watched them go in staggered silence.

'Very touching!' said Roger as he fingered his aching jaw. 'Perhaps I should start a dating agency.'

15

'You are going through a rough patch. After all this upset why not give your aunt a ring, and see if you can borrow her flat for a week?'

Good idea, thought Roger. I'll take Betty.

He loaded his mother's case and camp bed into her car. She had over an hour's drive back to Leeds and he wanted to make sure she got home before the heavy traffic.

'And cut the grass darling. If you decide to sell the house, it's better to have a tidy garden.'

He watched his mother's car until it disappeared out of sight. Sell the house? Where was he supposed to go if he sold the house? Perhaps Jack and Rosemary could put him up and he could re-acquaint himself with his own furniture. Alternatively, he could see if there was room for him at The Chained Bull. Would old man Murgatroyd even notice his presence? The thought amused him.

Suddenly Roger felt better. A kind of euphoria ran through him. He had no idea why he felt good, but he went back into the house light on his feet and cheerful with the hunch that he was starting a new life. After catching up with a few jobs he made himself a sandwich and removed the Sunday Mirror wrapped around Cyril's gift bottle of grog. Surprise, surprise – it was a first class Valpolicella. Roger found a bottle opener, opened it, and poured himself a large glass whilst examining Cyril's good luck charm. Brass he thought – and big Cyril hasn't brought me much luck so far.

Upstairs the window was still open after his mother's clean up, and a breeze had scattered papers all over the floor. Roger carefully gathered together his prized drawings and planning projects, and placed them on the desk with Cyril's good luck charm plonked on top. Swinging on a bulldog clip Roger spotted his weekly lotto entry. He managed a syndicate shared with three school pals, and although winners were contacted automatically, Roger liked to check. He smiled, rubbed the amulet, opened his laptop, and found Saturday's Lotto results. Line after line – not a chance. Hardly more than half a dozen draws in total. Then on the very last line the hair stood up on the back of his neck. Five draws plus a bonus point. He checked again. Yes, on the last entry, definitely five draws and a bonus point, and no mistake. They had won one million pounds between them. £250,000 each.

He poured himself another glass of Cyril's wine and sat on the office chair dazed by the possibilities. His financial problems solved, and an opportunity to fulfil some of his dreams and ambitions.

What a laugh! If Rosemary had chosen to leave him then she couldn't have picked a better time. To hell with her.

2. Blast Off

One cannot describe the feeling of exultation when good fortune follows bad luck. On Tuesday morning Roger awoke riding high on a cloud. He exceeded his 50 morning press ups, and almost knocked a hole through the mirror shadow boxing. He was going to make it a good day.

He contacted National Lottery for his claim to be processed, and checked all was in order before phoning the syndicate. Howard, Mick and Malcolm. All pals from school who had kept in touch. Winning the lottery would blow their minds.

Howard and Mick were both ecstatic. For forty minutes the telephone line sizzled with their respective plans of what they would do with the money. Malcolm was more reticent. He checked lottery results every weekend and knew they had won. He worked with his father at their opticians in Salford, and to his family's delight had just married an 'all Jewish girl'. Roger reckoned that Malcolm's father and new wife would relieve him of the worry of how to dispense his winnings.

Roger's claim had to be verified before the lottery money was paid into his account. Nevertheless, he thought he would start the ball rolling with his credit card. He caught a bus into Manchester and visited Nationwide where he settled arrears on his mortgage. At the same time, he wrote out a forward dated cheque covering repayments for the next 12 months. That sorted Roger treated himself to an excellent lobster lunch at Great John Street Bar, and then popped in to see Barney Hoffman.

Barney was a lovely man who should have retired years ago, but he was 'old school' and loved his jewellery business. He never forgot a face, and remembered Roger – without the swollen jaw and black eye. He adjusted his glasses and made a pointed inspection of the offending eye. Roger placed big Cyril's amulet on the counter.

'Mr Hoffman, this is brass, isn't it?' he asked. Barney was getting short sighted and he took the amulet to the window.

'Hmm – interesting. Where did you get it?'

'It was just a little something that hit me in the eye,' said Roger. 'Is it worth anything?'

'Yes, young man it certainly is worth something. You are in luck because it could be worth more than your black eye. You are looking at a beautifully fashioned piece of 18 carat gold and by chance I've got a gold chain to match it perfectly,' and Barney fumbled under the counter and laid a scored chain alongside the amulet.

'Done!' said Roger producing his credit card, and he walked out wearing big Cyril's good luck charm around his neck. His new identity.

£250,000 is a considerable sum. Before going overboard Roger wanted to put his parents in the picture. He arrived home and waited until 7pm before phoning. His father answered and didn't sound at all pleased to hear from him. The trouble was his father had no sense of humour. Nevertheless, his parents got along well together and were a happily married couple. Roger often thought that they were even more happily married when the bank moved his father to Leeds, and they left Roger behind to study at Manchester Technical college. Unfortunately, his results at Manchester Tech hadn't exactly pleased his father either. He knew his father's advice would be to safely invest the whole £250,000 but Roger had pre-decided (with a struggle) that £100,000 was enough to invest. The rest was 'marching money'.

'Dad good news! I paid off the mortgage arrears and I won't be needing that loan.'

'How did you manage that?' asked his father suspiciously.

'Somebody made me an offer I couldn't refuse.'

'And who was that?'

'Betty from The Chained Bull,' and Roger collapsed laughing.

'Not funny,' said his father, but congratulated him when he heard of the win and as anticipated recommended Roger be sensible and safely invest it all.

His mother was thrilled for Roger but offered him her usual cautionary advice.

His father's parting shot was 'Don't let this win spoil your career son.'

What career? Roger asked himself. The lottery win added up to more than 8 years pay working for Town Planning.

Completing an architect's course had been a bit too exacting for Roger. Much to the disapproval of his father he had jumped ship in favour of easier exams leading to draughtsman. Sitting at his office desk Roger reminded himself of his own work. Plans portraying castles and grandiose country mansions. A sketch of a cathedral with spires towering above the whitewashed city of Ostuni. Another picture depicted a quaint old Norman church in a dusty tree lined square (it had to be France), and a brilliant interpretation of his own dream property – a Spanish style hacienda built on a cliff top with its wide veranda overlooking the sparkling waters of the Mediterranean. This was the kind of undertaking he enjoyed getting his teeth into. Not the tedious work he had been compelled to do in a stuffy planning office.

A loud hoot diverted Roger's attention to the window. Mick's white van had parked on a double yellow line outside. Mad Mick – the man with the van. Mick stood at the door armed with a pack of San Miguel and came into the kitchen giving Roger a big bear hug. Mick was 6 feet 2 inches tall, with a big smile and black crinkly hair. He hadn't a care in the world and didn't treat anything seriously.

'Hey mate – just bumped into Bob. Sorry to hear about your split with Rosemary.'

'I didn't mention it this morning,' said Roger. 'Why spoil things? It's my problem.'

'Well mate I know how upset you are, but you will get over it. The good news is that you are a free man again. I've had a word with Howard and Friday is big celebration night. We can all get sloshed, and you are now rich enough to pull the best talent in Manchester.'

In their school days Mick, Roger and Howard were a formidable trio; Mick and Roger were experts at getting into trouble, while Howard was an expert at getting out of it. Mick poured a couple of beers whilst Roger related the dire events that had befallen him over the previous week. Mick was the champion organizer of Friday nights out. Unfortunately, whenever he organized anything, you could bet it would end with trouble, leading to some sort of female entanglement. A good example being Malcolm's stag weekend in Dublin.

'I don't think Malcolm will be joining us on Friday.'

'No, I don't think he will,' and they both laughed.

'And do you think Joan will allow Howard to come?' They both laughed again.

Mick looked at his watch. 'Time for me to depart. Tonight, I will be in the arms of the law. I've got a date with a sexy policewoman who gave me a parking ticket yesterday.'

Mick drove off. There was a crack of thunder, followed by a deluge of rain. Roger picked up the Sunday Mail (as yet unopened) and browsed through temperatures in Europe. Portugal and Rhodes both looked pretty good, and the South of France was unusually warm for early April. Inevitably his mind strayed towards his aunt's apartment in Nice – a regular family holiday destination. He last visited Nice with his parents when he was 15 years old. His father drove down in the car and from what he remembered Nice was the ideal centre for making excursions to numerous charming little towns and villages. Food for thought. He would sleep on it.

But sleep didn't come easily. He tossed and turned all night with the events of the past few days unrolling in dream after dream. A woman looking a lot like Rosemary (but wearing black stockings and black suspenders) constantly appeared in his dream, luring him towards her and then evaporating as he reached out for her. He awoke drenched in sweat with a rock-hard erection. What a shitty night – ridiculous!

Roger got up, had a hot shower, and sprayed his male parts with ice cold water. He had breakfast and sat on the only chair in the empty lounge contemplating his next move. Top of the list had to be a holiday. He googled temperatures in Nice. 72 degrees Fahrenheit expected by mid-day. Decision made. He picked up the phone and rang Aunt Evelyn.

Aunt Evelyn was his father's elder sister. She had married an army major and accompanied him worldwide on various overseas postings. Widowhood had not deterred her from further travel, and his aunt never stayed home in England for long.

'Roger dear boy, you have just caught me in time. Next week I am going to Melbourne. Drop in about five tomorrow and have some tea with me. I haven't been to the apartment for ages so stay there as long as you want. It saves me a trip because I need to make sure that *Monsieur le caretaker* is keeping the place in good nick.'

'See you tomorrow at five,' replied Roger. 'I'll bring a little bottle of something.'

Back to the laptop, and within minutes Roger had booked a Saturday morning flight to Nice giving himself a week to deal with outstanding arrangements before he went.

It was two years since he and Rosemary had taken a holiday. Buying the house had decimated spare funds. Why not make it a real holiday and travel around France for a month using Nice as his base. More food for thought.

He needed new clothes. His wardrobe was getting depleted and whatever his past extravagances new clothes wasn't one of them. Time for a shopping trip.

A call to the garage confirmed that the car was still under repair, so Roger caught the bus into Salford and called to see Malcolm. Malcolm was hidden behind a screen conducting an eye test, but he found time to give Roger a hug and a handshake and introduce his father who promptly swung into a sales pitch and sold Roger a pair of designer sun glasses, plus a spare pair in case he lost the first.

Across the road was Maximillion Menswear owned by Malcolm's uncle. Roger knew Max through frequently bumping into him and Malcolm at Manchester City Football grounds. Thanks to their Saturday meetings Malcolm and Roger became friends and before getting involved with his new wife, Malcolm regularly joined the trio on their Friday night escapades. Maximillion's was normally too expensive for Roger, but Howard shopped there regularly. Max stocked the best brands of clothing together with his own stock of worldly wisdom, and listening to these little gems of enlightenment was all part of the shopping scene when you visited Maximillion's.

Today Max was out and his daughter Claire was in charge. "Crutch crusher Claire," Howard called her. She was a tall, thin girl with hair piled so high that it added at least six inches to her height. Her personality was way over the top, and she dominated customers the moment they stepped through the door. But when it came to style and colour, Claire had absolutely brilliant taste and most of the shop's clients relied on her to help them choose anything special. Today was big welcome day – she knows something, concluded Roger.

'Roger – how a-a-a-are you? You have come to see

me so I can make you a star?'

'If you can turn me into a star, I will make you my co-star,' replied Roger, 'and we will be going to Nice,' he added.

'Light weights,' she said. 'Something light-weight and chic for the South of France. And I can just picture you in one of our new exclusive jackets.'

Roger bought two buggy lined semi plain Boss jackets – a stone colour and a silver-grey shadow check, which Claire then teamed up with a dark navy short sleeve shirt, and a multi coloured print.

'Trousers,' asked Claire. '34 waist and I think 34 inside leg – let's check.'

God – if she pushes up much harder, I shall swallow my balls thought Roger.

'Claire, I've already had the snip, you aren't sending me to Nice a eunuch, are you?'

'Sorry darling. We have to be accurate you know,' and Claire rolled up her tape measure and picked out a pair of chinos and a couple of pairs of jeans trousers which would be perfect when worn with either the jackets or shirts.

Roger added two pairs of shorts, some T shirts, a zippy travel jacket with lots of pockets, a pair of loafers and a pair of sandals. He was about to close the books when he noticed a Pal Zileri suit on display – a magnificent midnight blue which had to be just his colour. Roger tried the suit on, and it fitted perfectly. He added a pale blue shirt and a sparkling white shirt for good measure plus two matching silk ties. If he attended a job interview wearing the suit and a suntan, he would knock his interviewer's silly.

Claire's eyes had turned into cash registers, and she was about to suggest something else when Max walked in through the door. He eyed the array of garments on the table and said to Claire 'Parcel it all up and knock 10% off the total,' and putting his arm round Roger's shoulder steered him into the back room for a coffee.

'Listen,' he said, 'I am going to tell you something. You boys have had a bit of luck. So that's good – we all need a bit of luck. But as I said to Malcolm – money is like a woman, if you don't look after it you lose it. And you boys have got to wake up to yourselves. These nights out get you into trouble, and as I said to Malcolm – you can't do it. You are a married man now. You've got responsibilities.'

Roger listened and couldn't argue with the logic. He wondered how much of Max's advice was directed towards him because Malcolm was always the serious one who never put a foot wrong, and he had to admit that their disastrous stag night in Dublin had gone off the rails largely thanks to himself and Mick. Still – it was always worth listening to Max, especially when he got into full swing relating his pearls of wisdom.

They finished their coffee and Claire had parcelled everything neatly on the table, together with the bill, which even with the discount totalled £2,100. Max accepted a forward dated cheque.

'Money will be in the bank by the weekend,' said Roger. 'This little lot should last me until Autumn. If funds run out Claire has a job lined up for me with her favourite rapper group.'

Max ordered a taxi and Roger piled in with his purchases and said his goodbyes. Sitting in the back of the taxi heading for home Max's little lecture got him thinking. What sort of responsibilities did he have now Rosemary had made him into a single man?

As the taxi drew into the village Roger redirected the driver to Zorba's. He topped up his alcohol stocks with 6 packs of San Miguel, 4 bottles of Chablis, 4 bottles of Merlot, and 4 bottles of Dom Perignon Champagne, which were ice cold straight out of the cooler.

'Obviously things have improved since Sunday,' said George, raising an eyebrow as he helped Roger carry the bottles to the taxi. 'Invite me to the party.'

When the taxi arrived at his house Roger made several trips transferring his acquisitions into the house and onto the empty lounge floor. His mobile rang as he settled up with the taxi driver.

'Where are you? Joan and I are two minutes away,' said Howard.

'Pop in,' said Roger 'I have just got back.'

Within minutes Howard's Volkswagen drew up onto the drive. Howard had no idea what he wanted to do when he left school. He started work in a sports shop and now ran a chain of shops selling sports equipment. He seemed to be home more than he was at work. A typical Howard cushy number.

Joan greeted Roger with a hug and a kiss. Roger liked Joan. She was good fun, and easy to get along with. She was also close friends with Rosemary, and you could be sure that she would be well aware of exactly why his wife had walked out on him last Friday, but he was equally sure that Joan would keep that information to herself.

Howard breezed in looking perky. 'So, are you starting a menswear shop or an off licence?' he asked looking at the display on the lounge floor.

'Could be either. I'm relying on you two to supply me with a sense of direction.'

'Well, you won't find a sense of direction on your boys' nights out, and you won't find it in the gym either,' said Joan, giving him a dig in the stomach.

'Ignore that,' interrupted Howard. 'We bring glad tidings – I am going to be a daddy.'

'Well congratulations. This calls for dual celebrations. If it's a boy, will you call him Roger?'

'Not if I have anything to do with it,' said Joan. 'And we won't be calling him Howard either.'

'Cheers,' replied Roger and opened a bottle of the Perignon Champagne.

Howard and his wife were going house hunting. Both were in high spirits, but as they enjoyed their champagne Roger sensed a change in his friend. He was a bit subdued and trying not to show it.

Eventually, looking sheepish he said, 'I hope it's OK with you but we have changed plans for Friday night. I am bringing Joan, and Malcolm is bringing Ruth, so I thought I would book a meal somewhere special where we can all celebrate together.'

'You mean a change from Mick's celebration shindig?'

'Exactly,' said Joan. 'So why don't you give Rosemary a ring and ask her to join us. You are not going to give up on her, are you?'

Roger didn't answer. But it flashed through his mind that although he was distressed by his wife's unexpected walk-out he did not want to turn the clock back. So much had happened during the past six days that Rosemary's departure already felt like six months ago.

'Right,' said Howard. 'We are off to look at our dream house. See you on Friday.'

Roger cleared the lounge floor of drinks and refilled his fridge. He performed a thirty-minute fashion parade in the hallway and satisfied with his purchases he carefully stowed them away in his wife's spacious wardrobe. He phoned George who gave him a lift to the gym. They had a good training session followed by a pasta at the local Italian. After a few beers Roger concluded that this single life wasn't going to be bad at all and he retired happy with that thought.

A car had to be next on Roger's shopping list. He had shared Rosemary's old Toyota for long enough and when it was repaired, she could keep it. There was a multitude of garages and car dealers situated on the ring road and the local bus landed Roger right in the middle of them.

Unsold cars, new and second hand, were parked in rows stretching as far as the eye could see. Uncertainty over Brexit, and media hype about electric, had killed standard trade stone dead. Roger wasn't a car man and he soon realized he had too much choice. He toured the garages for over an hour. He looked at Fords, Audi, BMW, Mercedes. Too many cars that looked too much alike, and he was uninspired.

The car salesmen didn't inspire him either. Obviously

used to better times most of them sat in their showrooms crouched over laptops and didn't appear to have the energy to get off their bottoms. After asking two BMW salesmen if they were cripples, Roger found himself on Brown's forecourt, a small struggling family business squashed between two of its more flamboyant rivals.

Rumour had it that Brown junior had decimated the garage profits and run off with his uncle's much younger wife. Whatever the truth behind the story, Brown's Garage appeared to have a lot of cars to sell, and too few staff to sell them. Mr Brown senior stood alone, listlessly wiping a watery eye, and seemingly holding the fort with the task of dealing with all potential customers.

A flash of white caught Roger's attention. Tucked away behind a row of four by fours was a sight that lifted his spirits. A car that was different, and captured his imagination. The Alfa Romeo Convertible shone sparkling white enhanced by its black convertible top. The sales placard inside read 'Registered 2016. Automatic. One owner. 26,000 miles. £29,000.' Roger knew very little about cars, and nothing about Alfa Romeos, but he walked around the car thrilled by everything he saw – the colour, the style and the name badge.

A loud sniff at Roger's shoulder told him Mr Brown senior had joined him.

'That's a Spider,' he said sadly. 'It's a lovely car. The man who owned it died very young. His number plate alone must be worth at least another £1,000.'

Roger looked at the number plate. L27 ROG and that clinched it. This car had to be fate. His age and his initials.

'Can I take the car out on a road test?'

'Well, I can't leave the garage,' said Mr Brown drearily 'but my assistant will accompany you if I can find her.'

Ten minutes later, a highly colourful figure burst into the showroom and introduced herself.

'I'm Ana,' she said with a shake of her green streaked hair. 'Let's go!'

She skilfully manoeuvred the Alfa Romeo out onto the forecourt and beckoned Roger into the driver's seat. Within five minutes Roger was master of the controls, and within another ten minutes he was speeding smoothly along the motorway and knew he loved the car and must buy it. He didn't talk but concentrated on driving the car hard, and after half an hour of putting the car through its paces they were back in Brown's Garage.

Ana was all business. She took off her jacket, sat him down at a table, and produced a wad of papers to sign. Roger had been so involved driving the car that he hadn't taken much notice of her until he suddenly realized she was extremely attractive in an offbeat way. The first thing he noticed was that minus the jacket her sleeveless blouse displayed a magnificent pair of shoulders with a large tattoo on her left shoulder. There were rings on nearly every finger, double earrings in one ear, and a small ring through the side of her nose. Sitting across the table she half smiled and said nothing, but Roger knew that she knew exactly what he was thinking.

Papers signed, bank transfer arrangements made, the car would be ready for collection on Monday. Because part exchange was not in the deal the garage authorized a

£1,500 discount plus free servicing for one year. Roger was cocker-hoop but tried not to show it. He looked at his watch and remembered that he was due for tea with Aunt Evelyn at 5.00.

'Can I give you a lift home?' asked Ana. 'I am going your way to meet a client.'

She used her satnav to find his house, driving very fast, and breaking all the speed limits on route.

'May I use your loo?' she asked, as they arrived at his door.

'Be my guest,' said Roger pointing down the hall. 'Last door on the right.'

'Have you just moved in?' she asked as she passed the empty lounge.

'No – but I needed to sell the furniture to pay for the car.'

On the telephone stand his answer-phone light was blinking.

'Hi Roger. Sorry but no piss up on Friday night. Malcolm and Howard are bringing their wives. Since I don't fancy playing gooseberry, my sexy police lady will be coming with me. Hope that doesn't leave you stranded.'

It blooming well does leave me stranded thought Roger. It means I'm going be the gooseberry. The loo door opened and Ana appeared and stood completely still, looking him in the eye without saying a word. Unexpectedly her face lit up into a smile.

'Come on Mr Kelly – what really happened to your furniture?'

'It's a long story,' said Roger. 'But my wife eloped

with the furniture and a lot of other things besides. Sadly, I don't think I am much of a woman's man and I doubt whether I ever will be.'

'If you say that too often you will believe it,' she said, and took his arm. 'And it all depends on the woman.'

Her English was perfect, but there were distinct traces of a foreign accent when she spoke. She smiled again and they shook hands. Her handshake was cool and firm, and an unexpected tingling ran up his arm.

'Lovely meeting you Roger. Enjoy driving your Alfa Romeo, and contact me if you need help.'

As she got into her car Roger about turned, knocked on the window, and opened the car door.

'Ana – I have a celebration night planned for tomorrow and I will enjoy it twice as much if you will come with me.'

She took his hand again and said, 'I thought you would never ask.' Without thinking he leaned over and kissed her on the lips

'If you can make it here for about 7.00 you can leave your car on the drive and we will take a taxi into town.'

'7.00 o'clock,' she said and kissed him back. With his heart thumping and his head pulsing Roger returned into the house. That's a first for me he thought. It must be Cyril's amulet. He picked up the phone and called Howard. Joan answered.

'Joan, when Howard gets home can you ask him to increase tomorrow's table booking to eight?'

'Oh Roger – I am so pleased. We will look forward to seeing you both tomorrow.'

That surprise should add a bit of fun to the evening

thought Roger. Joan thinks I am taking Rosemary.

He was going to be late for Aunt Evelyn. He picked out a bottle of Chablis and walked the mile to her house at a brisk pace. When he arrived his aunt was already entertaining a friend who had called unexpectedly. The friend reminded him of an old bulldog with the beginnings of a beard, and jowls that shook as she talked. She was conducting a high-pitched monologue about her starring role in a local stage production (Ali Baba thought Roger) and his aunt was unable to interrupt the flow.

Talking was going to be impossible. He listened for a while, ate a couple of sandwiches, then collected the flat keys for Nice and politely made his excuses. His aunt followed him to the door.

'I'm so sorry darling, I didn't expect a visitor. She is an old friend and I just cannot be rude to her. You and I will catch up when I get back from Melbourne.' She gave him a hug adding, 'and while you are in Nice, please, do try to stay out of trouble.'

On his walk back home he chuckled at his aunt's farewell advice. If only she knew half of his troubles. Home early he had ample time to give free rein to his visions of the days ahead, and concluded that if he could possibly avoid getting into a mess on his travels it would make a pleasant change.

Next morning, he was a powerhouse. The garage was a shit-hole – full of rubbish. Roger spent the morning clearing it into his neighbours skip which was half full and awaiting collection. He had no idea how long he would be away on holiday. The garage lock was dodgy and needed something stronger to keep his new car safe.

He arranged for Alex's recommended locksmith to come to the house and fix a double lock on the garage door. The house burglar alarm was due for servicing, and the security engineers were free to come on the same day as the locksmith so Roger ordered an alarm to be fitted in the garage at the same time as they serviced the house alarm.

His back garden overlooked parkland and some trees were spoiling the view. He set about trimming the trees and uprooting bushes, and added the cuttings to the rubbish in the skip. Time flew by. Keeping busy helped lessen the queasy tremors which kept attacking his stomach. Apart from a few Friday night escapades, Roger hadn't dated anyone since he first started taking Rosemary out ten years ago, and he wasn't sure how well he would handle tonight.

Howard had booked the Beechwood Restaurant which was currently the 'in' place to see and be seen. Roger decided to wear his new midnight blue suit and set it off alongside the startling white shirt with the cutaway collar. No tie, and the shirt unbuttoned just far enough to show a glimpse of the gold amulet. If you've got it flaunt it, he thought. He checked the results downstairs in the full-length mirror.

'By God Kelly you are a handsome devil. Whatever are you worrying about?'

Ten minutes early a red Mercedes Coupe drew up onto his driveway. It had to belong to Ana because the car had her initials on the number plate. When she got out of the car, he was dumbstruck. This was not the uniformed salesgirl who had given him a lift home.

In her high heels Ana stood almost up to Roger's ear. A pale coloured stole covered her shoulders and enhanced a shimmering self-patterned green dress with a high split showing the full length of a slim sun-tanned leg. She looked to have been poured into the dress leaving very little to the imagination, and Roger's imagination ran wild.

Ana stood looking at him, holding his gaze and smiling. He noticed she had replaced the gold ring in her nose with a diamond stud which glittered as she moved.

'I didn't know I had a date with a film star,' he said.

'Ah – but when I used your loo, I knew I wanted a date with the leading man.'

Roger didn't break the spell by ordering a taxi. He locked up, got into the car beside her feeling completely relaxed, and certain that whatever the success of the evening Ana would prove to be a milestone in his life.

The Beechwood Hotel was situated on the outskirts of Wilmslow and heavy traffic stopped Ana from breaking the speed limits. She was a skilful driver but he saw that she wanted to concentrate, so he sat back and contented himself by admiring every detail of her face, her figure, her dress, her poise. How was it that he, a cuckolded husband, could be so lucky as to be with such a desirable woman only seven days after his wife had walked out on him?

They arrived at the hotel later than planned, and everyone was grouped together in the bar waiting. If Roger had wanted to create a sensation, then he could not have chosen better than Ana. Joan looked shell-shocked, whilst Howard and Mick were stunned into silence. Ana met them all with easy confidence and grace, and Roger could see that the novelty of the situation appealed to her.

Friday night was the night for beautiful people, and the Beechwood Restaurant was in full swing as they were led to their table. Walking from the bar Roger caught a glimpse of himself and Ana in a mirror. The cut of his new suit made him look a million dollars, and with Ana beside him looking a million dollars they were attracting a lot of attention. At the table Ana removed her stole and her backless dress was sensational, revealing a tattooed rose climbing down her back and almost joining the tattoo on her shoulder. There was a hush from some of the poser set at nearby tables, and Roger judged that whether tattoos were fashionable or not Ana had upstaged most of the glamour queens draped around the restaurant.

Dinner went well. The wine flowed, the meal was good, and the night was obviously a special celebration. Mick's police lady had entertaining stories to tell about Manchester's underworld, and Ruth sitting on the other side of Roger told him all about her ambition to live on a kibbutz in Israel whilst Malcolm sat restrained and said nothing. Roger drank little and listened a lot.

Howard and Joan at the other end of the table couldn't question him, and Ana handled everything perfectly by side stepping all attempts to extract personal details about herself and how she met Roger. With drink inside him Mick was not to be deterred either, but he also drew a blank. Mick used to boast about spending the night with his lady friends in the back of his van, and Roger reckoned that at the rate Mick and Wendy, his police lady, were downing their booze the van would be their resting place tonight.

As the evening drew to a close the head waiter handed Roger the bill. Being singled out as head of proceedings was a new experience. Throughout the meal the waiters had chosen to check with him if the table were happy with their meal, or if they needed extra drinks. Ana took the bill from him and checked the totals and split the cost into four. When everyone said their goodbyes, Roger was aware that one way and another the evening had increased his status, and he liked it. Life was moving on and his friends were moving on with it. He had split with Rosemary, Howard was going to be a father, and Malcolm was a much-married man. Max was right – those boys' nights out were coming to an end, and perhaps the days of 'Roger-the-bodger' were coming to an end as well.

As they drove home Roger said, 'I have got to thank you Ana. Tonight, was awkward for me but you managed the evening brilliantly. My only regret is that I left it all to you and we haven't had time to get to know each other.'

'Let's miss out all that boring stuff reviewing each other's lives,' replied Ana. 'I like you the way you are, so let's take the rest as it comes.' The roads were clear and they were back at Roger's house just after 11pm.

'I won't come in,' said Ana. 'I have had a lovely evening, but I have a hard weekend's work ahead. On Tuesday I am free. If you would like to take me for a spin in the Alfa Romeo it's my turn to buy lunch.' She put her arms around Roger and kissed him.

Her lips were cool with a taste of wine, and the tip of

her tongue flickered inside his mouth. They kissed, and they kissed again, and when she broke away, he could tell this was no ordinary kiss for either of them. Roger didn't push it. He was elated to be seeing her again.

He watched her car disappear. This is some woman. She is beautiful, she is intelligent, and she is confident enough to charm a group of people she has never met before. He guessed Ana was only in her mid-twenties, and yet she was already the owner of a new deluxe Mercedes Coupe with her own number plate. She has to have a story thought Roger (unless she has a sugar daddy) but whatever that story she isn't going to share it.

Roger wasn't tired and it was too early to retire for the night. Visions filled his head, and in his office, he began sorting through file after file of past work never completed. What could he have accomplished if he had stuck at it, and what could he now accomplish with the lottery winnings to back him up?

It was 2.00 am before he eventually got into bed, by which time he had a good idea of where he would make a start.

Saturday was a grey day. Roger started thinking of the Saturdays he had enjoyed playing football with the club, and swore he would return with a vengeance. He was not going to let his wife's silly affair stop him from playing. He gathered together his drawing board, sketch pad, and pencils and went outside.

The house and garage were separated by an archway which led to the back garden. After taking some measurements Roger calculated that an extension could be built over both garage and archway which would give him room for an office and gym overlooking the garden. The telephone rang.

'Mr Kelly zis is your joiner Mr Koshinski. I 'av ze truble vid ze Wednesday but I come now if you iz free and I fix ze locks.'

'No problem,' said Roger. 'The sooner the work is done, the better.'

The joiner worked well encouraged by a few whiskies and the promise of a cash payment. By the end of the day all the house window locks had been replaced, and there was a new double lock on the garage door. Koshinski claimed he was a professional builder in Poland and confirmed the feasibility of the planned extension.

'Unfortunately, I 'ad to leave Poland,' he explained. 'I 'av ze truble vit lotz of vimin 'aving ze babies. Now I keep ze lock on my cock.'

'Well, I hope the locks on my windows are an improvement on the cock locks you used in Poland Mr Koshinski,' said Roger as his joiner departed.

Roger returned to his extension plan entertained by the thoughts of Koshinski's cock lock. By evening the plan was drawn up and complete. He sat back pleased with the results. The most practical design he had produced in years. So why hadn't he ever attempted to do this when Rosemary was studying for her advanced teaching exams? No wonder she had gone flitting off with little Jack.

With five days to go before his holidays Roger had a busy week ahead of him. Monday morning he appeared at

Brown's Garage as they opened for business. He tied up all the details, made sure he had a full tank of petrol, then set off on a marathon drive to give the car a good run. When you are used to driving an eight-year-old Toyota, owning an Alpha Romeo takes you onto another planet, and Roger drove like he was on another planet. He sped up the M6 and down the A65 to Skipton, then back home through Colne and Accrington to test the car at a varying pace. When finally, he reached home and parked on the driveway he was completely satisfied with the car's performance, and delighted he had bought it.

The thoughts of seeing Ana next day excited him and he suffered from a few unwanted tremors in the stomach. She didn't disappoint him. Ana arrived on time in a Brown's courtesy car. She looked chic and sexy dressed in a tight blue sweater and short check skirt, and her long legs looked stunning as ever in a pair of flat designer walking shoes.

Roger was thrilled to see her, and his heart rate pumped to danger level. They drove to Southport and walked and talked the whole length of the promenade and beyond. They stopped and kissed. Hand in hand they were both enraptured by each other's company, and loving the warmth of the Spring Day. They shared a fresh fish platter in Southport's best fish restaurant, and then drove back to Salford Quays where they spent the afternoon admiring the Lowry paintings in the Art Gallery. Manchester centre isn't the safest place to leave a new car and Ana suggested they go back to Roger's house and swap cars, because her courtesy car would attract less attention than the Alpha Romeo. She took over driving, and again he was pleased to sit back and play passenger, absorbing everything about her.

Manchester on a Tuesday night was quiet. They had drinks in the Gay Village and wandered around China Town. Ana chose a restaurant where she was so well known that she was bowed in at the door, and the proprietor came over specially to welcome her and escort them to the best table. She didn't explain any reason for this, and again Roger sensed there was a story and another side to her life.

The day had been wonderful. He loved her company. They had laughed and talked, and exchanged interests in everything from music and art to travel and sport, but he still knew no more about Ana than when she accompanied him on his first test drive in the Alpha Romeo.

Travelling back home Roger guided her to the edge of the village where they parked by the stream and watched bats circling the derelict corn mill in the fading light. She was in his arms and the chemistry between them was like fire.

They kissed and her tongue was deep inside his mouth. They locked together in their embrace, and the softness of her lips and the sweet taste of her was electrifying. He slid his hand underneath her sweater and she shivered in response.

Her breasts were small and firm, and her nipples pressed hard into the palm of his hand. She opened her mouth and their mouths melted together in complete abandonment and Ana's hand dropped down frantically and grabbed hold of him and squeezed. Roger could not stop himself – he exploded in a depth of climax he had never experienced before.

'Oh, my darling,' she said. 'Roger, Roger, my darling' and she kissed his lips, his nose, his cheeks, and held him close to her.

'Let's go home,' he said.

When they arrived outside Roger's house Ana said 'Roger, I'm sorry but we stop here. I want to spend the night with you, believe me I cannot tell you how much. But I'm not going to. This is only our second time seeing each other. I work in two jobs. It makes life complicated, and at the moment your life isn't without complications either. Come back to me after your holidays Roger – I will be waiting for you.'

She reached in the back of the car and gave him a new road atlas. 'A little present to make sure you don't get lost. I'm out of town for the next few days. Enjoy your holiday and don't forget me.' They kissed long and hard, and when Ana drove away Roger felt his new life was disappearing before it had even begun.

Next day it was hard to concentrate. When the engineers arrived early to check the alarms' he had clean forgotten they were coming. By mid-morning the house alarm had been checked, and a new alarm fitted in the garage.

Roger then set out to tie up a few loose ends. The Toyota due back from repair was now ready, and he motored over to the garage and paid the excess insurance and also arranged to leave the car at the garage until Rosemary collected it. He thought he had better relay this piece of information to her, which meant a visit to see his mother-in-law.

He phoned, 'I am coming over with the dog basket, and Rosemary's car keys.'

'I shall be out,' she said.

'Good,' replied Roger. 'I will leave the keys and the basket in the porch. Tell your daughter that the repairs are paid for and the car is at the garage awaiting her ladyship's convenience.'

As he drove up to the house, he saw the front bedroom curtains move. He parked the Alpha Romeo in full view. That will give old horse face something to think about. He dropped the basket and keys inside the porch, and just for fun rang the bell three times.

Obligations fulfilled he dropped in to see his local bank manager. Another of my fans mused Roger. Fortunately, the bank wasn't busy and the manager made an effort to see Roger straight away. He was a frustrated little man hiding behind a barricade of sarcasm.

'I am pleased to see we are no longer banking with you Mr Kelly,' was his opening remark. 'Although at the rate you appear to be dispersing your winnings there is no guarantee that we may not find ourselves in the same situation quite soon.'

'Don't you worry about it,' said Roger. 'My investments are providing me with a lot of interest,' and he pointed to the car outside. He completed his business and left the bank manager with a big wink and a smile.

Back home he sorted out a couple of suitcases and got itchy feet. He couldn't wait to get away. He longed for two or three weeks on his own away from everything with time to think. Roger had a reputation for not taking life seriously, but it could never be said that he wasn't organized. Very soon he had put together an array of everything he wanted to pack for Nice, all laid out neatly on the spare bedroom floor. Except for his football boots. But did he need them – why would he think of taking football boots on holiday?

Holidays or not he remembered he had left his expensive pair of Nike Superfly in the club locker. The club lockers weren't very secure, and he would be annoyed if somebody adopted the boots in his absence. He checked his watch. Just after 5.00 pm. The club should be open for tonight's practice match by now. Roger hoped he could be in and out of the club without meeting anybody, but when he drew into the car park the first person he saw was Jack Fearnley holding court with Bob and three of the team on the club veranda. As he opened the car door they stopped talking and looked at him, and at the same time a bundle of fur launched itself at him, jumping up, licking him, running around in circles and barking excitedly with its tail wagging a hundred to the dozen. Roger hugged him, patted him, scratched him behind the ears, gave him a soft left and right swing, and said, 'now then old boy'. He hadn't realized how much he had missed Scott during the last two weeks.

Jack looked as though he was going to have an accident in his trousers, Bob looked embarrassed, and his three team mates found something interesting to gaze at around their boots. Roger walked onto the veranda exuding the best Roger nonchalance he could muster.

'Good to see you all. Sorry I've missed a few matches but I thought it would give someone else a chance to hug the limelight.'

'Good to have you back,' said Bob, shaking his hand. Roger shook hands with the rest of the team gripping Jacks soft hand with an extra hard squeeze.

'Can't stay,' said Roger. 'I'm here to collect my boots then I'm off on holiday.'

'Where to?' asked Bob.

'South of France,' said Roger.

'How long for?' asked Bob.

'Not sure. I have been made an offer I can't refuse,' and with Scott barking at his heels, he stepped jauntily into the clubhouse and collected his boots.

He felt a lot less jaunty about leaving Scott. As he stepped out of the clubhouse Jack tried to open his mouth, but Roger interrupted him, 'No problem Jack, it all comes with the furniture. Just make sure you look after my dog,' and he walked over to the Alpha Romeo leaving behind a group of baffled and envious faces. Well, fuck the lot of them. A fine bunch of pals they were.

But halfway home events caught up with him. Perhaps it was a delayed reaction to the past weeks. Suddenly Roger began to cry. Tears streamed down his face and he started to sob uncontrollably. Rosemary had been his friend for 10 years. He had lost her and the dog, and all the great guys he played football with. He sat at the roadside and wept, and wept, until there were no tears left. A concerned passer by stopped and knocked on the window, and he had to reassure her he was alright.

That made him move, and he drove back home totally drained. He hadn't cried since he was 12 years old. He garaged the car, missed eating, and retired straight to bed where he slept solidly for 10 hours. He awoke with a clear head and a different perspective. There was no going back – his break with Rosemary was final. He was going to move on.

Two years was too long without a holiday. Normally he travelled light, but on this occasion, he was going away prepared for anything. He needed his laptop, sketch pads and drawing materials, and he put together a folder full of half-finished projects including his dream hacienda and the newly planned house extension.

All his Maximillion attire would accompany him to Nice, even his new suit although he couldn't imagine wearing a suit whilst on holiday. This added up to two full suitcases, and after checking airline tickets, euros, and passport, Roger reckoned he had packed the lot. Then he noticed two shallow corner spaces in his largest case. Perfect for his football boots. Into the case they went, and that was the final touch.

Packed and ready a day in advance, he went for a six-mile run. He ate a light evening meal at 7.00, got showered, and relaxing in front of television in his dressing gown. He would buy a new TV and choose some furniture after Nice – hopefully when he had engaged in some sort of dialogue with his wayward wife.

He was enjoying his second whisky when he heard a car drawing up. Ana's red Mercedes was parked on his driveway, and she hurried out looking dishevelled carrying a small case.

'I couldn't wait until after Nice,' she said. 'So I've brought my toothbrush.'

The fire sparked immediately. There was an

explosion, and they were in each other's arms, half stumbling onto the lounge floor with the television still flickering.

Ana's sweater, jeans, and underwear were scattered on the carpet, and the feel of her and the smell of her perfume swamped Roger's senses as she pulled him inside her. Her fingernails tore into his back, she was kissing his neck, and his arms were tight around her as she climaxed within a couple of thrusts before Roger climaxed with her. They lay together, joined together, with hearts still thumping.

Ana said, 'You would never believe me if I told you how long I have waited for that.' And then she said, 'Please, take me upstairs,' and hand in hand he led her up to the bedroom, and the bed, where he was erect, and ready for her again immediately.

This time Roger seemed to be driven by some supernatural force and he made love long and gently putting everything he had ever learned into his kisses and caresses. They moved together slowly in thrilling rhythm, gradually building up to a plateau of passion that brought them together in ultimate satisfaction, leaving them both spent and fulfilled.

How often can early love making reach a peak of compatibility so soon and so easily? As they lay back relaxed Ana and Roger knew that together they had experienced something quite unique. Roger was also aware that until now he had never really understood what sex meant during the whole of his seven-year marriage.

Roger slept soundly with Ana beside him. In the morning she woke him with a coffee, having already showered and wearing his dressing gown.

'The gown looks better on you,' he said. But when she sat on the bed with her coffee, he found himself unfastening the straps so he could look at her. He traced the rose tattoo with his finger travelling the length of her back.

Very soon she was lying on the bed smiling at him, naked, whilst his eyes roamed the full length of her lightly tanned body. He admired her smooth flawless skin and the gentle curve of her hips. Ana's breasts were small and pert with rose coloured nipples which glowed in the morning light, and her long slim legs were the legs of an athlete with shapely calves and firm thighs.

He kissed her breasts, and she gently scratched the back of his neck as his kisses wandered fleetingly over her flat stomach and the triangle of soft blonde hair around her pubis. And then she was pulling his head down. He knew what she wanted him to do but he had never done it before. As she opened her legs he kissed gently around and then let his tongue separate her lips until he had found the vital spot which swelled in response.

Ana shivered, and he lifted her buttocks and moved to her vibrations as he licked harder and faster. Her stomach muscles tightened, and she pulled his face down hard until he was wildly moving even faster and stronger. She shouted 'Roger' then her whole body shook as she climaxed. He quickly entered her, and his thrusts were strong and deep until he felt her extended tremors as his own body discharged into a final orgasm.

For a long time they lay very still, drifting, letting the

warmth of the aftermath circulate through mind and body.

'Did the earth stand still for you?' she asked.

'The earth stood still for me ever since I met you,' said Roger.

It was mid-morning before they stirred and abandoned the bed. Roger cooked an omelette, bacon, and hash browns. They sat eating in the kitchen which apart from the bedroom was the only comfortably furnished room in the house. With the outside doors open leading to the garden, and the sunshine filtering through onto the kitchen table, their brunch was a pleasant experience. Ana had a good appetite. She sat opposite him sparkling and composed, doing full justice to his culinary efforts.

'So, what's the second job that keeps you so busy?'

'You wouldn't understand it if I told you, and you won't like it. But I left Manchester University with degrees in languages and Business Economics, and I wasn't prepared to accept some minimalistic salary while I climbed up the corporate ladder. I have made my own way independent of all that, and with a bit of luck I will soon be a co-director at Mr Brown's garage.' She smiled at him across the table, 'My second job means I have to travel a lot, and nothing is going to stand in the way of my ambitions. If you can understand that then you will be the man in my life.'

It felt like she had thrown down the gauntlet. Time for him to get out there too and become a success.

'You know the answer to that,' said Roger. 'And I will cook you another omelette.'

Ana stayed until lunchtime and when she left neither of them wanted to part. He wanted her to come with him to Nice, but she couldn't, and Roger knew that he was going to start this much needed holiday with a hankering after Ana and an incurable ache. Apart from Ana's mobile number and email address he didn't know where she lived, and her personal life was still a mystery. It worried him but he had to accept it.

During the afternoon Howard phoned, and then Mick. Both wished him a good holiday, and the rest of the day faded into obscurity in anticipation of next morning's departure.

On Saturday morning Roger caught the flight to Nice. He intended staying a few weeks. But he didn't stay for a few weeks – he stayed much longer. And who could have forecast that the man who went away on holiday could possibly become the man who eventually returned. And who could have forecast the circumstances in which he would become involved, or the events that would shape the man he became.

3. Ana

She had never experienced anything like this before. He thrilled her, he excited her, and Ana knew that until she saw him again her whole mind was going to revolve around him.

There were complications, and she guessed that the worst part had yet to come. Roger was very vulnerable until his marriage was settled. But that was to be expected, and did it matter? She wasn't without complications and surplus baggage herself. The worst of it was – how could she explain it? What would his reaction be, what would any man's reaction be?

It had started as a bit of fun when she was studying at Manchester University. Funds were tight, and her and Kata had conceived the idea of acting as escorts. Dinner dates with men needing a partner obviously had its dangers, but if you laid out the ground rules in advance most men accepted the conditions. The majority of dates were with travelling businessmen who needed to show off a partner at a function, but there were far more lucrative liaisons where Ana and Kata's knowledge of languages meant they found themselves translating at some very prestigious venues.

On such a date she met Jakub. He couldn't speak English and he was substituting for a colleague who could. Jakub was tall, handsome, married, and Polish, and for one week Ana missed lectures in order to guide him around the business community.

And the inevitable happened. She fell for him, and they had an affair. As Ana drove to work it struck her that

Roger reminded her a little bit of Jakub. Both were well built, and both were fair – but looking back no matter what she felt for Jakub couldn't even vaguely compare with this feeling she had for Roger.

Between her and Kata they built up a successful business. Her absences from Brown's Garage were tolerated because when she was called upon to translate at meetings and sales conferences, she regularly used the opportunity to sell cars for Brown's by carrying a file of specially discounted luxury vehicles. Browns had done well out of her. Another peg up and she could concentrate 100% on developing the car business here in Manchester. Meeting Roger meant she wanted to be home more, and escort dinner dates were now going to be a thing of the past.

As she walked into the car showroom something felt wrong. And when Mr Brown called her into his office and introduced her to his son Ana saw her years of work and possible promotion disappear into obscurity. This was the lover-boy son who had come back into the business, and Brown senior was overjoyed to have him back.

From the moment she met him Ana had enough experience to know that the son was trouble. He was tall and gangly with ginger hair flopping over one eye, and a fixed gaze with a set smile. All week he dropped files on her desk wanting details of past sales, and details of customers who had purchased cars whilst she was attending London meetings. On Friday evening she was sat at her desk tying up the week's work when he came with his set smile and plonked a huge file on her desk. He then put his arms around her and put both hands on her breasts. Ana got up and smacked his face, and then wiped off the smile with the second smack. She picked up her attaché case, gathered up her lists and walked out. It was no use deliberating. The son was an arrogant slob, he would always be an arrogant slob, and if she wanted to stay with Brown's she had to work with him.

Although Ana was upset, she was tough. What concerned her the most wasn't just the loss of a very good wage but the wasted years of effort she had put into supporting Brown senior who was hopeless working on his own. Ana wanted to tell Roger everything – but how could she, it would only open other doors which needed further explanation. If only he was here now – she could imagine his arms around her, and the way she was able to talk to him. She could make him understand.

When she walked into their Manchester office Kata was still working.

'Scottie McDonald is back on the books if you want him. It means travelling all over the globe for a couple of months, but he always puts us up in good hotels and pays well. Last time I went with him there were a few 24-hour stints to contend with.'

McDonald sold farming machinery and spent a lot of time in Germany and Russia.

Travelling away was the last thing Ana wanted. McDonald was a workaholic with the cracked face of a walnut, bad teeth and a breath like a donkey. Ana hated Russia but she was going to need the work because she could not cover her commitments otherwise.

She returned to her apartment feeling sad. All her plans had gone to pot. She had met somebody wonderful who she wanted to be with and the opportunity was going to be snatched away from her.

On Monday Ana set off on a three-day trip to Düsseldorf, to be followed by Berlin and Frankfurt. It would be a long time before she would meet Roger again.

4. L'école de l'amour

Another glorious morning of sunshine on the Cote d'Azur. At 7.30am Roger completed his morning run on Promenade des Anglais, returned to the apartment and jumped straight into the shower. He inspected himself whilst he shaved. What a fabulous suntan. Only his second week in Nice and he could pass as a local.

Aunt Evelyn's apartment was situated just off the Rue du Congress within a stone's throw of Hotel Negresco. Handy for the seafront and handy for shops, it suited Roger's holiday plans perfectly and he loved everything about it. A second-floor serviced apartment. Light and spacious by French standards with two bedrooms and a very large open plan kitchen and dining area. Roger had dragged the large dining table to the window and spread out some of his plans and sketches. If he strained his neck, he could just see the sea, and with the balcony window open the sounds and buzz of French life which arose from the outside street added inspiration to his penmanship. Behind the block a new secure car park had recently been built. A big improvement. He remembered from years ago that his father used to have a hell of a job trouble finding a parking space.

Nice was a good choice – he felt alive here. He explored the bustling streets and colourful markets, went window shopping on Rue de Paradis and Avenue de Verdum, and dined in any number of excellent cafés and bistros around the old marketplace.

He made trips to Antibes and Menton, and earlier in the week took the train to Eze making the arduous two hour climb from Eze seaside station up to the medieval village high on the summit. The views from the village were amazing and the air was like nectar. This was the kind of experience he came for.

The trouble was wherever he went he could not stop thinking about Ana. She stayed with him night and day, his mind constantly wandering back to their last night of love making. During the first week he couldn't stop himself from bombarding her with emails, but the intensity of their relationship was disappointedly lost. After making numerous calls he had spoken to Ana twice but each time the line was bad and their conversations stilted and formal. The same applied to text messages and emails. She was working in Berlin, then Frankfurt and twice in Croatia. She would text a selection of scenic city photographs but never explained what she was actually doing there. And how could she be travelling Europe when she was supposed to be working for Brown's garage? Weird – it didn't make sense.

Roger sat at the open window dipping a freshly baked croissant into a dish of apricot jam. Only the French knew how to make croissants and baguettes that tasted as good as this. Another week's holiday still to come but it was a bit concerning that after extensive deliberation and two weeks of his own space, he still hadn't any idea how he was going to fulfil the dreams and ambitions he had envisaged when he first won the lottery. In the café opposite, the owner and his wife began their daily argument with arms waving and their voices drifting up through the window. He wished he could understand what they found to argue about. He and Mick never learned much French because they fooled about during Fanny's French lessons and spent more time banished from Fanny's classes than they did attending her lessons. A pity – French life suited Roger brilliantly but it would suit him better if he could speak the lingo.

He finished his breakfast. The apartment provided him with almost everything. Cupboards were stacked with towels and clean sheets, and if he stayed a life-time it wouldn't be long enough to read half the books the major had accumulated. Conrad, Hemingway, Steinbeck, Kipling, Churchill's memoirs, travel magazines and books on languages. The place had smelt a bit musty when he first arrived, and a lingering aroma left by Maria the cleaner didn't help. She suffered from BO probably originating from great tufts of hair sticking out from under her armpits. Since he couldn't get rid of the smell, he had to get rid of Maria and Monsieur le Caretaker promised him someone different to service the apartment.

Today his bag was packed with camera, sketch pad and pencils. When the new cleaner arrived, he planned to catch the bus to Villefranche, and from there walk to Cap Ferrat and visit Villa Rothschild. There was a knock at the door and he was greeted by two large eyes and a smiling face.

'I is Elissa. I here for cleaning your apartment.' Plump golden-brown thighs extended below her mini skirt, and her rear view revealed buttocks to die for.

'What happened to Maria?' asked Roger.

'She going back to Spain for having baby. I now clean all flats. *Le patron* think you like me better.' Le patron was dead right thought Roger as Elissa carried her bucket and cleaning materials into the apartment. Whatever was a stunning girl like this doing cleaning his apartment? Her T-shirt must have got damp because it was moulded to her body revealing beautifully shaped breasts and the dark outline of her nipples. Roger felt a twitch in his lower regions and mentally postponed his trip to Villefranche.

As Elissa moved around mopping the floor, she was determined to tell him everything about herself.

'I is Lebanese from Beirut,' she told him. 'Working there very bad – plenty trouble. Bang! Bang!' and pointed her finger at Roger and laughed. 'I is married to one Lebanese man who is real bastard. He work in Dubai and never sending me money.'

Roger listened, trying hard to keep his eyes off her nipples which seemed to be attempting to exit her T-shirt.

'You play football?' she asked holding up his football boots. 'I loves football,' and she proceeded to recite the merits of her favourite international football players starting with France and going on to exalt the praises of Italy and Spain. There was no stopping her. By the time she had completed her football soliloquy half the morning was gone, and she gathered together her cleaning materials ready to depart.

'I here again Monday,' she said, and with a calculated wiggle she left. Roger picked up his backpack and set off in the direction of the old port laughing as he walked along. That was a bit of unexpected excitement – a domestic porn show. If Elissa is married to 'man bastard' from Beirut then she must have a pretty good idea that her tight T-shirt and short skirt would be sure to arouse lustful reactions from another male bastard like Roger Kelly.

Sunshine and clear blue skies followed him as he climbed the Colline du Chateau and wandered down to the Quartier du Port. The old harbour unfolded into a picture of white sunlit buildings with red and yellow facades, and boats of all sizes lazily bobbing up and down on a turquoise sea. He was struck by the resplendent colours of a blue and gold luxury yacht called Marigold flying the British flag. He took a photograph and sat down to create a rough sketch. On deck a woman was stretched out sunbathing in the company of her two Dalmatians. She was very thin and had toasted herself to the colour of old leather and it made Roger wonder if there was any danger of the dogs mistaking her for a piece of meat.

He sketched in the Dalmatians but left the woman out, and after taking some time to draw the whole ship he moved to a different angle and drew the deck area making a special feature of the Dalmatians. Relaxed, with the warmth of the sun caressing his shoulders Roger asked himself just how successful one had to be to buy a boat like the one he was drawing.

Back at the apartment he enlarged his sketches using strong lines in charcoal.

He then took out his travel box of water colours and added colour to small, isolated items. The ship's railings. The Union Jack. The dog collars on the two Dalmatians.

He treated his sketch of the deck area differently and painted the whole of the deck making a special feature of the two Dalmatians and adding a couple of the deck hands. It was well after midnight when the pictures were nearly completed, and he reckoned that even Monet couldn't have done a better job.

Next day he targeted Grimaldi Castle at Cagnes-sur-mer and spent the morning in the castle's art gallery admiring portraits of the cabaret artist Suzi Solidor as painted by her lesbian lover. In the afternoon he walked the town before visiting musee Renoir. An attractive American woman shared his enthusiasm for the paintings, and they finished the afternoon together eating rotisserie chicken and chips in the square. Too bad she had a husband waiting for her at their hotel.

At the end of the day Roger hit the gym for an hour. He had joined on the third day of his holidays and alternated his morning runs with a training session every other day. It wasn't the friendliest of gyms even though it was one of the best equipped. Body builders who worked out with the weights were lost admiring themselves in the mirrors, and few people acknowledged him apart from a small group of North Africans who always watched him when he was training on the punch bags. Tonight, he was surprised to be confronted by two of them.

'Anglais – vous jouez le foot, oui?'

'Yes – I play,' said Roger.

'Demain vous jouez le foot avec nous?'

Was this an invitation or a command? Roger's knowledge of French was too skimpy to fully comprehend the offer, but nevertheless he was delighted by the idea of a game of football and flattered to receive the invitation, so he accepted.

Next morning, he slipped into his Nike boots, got lost twice looking for the football ground, and arrived when the game had already started. He immediately realized he was going to be the only white face on the football field, and this was emphasised when the game stopped and the players clapped as he walked onto the pitch.

There were wives and children sat around in little groups on the side lines and they all clapped too so that Roger began the match mortified – judged to be a star before he even had time to twinkle.

It was a game like no other. Amine from the gym positioned Roger as inside right and away they went, tearing around the field hell for leather. Defence and rules of 'off-side' were non-existent. Most players were Algerian or Moroccan, and half of them were teenagers. Scoring goals was the sole object of the game and even the full backs finished up in forward positions. Thanks to a couple of long shots Roger scored twice in the first half, and once in the second, and was applauded each time with clapping, and a cheer of Anglais. By the end of the match the temperature had climbed to the 70's, and Roger walked stiffly off the field happy but dead beat.

He was astonished when a woman wearing a dark shawl and head scarf detached herself from the sidelines, took his arm, and guided him back to a group of ladies preparing a barbecue. It took a minute to recognise Elissa, covered from head to foot in black, and definitely not the sexy little thing who had mopped his kitchen floor.

Saturday morning football was obviously a party with groups of wives preparing an amazing variety of food. Fish tagine, couscous, chicken, meatballs. Large quantities of spicy delicacies were piled onto Roger's plate, and the ladies watched closely and nodded their approval with every mouthful he ate. Amine poured him a 'Spéciale' Moroccan beer from a cool bag, and a serious little girl with dark pools of eyes like saucers came to gaze at him. Radios played, dogs barked, children cried. The whole gathering got noisier and noisier. Everyone shouted rather than talked, and Elissa and the wives never stopped laughing.

The party lasted all afternoon and Roger enjoyed every minute of it. When he got up to leave there was another round of clapping as Elissa took his arm and they set off in the direction of their apartments. The situation was a hoot. With her face almost covered by her black head scarf she clung to his arm chatting away like a long-lost lover. She was assigned a ground floor room on the opposite side of the block, and before parting she squeezed his arm and turned to him with a hug.

'You very good footballer Roger. I like see you play. I come again to watch you,' and she floated off down the corridor. This holiday gets better thought Roger. The last thing he wanted was an involvement, but you couldn't knock it when a little sex bomb had you in her sights and promised a future liaison.

It had been an amazing day but so far most of his evenings had proved uneventful. During his first week he had paid a Saturday visit to Monte Carlo and spent an evening drinking over-priced lagers whilst watching the rich and famous arrive at the Casino. Tonight, he checked out Nice on Google and found a casino situated very near Hotel Negresco. Last time he forgot his passport – this time he remembered it and decided to add some excitement to the evening by testing out his luck.

It was early evening, and the casino was quiet. Roger had no trouble getting a seat in the restaurant with a good view of the gaming tables. The food was excellent. He enjoyed a starter of fruits de mer, followed by blanquette de veau with French fries and a side salad. He took his time lingering over a bottle of Chablis as diners filled the restaurant and the gaming tables started to get busy. He enjoyed watching people. Roger had never gambled. On odd occasions he and Mick had visited Grosvenor Casino together after one of their Friday night shindigs. Roger used to eat free sandwiches and have a laugh whilst watching mad Mick lose his money playing Blackjack. Tonight, was different. It was his turn to have a flutter, and he rubbed Big Cyril's amulet before buying one hundred euros worth of chips and joining the players at the roulette table where most of the action was taking place.

Piles of chips were scattered all over the table, and he recognised the sun burned woman from the Marigold nursing her little pile and on a winning streak. Standing watching her was a tall fair man wearing a white linen suit and flowery bow tie. The expression on his smooth baby face indicated complete boredom, as if he didn't care whether she won or lost a couple of million.

Roger had dressed well. If you haven't been born with blue blood in your veins, then dress as though you have. The casino emanated fashion. Suits, jackets, Dior dresses and the flash of gold bangles. Sun tanned shoulders displayed in backless flowing gowns with young divas hanging onto the arms of men twice their age

– all competing to see who could reveal the most cleavage. This was the real deal. He absolutely loved it. The buzz, the glamour, the spin of the wheel, and the rattle of winning coins at the slot machines. Manchester Grosvenor wasn't in the same league.

Majesty in a mohair suit created a stir as he plonked himself down at the roulette table. Massive shoulder pads doubled the width of his jacket emphasising the power image, and his tall glittering lady friend sported a massive gold necklace bouncing between her massive breasts. Both the necklace and the breasts looked large enough to compete at Cannes Film Festival. If she has had 'implants' in her breasts, would they have to be made of gold he wondered.

Another seat came free, and Roger sat down and placed his first bet. He knew absolutely nothing about the rules of roulette, so he played safe and bet even money on black and black won. He doubled the money – and black won again. Next bet he changed to doubling up on red and that won too. One of the stewards was watching him closely and caught his eye. 'God he's built like a brick shithouse' – 'if he coughs, he'll split his dinner suit', thought Roger. Roger took a breather and watched for a while.

'Shoulder pads' was betting big and losing heavily while 'Sun-burn' from the Marigold got bored and vacated her seat. An overfed, over-loud American took her place and after 15 minutes of listening to how it was done in Las Vegas Roger was ready for a breath of fresh air. He made a last 10 euro split bet (with no idea what he was doing) and won at odds of 17 to one. When his chips were cashed, he had made a straight 200 euros profit on the night. Not as exciting as a lottery win but not bad for a first-time novice.

He slept late then logged into the morning mail. Invariably there was an amusing message from Mick addressed to 'Roger the podger' confirming Mick's belief that a holiday break in Nice would provide Roger with a succession of young bed-able French starlets. This morning he opened Mick's email and wished he hadn't.

> *Hi Mate.*
>
> *We went back to The Beechwood Restaurant on Friday and were served by the same waiter. The waiter knew Ana. Take a look at this – thought you might be interested.*
>
> *www.escortsbilingual.com*
>
> *Hope all is well.*
>
> *Cheers,*
>
> *Mick*

Roger logged onto the link and Ana's face greeted him alongside a face which might have belonged to her twin. The link answered a lot of questions and he wasn't happy about any of the answers.

Ana and Kata – multilingual escorts from
Croatia.

Fluent in Russian. German. Dutch. Croatian. English.

Specialists in Eastern European events.

Available for – Business functions. Red Carpet Social Events. Weddings. Sales Meetings. Dinner Dates.

Strictly a non-sexual escort agency.

200 euros an hour plus expenses covering all travel.

Foreign arrangements and large functions negotiable.

A bolt of pain shot through Roger's stomach. She had said he wouldn't like her second job and he didn't. The word escort conjured up a picture of Ana on a one-to-one dinner date, and then he imagined her in bed with someone else and he felt sick. He tried to tell himself to stop imagining things. But the news wouldn't go away. What client was going to pay 200 euros an hour to an escort without expecting personal services in return? He couldn't stop thinking about it and the image of Ana on the internet spoilt the rest of his day.

The following morning, he was still trying to digest the newly acquired information whilst having breakfast in the café opposite. Why did women make a bonfire of his emotions? The café proprietor's wife collected his coffee cup and patted his cheek. The day was destined to go badly. He lingered too long over the picture of giving him a beaming smile. Perhaps his future lay with older woman. If his love life didn't work out, he could become a gigolo. He could join Ana's escort agency.

He took the bus out to *Cimiez* and *Musée Matisse* a naked lady called 'Odalisque Harmony in Red', and a little battle axe of a French woman complained he was blocking her view. Roger smiled, and stood back politely, and accidentally trod on the woman's toe. Amidst cries of pain, she hopped around the gallery on one foot loudly complaining about him. A French farce ensued – and unfortunately, he laughed. There followed an unwelcome focus of attention *à la française* all centred around Roger, so he decided it was the right time to make a quick exit out of the gallery. Obviously, the French didn't share his sense of humour, and what's more the irritating French woman reminded him of Rosemary's mother.

Leaving the gallery, he wandered around Parc des Arènes and the Monastère de Ciemez until he got caught in the first deluge of rain since leaving Manchester and made a beeline for the next bus back to Nice. The bus driver was loud mouthed and unpleasant. He was rudely abrupt about Roger's dripping wet clothing and as Roger got off the bus at Nice centre he whispered '*merde*' in the driver's hairy ear.

What followed was unbelievable. Who would have thought one little word could produce such startling results. The driver jumped out of his seat seething with rage and exploded into screams of abuse. Purple faced he looked in danger of a heart attack as he followed Roger off the bus hurling French insults after him, and alerting oncoming passengers to the short comings of *les Anglais*.

Time to call it quits. Back to base where he shed his wet clothing and reflected on what had been a bad day but a good laugh. Thinking about Henry Matisse he seemed to recall that the artist started life as a draughtsman before becoming better known for his art. Matisse was also a philosopher. One of his quotes was 'Always learn to walk on firm ground before you try walking on a tight rope'. Now how could that quote apply to today's bit of trouble he asked himself?

Roger's trip to the gallery and Mick's email put the tin hat on it all. After two weeks he had had enough of his own company. He pictured Ana lying beside him. Her steady gaze, her green eyes and the sweet taste of her mouth when they kissed. All his dreams and aspirations were wrapped up in those few days and nights they had spent together and he had to get back to see her again.

His flight home was booked for Sunday which left him with five more days. He walked to Cap Ferrat and spent half of Tuesday looking around Villa Rothschild. Onwards from there to Beaulieu-sur-Mer for late lunch, and by the end of the afternoon his sore feet just managed the return journey to Villefranche where he collapsed with a beer on the veranda of Hotel Welcome. Temperatures had again crept into the 70s and Roger had walked for six solid hours.

Too tired for the gym, he landed back at Aunt Evelyn's apartment and drifted off in the cool of her air-conditioned lounge dreaming dreams of an unavailable Ana in some distant foreign land. He was awakened by a dig in the ribs and opened his eyes to see Elissa's sun-tanned thighs erotically displayed in an even shorter than short micro skirt.

'I no think you here Roger, so I come in to leave this'. She handed him a parcel and when he unwrapped it, he was astounded. She had borrowed the two pictures of the Marigold yacht and had them framed. The framing was enhanced by a blue border running around each picture and cleverly designed to set off his seascapes. The result was sheer magic. It elevated his work into a different class.

'I have friend who do this for very little money. He say he make portable for you.'

'Portable?' said Roger 'You mean portfolio?'

'Ah sorry, is portfolio. He make portfolio for you. I take you to his shop.'

Ideas floated through Roger's mind as she spoke. The framing was superb and gave him ideas which opened up possibilities he hadn't thought of before.

'Elissa – these frames are fantastic. How can I thank you?

'I like you make picture of me,' she said. 'I like you paint picture with no clothes'.

Roger woke up. His mind leapt from Ana to picture frames, and from picture frames to Elissa without clothes. Nevermind Matisse – here was his chance to become the new 21st century Kelly-Toulouse-Lautrec.

'Come and have dinner with me Elisse and tell me about Beirut.'

'I love having dinner with you Roger, but first I use your shower because my shower no good' and without waiting for a reply she pulled off her T-shirt, dropped her skirt, and vanished into the shower-room. Five minutes later she was back with a towel wrapped round her hips, leaving her magnificent, pointed breasts in full view.

'You like?' she asked, and winked at him. 'You see again later,' and she disappeared leaving an electrified Roger to curb his lust. Suddenly dreams of absent Ana evaporated. After two weeks of eating on his own he was going to enjoy Elissa's company and anything else that went along with it.

He took her to Restaurant Acchiardo on Rue Droit, just off the old marketplace. It was a fun place where he had eaten before. Very often you shared a table with half a dozen other diners, but the food was consistently good, and they both chose dish of the day which was casserole of octopus cooked with garlic and aubergines. Across the room were a gay couple who he had shared a table with on his last visit. One partner had made the other jealous by paying too much attention to Roger. Sitting with Elissa in her tight bra-less sweater he didn't think that tonight either of them would have much doubt as to which side Roger was batting on.

Elissa bubbled with vitality. She was a great talker, she depicted life in Beirut, and she was amused about everything. She squeezed his leg, whispered in his ear, and you would think they had been together months instead of this being their first night out. It was the sort of boost he needed.

As they walked along the promenade he asked, 'How old are you Elissa?'

'I nineteen,' replied Elissa. 'Man bastard he thirty-nine. Marrying me when I am only sixteen. My father's fault – he bastard too'.

'So how long will you stay working in Nice?'

'When man comes back from Dubai I go back to Beirut. No go back he come and fetch me. Perhaps kill me – and you too,' and she collapsed into peals of laughter.

If this was a warning it didn't trouble Elissa. She took his hand and climbed the steps to his apartment, and once inside indicated exactly what she had in mind by walking straight into his bedroom.

'No clothes Roger – I like no clothes,' and she stripped off and pressing against him, unbuttoned his shirt. As he dropped his Maximillian trousers, he reached for her but received a push and found himself on the bed with Elissa in charge. She was soft and incredibly gentle and began moving up and down his body covering him with soft butterfly kisses. An old army veteran had once told Roger that to experience love making with an Arabian woman is an experience like no other. Love to them is an art. Part of their culture. An aptitude not understood by women in the West. Roger gave Elissa top marks.

'You have very nice cock Roger. Not too big and not too small. I like him' and taking him in her hand she extended the butterfly kisses up and down his penis, and covered the bell-end with her lips. Roger was still the fastest gun in the west and to his annoyance lost control and spurted two weeks of abstinence into one release. To his surprise Elissa was jubilant. She sat up straight, clapped her hands and laughed.

'Ah Roger you is too quick. I show you how I make

you slow,' and she caressed and coaxed him into recovering his erection, then sat astride and inserted his penis inside her.

'Now Roger you is staying very still, and I is moving very slowly, and you see – we have good fuck'.

What followed was every bit as good as the old army veteran had portrayed. Elissa made love as though she was in love with him. She prompted him, talked to him, guided him and melted and fused with his every movement. There were no explosions – no strained efforts to grasp moments designed to bring their lovemaking to a climax. By the end of their session Roger's every nerve end tingled and he was enthralled by Elissa. She left him with a promise of more to come, and his stay in Nice suddenly took on new dimensions.

Next day he was introduced to the picture framer, who for very little money put together a striking portfolio of sketches and plans which Roger had brought with him to Nice. To thank Elissa for her trouble he wanted to buy her a dress, and they set off to shop down Rue Paradis but she wouldn't hear of it.

'You no waste your money Roger. I take you to special place where good clothes is very cheap,' and behind Gare SNCF in a half derelict building they entered a warehouse full of designer names and clothing of every description. He bought two stunning dresses for Elissa and a cream Havana style suit for himself. In the evening she cooked a Lebanese meal climbing the stairs to his apartment balancing red hot plates on top of a tray of Kibbeth meat balls. She went downstairs and returned with dishes of hummus, rice pilaf, and salad. They ate a wonderful meal on the balcony with the blue of the sea a pale glimmer in-between the adjacent buildings.

She cleared away the dishes and said, 'I will be back,' and when she reappeared in her new orange dress Roger knew it was going to be game time.

'I like you take photograph of me then I take dress off,' she said. He photographed her then slowly unzipped the dress.

'Now,' she said, 'tonight you see me and another day you paint me'.

The light was fading and she stood in the shadows with her breasts just catching the light. She lay on Aunt Evelyn's large leather sofa displaying the firm round cheeks of her buttocks, and then sat with her legs slightly parted for him to glimpse the dark triangle of her pubic hair. Roger watched her with fire in his groin. When he couldn't watch any longer, he moved to the sofa and she held him back and laughed.

'Remember – is gentle Rodger, is always gentle,' and during the next hour of love making Elissa was like liquid in his arms. She touched him and she kissed him.

Her legs were wide open and wrapped around him, then she changed position and squeezed him tight inside her with both her legs fully closed. Even when he felt her climax it was part of a fluid movement which continued to flow with her looking at him, talking to him, and still caressing him. She turned him on again and again, and at times he felt she was more interested in pleasing him than satisfying any carnal desires of her own.

She stayed the night and left early. Roger lay in bed and dismissed all thoughts of the future. Why the hell couldn't he have met her in the first few days of his holiday, and his mind started to tick over – his three weeks would easily extend into four and longer if he wanted. He ate breakfast and had an idea.

He parcelled the two framed pictures of the Marigold into his backpack and walked down to the Old Port to check if the yacht was still docked there. The tall, bored man he had seen at the casino was standing alongside the gangway busily filling buckets with water. He had swapped his white linen suit and bow tie for an extra tight white linen shirt and squeezed into a pair of shorts at least two sizes too small. With his white socks and chubby hairless legs his appearance was that of an overgrown schoolboy, and a navy baseball hat (like a school cap) completed the schoolboy image.

'Excuse me,' said Roger, 'are you the owner of this boat?'

'Absolutely,' said the man and fixed a pair of guileless blue eyes on Rodger.

'I thought you might like to take a look at these,' said Rodger producing the two framed sketches.

'Absolutely, old boy,' said the man, 'let's pop on board, shall we?' and he led the way across the gang plank. 'Teresa darling, come and look at these,' he shouted.

A sun-baked Teresa emerged from below with the two Dalmatians close on her heels.

'Darling, these are awesome,' she said, ignoring Roger. 'Oh darling, just look at Nero and Salome.' Nero hearing the sound of his name immediately got on his hind legs and amorously fastened himself around

Teresa's arm.

'Naughty doggy,' she said patting Nero on the nose. 'Aubrey darling, I just love these pictures. Will you buy them for me darling?' and still ignoring Roger she fluttered her eye lashes at Aubrey who appeared to be on another planet.

'Absolutely,' he said, 'How much was that picture we bought in Antibes darling?'

'That was 700 euros darling – and it wasn't even framed.'

'Absolutely,' said Aubrey. He turned to Roger and produced a wad of notes from the back pocket of his shorts. 'How about 600 euros for the two old chum?' and handed the pictures to Teresa then peeled off twelve 50-euro notes and gave them to Roger.

To Roger's amazement Aubrey then turned to him and putting his hand on his shoulder in a confidential manner spoke quite loudly in his ear

'You're a lucky young bugger, alone in Nice with the chance to shaft all these young French birds,' then without even a cheerio he nipped Roger's bottom and disappeared below deck. Teresa ignored the remark (and the nip) and stretched out on a sunbed as though Roger didn't exist. Crossing the gangway it was a puzzle to Roger figuring out how the other half lived. Were there many potential customers who would pay him 600 euros and nip his bottom? What a laugh – the mind boggled.

Boats sailed in and out of the port, and the ferry for Corsica came and went. Roger sat on the harbour side contemplating his success. One rose didn't make a summer and if he was going to make a business out of sketching boats, he would have to sketch a hell of a lot of boats. Still – he was elated by selling the pictures of the Marigold, and was there the makings of a wider enterprise he could set up in Nice? It was worth thinking about.

On Tuesday's trip to Cap Ferrat he had spotted a villa which intrigued him. Set back on the cliff top between Nice and Villfranche it looked more like a castle than a home. Like most large properties it was almost completely surrounded by trees ensuring that the owners were hidden from prying eyes, nevertheless such an unusual building merited a closer look. Half an hours walk along the wooded hilltop and the nearer he got to the villa the more it looked like a fortress. There was massive security at the entrance, which was blocked by an impact proof iron gate, and a twelve-foot-high wire fence surrounded the house and grounds. He was surprised by how peaceful it was. Two large black saloon cars were parked on the driveway but apart from that there were no other signs of life. The house was majestic but austere, and reminded him of something out of a Bronte novel. Illustrating it would be a challenge – but what an achievement if he could do a good job and flog the picture to the owner. His father (and old rumble tummy in Town Planning) wouldn't believe it.

There were several good vantage points where small trees and clumps of bushes offered a hidden spot from which to operate. After an hour's preliminary work, he stepped out into the open and took photographs until a reflected light from an upper window warned him that he was being watched through binoculars. An armed security guard suddenly appeared from nowhere and started moving towards him. Roger stowed away his pencils and pad and walked back into Nice. Not a good time to get himself shot. He would resume work another day.

In the old market place the stalls were bustling with tourists. He sat amongst the lime trees with a beer admiring the flower displays and watching locals carefully selecting the day's fruit. Every café and restaurant lining the marketplace was busy. Every stall of vegetables, antiques, books, towels, was beautifully laid out so each display created an independent picture – every stall a manifestation of art and the afternoon sun lit up the market and shoppers like a scene from a stage show.

This was everyday life in Nice and Roger loved it. Ideas were beginning to take shape and thoughts of regular liaisons with Elissa added to their appeal. An extended stay here could turn out to be an exciting prospect.

On the apartment table Elissa had placed a rose in an empty wine bottle, and another one by his bed. The whole place had been cleaned until it sparkled.

He had missed his morning run and made up for it by having a mammoth session in the gym. On the punch bags and speed ball he was in championship form, and while taking a break he observed the '*brick shithouse*' from the casino bench pressing enough weight to sprain an RTR Tractor. He half raised his hand to Roger in silent salutation.

It was late when he knocked at Elissa's door and there was no reply. In Roger's mailbox a card from Australia informed him Aunt Evelyn had met a 'golden oldie' with whom she was drinking under the table and she was unlikely to be home any time soon. Aunt Evelyn had the right idea – sod it, and he rang Jet 2 and cancelled Sunday's flight. He was busy making adjustments to the mini castle when Elissa used her key to slide in as though she owned the place, and laughingly bit his ear.

'Tonight, is celebration night,' said Roger, 'I sold the pictures.'

'I like celebrate pictures. So, where you take me?' She found a chilled wine in the fridge, poured out two glasses and gave him the Elissa wink. The cool wine and the wink took immediate effect on Roger anticipating the onset of another lesson from '1001 Arabian Nights'. However – today was his lucky day, and he put the sex lessons on hold until after a trip to the casino.

'I very like the casino,' said Elissa, 'and tonight I wear my new black dress for you.'

She promptly did her strip-trick and bared all before using his shower and returning downstairs to get changed.

At the casino, Roger ordered a bottle of champagne and was again shown to a restaurant table overlooking the gaming. The food was excellent and superbly presented, and the bottle of champagne came surprisingly well priced. Elissa looked stunning in her new black dress and as Roger guided her down the restaurant steps the world was his oyster and he was in the right mood for a rip-roaring evening.

Making their way between tables they passed the '*brick shithouse*' standing stiff as a board in his dinner suit. He acknowledged Roger with a slight nod, never letting his face slip.

Elissa whispered in Roger's ear, 'That man Monty. Him working for very dangerous man.'

'How do you know?' asked Roger.

'I know,' she replied.

Roger bought 200 euros worth of chips and gave half to Elissa. From then on there was no holding her back. She played the slot machines, she had a round of Blackjack, and when she eventually sat down at the roulette table it became clear she was no stranger to the game. Using a variety of intricate compilations, she won and lost and won and lost insisting on using her own money to top up with another 200 euros which she lost within an hour. She laughed non-stop entertaining players at the table with absurd comments, and flirting with a fat man (dripping with wealth) who was trying hard to catch her attention. A hard-faced woman with massive arms and dangling earrings watched Elissa enviously, whilst the serious faced croupier unmistakably found Elissa's effervescence distracting.

Thursday was a quiet night in the casino. It hadn't the same buzz of the previous Saturday and after an hour at the roulette table Roger began to get bored. He had neither won nor lost, and was finishing with pretty much the same number of chips as he started with so he went for broke, doubled up and made a straight-up bet on number 17 and won at the brilliant odds of thirty-five to one.

'Hell-fire, I've done it again,' he said. Elissa went ecstatic, jumped up and knocked over her fat admirer's cocktail. Roger gathered up his chips to cash in and

Monty's questioning eyes followed him all the way to the desk. Outside was still warm with clear starlit skies. Walking back to the apartment it struck Roger that he had accrued more money from selling his pictures and gambling than he had spent during the whole of his three weeks in Nice.

When he unzipped Elissa's black dress, she was more desirable than ever. But tonight, wasn't going to be a games night, and he picked her up and dropped her on the bed taking charge of the evening's lovemaking. He held her back and copied Elissa's technique, moving around her body with kisses and gentle bites. She wriggled with delight, and he felt her wet and ready for him straight away.

'From behind Roger – I like from behind,' and she knelt on the bed with her firm round buttocks facing him. As he lifted her buttocks to enter his hand slipped round where he could comfortably caress her as he moved. Elissa was never still. She shifted and turned with his thrusts, always fluid, always in tune, co-ordinating her movements to grip and squeeze which added to their pleasure. They lay together side by side and their slow rhythmic love making lasted into the early hours of morning.

He had promised to paint Elissa on Saturday. In the morning he played football and when he walked onto the football pitch he got the same greeting as the previous week and received the same shouts of '*Allez l'Anglais!*' when he scored. Amine told him it was the last game of the season – no more football until October. At the end of the game Roger felt quite emotional shaking hands with all of the players and there were claps from their wives as Elissa trotted onto the field and commandeered him.

What an experience! Football with the home team would never be the same again.

Roger needed to catch the afternoon light in order to paint well. He had no problem painting nude figures. He had painted nudes before at evening classes in Manchester. But capturing Elissa's facial features and doing full justice to her was going to be a challenge he wasn't sure he could meet. And then again how long could he keep his distance from a nude Elissa while he painted her. This wasn't a fast-fading model from Manchester old enough to be his grandmother.

At the apartment Elissa said, 'We have shower Roger,' and after ten minutes of shower games she had soaped away enough of his cravings to allow a workable degree of concentration. As ever Elissa was bubbling over and if he was going to paint her the big problem would be getting her to keep still. He took photographs covering different angles, and found a position where she turned away from the camera and he was able to complete a rough pre-sketch without worrying about accurate facial details. Everything – her eyes, her mouth, the shape of her face and the teasing smile were perfect. As he started painting, the light caught the tinges of blue in Elissa's short dark hair and Roger recalled the words of a song - *'softer than the down on a blue Raven's wing'*. His paint brush hovered around the flat contours of her stomach and suddenly he had to remind himself – Elissa is married to 'man bastard' and this affair is not meant to last. With that stroke of the paint brush Roger made a decision: life is a journey not a destination – enjoy the affair before something happens and it fizzles out.

So began the most mind-blowing, lottery-blowing four weeks to exceed anything he had ever imagined. He called at the airport and hired a Mercedes. He wined and dined Elissa nightly and in spite of her protestations bought designer outfits from the most expensive shops on *Avenue de Verdun* providing something new for every casino visit. They drove everywhere visiting as many tourist destinations as time would allow. Most days Elissa finished work by lunchtime and it allowed time to see Grasse and pay a return visit to Eze and Cagnes-sur-mer showing her around the museums and art galleries.

Some afternoons were spent on the beach where he hired chairs in close proximity to restaurants serving lunch, and they dined on oysters and champagne. One day they dressed to be noticed and drove to Cannes, walking the promenade trying to spot the rich and famous and ate a ludicrously expensive evening meal in one of the sea front hotels. The evening ended on a note of embarrassment when Roger found he had forgotten his credit card and it took Elissa's French, and Roger's positive assurances, to persuade the hotel manager into accepting that a delayed cheque would be forwarded to the hotel later.

On the second weekend they took the coast road through Menton then over the border, and driving into Sanremo where they stayed for two nights. Sanremo was disappointing. Shabby and run down. Gambling at *Casino di Sanremo* was even more disappointing because Roger lost money both nights. Fortunately love making in the king-size bed at the Grand Hotel compensated for the casino, and the Grand Hotel's restaurant lived up to its acclaimed five-star reputation. Roger was spending money like he had never spent money before and he didn't care.

Back in Nice they found a small Lebanese café off the tourist trail where there was music and amazingly good food. They twice went back to Restaurant Acchiardo on Rue Droite and there was La Baie d'Amalfi on the corner of Avenue de Medecin where Italian food was a step above the usual pizzas and spaghetti. But most of all there was Elissa - so amusing and unpredictable, you never knew what she would do next. Regularly she added spice to their meals by suddenly gripping his leg under the table and whispering something suggestive to turn him on. He got wise to this and halfway through eating he would do the same to her, and the more graphic the suggestions he made the more she laughed and loved it. Any sex experience that Roger had lacked in married life he was fast acquiring with Elissa, in fact sometimes he wondered if she was coaching him for a diploma.

The weeks flew by. There were early evening sessions working with Elissa on her painting, and on several mornings, he approached yacht owners showing his portfolio of sketches but there were no takers. At the old port he passed two artists who were set up to paint views of the boats docked in the harbour. Both artists were good – very good, far better than he would ever be. If he was going to pursue illustration on a profitable basis his own speciality was buildings, and he needed to develop that side of his work accordingly. But there was no rush to do anything. Life was sweet.

He went back to the fortified villa outside Villefranche. He worked unhampered for two mornings, sectioning the villa and grounds into adjoining views. On his third visit the black saloon cars were parked on the driveway and the security guard waved him off before he had time to even put pen to paper.

There was plenty of time for training sessions. He never missed a day alternating a run one morning with a visit to the gym the next. Mick continued to address cheery text messages to 'Roger-the-bodger' and home news from Howard told him Joan was suffering from morning sickness, and their house hunting had been put on hold.

But Ana – Ana was puzzling. Nothing from her, then three or four emails would arrive in a row. Always apologetic, always busy, always corresponding from some far-flung city. He couldn't complain that she hadn't warned him, but he realised that if he was home Ana wouldn't be around when he wanted her, whilst here in Nice he was having a ball and thoughts of an absent Ana and Manchester life receded a little further away every day. But the music couldn't play forever. There was an urgent voice mail from his parents – when will you be going home?

Roger phoned his father who was out playing golf. His mother answered and came straight to the point.

'Your father thinks you should go home and get things sorted out. Rosemary phoned for your address. We got the feeling that her affair with that man is over, and I had quite a long talk with her'.

'Well, I am glad she talks to you,' said Roger, 'because I haven't heard a dicky bird from her.' Suddenly the reminder that the house and their affairs would have to be taken care of loomed like a dark cloud on the horizon. And Rosemary had his email address – why phone his mother? He didn't wait long for an answer. Three days later he received an unwelcome letter.

Dear Roger,

I have moved back into our house.

Everything of yours is exactly as you left it, and will remain so until we have sorted things out between us.

St Mary's have promoted me to Assistant Head which means a lot more work and a lot more responsibility. I am very busy.

I know I must have hurt you leaving you the way I did. However, you must take some share of the responsibility Roger. It seemed as though you were never going to grow up or learn from your mistakes.

We will discuss everything when I see you.

Rosemary

Roger's first thought was 'Damn! There goes my love nest with Ana.' And his second thought was – 'what love nest?' He ate an omelette and fries in the café opposite, and sat thinking about it. Returning to married life was a 'no-no'. So where was he going to live? No home, no job, and Ana floating about all over the globe.

He walked along the *Promenade des Anglais*. Deck chairs on the beach were nearly all occupied by sun tanned bodies. The sea wasn't warm yet, but plenty of bikini clad bathers were testing the water before risking a swim. A click of glasses and the hum of quiet conversation followed Roger as he passed some of the fashionable sea front cafés. The four o'clock wine drinking set who congregated every afternoon to see and be seen had already taken over the shaded spots evaluating everyone who walked by. A couple of women with painted faces and ruby red nails (both old enough to be his mother) flashed him a smile. Yes, all of this was great, and he had had a terrific holiday but after six weeks he needed to get home and straighten out his affairs besides taking stock before his little pot of gold ran out.

He turned around and headed back to the apartment. Most weekend flights were fully booked but he found a late afternoon flight on Sunday which would get him into Manchester at about 9pm. He sat at the table flicking through his recent handiwork. He had finished painting Elissa. It was a good painting, but it didn't look a lot like her. On the other hand, detailed sketches of the mini-castle at Villefranche were superb – they would look impressive in anybody's portfolio. Let's face it, he trained to be an architect and finished up as a draftsman. – he loved buildings.

Tonight, Elissa looked breath-taking in her orange dress. He took her to the Yacht Club where the restaurant had superb sea views. She was quiet when he told her he was returning home to sort out his affairs and she didn't believe him when he said he would be coming back to Nice. The night temperature was still warm as they walked slowly back to the apartment with his arm around her. Suddenly she stopped, and threw her arms around him and kissed him passionately full on the lips as she had never kissed him before. They made love and it wasn't a game any longer.

She stayed with him all Saturday night and the following morning. She remained serious while she watched him pack, and it wasn't until he was ready to leave for the airport that Elissa bubbled over into being Elissa again.

As he got into the car she said, 'You see woman when you go home?'

'That is part of the plan,' said Roger.

'Well, you show your woman all the things I teach you and do good?' and she was still choking with laughter as she waved him goodbye.

5. Home and Away

There was over an hour's delay before take-off. After returning the Mercedes to Avis.

Roger sat in the airport lounge waiting impatiently with too much time to think.

He arrived late into Manchester and booked straight into Holiday Inn Express. Awakening to a typical grey day Roger still hadn't formed any plans and postponed taking a taxi until mid-morning. A look at the morning papers confirmed that nothing had changed. BREXIT was still the big story, and the newspaper headlines repeated themselves with monotonous regularity depending on which paper you picked up.

He calculated Rosemary would be at school until well after five giving him ample time to look around and make decisions before they met. Roger had no idea when she had moved back into the house, but she certainly hadn't wasted any time. It was raining as he got out of the taxi but the neat array of flowers in the front garden presented a well-tended picture, and when he walked into the hallway there was the fresh smell of paint. The lounge was newly carpeted with curtains to match, and a sparkling 40-inch screen Sony TV overlooked the new pale green suite. So where had she found the money to do all this?

A phone call to Brown's garage was answered by a bright sounding female voice who informed him that Ana no longer worked there, whilst Escorts Bilingual office in Manchester replied with an automated recording asking him to leave a message.

So that was that! Catching Ana was a dead loss but worth a try and he might just as well settle for the fact that you fall out of bed on the wrong side if you try to jump into bed with a partner who works hundreds of miles away. Some romance!

Roger adjourned to the kitchen and made an Earl Grey tea to wash away his greasy hotel breakfast. He opened the fridge door and three ready meals fell out. Rosemary never was much of a cook. Roger sat drinking his tea and thinking about the relationship he had had with his wife. She wanted a baby and blamed Roger when nothing happened. He started to chuckle when he recalled Elissa's parting advice and pictured himself 'doing good' with Rosmary while she lay there stiff as a wooden plank. That was it – he made up his mind. There was nothing here to keep him and nothing to sort out.

The Alpha Romeo sang like a bird as he backed it out of the garage. There wasn't much room in the boot so he was going to have to pack carefully. Upstairs he worked for two hours getting together things he might need. Extra clothes were packed straight into the boot without a suitcase. His printer, photographs and working materials fitted into the back of the car, and books, DVD'S and CDs were slotted in wherever there was room. All bedrooms had a fitted wardrobe and items left behind from the main bedroom transferred easily into empty space in his office. When he finally squeezed his Roberts Zoombox behind the driving seat, he was satisfied that the only things he was leaving behind was the house, his memories, and Rosemary. He wrote her a short note.

Dear Rosemary,

I am staying in Nice to start a new business. I may or may not be successful but until I come back to Manchester the house is all yours.

I don't think there is anything to sort out. What's past is past – you and I will always be pals.

Good luck with the new job.

Roger

When the note was written he felt better for it. Never burn your boats. As an afterthought he placed his sketches of the house extension alongside the note, and left them both on the kitchen table.

It was an astonishingly clear run down to Dover. By 7.00 he was through the tunnel and drove straight to Le Touquet and booked in at the Red Fox. As he walked into the hotel bedroom his mobile rang and Rosemary's voice came on the phone, 'Roger, couldn't you have possibly just waited to see me?'

'Couldn't you have just waited to see me Rosemary when you marched out with half the furniture and moved in with Jack Fearnley?'

There was a silence and the phone went dead. It was the first time he had spoken to his wife since she left him and he didn't feel a thing.

Next morning Roger lingered over breakfast and planned his journey. A walk round Le Touquet (once the playground of the rich) brought back memories of holidays with his parents which always started at the Red Fox before travelling further down the coast. He wanted to avoid Paris and picked up the A26 at Arras and drove nonstop to Dijon. The roads weren't busy, the car was a joy to drive, and with its spacious parking facilities he settled for a couple of nights in the Holiday Inn.

In the back-packing days of his youth, he had worked for four weeks picking grapes at a village just outside Dijon centre. He spent a day revisiting the city's sights, and whiled away most of the following day in and around Palais des Ducs relaxing with a beer and watching the flocks of cosmopolitan tourists.

He was late out of Dijon, held up by the traffic. At breakfast he had been adopted by an interesting couple from London who he met in the bar the previous evening. They lived three quarters of the year in Nice, and the husband was a keen yachtsman who according to his wife spent more time on his boat than in their much-loved house overlooking the ocean. Both conducted their accountancy business on the internet, and only returned to London to visit their daughters.

'John and Jane. Look us up and we will take you out sailing' and John handed Roger his card with the name of his yacht – 'Sky Fly' written on the back.

Roger journeyed as far as Avignon and stopped over in a cheap Motel rather than arrive late into Nice. He ate a burger and lukewarm fries reflecting on his lightning trip home. Worrying about women and living under the grey skies of Manchester was for the birds. He could make it work in Nice. If the South of France was good enough for the rich and famous then it was the right place for Roger Kelly.

Driving with the hood down on the coast road between Cannes and Nice, Roger was like a King returning to his Kingdom. When he reached the apartment's car park the gates responded to the security code, opening majestically for him to drive through and park between a Mercedes and a Lamborghini. Aunt Evelyn's apartment was his home. He would buy it from her.

Five times he climbed up and down the steps before the car's contents were fully unloaded but the moment he stepped into the lounge he sensed something was wrong.

Six empty wine bottles each containing a rose were dotted around the bedrooms and living area. Elissa hadn't put water in the bottles and the roses were wilting with petals scattered all over the floor and over his papers.

There wasn't an answer when he knocked at her door. He tried again later and still no reply. When he came to straighten up the pile of sketch work on the lounge table the painting of Elissa was missing. Also missing were multiple views of the fortified villa sketched outside Villefranche, and after searching around he turned to his portfolio where there was an empty space previously occupied by the picture of his own planned hacienda. They couldn't have disappeared. An immense amount of work was involved in both sets of drawings, and his hacienda was the product of years of imagination and adjustments.

There were no signs of Elissa. The weekend passed without any explanation until climbing the stairs he bumped into a cleaner he hadn't met before.

'Are you the occupant of number eight?'

'Yes Roger Kelly'.

'Pleased to meet you Mr Kelly. I have taken over the servicing for your apartment.

10am Mondays, Wednesdays, and Fridays if that's alright with you?'

'Elissa services my apartment,' said Roger.

'Is that the young girl who went back to Beirut? Oh, don't worry about her love she left on Wednesday. I'm from Liverpool. You can trust me to do a good job for you'.

So, Elissa had left. Not even a goodbye note, and surely, she hadn't taken his drawings. What use would they be to her in Beirut unless 'man bastard' was building a castle. Losing Elissa without saying goodbye was bad enough. Loss of his work too was really disheartening, and he could not believe that Elissa was responsible.

He phoned his parents. His father was surprisingly agreeable about the Rosemary situation and didn't shoot down his plans to set up in Nice. Next in line was Ana.

Last time he heard from her she was in Russia. He wrote a lengthy email to say he had been home and collected the Alpha Romeo, his wife had moved back into their house, and he had moved to France to start a business. Roger had seen Ana's website. He never stopped thinking about her, but with her work coupled with his new venture in France he couldn't imagine how they would ever get together again.

Ana was tired. She was so very tired. She had been involved in a meeting that went on for four solid hours. Translating had been a nightmare and then she had been stuck with a Russian who she had to suffer over dinner, and then make it quite plain she wasn't going to bed with him.

St. Petersburg was supposed to be beautiful. Ana found it rather shabby but perhaps she had been too busy to explore the place properly. The hotel was comfortable but the food was awful, and although Scottie looked after her very well the long hours and pressure to promote his business was harder than she bargained for. Roger's email came at a bad moment.

In her heart she knew that her work and his decision to set up in France were incompatible. But she clung on to the hope that some miracle would happen and she would see him again – even if it was many months away. When she received his email on her mobile, she excused herself and went up to her room and emailed him straight back. Would he understand?

Within 30 minutes, Ana had come back with a reply – the longest communication he had received from her in weeks.

My dearest Roger,

I cannot explain my situation to you. It seems as though I have forgotten you but you are never out of my mind. You are going to be very successful in France, Roger. I know you will be very successful. Work hard and please be patient with me.

I will not be travelling the world much longer

and then if you still want me, I will be with you wherever you are. I am going home to Croatia for two weeks. There are things I want to tell you but I need to have time to write properly so that you will understand.

You have all my love Roger.

Ana

Roger sat back and tried to digest Ana's reply. His feelings for her surged so strongly that his legs went weak. Two women had left him dangling in the air, and this woman who he craved for was far away in Russia. If he was going to buy a yacht, he would need to do a hell of a site better in business than he had done so far in his love life.

His mind full of Ana and Elissa he paid a visit to Elissa's picture frame man and had a photograph taken wearing a dark suit and tie. Next was the design for a leaflet and business card. The printing was as good as the framing and using superior quality paper Roger's business cards and leaflets turned out brilliantly. Every leaflet showed the suited photograph of himself above a small, sketched villa, and at the bottom of each leaflet a reproduction of the Marigold.

The wording on both his cards and his leaflets was printed in gold type.

ROGER KELLY. DRAUGHTSMAN. DESIGNER. ARTIST.
Add prestige to your property. Boats and ancestral homes a speciality.

The results were classy by any standards. He had no idea where to place the leaflets or where to place the business cards, but now he was prepared for anything.

For one hour each day he disciplined himself to listen to a French language CD from his uncle's collection or studied 'Teach Yourself French' discovered tucked away on a shelf in the apartment's mini library. He was going to succeed.

It was a still a novelty driving the car and he circulated Cap Ferrat, Monaco and Monte Carlo, taking note of prospective properties whose owners might like their opulent dwellings illustrated for the sake of posterity. He needed contacts. A stroll around the old port soon uncovered the whereabouts of John and Jane's 'Sky Fly' modestly anchored near the Yachting Club. It was a small trim boat built for a yachtsman who enjoyed sailing as opposed to owning a floating home. Roger took photographs and drew a rough sketch to work on at leisure. The Marigold had gone, and another luxury yacht was berthed in its place. A professional artist had set up nearby with easel and canvas, and if he wasn't actually painting the yacht, he was certainly including it in an overall harbour scene.

The Liverpudlian lady caught him as he climbed the apartment steps and handed him a large envelope.

'A man came today and asked me to give you this'

Roger opened the envelope to find inside the missing sketches of both the villa and his hacienda.

'What did he look like?' asked Roger.

'He was a big bugger. You wouldn't want to argue

with him.'

There were double security locks on the apartment door. To gain entry you had to have a key. That meant that while he was away somebody had put pressure on Elissa in order to walk into Roger's flat and help himself. Well, whoever that big bugger was Roger was going to find him. The most likely candidate had to be associated with the villa he sketched outside Villefranche which checked out on the internet as Villa Romano, and the owner's name Antonio Romano. Roger couldn't find a telephone number and became angrily frustrated by his lack of French.

It had been an unproductive day. In the evening he found his feet propelling him in the direction of the casino. He was going to miss Elissa and the idea that somebody might have frightened her to obtain the flat keys bugged him, and it bugged him more because he didn't know what to do about it.

Tonight, the casino was dead apart from the 'no hopers'. A few elderly ladies were engrossed working the slot machines, and a set of bystanders who didn't look to have two euros to share between them wandered listlessly around watching the players.

There was minimum action at the roulette table. Three shifty looking Albanians were clearly on a losing streak, and a thickly made-up woman with an ugly beauty spot leered at Roger as he took his place beside her. Over at the blackjack table Roger watched Monty (stiff as ever) giving a player a hard time for breaking the rules, and frog marching the man out of the casino.

Roger didn't plan staying for long but found he was

losing and wasn't going to be beaten. Switching back to his formula of betting on even numbers the wins began to accumulate again but it took two hours to turn a 200-euro loss into a 200-euro gain. He cashed in his chips. It was a good time to take a leak and call it a day.

Having a pee in the casino toilets was part of the evening's pleasure. They were the most luxurious, sweet-smelling facilities he had ever experienced. Above the wash basins was a better choice of toiletries than you would expect at the Ritz, and the walls and urinals were covered in bright shining steel – like walking into an air-conditioned hall of mirrors. Roger heard the Albanians coming as he zipped up his fly. Two of them shot through the door straight towards him. He spun round and kicked the first one just below the knee, and the leg collapsed. The second man close behind the first half stumbled and Roger stepped to the right and left hooked him to the solar plexus, chopping him behind the ear as he doubled up and fell on top of his pal. There was another loud scuffle at the doorway and Albanian number three hit the floor with a thump, followed by Monty close on his tail.

'Thought you might need a hand mate, but I can see that you didn't'. He spoke into his cell phone and two more security men joined him and between them they hauled Roger's would-be assailants off the floor and out of the cassino. In two minutes, he was back and held out his hand

'Monty Bell' he said. 'East-end if you hadn't guessed'.

'Roger Kelly' and they shook hands.

'You did well there mate, but make sure you watch

your back in future'.

'Well, I wasn't stood admiring the reflection of my penis when I dealt with those two' replied Roger, and Monty actually grinned as he walked back onto the floor.

Next day the rain fell down in buckets. Unable to go anywhere he completed the picture of Sky Fly with the usual touches of colour. Drawing yachts wasn't going to provide him with a living, but the contacts might be useful. Looking closely at mini castle Villa Romano there were final touches to be completed. Also, what was it that made the villa so important that someone entered his apartment solely to borrow a picture of the place? The villa was worth another visit.

Friday dawned brightly with the prospect of cloudless skies spilling over into a perfect day. Roger packed his shoulder bag and took the drawing of Sky Fly to be framed. It was late morning by the time he had walked back through town and along the cliff path to reach Romano's villa and the two black saloons were already parked on the driveway but otherwise there were no signs of life. He didn't bother occupying his previously concealed sketching position, but taking out one of the drawings he leaned against a tree and worked in full view of the upper windows. A flicker of light alerted him to being observed through binoculars, but nothing happened. If you had money, why would you live in a place like this? It was built like a military prison.

The morning was hot, very hot. He had forgotten his hat and he hadn't packed a water bottle. In a very short period of time his diagrams were completed, and it was too hot to hang around. He set off walking back to Nice along the main road with his mission unfulfilled.

He heard the villa's security gates open and close as he left, and the black saloon with its blacked-out windows crept past him and suddenly stopped twelve yards in front. A man jumped out and barred his way, and the saloon's back window rolled slowly down.

'Monsieur Kelly, you are looking tired. You have been busy. Please – jump in and allow me to offer you a lift into Nice'. The man barring his way was the armed security guard from the villa. The driver of the saloon was Monty from the casino. So, if Roger's conclusions were correct the man inviting him into the hearse was the dangerous man Elissa had mentioned.

As Roger stepped into the car, he hoped he wasn't en route to his own funeral.

6. Ana

Whenever Ana went home to Croatia it tore her heart in two. Luke was now nearly four years old. He was so affectionate, so loving. He would throw his arms around her and she would bury her head in his golden curls. She was his mother but he would never be able to call her mother – she had assigned that task to her sister when he was only six months old. Her sister and her husband adored him, and now nothing could ever be changed.

It was six weeks before she had realized she was pregnant. By that time Jakub had left for Poland and had been back with his wife and family for well over a month.

Ana didn't try to contact him. It had been her choice. She knew he was married, and she knew their romance was a casual one, so she wasn't going to risk spoiling his life when it would be of no benefit to herself anyway.

After completing another six months of studies in Manchester, she went home and joined her mother and sister in their family house at the top of the cobbled streets of Rovinj. Her mother was wonderful – she had always been wonderful in the way she had forfeited so much for Ana and her elder sister after their father died.

When she knew Ana was pregnant her mother accepted it without fuss. Baby or not it was a relief to have Ana home after nursing Petra through 18 months treatment for breast cancer. Petra had recovered. It was a celebration all being together again and although sleeping space was cramped, they managed very well with Ana and the baby sleeping in the attic bedroom.

What a relief it was getting out of Russia. No amount of money would persuade her to undertake another trip like that again. She sat on the beach wriggling her toes in the warm sand. Petra and Luke were in the sea, both trying to balance on a dingy and falling off with Luke gurgling with laughter at every fall. He was a very healthy little boy and taking responsibility for him had helped Petra gain a new lease of life.

They came out of the sea radiant. Luke ran to Ana and dragged her into the water for her turn to fall off the dingy.

It was two months after Ana's baby was born that Petra got married, and her new husband joined them in their small family home and the house became much smaller.

It was a blow to Petra when she discovered she couldn't have children, and it made sense for her to look after Luke so that Ana could return to Manchester and complete her final year. Petra's husband was a fisherman. He was never sure how much he would earn. When Ana returned to university her escort business was more important than ever. She needed all the money she could get to help support her mother and sister whilst also covering university expenses.

Ana had always loved Rovinj. She loved its picturesque simplicity and basic local life – and she loved the way the town remained unspoiled in spite of its reliance on tourism. But once you had experienced university and acquired a degree, you outgrew your birth place. Even the thoughts of Rovinj's tennis club and sun kissed days on the beach couldn't tempt her to abandon the thrill of success and the sheer thrusting ambition that took over her life amidst the grey hustle bustle of Manchester.

Mr Brown and his failing garage were manna from heaven when she walked into the job on the same day she received her degree. She managed to successfully fit selling cars and the ever-growing demands of the agency into one very profitable package by working non-stop. The rewards were immense. Inside one year she had leapt into a top executive wage bracket – an outstanding accomplishment for anyone fresh out of college.

Meeting Roger had never been part of her plans. Sitting thinking about it the whole escapade was ridiculous. The agony of walking away from Brown's after two years of building the business, and then the past three months fighting to fill the financial gap. It was senseless to still be mooning over Roger after weeks of exhausting hard work. A few days of an intense affair with someone she hadn't seen again for over three months, and yet she still couldn't get him out of her mind.

Petra and Luke brought the dingy out of the sea after a final dip. Luke was hungry – she could tell. They deposited the dingy in their back yard and then they collected her mother and Ana took them all to the nearest café for lunch. Eating out in Rovinj was so cheap, and the fish was so fresh. She watched her mother as Luke tucked into his food and used his knife and fork unaided. Becoming Luke's grandmother was a new lease of life to her as well as for Petra, and although Ana was happy for them both she was envious of how well they looked, and how enraptured they were with her son. The son who could never be her son.

She could tell by his emails that Roger had met someone. Starting a business was not the only thing keeping him in Nice. She didn't expect him to be a monk – she wasn't a nun. But the few liaisons Ana had time for on her travels were disappointing and unimportant. Given time perhaps her relationship with Roger would have fizzled out. What Ana knew for sure was that those few days they had spent together were so perfect that they were a love affair in the making. They had been so happy together that both of them knew they had hit upon something very special. Would Roger be able to find that so soon with anyone else?

In the evening she made up a four with Petra, her husband, and his fisherman friend. They had been out together four or five times previously, and the friend had fallen for her straight away. She insisted on going Dutch and paying her way and the more Ana tried to cool the relationship the more attracted to her he became. Today he had sent a bouquet of flowers before he arrived. She looked across the table at him. He was younger than her – he was a lovely man. His deep tan enhanced the depth of his startling blue eyes, and the broad shoulders, colourful shirt, and large gold earring reminded you of a pirate starring in a technicolour film. She would love to go to bed with him, but if she did in his eyes, it would be a commitment and she didn't want to hurt him. Her affair with Roger had left her with a deep intense longing in her groin which sometimes seemed unbearable to live with. Unconsciously she would often find that she was caressing herself to ease away the ache, and lying in bed with her thoughts made that ache ten times worse.

Petra took Luke to the nursery and Ana walked up to the church with seagulls accompanying her all the way. She used to spend hours there when she was very young. It was a beautiful church. Simple, peaceful, and the venue for visiting choirs who made exchange visits, and gave choral performances all over Croatia.

The morning started off grey with a hint of rain. The stone cobbles were slippery and twice Ana lost her footing and managed to stop a serious fall. Today there was nobody in the church and quiet recorded music added to the tranquillity. Ana wasn't religious, and it was many years since she sat here inside the church. There was a lump in her throat as she remembered her childhood. Her father. Carefree days of play with her sister, and now perhaps something missing in her life which in her heart she wanted so much.

She bent her head and prayed. Outside the clouds parted and the strong July sun broke through. The first beams shone through the church window directly onto Ana, and her clenched hands were like holding a lamp light in front of her.

At that moment Ana knew she was going to see Roger again.

7. The Contract

If Roger had expected to meet a gun toting Al Capone, he was disappointed. The man inviting him into the back of the car looked anything but dangerous.

'An ice-cold beer, a whisky, a fruit juice? Tell me your pleasure Mr Kelly?'

At the touch of a button a mini bar appeared. His host was probably in his mid-fifties. Dark haired and clean shaven. Slim – dressed in an immaculately tailored linen suit, with an intense smile displaying a set of pearl white teeth. Roger chose a bierre blanche, and sank back in the cool comfort of the air conditioning curious to know what was coming next.

'You seem to have a consuming interest in my property Mr Kelly, perhaps you would like to tell me all about yourself.'

'Well after entering my apartment, you know more about me than I know about you Mr Romano.'

'I must apologise. My business is property. I own hotels on the Côte d'Azur. I rent out villas. I have shares in the casino where you play roulette, and I own the gymnasium where you train. When someone takes photographs of my home and makes numerous trips to sketch details of my property, I have to know who they are. I don't think that is unreasonable – do you?' The Italian accent was strong.

'You see – you are an enigma Mr Kelly. You gamble, and you always win. You appear to be what you English would call 'a hard man'. You train in the gym. You box. And you had no trouble despatching our Albanian friends when they sought to relieve you of your winnings. You are a footballer with half of North Africa amongst your loyal followers – including our little friend from Beirut. So, who are you? What are you doing in Nice? Perhaps you are a member of Manchester's notorious Quality Street Gang – here to suss me out.'

Roger felt confident and laughed. 'I am interested in architecture Mr Romano. The design of your villa is unusual.'

'That tells me nothing Mr Kelly. Grant me the privilege of entertaining you to lunch, and we will talk further,' and with a curt instruction 'Da Mario's' to Monty the car changed direction, travelling above the wooded cliffs and skirting the edge of Villefranche. This is the man who sent the 'big bugger' to my apartment thought Roger. He wants something and he isn't going to find me a push-over.

There was a flurry of attention at Da Mario's. Antonio Romano obviously had a reputation which demanded attention and the head waiter nearly fell over himself as he led them to a shaded table under the trees. Glancing through the menu, and listening to the hum of quiet conversation at scattered tables this was a meeting place attracting discerning diners. Mr Romano didn't intend cutting corners. It was a lunch meant to impress – but why?

'A family from Naples Mr Kelly. Good Italian food. I hope you like it.'

'Thank you, Mr Romano. Italian food suits me admirably' said Roger 'And of course it is a pleasure to learn how you believe I can assist you.'

108

Sitting opposite Antonio Romano Roger couldn't help but admire him. He exuded an understated aura of power. He was a handsome man who paid a lot of attention to his appearance. His hands were manicured and sideboards carefully trimmed. There was a brief glimpse of gold amongst the pearl white teeth, and the single gold ring on his left hand perfectly matched the large gold watch which drew your attention without being ostentatious. Looking through the wine list Romano obviously enjoyed being noticed. Diners paused their lunch to determine who was getting the VIP treatment, and Roger got a kick out of the perceived importance he was sharing with his host.

'You see business is not just about making money Mr Kelly – it's keeping it once you have got it. You tell me you are interested in architecture. I too am interested in architecture. I engage a recommended architect. He sits on his arse and charges me money whenever he takes a shit. So, then another architect. He pretends to work while he is shagging my secretary. He thinks I am naïve. He offers me copies of designs he sold to someone else – so I get rid of him, together with my secretary. I pay good money. Tell me – why these problems?'

A bottle of Italian white arrived at the table together with a superb array of grilled fish in a succulent sauce. Monty and the security guard sat smoking, overlooking the scene from a distance. Antonio Romano was a small man, and Roger wondered just how confident he would be operating alone without his tough guys backing him up.

'So how does this concern me Mr Romano?' asked

Roger.

'It doesn't but it could. Perhaps you acquaint me with more about yourself and I make you an offer – you are an interesting man Mr Kelly'.

Roger began to see where the conversation was leading. It would be fascinating to know what the offer might be, but did he want to get involved with this man.

'Your little Elissa was very loyal. She showed your portfolio to prove you had no ulterior motive in staking out my property. But let me be clear – I cannot allow details of Villa Romano shown around, and I must ask you for all copies please. What does intrigue me is another piece of your work. Bruce' – he clicked his fingers and the villa security guard came to the table handing over a small attaché case. Romano delved into the bag and brought out a print of Roger's hacienda.

'Tell me about this,' he said.

'A product of my imagination,' said Roger. 'Perhaps my future home when I become as successful as you.'

The waitress cleared away the empty plates and returned with two dishes of pasta and a carafe of red. It was the best pasta Roger had ever tasted. The flavours circulated his taste buds and accompanied by the soft red wine induced a gastronomic high.

'I must thank you for bringing me to this restaurant Mr Romano. I have never tasted better food'.

'Simple but special. Now when we finish lunch, I would like to show you something else special'.

Fruit, cheese and coffee followed, and if the meal had been intended to seduce Roger it succeeded. In the car Monty took a route back to Villefranche in the direction of Monte Carlo and stopped on a scenic slope with a panoramic view of the town and the sea.

'This wedge of land is invaluable,' said Romano, 'and it belongs to me. On each side you see the most prestigious villas in the South of France. Villas owned by industrial leaders, film stars, statesmen. My wife and family live in Naples, and I spend half my life in Naples. I want to build a very special home here. A break with tradition. A modern construction of light and artistry, where good taste and elegance will elevate my property to the same status as that of my neighbours.'

'Mr Romano – I am only a draftsman. I enjoy illustrating buildings and boats but this is a job for an architect who is a master craftsman. I have never worked on anything to match what you are planning'.

'Now this is your chance Mr Kelly. Do you always want to work in the shadows?

I see your work – what do you call it – your hacienda? It is imaginative, it is elegant, and I see it here in this place on this cliff side. I am an experienced businessman and I think at last you are the man to give me what I want.'

'And supposing my finished design falls short of what you want?'

'Then I don't buy it. It is simple as that my friend. I give you the opportunity and if you succeed in pleasing me, I pay you a lot of money. In addition, you win possible clients moving to the Cote d'Azur who will admire your design, and seek to discover the name of the designer. Suddenly you are an important person – you command respect.'

They walked the strip of land together. The location was perfect. It was everything Roger had dreamed of. After tedious hours in the planning offices sat glued to a computer, falling asleep at his desk, with a vision of using his years of study to create something magnificent – finally that opportunity was being offered to him right here and now.

He noticed an area had been levelled out. 'And how big do you want it?' he asked, pointing to the flattened space.

'That is big enough. Perhaps with six bedrooms. You decide.'

Monty produced two chairs for them and they sat on the cliff edge admiring views of Villefranche and the distant rooftops of Nice, shimmering in the heat haze.

'I make you this offer Mr Kelly. You create for me your hacienda. The design, the interior, the grounds. I pay you 600 euros every week you work for me. When you have finished I make you an offer to buy.' He handed Roger a card. 'Think about it over the weekend. Phone my office with your bank details and I will pay the first 600 euros directly into your account.'

Roger handed him the plans of Villa Romano. 'With my compliments Mr Romano and thank you for your hospitality. If I undertake this work, it will be completed within two months. But please understand I will be creating for you my own dream, my own vision. A hacienda which may not impress your neighbours and won't keep you safe in a fortress. Barbed wire fences and metal gates will not be a part of it, and it is an open plan which cannot be protected by bodyguards. My plan is for a villa you can live and relax in. To experience sensuous peace when you step outside and enjoy clear views of the sea and the glorious landscape which surrounds you. This is what I visualize – otherwise I cannot take your money.'

For a minute Antonio Romano was struck silent by the show of independence.

'Very well my friend I am in your hands. You are an honest man,' and he gripped Roger's hand in a surprisingly strong shake – particularly surprising because Roger realized that the middle finger of Romano's right hand was missing. When they dropped Roger off in Nice centre, he shook hands again with all three of them. Dangerous man or not he was satisfied that he had made his point. Roger intended to be his own master.

Consumed by fire he collected the Alpha Romeo and drove back to Villefranche. Over and over again he paced the strip, examining it from different angles and contemplating how to plan his design most effectively. He stayed until dusk and watched the sunset. Next morning, he drove back again at 5.00 am simply to calculate the sunrise, and where best the master bedrooms captured the early morning light.

In the apartment he stacked all previous work under the dining table, and spread his hacienda on the table top extending the picture to left and to right experimenting where best he could increase size and where best he could alter the external layout. This was going to be a masterpiece, a mind-blowing triumph. Nothing was going to distract him.

By the time he telephoned his bank details to Romano's

office Roger had a strict working routine lined up. An early morning run, work through until mid-day, a swim followed by late lunch, then back to work until early evening when he would take a stroll or visit the gym.

Five days later his commitment started to pay dividends and the Romano hacienda was taking shape. He had a feasible outline of the building and had put into place a corresponding internal room plan. He was working fast, he was working effectively, and all the while his mind was overflowing with ideas which were coming so quickly that they were sometimes difficult to keep abreast with.

There was a letter in Saturday's mailbox which when opened contained a brightly coloured card of Parisian night life, with clubs, shop fronts, and exotic bars lighting the sky and waterside. But the card was not Paris it was Beirut, and on the reverse side Elissa wrote 'I is very sorry Roger. I never forget you'.

He propped the card on the sideboard then rummaged under the table until he found the photograph of Elissa in her orange dress. He placed the photograph next to her card and sat thinking about her. He felt sad – he was going to miss her. Thanks to her he was working with the 'dangerous man' and he wondered what she would think about that if she were here now. One thing for sure – he wouldn't be able to concentrate on Hacienda Romano with Elissa giving him sex lessons.

He was ready for a break and sitting looking at her photograph drew his attention to the framed picture of the Sky Fly also perched on the sideboard. He had meant to give John and Jane a ring earlier but had got bogged down. John answered the phone and sounded pleased to hear from him.

'Roger – good of you to call. We are just on our way down to the yacht. It's too calm for sailing but why don't you join us for a drink and a catch up?'

The prospect delighted Roger. They were an entertaining couple when he met them in Dijon. He was pretty sure of an enjoyable day in their company, besides which his picture of the Sky Fly might lead to a few useful contacts.

He dressed carefully in his new Armani shorts and T-shirt and slid into his Maximillion loafers. 'Yep – he was looking good' and making sure leaflets and business cards were packed together with Sky Fly, he set off for the harbour in high spirits swinging his Ted Baker document case.

Disappointingly John and Jane had company when he arrived at the yacht, and when introduced to Charles and Hilary he knew from the start they were going to be hard work. John and Jane first met when serving as officers in the RAF, and that was where they encountered Charles. With a red face and twirling moustache, he was a typical old-fashioned caricature of an RAF pilot. He left you in no doubt that everything was 'cricket' or it wasn't, and after firing a few questions at Roger he didn't class Roger as 'cricket'. His wife wasn't much better. Hilary was a tall angular woman with a shrewd tongue which would command the uneasy respect at any social gathering, and when she wasn't dominating the conversation Charles stepped in to take her place. Out of courtesy Roger sat listening but was absolutely bored stiff by the pair of them.

Jane put together a delectable array of sandwiches, with chicken drumsticks, salad, choice of cakes, and glasses of chilled Sauvignon Blanc.

'And what are you intending to do with yourself here in Nice?' demanded Charles.

'I came here on holiday and decided to stay,' Roger replied. 'I am a draftsman and illustrator. I subsidize my stay by sketching yachts and properties.'

'You won't make a living out of that old chum. Who the hell is going to buy them?'

'Surprisingly quite a few,' said Roger. 'At the moment I have a big job in hand designing a villa for the owner of a string of properties.'

'Who is that?' asked Charles 'Not that bastard Romano I hope?'

'Exactly,' said Roger. 'A very courteous man and a very powerful man I believe.'

'A bloody villain! An absolute scoundrel! I wouldn't touch him with a barge pole. Have you a contract – for what it's worth?'

'No contract – weekly payments for work in progresses. Better than a contract.'

'Well count yourself lucky,' chimed in Hillary. 'We sold him one of our properties and he renegaded on his payments. We finished up thousands out of pocket.'

Charles enlarged upon that bastard Romano, and Roger found himself liking Antonio Romano more and more with each affirmed loss that pompous Charles said he had suffered. Memories of their business dealings seemed to unsettle them, and after swallowing as much

116

wine as was available Charles and Hilary made their excuses and left Roger alone with his hosts.

'Sorry about that,' said John. 'We hadn't expected them. Charles is an old comrade and gives me quite a large lump of his accountancy business. He's a good sort really but just a bit self-opinionated. An exceptionally good pilot and squadron leader, but unfortunately a bit of a bore.'

'Mind you – he is right,' interrupted Jane. 'You do have to watch yourself when dealing with Antonio Romano. He is renowned for being a real rogue.'

'No problem. I am a rogue myself,' said Roger. 'Anyway, it's a pleasure seeing you both. Thanks for the invite and here's a little something I sketched for you.'

They were captivated by the picture of Sky Fly, and Roger knew his gift had done the trick. John and Jane would be good contacts if he stayed working in Nice.

The Sky Fly was a cracking little boat. A four-berth yacht with enough space to move around, but not too big for two people to handle on their own. John told stories of his flying experiences, and how he and Jane set up in business when they finished their RAF service. He asked Roger questions and pointed out differences in French tax laws – particularly what might happen when the UK withdrew from the EU. They were sceptical about the business Roger was trying to build but John thought he might be able to help. He took a supply of leaflets whilst Jane insisted that as soon as Roger was settled, they would install an easy bookkeeping system for him, and make sure he was on the right track.

They were a worldly couple – straight, without airs

and graces and Roger felt he could open up and ask their advice on anything. Sitting on the boat basking in the sunshine, conversation ranged from books to foreign travel, and from Roger's marriage break-up to his business involvement with Antonio Romano.

'Next time we see you we must show your round the yachting club,' said John. 'There's quite a bit of social life attached, and it's a useful club for networking.'

Roger left with a lot to think about. He had had a brilliant day, and as he wended his way through the tourists on the harbour side, he was convinced that, despite all of the warnings, Antonio Romano would serve him well. Romano was a man to be reckoned with – more work would follow.

He phoned home and wrote a long email to Ana bringing her up to date on his progress. By now he had reconciled himself to an internet romance with her – in today's world that was how many people seemed to conduct their love affairs. In fact, two Japanese youths being interviewed on TV told the reporter that they didn't need girlfriends because they were completely attached to their mobile phones. Well sod that! Roger certainly wasn't in love with his mobile phone – in fact it was a damned nuisance always 'pinging' away in his pocket.

Roger threw himself into work. He trained hard, soaked up as much sun as possible, and never missed his hour of French study. Midweek he was struggling with the problem of where to fit a swimming pool into Hacienda Romano when John phoned and invited him to join them at Friday night's dinner dance at the yacht club.

'Relaxed dress,' said John. 'Jacket but no need for a tie. And by the way I have a nice surprise for you'. A nice surprise thought Roger. Don't tell me they have found me a French *femme fatale.*

Friday arrived and he had an easy day. He was already approaching a stage where he needed to consult with Romano to get approval on the general villa layout. He had just finished lunch when his mobile rang, and as he answered he was struck by a strange premonition. Rosemary's unmistakable voice greeted him.

'Roger – I have just arrived in Nice. I have booked in at the Hotel Windsor. Will you meet me there?'

'I wish you had let me know you were coming,' said Roger. 'I have an appointment this evening but expect me in an hour'.

It was nearly three months since he had seen Rosemary. After their short exchange on the telephone Roger would never have believed that she would come to Nice. Her visit was the last thing he wanted at the moment, and as he walked into the Windsor Hotel, he had no idea how either of them would react.

There are many stories of couples meeting years after a split and when they meet again it is as though they had never spent a day apart. It was like that with Rosemary. She might just have arrived home after a day's teaching at St Mary's. He was pleased to see her and kissed her. Rosemary was still the same Rosemary he had married seven years ago – attractive, sensible, and the perfect English rose who you would be proud to take home and introduce to one's mother. In the absence of anything traumatic, Roger concluded that really his wife was the sister he had always wanted and never had'.

She told him about her new post at St Mary's; Roger described the designer job and plans for setting up an agency. He didn't mention Jack Fearnley and Rosemary never asked about Ana. God, wasn't this a fiasco? After all that trouble and upset here he was sitting talking to his wayward wife without even a thought of the humiliation and turmoil she had caused him. Don't let anybody ever tell me to treat life seriously again thought Roger – life is one massive contradiction.

It was difficult to understand why Rosemary had travelled to Nice and it was difficult to know what she wanted. One thing was apparent – she hadn't expected their meeting to turn out to be so amicable. She was surprised when he asked her to accompany him to the yacht club, and even more surprised when he turned on the charm, complimented her on her dress, and told her she looked perfect for the occasion. Roger checked the time. John and Jane were expecting him at 6.30 for a look around the club before dinner. Aunt Evelyn's apartment was a short walk from the Windsor, and again he sensed Rosemary had a moment of bewilderment as he opened the car door, stood back, and invited her to step into the Alpha Romeo.

They drove along the coast road with the open top creating a cool breeze. He loved the drive, and he could feel Rosemary's excitement as they descended down to Quartier du Port and she caught her first sparkling sea views of the bay, and the lines of yachts with their white sails illuminated by the late sun.

Roger and Rosemary walked into the yacht club bar holding hands like a couple of young lovers. John, looking cool and suave in a white cruise jacket never batted an eye lid when Roger introduced his wife. Jane welcomed Rosemary with a smile and a kiss, but when she gave Roger a peck her eyes danced with amusement. Jane was nobody's fool, and after sitting on the Sky Fly listening to Roger's account of his broken marriage Jane knew that all was not as it appeared to be.

The yacht club was an impressive place. A quintet played a tricky jazz tune which livened up the bar. Smartly dressed groups of all ages were scattered the length of the room taking pre dinner drinks, and dining tables had been arranged either side of the dance floor with sliding windows fully open to invite in cool air and the sound of the ocean. Roger had eaten here twice before without realizing the diverse range of activities club members could enjoy. After a quick drink John and Jane gave them a comprehensive tour of the power boats and rowing section, and Roger began to see the potential for expanding social life and business contacts if he became a member.

No doubt about it – he had to join.

'And now for the surprise,' said John as they passed through reception. Taking up a large space on the club notice board Roger's face gazed out benignly from his promotional leaflet. The leaflet could not have occupied a better spot.

'I managed to fix another of your leaflets on the board in the health spa and one in the gym,' said John, 'and for that you can buy me a double brandy'.

'Have you shown them the gym yet?' asked a familiar voice.

Charles, dressed in a wine-coloured cotton jacket and bow tie, stood directly behind them self-important as ever. Without hesitation he introduced himself to Rosemary, nodded to John and Jane, and accompanied them uninvited for a look at the club gym.

'A damned fine gym,' he said. 'I get in here at least twice a week. And when my lad is home from Oxford, he keeps up his rugger training with a session here every day. How about you – do you play rugger?' he shot at Roger.

'I'm not a rugger man, nor golf,' replied Roger.

'Pity! Damned good game. It's important to keep yourself fit you know,' and turning to Rosemary. 'A bit of training will keep your husband out of mischief – stop him from getting too involved with those villains he does business with.'

Roger made no comment. It was a well-equipped gym but minus the boxing gear.

If he became a club member, he could quite see himself splitting his training between boxing at his present venue and two weekly sessions here at the yacht club. Charles commented authoritatively on various pieces of equipment, and as they passed by a chinning bar Roger stopped. Rosemary knew what he was going to do, and Roger knew that Rosemary knew what he was going to do, and it amused him to watch her cringe. He whipped off his jacket, jumped up to the bar, and to every one's astonishment (except Rosemary) he performed 15 chins in quick succession. He dropped down, put on his jacket and placed his hand on Charles shoulder.

'You see Charles it's all very well stamping on the heads of chaps in a rugby scrum, but you have to be strong enough to stand toe-to-toe when dealing with villains, and look them in the eye.'

Charles was thunderstruck; John was mildly embarrassed; Jane was in stitches; and Rosemary fell deadly silent.

'I'll see you all later,' said Charles and departed without a word.

'That was a turn out for the books,' said John grinning at him.

'An absolute hoot,' added Jane.

'Sorry, I couldn't let the moment pass. Unfortunately, I am an embarrassment to my wife as always' (and nothing changes, he thought).

John had booked a good table. Far enough away from the band to enjoy easy conversation and in a good position to be part of the action. As he and Jane had a quick word with a nearby couple, Rosemary said coldly: 'I suppose you know that that was completely the wrong thing to do', but before Roger could reply, John and Jane were back ordering drinks.

Everybody liked Rosemary. She was an asset at any social event. Very soon she was discussing education, and questioning Jane about life for a woman in the Royal Air Force, and conversation flowed smoothly without fake humour or forced laughter.

There was something quite magical about the evening. Tiny lights marked the ballroom floor and there was a small modestly lit lamp on every table. It was still quite bright outside so that the open windows, and shaded interior, created the balmy impression that you were dining outside but under cover.

'Do you know many people here?' asked Roger.

'Yes and no,' said John. 'We aren't great socializers and most of the British set we recognise by sight or through business'. He pointed to Charles and Hilary on the far side of the room with another couple. 'Charles is in finance and so is Carrington-Brown. They are both in the big league and left us behind years ago. We have to struggle to keep our clients happy, and Jane and I put in some hellish long hours.'

'And as you can see, we are early diners,' added Jane pointing to the half empty tables. 'Force of habit I am afraid – we get too hungry for dinner at 8.00.'

A lot of drinkers had spilled out from the bar onto the outside terrace, and glancing around Roger couldn't spot many people who looked French. Rosemary must have come to the same conclusion.

'Tonight, has quite a British feel about it. What's happened to the French?'

'I would say at least two thirds of club members are local French,' said John. 'The club holds this sort of a do once a month, and it's mainly full of expats – finance, insurance, or retirees who have taken a golden handshake. French members are more concerned with pottering around on their boats, and a lot of the big business regime meet in the restaurant on a lunchtime – long lunches, when we hard workers only have time for a sandwich. Apart from that the rowing team is almost 100% French.'

The meal went well. Courses were served at a leisurely pace and service was good. The band started up again playing 'My Way' with a Frank Sinatra look-alike on the piano, and as the meal ended all four of them temporarily vacated their table to watch the sunset from the outside terrace. Leaning on the balustrade, with views of the harbour and music in the background, Roger was mesmerized. Tonight ticked all the right boxes. He was enjoying Rosemary's company without being involved with her. And more importantly, he had formed a pretty good idea of what being a member of the Yacht Club in Nice was all about, and he liked what he saw.

The spell was broken when Charles and his wife joined them, accompanied by their fellow diners. With a few drinks inside him Charles had become pleasantly affable and introduced both Roger and Rosemary to the Carrington-Browns.

'Ah – I take it you are the man who can chin the bar 15 times straight off?'

Edward Carrington-Brown was a charming handsome man. Well over 6 feet with dark iron-grey hair, and a neat moustache. He oozed confidence and success, and he radiated the kind of personality that would captivate the ladies. Helen, his wife, had the slightly dispirited look of an attractive woman who has had to overlook her husband's affairs, and now worries about her own fading appeal. Roger was drawn to her immediately – he found her extremely feminine and dangerously vulnerable. Their eyes met and Roger knew he was in trouble.

Everybody started talking to everybody else. Rosemary was taken over by Edward and Charles, and Helen was sharing a joke with John and Jane. Roger found himself standing alone beside a well-oiled Hilary who was overlooking the dance floor and jigging on the spot. She's pissed thought Roger. Her tall thin frame was moving about like an uncoiled spring, humming to herself, with her head nodding to the music. Late diners were still drifting from terrace to tables when a group of very young and very noisy French arrived on the scene. They were a delightfully happy bunch. They crowded onto the dance floor, the band hotted up the tempo, and soon the dance floor was a mass of gyrating beautiful people all doing their own French thing.

'Come on Rog – let's dance,' said Hilary, and taking hold of his hand she pulled him onto the dance floor and began jumping around like a runaway stallion. She threw her arms up, kicked her legs, swinging her non-existent hips and shouted 'woo, woo' with every movement. She looked ridiculous. With arms and legs working like pistons she grabbed Roger and spun him back and round again in 60's jive style, and with no option but to let himself go Roger joined in and gave it his all.

The French have a different sense of fun to the English and love anything a bit off-beat. Hilary's energetic exhibition cleared a space, and the young crowd shouted and clapped and stamped encouragingly until the music ended. Roger gave a little bow, and as they made their way to the terrace it amused him to think that Charles was unlikely to class his wife's performance as 'cricket', and to Rosemary his own performance would be a downright social disaster. Quite wrong!

'Bravo darling, bravo!' enthused Charles to his wife, and Roger too was surprised to find himself the centre of attention, with compliments from all directions.

'I'll say one thing,' said John, 'everyone should be able to put a face to your leaflet after that outstanding performance'.

'Congratulations,' added Edward. 'I think that ranks alongside today's 15 chins. Let's get you signed up for club membership before you knacker yourself.'

The musical tempo slowed down and Roger led Rosemary onto the dance floor. She was very quiet. They had always danced well together, and when they moved to the music he got the same familiar feeling as when he first walked into the Windsor.

They danced closely, and the soft smell of her hair blended with her perfume and the freshness of her skin. He knew Rosemary was a prize catch for any man. He had been the envy of all his pals when they first got married, but as they moved together and he held her to him, something had gone – he could have been dancing with anybody because he couldn't feel a thing for her.

Other couples had joined them on the Terrace, and when Edward commandeered Rosemary the danger moment materialised. Almost without asking he was dancing with Helen and she was smiling up at him soft in his arms.

'Do you like the band?' she asked.

'A good band – but I don't think much of the singer.'

'No – but he's a nice pianist,' said Helen.

Roger smiled at her. 'I wouldn't know – I've never seen it,' and she laughed.

'Now that, young man, is just the sort of joke you don't make the first time you dance with somebody from the Yacht

Club.'

'I know,' said Roger. 'But I felt it would help me get to know you better'.

She looked startled – then she pressed close to him, and he felt her shiver as his hand touched the small of her back. What can you do about chemistry? She was at least ten years older than him and the wife of a charming guy who he liked and respected.

But the chemistry was strong – she felt it too, and the familiar ache in his groin was back again. When did he say he wasn't much of a woman's man?

'Do you know the Davisons very well?' she asked.

'Who – John and Jane? We met for the first time a few weeks ago in Dijon. John has been helping me with problems setting up my business.'

'And your wife – she is lovely. Will she join you in Nice?'

'That's very unlikely. My wife is ambitious and has her own career'.

'That can be lonely,' said Helen, 'Edward travels extensively. It's lonely for me, but not for him. But then again life is different for men, isn't it?'

'Not always,' said Roger. He felt the receptive warmth of her stomach and thighs through her thin dress, and she made no move to separate and pressed into him as he grew hard. Three bottle blondes standing on the side watched them closely. They stayed together for three long dances and Helen's breathing was heavy against his neck. If they weren't careful, they would be noticed.

'I never want to end this dance Helen, but we had better join the rest.' She gripped his hand hard and fleetingly brushed his lips. John and Jane had returned to their table and watched them as they left the dance floor. The tempo changed again and young French hipsters flooded the floor.

'This club reminds me a little of Hong Kong,' said Jane. 'Some nights were full of ex-pats – little England in a foreign land. There was more drinking than dancing.'

'Sometimes I was still half-cut next morning,' added John. 'And as for Charles – how come he never pranged a kite was a miracle. He never went to bed.'

Everybody returned and brought chairs round their table. Roger sat back and listened. Charles and Hilary were not too sloshed to cross question Rosemary about her new teaching job, and becoming an assistant headmistress so young earned her their respect. Definitely 'cricket'. But it was Edward Carrington-Brown who held the floor most of the time. His travels, his jokes, his experiences were spell binding. He was such an effective speaker one could listen to him for hours, and just watching the man was enough to engender an unfettered loyalty that might take you wherever he chose to lead.

What am I playing at? Roger asked himself. Don't be such a bloody fool. Don't even dream of having an affair with this man's wife.

He looked across at Rosemary sitting next to Helen. Rosemary was younger, more striking, and more vivacious. By comparison Helen's delicate features were almost wan. She was not a woman who would stand out in a crowd but there was something so gentle and graceful about her that he felt himself drawn to her like a magnet, and the lingering appeal in her eyes was going to stay with him.

The party broke up. Charles and Hilary were sharing a taxi with the Carrington-Browns, and Helen didn't look at him when they all shook hands and said their goodbyes. Rosemary and Jane disappeared to the loo. Roger wanted to share costs for the evening but couldn't persuade John to even accept a small contribution towards the wine.

'Return the compliment next time,' he said. 'A great evening – glad you could both join us. I'm not sure it has brought the pair of you any closer together, but at any rate you will know a few faces next time you come to the club. A word in your ear – go easy with Helen. She is a lonely woman. Edward is a terrific bloke but he goes his own way, but that doesn't mean to say he will be all that happy if someone borrows his wife.' He grinned at Roger. 'That apart – bring me your books and we will set up an accounts system as soon as you are ready. It's easy to lose out when setting up business in France.'

Jane returned with Rosemary and they were thick as thieves. As he received a parting kiss on either cheek, he wondered whether his good name had suffered from tales in the toilets about his escapades in Dublin.

The evening had been a great success. He had established a presence at the club and taking Rosemary had been a good move. They drove along the promenade in the balmy warmth of the evening. The shore lights lit their way to the Windsor, and the town's late-night buzz was as lively and compelling as ever.

'You can see why I want to stay in Nice can't you?'

'Whether you stay in Nice or come back to Manchester, I don't think you will ever change Roger.'

'What made you think I was going to change?' asked Roger. 'You should know – one doesn't change – one grows deeper.' They arrived at the hotel, and Roger got out and opened the door for Rosemary.

'It's been a great evening and lovely to see you. Tomorrow let's have breakfast together at 10am and then let me show you some of the sights. And bring your bikini – or perhaps not.'

He kissed her cheek and got into the car laughing. If he hadn't changed nor had Rosemary. Once a schoolteacher always a school teacher, but either way he intended to be headmaster.

The weekend flew by. Breakfast in his favourite café opposite the apartment was a good start. The proprietor's wife beamed when she saw him, kissed him on both cheeks, and didn't charge them for coffee. Looking round *Musée des Beaux Arts* was interesting and took up most of the morning. In the afternoon Roger collected the car and took Rosemary to see the proposed site for Hacienda Romano. Too hot to sunbathe, they ate lunch in Villefranche, and waited until later before joining the lines of suntanned bodies on the beach. All very civilized thought Roger. They separated for siesta and in the evening walked to the old town where Rosemary sampled octopus for the first time, grilled and served with rice and an accompanying tomato-based sauce. She rated it her number one dish of the year. It was like old times; in their post student days trying out local dishes on holiday had been fun. Rosemary enjoyed adventurous eating even if she was a lousy cook.

On Sunday they set off for St-Paul-de-Vence. It was top of Roger's 'want to see' list but holiday traffic on route was a nightmare and parking the car even worse. In spite of crowds of tourists, the village of St-Paul-de-Vance was enchanting. They walked the ramparts and sat eating sandwiches next to a flying statue, half man and half bird, which commandeered the beautiful setting below. Rosemary's knowledge of French was invaluable. She translated every interesting placard on display in the art galleries on rue Grande, and Roger learned the histories of Chagall, Bonnard, Miro, and a lot more about Matisse.

It was a good day. Traffic returning to Nice was terrible, and after struggling behind queues of tourists for over an hour Roger stopped the car at a café outside the city boundaries. He was on his second beer when Rosemary pointed out a lone figure opposite.

'Who is that man watching us? He hasn't taken his eyes off us ever since we got here.'

Sitting immobile in the company of a giant-sized Coca Cola was Monty who gave them the slightest nod, but then raised his hand in acknowledgement as they left.

'Not the friendliest chap,' said Roger 'He is bodyguard to the villain I am doing business with.'

'That sounds like the sort of acquaintance to impress your friends Roger.' There she goes again, he thought. Our relationship really is bizarre. If she has come here to seduce me this must be a new way of setting about doing it.

Overall, Roger was pleased with the weekend. She had taken the trouble to come and see him, and he had done his best to entertain her. They were good pals and he was happy to let things stay the way they were. When they eventually made it to the *Boulevard des Anglais* he turned off on Rue du Congress, drove into the secure car park, and took Rosemary up the stairs to see Aunt Evelyn's apartment.

A big mistake. By the time he had made them both a coffee, Rosemary had rummaged amongst his sketches and found a nude photograph of Elissa and paired it up with her photograph on the sideboard. He kicked himself. He should have had the sense to stick the nude photos out of the way and into a drawer. Strangely enough Rosemary was amused, and carefully examined the photograph before commenting.

'Some lucky lady will have to be good to compete with this one. Congratulations!'

'Would you like a slice of cream cake to go with your coffee?'

'No thank you!' said Rosemary. 'I will miss out on the cream cake – I have something else in mind'. Suddenly a warning bell rang in Roger's head.

'I am sure you have been wondering why I came to Nice. Well, I came to ask for your help Roger. I have got us into debt. Our new furniture cost over £20,000, and I have had to help Jack out because he got himself into serious trouble by overspending on his credit card. I badly need £50,000, and that should cover everything.'

'You must be fucking joking,' exploded Roger. 'You walk out on me for that little shit, then you come over here and ask me to finance the pair of you. What sort of a soft touch do you think I am?' Rosemary sat calmly and took another sip of her coffee.

'Before you lose your rag, think about it: you can afford it – I know about your lottery win. And it will cost you a lot more if we split up and I claim half of everything I am entitled to if we enter into divorce proceedings.'

Roger was shaken. After such a pleasant weekend this was the last thing he expected.

'Rosemary – is that fair? You walked out on me. Furthermore, I never looked at another woman while we were married'.

'Well, you haven't wasted much time since. After your little interlude with the escort girl you forgot to change the sheets before coming on holiday. And,' she said, pointing to Elissa's nude photograph, 'this doesn't seem like a heart broken effort on your part to win me back. Let's face it Roger – if I hadn't had to waste a lump of our savings bailing you out of a police cell in Dublin none of this need have happened.'

He had run out of words. His wife's lecture brought back weeks of misery he had left behind, and a Dublin disaster which was not his fault. It was hard to believe that this was the same woman with whom he had spent the last three days.

'I will leave you to let it sink in.' Rosemary got up. 'Thank you for the weekend. Think hard about what I am asking. It will save us both a lot of trouble and heartache because taking these matters to court is a long and tedious procedure.'

Roger woke up, and a cold fury enveloped him.

'I don't need to think about it. I covered the house mortgage, and you won't get another penny out of me.

Take me to court and I will fight you tooth and nail – and don't forget, if you lose you will be even deeper in debt. As for Jack Fearnley – that bent little sod won't dare to put his nose outside the door because if I get hold of him I will skin him alive.' Rosemary's calm expression disappeared. She was startled, he frightened her.

'Go and stew in your own juice Rosemary. The legal proceedings will add to your newly found status at St Mary's, and I will make sure they hear all about it. I will make your life a bloody misery. Now get out of my apartment.'

She couldn't leave the room quickly enough. He heard her footsteps disappearing down the stairs at a running pace. So, this was the devious wife he had been married to for seven years. Lovely Rosemary who everybody loved. She made a fool of him when she left him, and she had made a fool of him here in Nice. He sat fuming.

He had always played it straight, but he was getting tired of playing it straight. If you had to get along by bending the rules in life then so be it – in future he would bend the rules. And Rosemary – she wouldn't know what hit her.

8. The Reckoning

Roger Kelly was not the same Roger Kelly who left England three months earlier. He was coolly confident. He slept like a log and was out of bed by 6.00 am and got down to work without delay.

He wrote a standard letter dissociating himself from his wife and all future financial transactions. He emailed copies to the head offices of HSBC, Nationwide, Npower, North West Water, Amazon, and Easy International Credit Company. He backed all emails with copy letters to be sent by post, and made a note of several telephone numbers. Fortunately, Rosemary had her own separate credit card but correspondence directed to Easy International would set alarm bells ringing. When it came to overdue accounts they were lethal, and Roger guessed that the new furniture would have been bought via Easy International with payments still outstanding.

Two hours later he sat back with the job complete. He checked to make sure Rosemary had booked out of the Windsor to catch her early morning flight, he ate a light breakfast, then went to the gym and gave the punch bags hell.

Workwise he was at a crossroads. Until he could verify his plans for the hacienda there was no point in going any further. Five times Roger rang Antonio Romano and five times he received a put off from Romano's secretary. When eventually they spoke, he grudgingly agreed to meet Roger at the yacht club mid-week.

'One hour Mr Kelly – no more. I expect there to be a

good reason for this meeting.'

Not a good time to take offence. Instead, Roger ran the car to Villefranche and re-checked his measurements, then returned to the flat and made a few amendments. If he could get some answers, he would be sailing full steam ahead.

The day was hot. Well into the high 70's. He bet Romano would be wearing a suit so Roger dressed accordingly in his midnight blue Pal Zileri and added an Armani tie to match. He arrived at the Yacht Club with time to spare and found Romano had already beaten him to it. He was impatiently sitting in the cafeteria sipping a fruit juice with Monty reading an English newspaper a couple of tables away.

Roger got straight down to business. He spread his two major plans out on the table. He pointed out that the hacienda was a single floor property and if six bedrooms were required it meant invading the roof space. Plan one was sketched as a single storey, and plan two was repeated with the addition of two dormer bedrooms which necessitated an internal staircase.

A wrap around wide wooden porch allowed ample room for tables and chairs with entry points from lounge and dining area, as well as from four corner bedrooms.

A swimming pool at the back of the property would interfere with views of the sea from the porch whereas a pool situated at the side of the villa would be more practical and could be built independent of the main building. Alternatively, it was possible for the pool to be built as an undercover extension of the property – easier to clean, and easier to manage. Two separate plans illustrated both options.

Romano asked probing questions, and pointed out possibilities. They agreed that the cliff top situation obviated the need for security, but the front of the villa leading to the main road needed a fence to preserve privacy and discourage intruders.

At the end of the hour Romano consulted his watch, nodded to Monty and pulled back his chair.

'I am happy with what I see Mr Kelly. You are my man.' A group engaged in a business meeting watched as they left. It was definitely a boost to his image to be seen dealing with a man like Antonio Romano.

Antonio Romano was impressed. He got into the car and sat back deep in thought. He liked the prospect of a residence which he could oversee from the beginning, and equally he was intrigued by the man who was designing it. This man had talent, and success in Romano's life depended on manipulating talent. Monty didn't say anything. You didn't say anything to Romano – you waited for Romano to say something to you.

'So, what do you think about our friend Kelly?'

'A bit of a loose cannon,' said Monty. 'He is his own man and he knows how to look after himself.'

'His plan of the villa is brilliant. And he's landed a connection with the yachting fraternity – did you see his pamphlet?'

'A stuck-up bunch,' said Monty. 'He's welcome.'

'He puzzles me,' said Romano. 'He hasn't tried to tap me up for money yet. What's his weakness then? If he doesn't love money, I can't buy him.'

'Women,' replied Monty. 'He loves women. On Sunday he was with a classy bird who looked like his wife. She was wearing a wedding ring. They didn't look too happy with each other either.'

'Ah woman trouble. He is here and she is in England. That gives us something to work on. Mr Kelly is a useful man – we might like to have him on board.'

'Are we on our way now to sort out the Heinsberg problem boss?'

'We are on our way to sort out the Heinsberg problem Monty. We will crush his balls until the little bastard gives us what he owes, and something besides,' and they both laughed.

The meeting with Romano had progressed well. But Rosemary's visit unsettled him. He was even more unsettled when he discovered two photographs missing from the pile under the table. Gone was the teasing photograph of nude Elissa sat astride a chair, and gone was the souvenir photo of him and Elissa in Casino di San Remo with their arms wrapped around each other. If there were two damning photographs which could be used in legal proceedings then Rosemary had picked a couple of winners. There was nothing Roger could do about the photographs, but could he obtain proof that little Jack had moved into the house with Rosemary? Roger phoned Mick who typically relished the whole situation.

'Well done mate,' he said. 'Those photos sound like they are worth seeing. You're a pillock for entertaining Rosemary, but leave it to me. I'll see if I can catch Jack and take a compromising snap of him on the job inside your property,' Speaking with Mick was always good for a laugh. He was still involved with his police lady and Roger imagined the pair of them sneaking round to do a bit of detective work. Besides, Mick had plenty of experience of women suing him. He was an expert.

Cheered by the thought, Roger threw himself back into a steady working routine.

Most days he ate in the café opposite where he was now almost a member of the family. From there he was straight back into the flat without wasting time. He was a man with a mission. He concentrated 100% on planning Hacienda Romano, and spare time in the evenings was spent on the balcony swotting up hard on his French.

John forwarded him an application for membership to the yacht club, which Roger filled in and returned. Thoughts of the yacht club reminded him of his dance with Helen. Some dance – a fornication foxtrot. Taboo!

Ten days after his weekend with Rosemary he received a letter from her solicitor.

As joint owner of their home in Manchester Roger was legally bound to share all costs relating to maintenance of the home, even though he chose not to live there. The solicitor gave official advice that his wife would be putting into place divorce proceedings within the next few weeks, and police action would be called upon if in the meantime any attempts were made to threaten her.

Roger cursed Rosemary. The letter coincided with a call from Romano's office to meet at the site the following day. Roger had worked like a Trojan for weeks and was near completion of the whole project. The serious ramifications of the solicitor's letter stayed with him and he couldn't clear them out of his head.

Thursday morning Roger turned up at the site. Romano and Monty arrived at 11.00 and two French landscape gardeners followed. The question of dormer bedrooms had been shelved, as had the need for a swimming pool. In its place Romano chose a summer house with little more than a paddling pool in front of it, and some basic facilities within. Roger was called to agree a rough plan with the gardeners on how best the grounds could be effectively divided up into garden and useable space, bearing in mind the change of layout.

The meeting had a party atmosphere about it. The gardeners couldn't speak English, and Roger couldn't speak French. Translation was a problem, and Roger wasn't sure if they had any idea what the hell he was talking about. The gardeners left but the meeting wasn't finished. Monty led the way down the cliff path to a shed like restaurant where three beers and a bottle of wine were ordered together with a large tray of shell fish. Romano sat at ease with his drink.

'So how long before plans are completed Mr Kelly?' His mobile rang and he went outside to answer the call. Monty, with thigh muscles bulging through his shorts, sat bolt upright staring hard at Roger with his penetrating gaze. Unexpectedly, he leaned forward and patted Roger's shoulder.

'You're in luck. The boss has some extra work for you mate.'

'Don't tell me he wants an extension for some more of his family from Naples?'

'Don't be a schmuck mate. The new villa has nothing to do with bringing his family over here. The place is all about setting up his mistress in style.'

The cool beer slid down like nectar and worries about the solicitor's letter were temporarily shelved. Roger relaxed. Romano returned to the table and raised an eyebrow at Roger.

'Less than two weeks – and everything will be finalized' Roger assured him.

'And tell me Mr Kelly – what are your plans for the future. Will you return to England or will your wife join you here?' With two beers and a glass of wine inside him Roger saw no reason to keep his marriage a secret.

'My wife left me months ago. She was here last week to blackmail me. She wants half of what I own in order to live in my house with her new lover, and her solicitor is making life very awkward.'

'Expensive,' said Monty.

'Expensive,' agreed Romano. 'All you need now is your little friend's husband from Beirut coming over here to shoot you, and we lose a valuable architect.'

It amused the pair of them. There were no conciliatory words of advice nor further comments, and no mention of extra work. When the plate of shellfish was empty, and only a drop left in the wine bottle, they got up to leave. Today they climbed into a four-by-four Citroen.

'Where's the saloon?' asked Roger.

'Never advertise your presence, Mr Kelly. We like to keep them guessing. I will see you again soon. And with a '*Bonne chance!*' they drove off.

Roger stayed behind to drink a black coffee. Romano hadn't mentioned who 'them' were 'who he liked to keep guessing' and it was fun imagining what kind of gamesmanship was involved. Today's drinks had gone to Roger's head. The young waitress brought him a bitter drink which sobered him up completely, and he drove the car back without a wobble.

In the apartment he sat thinking. He had had an amazing run of good luck. The lottery win; the casino; the design work. The apartment was as good as his without costing him a penny and most of his aspirations were going to plan so what more did he want? He sat on the balcony taking in the last rays of the sun content but very much alone. He ate a sandwich, read a book, and was in bed early. His mobile rang. He was surprised to hear Romano's voice.

'Mr Kelly – you have a pencil and paper handy – you have, good! I want you to ring this number tomorrow morning. A solicitor in Manchester, a friend of mine. He will look after you.'

'Is this going to be costly Mr Romano?'

'Not as costly as losing half of what you own Mr Kelly,' and Romano rang off.

Romano's solicitor was abrupt and impartial to the point of rudeness. For a solid hour he asked questions without providing any answers. After an hour's grilling the voice at the end of the phone made no effort to reassure nor advise. The only instruction was – don't contact your wife and don't reply to her solicitor. The call drained Roger's energy – it was like a ten-mile run in the wind and rain. He spent the rest of the morning confirming facts by email, and forwarded a copy of the letter from Rosemary's solicitor to the mystery 'voice' in Manchester. The day felt good for nothing. He was uneasy about the whole interview. The man was a rude bugger, and would Roger have been better finding his own solicitor?

He walked the promenade, paid 30 euros for a sunbed, and went to sleep under the umbrella amongst the August sunbathers packed like sardines on the beach. He sat in the apartment thinking about Ana. Her promised letter to explain things never happened and instead her weekly emails got shorter and shorter. Perhaps the escort work had involved her with the Russian Mafia – and then it struck him. Never mind Ana, what about himself? For all he knew, he might be involved with the Italian Mafia.

He got changed and walked up the Avenue Jean Médecin to the Restaurant Baie d'Amalfi. There was one table available by the door, a cool spot, but almost on top of the next table where a young French couple were perusing the menu between phone calls. Roger ordered peppered steak, French fries, and side salad with a half-bottle of house red. The couple were still deliberating their choice as Roger finished his steak and ordered a tiramisu.

Baie d'Amalfi was not a touristy restaurant. Glancing around, most diners looked to be French and regular customers. In the far corner Roger noticed an outstandingly beautiful woman totally involved with her partner – the back of whose head looked vaguely familiar.

When Edward Carrington-Brown stood up to leave he spotted Roger and came over to shake hands and introduce his secretary who was just as charming as she was beautiful. Very English and very refined.

'Everything alright with you?' he asked.

'Yes – more or less,' replied Roger.

'You don't sound too sure. Well don't forget – any problems I can help you with, get in touch. You know where to find me.'

What a hell of a nice guy thought Roger. The woman was obviously a lot more than just his secretary, and she was obviously enchanted by Edward. Roger thought of Helen and felt sorry for her; any woman would struggle to keep tags on such a man. But attraction was a funny thing – if he could choose between Helen and her husband's secretary it would be Helen every time. Roger retired for the night relieved that he didn't have Helen's telephone number otherwise he might have been tempted to give her a ring.

Work for Romano was completed by the end of the following week. It was a milestone in Roger's life. The culmination of an ambition and a dream. Accepted or refused, paid for or not, none of that really mattered. He had finished a piece of architecture to be proud of and nothing could take that away from him.

Elissa's picture frame man put together a presentation folder – one set of plans for Romano, and another copy for Roger. Romano was in Naples and Roger left a set of plans at his town centre office which turned out to be located behind a letting agency run by a guy called Eric and his gay partner named Melvin.

Roger had expected a prompt call from Romano when he returned – but nothing happened. In fact, for the next few weeks nothing happened full stop. Nothing came back from his solicitor, nor Mick, and he didn't hear from Rosemary's solicitor either.

Chasing after Antonio Romano was definitely not on the cards. Roger had fulfilled his part of the contract and it was now up to Romano to get in touch with him, but after the pressure of completing his work by a set date the lull in response left Roger kicking his heels.

Membership of the Yacht Club was confirmed. Some social life at last. He had a work-out in their gym, and a meal in the club restaurant and spoke to nobody. In need of action, he tried a night at the casino where he lost 280 euros inside an hour. Checking his bank balance afterwards he was surprised to find that the 600-euro weekly payments were still being paid into his account.

When things started to happen, everything happened together. First a call from Monty asking Roger to meet him at their Letting Agency. Then a voice message from Mick to ring him back urgently.

'Hey Roger – what's going on? No signs of little Jack occupying your house, but when I checked up this morning a van was there removing all your furniture. Wendy says it's a firm that specializes in recovering goods from bad debtors. And Jack has just resigned as manager of the football club. Why would he do that?'

'Not guilty Mick,' said Roger. 'Not my debt and not my furniture. Can't think why Jack resigned – except that he's a lousy manager. Keep your ear to the ground and let me hear of any other news.' It looked like his letter to Easy Credit had done the trick. What would Rosemary's next move be? What would her solicitor's next move be? He gave big Cyril's amulet a good luck polish and crossed his fingers.

Monty was waiting for him when Roger arrived at their office the next morning. This time he was sat in a two-tone silver-grey Range Rover Sport. He moved over and offered the driving seat to Roger.

'Have a try at driving mate – see how you get along with left hand drive. The governor wants me to take you for a joy ride around some of his properties.'

With Monty directing they began a tour of Romano's coastal villas which stretched from Villefranche to Monte Carlo. All the villas were occupied. All of them were blue-chip properties with a swimming pool, and Roger guessed there must be multi millions of euros tied up in the ten villas they visited. During the trip he got to like Monty. He was still stiff, but he came over as a pretty genuine cockney who had worked with Romano for over ten years. At the end of the day, he dropped Roger in the town centre and gave him a friendly handshake.

'I don't know what Antonio has in mind mate but play it straight with him and he will play it straight with you. You won't work for a better man.' That same evening Romano telephoned.

'Mr Kelly, I trust you have had a good day. If you check your bank account, you will see that I have paid 12,000 euros into your account. Together with my weekly

147

trust payments you have earned 15,600 euros from me. Are you happy with that?'

Roger said he was more than happy. 'Good! I am pleased you are satisfied. Can we meet tomorrow?'

If Roger had harboured doubts about Romano, then those doubts had been dispelled.

With luck his dangerous employer had more work for him and if so, Roger was going to enjoy working with him.

The office at the back of the Letting Agency was surprisingly small. Officially Romano was not involved with the agency and paid them to handle his properties. Unofficially the agency was organized as a commission-based centre to administrate some of Romano's big property deals, and the land on which the new villa would be built was all part and parcel of the same set up.

'I would like to offer you a share of this without compromising your independence Mr Kelly. You continue to draw your weekly trust fee but it is paid by the agency. What you earn from private sketching is your business. Any information you pass on to me is our business – and you and the agency receive a shared 2% commission on any deal I complete. Work it out for yourself. 2% commission on a million-euro deal is 20,000. A nice hand out to share if we can make the sale.' It was a base from which to work, and the opportunity to share big pay cheques. The offer was too good to be true.

'And what else do you want from me Mr Romano?'

'Good question my friend. Yes – there is more. I need someone with a presence to visit the villas we let. Our clientele is almost 100% English. Most occupants arrive by car and collect their keys from Eric who handles all administration. There are special tenants – often friends of mine – who need to be met at the airport, and this would be part of your job.'

'And the rest of the job?' asked Roger. Romano laughed. He was charming, he was likeable, and his very presence was riveting. Every movement he made, his very precision – he was the sort of man who never missed a trick and by just simply watching him you learned a lot.

'Working together will be to our mutual benefit Mr Kelly. There are certain formal occasions where I would like you to accompany me. Image is everything. You are a well-presented English man and you are rapidly acquiring contacts. You will hear of opportunities that we can develop together, and to have you with me will inspire additional trust.' He led Roger into the front office and introduced him formally to Eric. Eric was razor sharp and would not be easy to work with, but he spoke perfect English and gave every indication that he was Romano's right-hand man. The rear office door was opened leading to a couple of parking spaces.

'And I believe you have already driven our latest acquisition which once belonged to one of our poor paying clients. The Range Rover will be at your disposal – roomier than your current transport, and giving you space for two lady friends, or even three if you so wish.' Romano had a sense of humour.

Quick decisions. A lot of the time he was going to be used as a 'front-man'. But did that matter? How much more could he learn from a man like Romano, rather than following the rules of 'cricket' with someone like pompous Charles.

'I will want to use my own accountant,' said Roger.

'Go ahead. No problem. All payments made to you will be made through the agency, and any time you wish to examine the books Eric will gladly take you through them.' They shook hands on it. The job potential was brilliant for Roger. The villas were something to keep him occupied, and the photographic and printing facilities would make art work ten times easier than working from his apartment.

After completing arrangements with Romano, he was well satisfied with his day and gave John Davison a quick ring to put him in the picture.

'Come along early tomorrow,' said John. 'We will soon get you sorted out.'

At the apartment came the first inquiry from a yachtsman who had just bought a new boat and Roger arranged to see him at the club in the afternoon. He phoned his father who sounded pleased, and mentioned that the £100,000 invested for him in pharmaceuticals had increased by over 7%. August was finishing better than it started.

The morning was well spent setting up an accounts system. If you were officially working in France then you played by their rules. Roger's lump sum and trust payments were recorded and entered into a separate business account. John set up tax and health payments, and an easy way to account for everything showing which expenses could legally be deducted if Roger was operating independently. No matter how Romano made his deals the letting agency worked solely on a standalone commission basis, and as such John assured him the system passed all necessary legal requirements.

Before setting off for the Yacht Club, Roger called into the agency offices to pass the new details to Eric. Eric was super-efficient, and most of the recommended items were already in hand. He had cleverly altered and re-designed the layout of Roger's leaflet to now include the agency telephone number, and a special space had been created for Roger at a desk in the front office where he would best be able catch the light. Roger mentally reviewed his first impressions. He liked the whole set up but he knew that he was not going to be anything like as independent as he had wanted to be.

The yacht owner from the club turned out to be a great guy. He was about the same age as Roger, loved football and was a total computer wizard. They enjoyed a beer together, and he showed Roger around the boat which would be moored at the Yacht Club for three months whilst he was in London. He paid 500 euros cash in advance, and Roger agreed to forward the finished picture to him in London.

As Roger left the club, he was surprised to meet Carrington-Brown stood outside admiring his car.

'How long have you had this little beauty, Roger?'

'Only about four months. I bought it before coming to Nice.'

'It's a lovely job. Does it bother you having right hand steering when you are driving on the right?'

'Left hand steering would be preferable,' said Roger 'but so far I have got along without pranging it.' Carrington-Brown was amused.

'Well, if you think about selling, I will pay you what you paid for it. Helen is moving back to England after Christmas and I think a little hot rod like this would suit her down to the ground.' He walked over to his own car then turned back and handed Roger his card.

'If you could spare an hour or so I would appreciate you calling round at my house.

'I have in mind an extension for an office. Tomorrow, I go away for a few weeks but Helen will look after you. You could take her for a spin and see what she thinks of the car. Make a change from the bitchy lot she meets at her coffee mornings.'

He grinned at Roger, shook hands, and smoothly departed in his top range Mercedes.

A strange request! Roger drove away, puzzled by it. 'Away from home?' 'Take Helen for a spin?' It was almost as though he was giving Roger the green light to have an affair with his wife. Edward Carrington-Brown was a man he admired and even if he was in love with his secretary, surely he had more respect for Helen than to make a suggestion like that. He was still mulling over his encounter with Edward when he arrived back at the apartment. As usual he had forgotten his mobile phone and missed a voice message from Mick. He phoned him straight back.

'Hey Roger – it looks as though the bird has flown. The house is definitely empty – there is nobody living there. I've looked through all the windows, front and back. Doors are locked, and I had a peek through the letter box and I think I can see a bunch of keys lying on the mat inside.'

That had to be good news. Perhaps Jack had carried Rosemary away to a desert island. Why worry? But it gave Roger something more to think about. He deposited his new accounting book on the sideboard and decided not to include the cash payment from today's computer wizard. He poured himself a double whisky, and then checked the mailbox downstairs – just one letter for him and he thought he recognised the handwriting.

Out fell the two missing photographs of Elissa, plus an accompanying note from Rosemary.

> *Roger you dirty rotten bastard. I hope that you and all of your gangster friends rot in hell.*

It was significant that Roger didn't bother to think twice what had persuaded his wife to return the photographs, nor why she referred to his 'gangster friends'. As far as Roger was concerned the Manchester solicitor had done his job, and from now on he couldn't give a damn what happened to Rosemary.

9. Life on the Edge

The dawning of a new day. Working with a man whose house was protected by security guards, a man who never went anywhere unless accompanied by one or two professional minders. The prospect appealed to Roger. Walking down to the agency's office he contemplated what he might be expected to do to earn his weekly trust payment.

Rodger's father could never be sure about his son. Just when he was on the right track, he did something damned silly. Married before finishing college, and now what a mess; probably divorce proceedings with hard-earned money wasted. And if Rosemary meant business Roger might find his little pot of gold disappearing faster than he had won it. What's more he wasn't convinced about this new enterprise of Roger's in Nice. But how could you feel convinced about anything Roger did?

September was the end of the French holidays. They were joining golfing friends in St Andrews at the end of the month, but if he booked now, they could fit in a week's sunshine in Nice and at the same time make sure Roger was looking after Evelyn's apartment. Since his wife never stopped worrying about their son's chequered career the visit might (or might not) quell her doubts. One good thing – he was a safe distance away from that crazy friend of his. That silly bugger Mick who drove a white van.

Flights from Leeds/Bradford Airport were fully booked. Sunday from Manchester offered better options.

He emailed Roger:

The two of us are coming to join you for a week. Arriving next Sunday around 12.30pm. Hope it doesn't interfere with your plans.

Try and meet us at the airport.

Your mother sends her love.

Dad

Roger had expected a visit sooner or later and he supposed now was as good a time as any. Pity they couldn't have made it a bit earlier, they could have watched Elissa giving him sex education lessons.

He waited for the Liverpool lady to arrive Monday morning and arranged for her to make up the other bedroom. Like old times – when they all used to visit Nice during school holidays. It would be good seeing them both but answering his father's twenty questions would be a real bind, and something he didn't look forward to.

He started the week by borrowing the Range Rover and rechecking the location of Romano's villas. Four of them were on six-month lease and their occupant's demanded privacy. Of the six remaining villas four were rented out for varying periods, and another two were kept free for Romano's special guests.

Administration of the villas involved cleaning services, gardeners, and special maintenance, and Eric employed an ever-changing number of part-time helpers to deal with the office work. Eric was a carbon copy of Romano minus the charm.

He paid close attention to every detail of his appearance, and some of Romano's power had rubbed off on him so that, underneath an exterior of fussiness and smiles, Eric displayed a ruthless edge. Judging by the size of the Mercedes parked at the back Roger had been correct when he counted Eric as one of Romano's right-hand men. But what office tasks he allocated to his partner Melvin was a mystery since Melvin acted very 'precious', and seemed to come and go as he pleased.

Roger was working in the front office when a communication from one of their maintenance team reported two tenants causing damage in one of the villas. Melvin flapped about until he found Eric who was straight on the ball, couldn't get hold of Monty or Bruce, and enlisted Roger's help to investigate the problem.

It was 11am when they arrived at the villa and the tenant and his wife were more drunk than sober. An indoor plastic screen and window blind were burned to tatters after an accident with the barbecue. Beer cans and bottles were scattered everywhere. A cushion and a newspaper floated in the swimming pool amongst cigarette ends, and the kitchen overflowed with unwashed pots and cutlery.

Eric didn't take prisoners. The tenants would lose the complete amount of their deposit and he wanted them out of the villa by lunchtime. The woman was a foul-mouthed amazon who screamed that the cleaners hadn't done their job. The man stood in front of Eric dwarfing him and gave him a push.

'A little prick like you isn't telling me what to do. We shall stay until the end of the month when our tenancy runs out.' At this stage Roger took over. The man resembled a barrel of lard with arms hanging down like pipe cleaners. Put him in a suit in front of a sales meeting and his immense bulk and grainy voice would impress everybody – a figure to contend with who could silence most opposition and act as he pleased. Stood wearing only his shorts he cut a ridiculous figure, a mountain of hot air convinced he could get away with murder. This was going to be fun!

Roger gripped the man's bicep until he winced. Told him what he was going to do to him, what the French police might do to him, and what he could expect their legal team to do to him, then frog marched the man into the villa and said 'Pack!'

He caught the woman's wrist just as she attempted to slap his face, and applied pressure so that she didn't risk trying another slap. 'Help him pack!' commanded Roger. He opened the boot of their Jaguar and loaded obvious belongings into the back. The woman began screaming and so he asked her if she wanted to take a dip in the pool whereupon she sat down on the floor and was sick. By now the man was too frightened to object to anything and he stayed inside gathering their possessions together into little piles. Roger took photographs of the mess and the damage and within just over an hour the couple had thrown everything into their Jaguar and gone on their way threatening legal action as they left. Eric had watched completely unfazed by the experience.

'What did you say in the man's ear?' he asked.

'It's unrepeatable in French,' replied Roger, 'but what matters is we got rid of them.'

He swerved round a corner too fast. That was tight – but he was used to tight corners. Getting rid of tenants who had messed up one of Romano's villas had been quite an enjoyable experience. Eric remained quiet and said nothing until they approached the office.

'Not all our awkward clients are as easy as that,' he said.

Roger itched to get started on a picture of the London customer's boat, but next day he was detailed to meet one of Romano's special guests at the airport. On meeting the guest his first thought was – 'this can't be serious'. The man he was picking up had stepped straight out of a 'Godfather' movie. At least twenty stone in weight, with the brim of his black Fedora pulled well down over his eyes, the man handed Roger his case, commanded 'Romano', then climbed into the back of the car and never spoke another word throughout the whole journey. On arrival at the villa, Romano was there to meet him, accompanied by three dubious looking characters all wearing dark suits and dark glasses. With a brief nod of the head Roger was dismissed, and he drove back and parked behind the office. He couldn't complain that this side of the job might turn out to be boring. Mick would love it when he gave him a run down on his new employment in the world of gangland.

Inspired to keep up with boxing training he bumped into Amin who he hadn't seen since Saturday football. Amin told him they had found a new football ground and would be playing Saturday mornings starting from October. Life in Nice was beginning to take shape. He had a solid half-hour on the punch bags, and then an hour on the weights. If he was going to be tackling jobs normally assigned to Monty, then he had better be fit.

Queuing at a nearby chicken take away he acknowledged a smiling man who seemed to know him. As the queue moved forward, he felt the man's hand stroke his bottom and with amazing will power Roger checked himself from downing the man with a right uppercut. Instead, he turned and politely said 'Fuck off,' and the man smiled back politely and replied 'Pardonnez-moi monsieur.' Roger carried his chicken and French fries back to the apartment insulted by the challenge to his masculinity. But the incident highlighted the fact that at the moment he was leading a womanless life and quite unintentionally Helen crossed his mind, and Edward's office extension. He rang Helen who after making numerous excuses not to see him arranged for him to call on a Saturday morning when their concierge could deal with him whilst Helen was out shopping. Probably a wise move. She had drawn a complete veil of formality over their interlude on the Yacht Club dance floor.

The Carrington-Browns home was surprisingly modest. A four bedroomed house in the suburbs. No swimming pool, a single garage, and a relatively small garden.

Helen hadn't gone shopping – she was entertaining two friends for coffee on the patio and Roger was invited to join them and introduced to Laura and Ruth.

'Jane darling,' said Ruth, 'you really are a dark horse.

Where have you been hiding this gorgeous man?' She is a bit of a dark horse herself thought Roger. A big woman with a mane of dark hair and flared nostrils which she had a habit of inflating, and snorting, whenever she laughed. Laura was quite different. Sophisticated, ponytail, and fair, with a slim figure and smiling grey eyes – very much like Helen.

'Laura is my younger sister,' said Helen. 'She visits us in Nice so we can shop on Avenue de Verdun where she persuades us to buy clothes which we can't afford'.

All three of them were wearing short sun dresses and Roger silently observed that Helen's legs looked the best of all three of them, and his mind raced back to how she had felt in his arms with her thighs pressing close to him as they danced.

'I had better show you where Edward is thinking of extending,' said Helen.

'I'm timing you darling,' shouted Ruth.

Edward's proposed office extension didn't make sense because the cost of the work involved wasn't worth the space gained. On the other hand, there was ample room to convert the single garage into a double, and copy his own idea of building a sizeable office on top which could be used as an additional bedroom if necessary. Helen avoided eye contact with him and left him to take the measurements.

When he re-joined the group Ruth said, 'We aren't going to let this gorgeous man depart without inviting him to next week's party are we?'

'Unfortunately, this gorgeous man has to entertain his parents next week,' said Roger. 'But I will gladly accept any invitation to join you lovely ladies another time'.

'Oh – he's smooth, as well as being a hunk,' said Ruth, and snorted. 'There's a party every week until I go home in October, so join us the following week darling. I don't know what the owner will do with the property when she loses our rent' – snort – 'she's been trying to sell the place for years.'

'If she wants to sell her house put her in touch with me,' said Roger. 'I'm not just a struggling draftsman. Introduce me to her at your party.' Helen conducted him out and stood admiring the Alpha Romeo.

'Edward tells me you intend to return home to England. What will you do there?'

'What I did before I met him,' said Helen. 'I worked in property before Sandbanks really took off. I will go back to the same job'.

'We can liaise,' said Roger. 'I will send you anyone who wants to live in Sandbanks, and you can send me anyone wanting to live on Cote d'Azur, and we will go for a spin in the Alpha Romeo – and you can drive'.

'Did Edward suggest that? It's his way of easing his conscience. He palms me off onto someone else whilst he is away romancing his secretary'.

'No one palms anybody onto me,' said Roger, 'I make my own choice, and only when I'm madly attracted to someone, even though I try not to be'.

She gripped his hand and held it tight against her thigh. He felt the same chemistry he felt on the dance floor, and the same reaction.

'I will bring you the plan as soon as its finished,' he said. And he drove away with the thrill of that one contact burning into his thoughts.

The week with his parents started off smoothly. It was great seeing them both, and he was determined to make sure they enjoyed a good week's holiday. When they came through the gate at Nice Airport Roger thought his father looked very tired. Work at the bank wasn't getting any easier, and his father wasn't getting any younger.

His mother was her usual attentive worried self, but when they arrived at Aunt Evelyn's apartment her doubts regarding Roger's tenancy vanished. The Liverpool lady had done an amazing job clearing Roger's clutter. The place was fresh smelling and spotless, and his cleaner had copied Elissa by arranging an empty wine bottle containing a flower in every corner of every room.

'I like the Range Rover,' said his father, 'I am surprised at you making such a practical choice. I thought you had bought yourself a sports car.'

'The Rover comes on loan with the new job,' replied Roger. 'But wait until you see the unpractical car I did buy. You can borrow it while you are here. It will remind you of that unpractical Triumph TR2 you used to own when you first met mother.'

Score card one nil thought Roger. Much as he loved his father there would be the inevitable fencing match, no matter how hard he tried to avoid it.

Roger didn't want to take time off work. His father and mother knew their way around Nice and would be happier wandering around on their own without him. Plenty of time to get together on an evening and head out to some of the restaurants he had discovered. He started

162

the ball rolling with his own omelette and side salad speciality, including plenty of '*herbes de Provence*' in the omelette, then finished off with a creamy cake from the café opposite. They spent the evening looking through Roger's sketches, and Roger explained how he made drawings of Romano's Villa, and how he landed the work to design Hacienda Romano. There was no doubt that his father was impressed.

'And where did the '*pièce de resistance,*' on the sideboard come from?' asked his father, pointing to Elissa's photograph.

'From Beirut,' said Roger. 'Elissa is from Beirut. It is thanks to her that I landed my first job painting the yacht. She has gone back home to her husband now – sadly'.

Luckily, Roger had made sure that this time any other examples of his '*pièce de résistance*' that might upset the apple cart were hidden away safely in a drawer.

His father and mother were well occupied during the day. They liked the Alpha Romeo and drove to spots they remembered from previous holiday breaks in Nice.

The Letting Agency was quiet. Roger sat in the front office and worked on the picture of the yacht, and completed a simple plan of the intended office extension for the Carrington-Browns. A serious, hard-working part-timer joined Eric to pour over the office account books. He spoke very little English, kissed Roger on both cheeks, and became so absorbed in columns of figures that Roger enjoyed three uninterrupted days racing ahead with his own assignments, and finishing work in time to spend late afternoon and evenings with his father and mother.

Roger took them to the Yacht Club. They ate out at one of Elissa's lively Lebanese cafés, and on Thursday night he introduced them to Restaurant Acchiardo down the *rue Droite*. As luck would have it his gay acquaintances were eating at an adjoining table. They were in the company of two new friends each nursing a small dog on his knee and all four behaved extravagantly 'camp', noisily attracting the attention of the whole restaurant. Eager to include Roger in the fun they glanced his way with every piece of humour.

'Some new friends?' asked his father.

'Bed mates,' said Roger. 'You have to keep up with modern trends.'

The meal was brilliant. Well fed, and mellowed by two bottles of Merlot, they returned to the apartment and sat on the balcony watching the activity in the street below. At 10.30 pm the phone rang.

'Mr Kelly – Roger, you are alone?'

'No Mr Romano – my parents are here.'

'Ah – I'm sorry, it's late. Please give them my regards. Tomorrow, we visit two of my hotels in Marseilles. I need you with me. 8.00 o'clock – is that too early?'

'8.00 is fine,' said Roger. To be included in any sort of involvement with Romano's hotels was news to Roger.

'And the marriage problem, is solved – yes?'

'I haven't heard anything from the solicitor – but thank you!' said Roger.

'The solicitor is not your problem Mr Kelly. See you tomorrow – you owe me'.

His father looked at him inquiringly when he put the

phone down.

'So, what was that all about?'

'Not quite sure,' said Roger. 'But it looks as though I am joining my employer on an inspection tour of his hotels in Marseilles'.

Retiring for the night, the words *'you owe me'* sat a trifle uneasily in Roger's mind.

Breakfast prompt at 7am next morning. His father stood on the balcony mesmerized as Roger joined Monty on the front seat of the saloon with its blacked-out windows and special number plates. Romano sat in the back with a character he introduced as his accountant who at a brief glance looked Italian. Due to the sound proof screen Roger couldn't hear any of the conversation from the back (which was conducted in Italian anyway) and since Monty wasn't very talkative Roger sat back contentedly enjoying the ride and the passing scenery.

Marseilles has always had a seedy reputation. Crime, pick pockets, poverty. But with the second largest population in France, it is listed as their second city, and on arrival at the port of Marseilles no one can fail to be impressed. Roger sat spellbound by the sheer size of the harbour and the vast array of boats as the car climbed the steep slope up to *Basilique Notre Dame*. If he was stirred by the views of the *Quartier du Port* in Nice then the views of the port here in Marseilles were even more sensational.

Romano owned two hotels in Marseilles and both hotels were due for a surprise visit.

'One hotel is good news,' said Monty, 'and the other

is a shithouse'.

The good news had to come first because the hotel they drew up alongside had a commanding view of the harbour, flew a host of international flags, and sat proudly on the cliff top sparkling white and pristine in the morning sun.

'All that glitters is not gold,' said Monty. 'Especially the little cunt who runs it'.

The cunt in question didn't look pleased to see them. Having been summoned to the foyer he took a full twenty minutes to arrive, hadn't shaved, and looked as though he had just tumbled out of bed. He flapped about, offering profuse apologies in French, and ushered them into the breakfast room where curious guests watched the four of them being seated at a hastily cleared table. The atmosphere didn't improve when a large American got up from his table, came over, and took hold of the manager's arm.

'Can you tell me how many times we have to complain about the shower before you do something about it? Are you stone fucking deaf?'

Croissants, cheeses and jam arrived at the table together with a large pot of coffee.

All three of them sat silently waiting for Romano to comment.

'Roger – you can eat an English breakfast – yes?' He snapped his fingers at the waiter, ordered the breakfast and looked at his watch. 'We will see!'

The manager was still jittering about – in and out of the kitchen. Actually Roger thought the food looked good. Plates being collected were clean which was always a good sign, and sausage, egg, bacon and toast arrived within seven minutes of placing the order – nicely served, and on a hot plate.

'So – I think the chef is the right man,' said Romano. 'Roger when you have finished eating you will circulate around. Visit the kitchen and take a look at a few bedrooms, and the shower which our American friend was complaining about'.

Roger set off on a 'tour de l'hotel'. The downstairs toilets and washing facilities were anything but sparkling and had a French 'pong' the moment you stepped inside. Decorations on the first floor were good, but fast deteriorating on the second and third floors. Roger had taken a key to look at a vacant bedroom. Not very well cleaned. Under the bed was grubby and the toilet was slow to flush. When he put a plug in the wash basin and filled it with water the water didn't drain as he pulled the plug out. And the American had plenty to complain about. His family were staying on the first floor in a supposedly superior room where the shower tray was leaking onto the bedroom floor and the smell was horrific.

Roger reported back. Romano and the accountant were sifting through the ledgers with the hotel manager hovering in the background like a stricken chicken. Roger visited the kitchen, which was immaculate, shook hands with the chef, thanked him for breakfast and joined Monty sitting in the sunshine by the swimming pool.

'You thought this hotel was going to be the good news didn't you mate?' said Monty. 'The next one will surprise you'. There was no sign of the hotel manager when they left. Roger wondered whether they had flushed him down one of the toilets, but remembering the state of the toilets he thought that might be easier said than done.

Monty drove the car down to the harbour front and was lucky enough to find a parking spot. Hotel number two looked anything but appealing. Outside a tattooed body builder with a shaven head was holding court with three admirers seated at a table on the cobbled pavement. The bodybuilder was pumped up to huge proportions – definitely steroids, and his admirers looked capable of robbing their own grandmother. The hotel entrance was shabby – and didn't even give the impression of being a hotel, but how different when you stepped inside. A stunning dark eyed receptionist, and a tall, smart assistant greeted them. In a flash the manager was there, smiling and welcoming. Even before inspecting the hotel, you knew that this man knew his stuff and ran everything superbly.

The hotel was small with 20 bedrooms. They sat outside on the only other table and were served a bowl of bouillabaisse – a magnificent fish soup. Apart from the inconvenience of handling the lobster shells without landing half of them on his trousers Roger had never tasted anything like it. This hotel had to be the winner.

They finished the meal with cheese and fresh fruit, then he and Monty walked the harbour front while Romano and his accountant discussed business inside the hotel.

'I haven't bumped into you at the gym lately,' said Monty 'Why not join me and Bruce one night. We throw each other around on the mat and practice a few holds. It's always useful. Especially for a man like you who gets himself into trouble at the casino'.

'My luck's run out recently. I'm giving the casino a miss.'

'Wise man,' replied Monty. 'I'm giving it a miss too. I can't be everywhere. If the boss wants me looking after his interests during the day, I can't be knackering myself on a night rescuing people in the casino toilets.'

'Snap,' replied Roger.

Two more tables had been placed on the cobbles outside the hotel, and now all four tables were occupied by diners, with another couple patiently waiting. Romano was ready to move. He congratulated the hotel manager, shook hands, and they made their way to the car in time to stop three urchins from sticking a knife point in the boot lock. Monty shouted at them and they disappeared like grease lightning.

'Private enterprise so young,' commented Romano. 'You see Mr Kelly it is the way of the world. Everyone from the very top to the very bottom is trying to steal something from somebody else'.

The car set off and Monty guided it along the busy front in the direction of Nice.

Romano pressed a button and the glass partition slid down.

'So, what views have we formed during today's visits? he asked.

'Well, you know my views on the scruffy little sod who runs 'The Cliff'. He's inefficient, and he's on the take,' said Monty.

'And you Mr Kelly?'

'Hotels are not my field Mr Romano, but I agree with Monty. One thing that you need to consider: before any manager can make a success of the hotel it's going to need money spending on it. The hotel requires new plumbing throughout – and how long will it take for you to recuperate the costs involved?'

'I like that,' said Romano. 'A man who considers my costs. Do you think I should sell it?'

'In a position like that overlooking the harbour one of the big groups will fall over themselves to buy it. And their management team are probably asleep over their computers. They won't sniff it until they have bought it.' A laugh came from the back. The accountant must understand English. Romano laughed and then Monty. The idea that the buyers wouldn't 'sniff it until they had bought it' appealed to Italian humour.

There were no stops on the way back and they arrived in Nice early evening.

'Have you a dinner jacket with you Mr Kelly? You will need one. We go to the Monaco Yacht Show next week.' The mind boggles, thought Roger, as they dropped him off near the apartment. Surely Romano wasn't buying and selling million-euro yachts.

'Two telephone calls for you whilst you were on your hotel run,' said his father.

'A Mrs Jane Davison and a Mrs Carrington-Brown. Both asked if you will ring them back,' and he raised an eyebrow.

'Marriage guidance,' said Roger. 'Another string to my bow.' He rang Helen and there was no reply. When he rang Jane, John answered.

'There's a breeze forecast for tomorrow. Would you

and your parents like to go sailing. Leaving about 10 am?'
Roger turned to his father – this should impress him.

'My accountant wants to know if you would like to go sailing tomorrow?'

'Tell him yes – we would love to,' said his father, and his mother nodded her assent and looked pleased.

'Enthusiasm all round John. Look forward to seeing you about 10 am.'

This will be a good day out, he thought; John and Jane will fit into father's image of English propriety.

'You better come and have a look at this,' said his father. In the kitchen was a bouquet of flowers addressed to his mother, and a bottle of whisky, a brandy, and two bottles of wine were packed with a note addressed to his father.

Sorry to borrow your son. My best wishes –
enjoy Nice. Antonio Romano.

Romano's generosity knew no boundaries. Typically, his father looked suspicious.

'I don't know what troubles you,' said Roger. 'This man is a gentleman. When did Barclays or Town Planning ever make a gesture like this? The only thing Town Planning ever gave me was the sack.' His parents retired to bed early and Roger followed. He had a lot to think about. Antonio Romano – what a man to be working with: the Hacienda, the hotels, Monte Carlo. Where else would he be included in assignments like this? Blow his suspicious his father – and doubters like him. Roger had hit the jackpot.

171

If he hadn't made such a fool of himself then the family day out sailing would have been an unmitigated success. John, Jane and his parents got on like a house on fire, and the Sky Fly set sail under perfect weather conditions in calm waters with the minimum of swell. Conversation flowed. There were drinks all round and the trip was swinging along happily until Roger turned green and dizzy with sea sickness. Everyone enjoyed a brilliant day sailing the crystal-clear waters of Cote d'Azur whilst he lay below deck wishing to die. After five hours sick as a dog the boat docked and Roger staggered onto the harbour side, his presence hardly noticed as his parents shook hands with his friends and exchanged addresses.

Driving back his father gave the impression that his son had let him down again. Instead of being seasick he expected a son of his to climb the ship's mast, sit in the crow's nest, and repel pirates. Roger had recently experienced repelling a 'bandit', and he now had the experience of sailing in the Sky Fly. If ever he made his millions, he swore that purchasing a yacht and sailing the high seas would feature the very last amongst his list of priorities.

The last day with his parents passed pleasantly. It was inevitable that there would be a detailed discussion before they left and Roger related the whole story of his wife's visit, and her attempt to extract £50,000 to finance the debts of her and little Jack.

'What are you going to do?' asked his father 'You can't stay in Evelyn's apartment forever.'

'For a start, I will go back to Manchester and sort the house out,' said Roger. 'But I can't go there yet. If you take the keys, I am hoping you can call there on your way to Leeds and take a quick look to make sure everything is safely locked away.'

'You don't think Rosemary might go back? Did your solicitor pressurize her to leave?' asked his mother.

'I don't know and I don't care,' said Roger, 'I don't know the solicitor – he was just a voice. But if Rosemary has fled the nest and if I never hear from her again then my solicitor has done a damned good job.'

'What about the bill?' asked his father.

'Nothing! He is a friend of Romano's. His services come free – Asda price.'

His mother looked as though she wanted to cry and his father sat stiffly, his face the picture of impending doom. Neither parent was assured that their only son was moving in honest circles. Whatever he did wouldn't be right so it might just as well be wrong. Roger poured out a couple of large whiskies from Romano's gift bottle, gave his mother an extra-large sherry, and decided on a fun evening.

'Why doubt my employer and yet put so much faith in banks dad? Look at the number of people who never recovered their savings from Northern Rock. And then the disgraced director of RBS who walked away with a 2.8 million pay-out. It seems to me that the top echelons of society get away with murder so they can question the ethics of everybody else.'

'You have a point,' said his father, and changed the subject.

It irritated Roger that bankers like his father, and financiers such as Charles, always suspected those outside their own privileged little circle to be villains. What sort of crap deals did Charles and his pals pull out of the bag, and how many simple souls were left financially worse off? As far as Roger could judge insurance, finance, and banking all existed on smart-arse deals tied up in packages which nobody but themselves could understand.

His father took the house keys, and early next morning Roger dropped his parents off at Nice Airport. Secretly he thought both of them were impressed by his progress. Too bad if they entertained doubts about his lifestyle, but they had enjoyed their holiday and looked a lot better for it. He drove back leaving the Rover parked in its usual spot behind the agency, and walked to his aunt's apartment. Helen had rung again and left a message. Please return her call – she wanted to see him urgently. As he dialled her number, he tried to guess what could be so urgent. The conversation that followed set his imagination racing.

He gathered together photographic equipment, sketching pads, and measuring instruments. He changed his shirt, gave himself a spray of aftershave, and jumped into the Alpha Romeo, arriving at Helen's forty minutes after their conversation.

Helen was dressed in a lemon cheesecloth shirt and short white skirt. She was cool, classy, and composed. God – she was wonderful. Edward must be mad to risk losing her. When she got into the car one sun tanned leg was dangerously close, and Roger had to concentrate to keep his eyes fixed on the road and his hand away from her leg. Fortunately, he didn't have far to drive and as they entered the grounds of her friend's villa on Cap Ferrat and the sheer magnificence of the estate banished all thoughts of anything else.

She had outlined details during their journey, but as they stopped outside the house Helen said 'Roger – these are very special friends. They are in one heck of a financial mess. Selling this place is the only way they can rescue their home in England and everything they have got. I know Romano is a tough cookie and specializes in tough deals. That's why I contacted you first as a friend I can trust.'

Three children ran out to meet them. They flung their arms around Helen - two boys and a girl of about three. The girl was the youngest, but there couldn't be more than a couple of years between each of them. Their father made Roger think of a top-class tennis player who had suffered a defeat and a week of sleepless nights, whilst his wife looked worried but determined to put on a brave face. She was gentile and very English – the sort of woman who would support her husband through thick and thin whatever the circumstances. He immediately liked them both.

Introductions were made. Carl and Tracy Delondis. And with both of the two boys dancing around Helen, and the girl's hand curled round Roger's finger, they all adjourned to the shaded patio overlooking a swimming pool, and two grass tennis courts.

'To sell a place like this must be heart breaking,' said

Roger.

'Some you win and some you lose,' said Carl. 'This time, I have lost out big time.'

A nerve ticked under his eye. Roger felt sorry for him. He bet that this man had worked hard for everything he owned. A maid appeared with a tray of drinks, and then the ladies and children disappeared whilst Roger heard how Carl had borrowed to extend his mining business in Nigeria, and got into trouble when the Government stepped in. He casually explained that he was millions in debt to the banks, and millions in debt to the Nigerian Government, with the added problem of a pay-out for more than three hundred unemployed workers.

'We flew over yesterday,' he said. 'I have got a week here to see if I can set up something to stall off my creditors. Then we have to get back to London.'

He took Roger on a tour of the house and grounds. Every step was a delight. This villa was serious money and Roger could not visualize any buyer willing to make a quick decision, given the figures involved. It took two hours of careful photography and back-up sketches before Roger was able to compose even the most basic pictures illustrating the beauty and the ambience of the property. To appreciate its splendour, you needed to live in it and be part of it. He would have to convince Romano to get out here fast before someone else did because Carl wasn't a man to hang about.

There were oysters and champagne waiting when he finished the photography. Helen had helped her friend prepare lunch and a dish full of lamb cutlets were placed on the table together with delicious side vegetables that

Roger couldn't distinguish.

It was a celebration meal rather than a tragedy. Helen's friends were perfect hosts.

Carl was the sort of guy you would love to have a beer with and listen to his travel experiences. He must be brilliant to have achieved all this, but he would have to be even more brilliant to save his business from the present predicament.

Helen hadn't seen her friends for over a year. The afternoon passed quickly and they talked and drank until the light began to fade. Before leaving Roger thanked them for lunch and wished them luck. He quietly took Carl to one side.

'I have no authority at the agency. I work free-lance as their draughtsman. Romano is a hard man to deal with but I find him very straight and very generous, and most importantly he gets on with the job. I will get things moving for you apart from which I can only wish you good luck.'

'A charming family,' said Roger as he and Helen got into the car. 'I hope I can help them – they feel like my friends as much as yours.'

He opened the sliding roof and the warm breeze ruffled Helen's hair as they set off for Nice. He diverted to show her the plot where Hacienda Romano was to be built and got a shock. A couple of diggers were parked on the site and in the half-light it looked as though work had already begun. That was impossible. It was only a few weeks since he had handed over the completed plans and how could Romano have got building permission passed so soon.

It was early evening and the heat of the day was reduced to a mellow warmth. Magic lights from the fireflies surrounded them with a symphony of tiny beacons, and chirping crickets had begun their evening chorus. Roger parked the car overlooking the cliffs and the distant illuminated rooftops of Nice.

'If Romano sells the property, I stand to make an enormous commission out of the sale Helen. I am grateful to you for putting this opportunity my way. But what puzzles me is why you didn't ask Edward? Surely, he is the perfect man to help with finance?'

'Two reasons,' replied Helen. 'You probably don't realize it but Romano is part of a very large consortium. When it comes to important property deals, they leapfrog over the ex-pats because Romano has the muscle behind him, and enormous financial back-up. That's what makes him unpopular with people like Charles. The second reason of course is because I wanted very much to see you.'

'I am flattered,' said Roger. 'After our one dance I thought about you a lot.'

'You know Roger – when we danced together Edward hadn't touched me for over three months. Can you imagine how that feels?'

'But he still loves you. If he was married to the woman who is now his secretary, and you were the secretary travelling with Edward, then the position would be reversed and you would be his mistress.'

'You're quite wise really, aren't you?' and she laughed.

'Count yourself as the first woman clever enough to

come to that conclusion'.

She turned her head towards him and they kissed, and she opened her mouth and they kissed again. His hand dropped to the inside of her thigh and she held it there.

'No further Roger. If we are going to have an affair then we are not starting it in your car. No disrespect – I love your car, but it's too cramped for passion. Besides which any time we meet has got to take place in the strictest secrecy, and you have to understand that from the beginning.' His hand was still on her thigh, and he wanted her badly. But their kiss reminded him of Ana. The same taste, the same all-embracing reaction which took over his mind and left him emotionally spent. Was that what he wanted?

'Helen, within the last six months I have lost three desirable women who all disappeared into the sunset. Now, a very attractive woman in love with her husband offers me secret liaisons – and in a few months' time she goes back to England. What am I to make of that?' She put her arms round him and kissed him again, and her tongue flickered in his mouth teasingly.

'You are going to think about it,' she said.

'I tell you what,' said Roger. 'Since you like the car so much you drive keeping both hands on the wheel. I can keep my hand on your leg – and let you think about it'.

She was amused. It was part of a game. They exchanged seats and Helen drove all the way to the Carrington-Brown residence with Roger's hand resting high up on her thigh. He made her laugh with his misadventures in Nice. The irate bus driver, and the French woman who objected when he stood on her toe.

But the story she liked most was the Dublin escapade when he rescued Mick from the Irish police, and had to be bailed out of the police cell. Helen wanted Roger as her lover, but there was another side to her that liked him as her amusingly immature friend.

He handed her the office extension plan. 'Give that to Edward with my compliments. Pro gratis for the business opportunity and the company of his sensational wife.'

As he drove away, he couldn't believe the decision he had just made. He had turned down the idea of taking Helen to bed. Was he losing his sex drive? But by the time he got to the apartment he concluded it wasn't a bad decision after all. He could keep Helen as a friend and still look Edward Carrington-Brown in the eye.

Time was short. Roger guessed it wasn't often a multimillion property came up for sale on Cap Ferrat. Monday morning, he was outside the Letting Agency waiting for Eric. They looked at the photographs together and Eric immediately located Romano. By the time he arrived they had printed off all the photographs of the villa and grounds, and fixed an appointment to see Carl Delondis.

With Monty at the wheel, they reached the villa mid-morning. Roger hadn't mentioned financial problems – that was Carl's business. He made the introductions and stepped back. Carl showed no signs of anxiety as he conducted Romano and Eric into his office, but their meeting seemed to last forever. After hours in the office, they came out, walked the grounds, and went back inside again. Tracy played the perfect hostess with the help of her maid. She was in and out of the office with coffee, sandwiches, and beers. At the same time, she kept her eye on the children, entertained Roger and Monty, and answered a stream of calls on her mobile.

'You will get used to this,' said Monty as they stretched their legs. 'There's always a lot of hanging around when these big deals take place. And just be prepared – the governor isn't always a bundle of joy if the deal doesn't go his way.'

On the face of it some sort of agreement was reached. When business was complete Romano looked satisfied. Carl showed subtle signs of relief, and Eric remained the smiling unruffled master of ceremonies.

They left with a warm handshake from Carl, and a significant nod from Tracy.

Speeding back to base Romano asked.

'Was that a contact you made through the yacht club?'

'It was from a woman at the yacht club – yes!'

'You have a special way with women Mr Kelly. Keep cultivating it.'

'You mean a special way of them landing him in trouble?' asked Monty.

'No comment!' said Roger. 'I appreciate your faith in me Mr Romano. I promise to keep trying.'

'Trying to do what?' asked Monty. Romano took over, incisive and brief.

'The day was good. This is a big one – we aren't going to fuck it up. Wednesday Morning, I want a presentation folder complete with information, photographs, and sketches, and the format must sell online. Eric – you follow up with a courtesy call.'

The car pulled up outside the agency. Romano got out, didn't say a word, and shook hands firmly with Roger before they drove off. Roger became Romano's man.

10. The Apprentice

Holidays had ended. No longer the architect of his own ambitions, his dreams of independence were put on hold; Roger had become one of the Romano team.

Every day was different. Working with Romano meant you were on call whenever he needed you, and usually he needed you for something urgent. Most times he was teamed up with Romano and Monty which could involve anything from debt collecting to assessing property. The intricacies and possible ramifications of handling the sale of the Delondis family's villa were mind blowing, and Roger set out to learn as much as he could as the sale progressed. The job was fun – and the more he saw of Antonio Romano, the more he came to admire him.

To work with him you had to share his sense of humour. Observations came out at the most unexpected times. When Romano's silent guest with the black fedora was ready to return to London, Roger collected the two of them from the villa and took them to the airport. As previously experienced, the guest was surly, rude, and hardly spoke a word. Yet when they arrived at Nice Airport, Romano treated him like royalty - literally bowing down to him and charming him all the way to the departures lounge.

'A miserable bastard,' he said when he got back into the car. 'He is what you English call a 'wet blanket'. I keep him around in case of fire – and money,' he added, and laughed. 'But Mr Kelly it is part of our job to keep miserable bastards happy'.

Before the Delondis family returned to London, three Russians came over from Moscow. They arrived on a Thursday and returned to Moscow the next day. Father and son. The father, old and gnarled with a scar reaching from his left ear down to the corner of his mouth. His son, more sophisticated (in a jacket big enough to cover a massive belly) with a red veined face and wet lips sucking an unlit cigar.

But star of the three was the statuesque blonde woman who had to be their minder. She stood over 6 feet 6 inches tall with legs like tree trunks, and muscles bulging underneath her tights. Shoulders and neck muscles matched the legs, and were crowned by a fair skinned face with perfectly chiselled features. Unfortunately, her eyes glared hate at everyone and everywhere she looked, and even Monty appeared uneasy when Roger transferred the three Russians into Romano's limousine and they set off to view the Delondis villa.

Next day he played taxi again and, accompanied by Romano, transported the Russians from hotel to airport. Afterwards on their return to Nice Romano said, 'Mr Kelly – do you think you could have charmed that Russian woman into bed? Have you a bed big enough? I give you special bonus if next time they visit us you fuck her without getting your balls cut off.'

'Thanks Mr Romano, but your bonus is safe' replied Roger 'and so are my balls.'

'These Russians – they have too much money,' said Romano. 'Soon they will have bought up half of Cote d'Azur, and half of London besides. However – I think we have successfully sold the Delondis villa, providing there is not a last-minute Russian circus. But always remember – the Russians can be unreliable and dangerous.'

Every trip with Romano incorporated a valuable lesson. A Russian Circus? What had he in mind?

Roger invested in a dinner jacket, dress trousers, dress-shirt and shoes. Monaco Yacht Show at the weekend, and a ticket for an evening function which must have cost Romano a fortune. For convenience Romano had booked a hotel room and following two meetings he and Monty returned to the hotel and got changed into evening wear, then made their way with Roger to what was described as Monaco's most exclusive yearly function taking place on reputedly the world's grandest yacht.

'We separate here,' said Romano at the door. 'Monty and I are known. You are an unknown face Mr Kelly. If you have a ticket to be here then you are a somebody, and you are a rich somebody. Circulate. See who you can meet. Tell them nothing. Let them speculate.'

To be left on his own was a gift from heaven. The yacht was immense. Three swimming pools, a cinema, and a gym to explore. The yacht was fitted with a helipad, bullet proof windows, and the restaurant and ballroom areas were all lined with gold panelling. Wealth and famous faces were everywhere with armies of white coated waiters dashing from room to room serving cocktails. How had Romano been able to obtain invitations to an exclusive event like this? A mystery.

Roger felt a surge of power pass through his body. If you played it right you could be anybody. He recognised

Rafael Nadal in the corner by the bar, and Johnny Depp was another face paying rapt attention to a 'way out' starlet with bright red hair. Roger stood back quietly enjoying his drink and taking in the scene. It was an eye opener viewing the wives and partners of the rich and the famous, all keen to outshine one another by wearing the most outrageous gowns. And the older the woman the more outrageous her dress. Combine the revealing costumes with drastically over-bleached hair and surgically adjusted faces, and some of these women were positively frightening. He decided that if he fancied anybody then the only likely talent would be one of the waitresses.

Men in comparatively modest dinner suits circulated the gold panelled rooms with their colourful bejewelled ladies. Probably yacht owners visiting Monaco purely for the show. There were no signs of the usual male cliques tucked away in secluded corners discussing business. Everyone was here purely to enjoy themselves and when Roger looked around Romano and Monty were nowhere to be seen.

As if by a universal signal, the ladies swirled their outrageous gowns and cocktail dresses onto the ballroom floor like a flamboyance of flamingos with their men smiling indulgently.

'Are you giving us a demonstration tonight?' asked a voice in his ear. A sun-tanned Edward Carrington-Brown stood behind him sporting an immaculate dinner suit and his most charming smile 'How on earth did you manage to obtain a ticket to this sumptuous event?'

At that moment David Beckham passed with Victoria

on his arm. He stopped and looked questioningly at Roger. Roger had shaken hands with him on many occasions when he played for Manchester United. There was no reason why he should recognise Roger, and it was obvious that he didn't. But it was also obvious Roger's face rang a bell and that David Beckham wanted to place him.

'Hi there. Surprise to see you here. How are you?'

'Fine thanks David. How's life with you?'

'Great man, great! Good to see you. Enjoy the evening' and Victoria bestowed Roger with a rare smile and swept her husband away. Roger turned to Edward,

'As a renowned gymnast, footballer, and architect one gets invited to these events Edward. Now I wait for a super-rich yacht owner to engage me at an astronomical fee to redesign his yacht.'

'You might wait a long time for that to happen,' said Edward. 'But on a more practical note, I understand that Romano has found a buyer for the Delondis Villa?'

A cautionary signal clicked in Roger's head.

'I wouldn't know Edward. I am attached to the letting agency to carry out design work. Romano's business isn't connected to the agency.'

'Oh, come on Roger – everyone is aware who is behind the letting agency. All the property belongs to Romano. Listen, I want to thank you for the design of my office extension. Let me pay you, I can't allow you to work for nothing. But here's a bit of serious business I can put your way. If you can find out for me who has made an offer for the Delondis Villa, and the sum involved, then a little group of us will make it well worth your while. What's more – I am impressed with you and a lot of other people are impressed by you too. Information from you gives us the chance to take over the whole deal, and I am sure that we could create a permanent place for you amongst us.

'Ah there you are!' a ruddy faced man and a woman dressed like a Christmas tree joined them.

'Allow me to introduce another Roger,' said Carrington Brown. 'Roger and Rene Mathews – Roger Kelly. Roger owns Mathews Building Investments which is the largest building corporation in the North of England. You two are neighbours. Roger here has his major offices and works based in Leeds.'

'Is this the young man you were telling me about?' asked Roger Mathews.

'This is our man,' said Carrington Brown putting his arm round Roger's shoulder.

'I have just been explaining how he might help us, and how I think we can help him' and as he spoke the compelling Carrington presence and seductive voice cut a magic path to future glory.

'I am very pleased to meet you lad' said Roger Mathews 'and pleased you can help us. We Northerners have got to stick together – and when you deal with a man from the North you know you are getting a straight deal.'

He was typical. A solid Northern businessman. Anything South of Watford would belong to the Londoners, but anything North of Watford would belong to Mathews Building Investments. Roger felt the tingle of power run through his body, and an iron will grip his mind. This was how it was done wasn't it? This was cricket! These were the underhand bouncers which secured the runs. Everything he hated.

'Tell me gentlemen – would you call it a straight deal if I sold one of your private contracts, or supplied confidential information about Mathews Building Investments to Romano, or any other of your competitors?'

Suddenly Edward Carrington Brown looked uncomfortable – he had lost control. Roger Mathews eyes narrowed, 'I can see we are wasting our time. This fellow doesn't know a good offer when he has the chance of one'.

'On the contrary,' said Roger smiling. 'I appreciate your offer. But as I have told Edward, I am not privy to the information you seek – but if I were I wouldn't be prepared to divulge it at any price.' Rene Mathews stepped forward and chimed in.

'Explain to this young man that money isn't the real problem. We don't want the wrong type of people occupying the villas on Cap Ferrat so we like to handle everything ourselves.' Her husband looked unperturbed by her interruption.

'I admire your honesty lad. But that's no use to me. Let me know if you change your mind. We've some big projects on the cards, and plenty of opportunities for an imaginative man to help us market them.' He sauntered off in the direction of the bar with his Christmas tree wife. Carrington Brown lingered behind.

'You know you could be making a big mistake old chum. You might be batting for the wrong side. Have a think about it. When I see you at the club let me pay you for the drawings, and by the way,' he smiled 'Helen enjoyed the spin in your Alpha Romeo. I am away for a month. You have my permission to take her for another spin.'

'I can't believe what you are suggesting Edward.'

'Well life for me is a bit complicated old chum. If you don't take her out then somebody else will,' and Carrington Brown followed his friends to the bar.

Unbelievable thought Roger. In Manchester gyms, boxing clubs, and night clubs he had met some pretty low life characters but the standards of this shitty lot took some beating. He changed from sedate cocktails to a double whisky, downed it in one go and ordered another. The encounter had surprised and disgusted him.

'I hope my father wasn't rude to you,' said an English voice which appeared at his side. 'Phillipa Mathews and you are Roger Kelly, aren't you?'

'Nobody was rude,' said Roger shaking her hand. 'I just never realized that business practice can be so surprisingly bent.'

'We are all secretly a bit bent – but how bent depends on where you are looking.' Phillipa gave him an open fresh-faced smile. She was wearing minimum make up which hardly covered her freckles, and gave the impression of a permanent smile due to slightly protruding teeth. He could imagine her riding the Yorkshire Dales on horseback.

'You must be the only woman here tonight wearing a lovely dress which suits you,' said Roger. 'In which case you are going to be the only woman I dance with.'

'That's very positive,' said Phillipa as he led her onto

the dance floor. 'You didn't even ask me.'

'I had to do something quickly,' said Roger 'Before you shocked me with some bent revelation and frightened me away.' She stayed with him all evening. Phillipa was fun, easy to talk to, and good to dance with. He was sorry when her father gave a wave to indicate they were leaving.

'I go home tomorrow. Look me up when you visit your parents in Leeds. If ever you do any work for us, you will be dealing with me anyway,' – and with a kiss on the cheek she was gone.

The night was still young. If you weren't dancing you were being plied with small plates of food and glasses of champagne. Roger made the most of the food but stuck to his whisky. The colourful gowns continued to swirl. The Monaco yachting set certainly knew how to enjoy the opulence of the occasion, whilst taking every opportunity to parade their own affluence. An awe-inspiring night.

It was late when Romano and Monty appeared from nowhere and gave Roger the nod. The evening ended. After five minutes Roger followed and met them back at the hotel. Straight away he sensed that their evening hadn't lived up to expectations.

'Was your night more productive than ours?' asked Romano 'Did you charm the woman we saw you dancing with? Did she reveal anything significant?'

'Sorry – a good dancer, but no revelations. On the other hand, her father thought he could persuade me to change career and become a spy. He believed I would roll over for the chance to join their old boy network.'

'Who was that?' asked Romano.

'Mathews Building Investments and Carrington Brown,' said Roger. 'An eye-opening experience. Two straight pillars of society. It was fun telling them to stick their offer.'

'Don't take it too seriously Mr Kelly. I know them both. It's all a game. But what annoys them most is that it's a game we win – and you are playing with the winners.'

It was late. They cleared the hotel room and Monty was in the driving seat on route back to Nice. Roger had time to reflect.

'Tonight, Mr Kelly you have been amongst the greatest accumulation of wealth that you will ever meet under one roof. Stars, Royalty, and the world's wealth, many of whom enjoy a tax-free life in Monaco.'

'And are quite prepared to fiddle you, as well as the tax man,' added Monty.

It was 4.00 am when Roger eventually got to bed. Another high point in his learning curve, and another high point if he considered where the night's offers might lead. And try though he may he just could not banish the thoughts of an available Helen.

With the Yacht Show and Helen colouring his dreams he slept most of the day away.

Weekends in Nice were still very busy. Many visitors preferred September to the intense heat in overcrowded August. Restaurants and popular venues were well booked, and since he didn't feel like going anywhere on his own Roger decided to catch up on home affairs, and take stock of the past few weeks.

On the terrace of the café opposite all tables were occupied. Roger settled for a late take-away of *poulet-frites*, and joined the inevitable queue without having his bottom stroked. Dancing and talking with Phillipa had set him thinking. During the last few weeks, he had been so busy that the absence of female company hadn't bothered him, but his night in Monaco made him realize that his friends in Nice were all part of an older crowd, and he missed pals like Mick and Howard to keep him company. Take Nice Yacht Club for example – where did he fit in? Most yacht owners were in a senior bracket, and the younger crowd who belonged to the rowing set were mainly French, and likely to slot Roger amongst the British ex-pats. And although he was admirably positioned to start his own business the approach by Carrington Brown and Mathews Building investments made him realize he was out of his depth, and he had a lot to learn before he could deal successfully with experienced business people like them. Living life in Nice was brilliant and so was working with Romano. But tonight, he badly needed a pal who he could talk to and offload some of his concerns. His parents were still playing golf in St Andrews, Mick was impossible to catch, and Joan sounded cool towards him when she answered his call. He spoke to Howard and learned that Rosemary has parted from little Jack, given up her teaching job, and fled to Scotland. She had told Joan a frightening tale of intimidation which she blamed on Roger. That apart Howard was only interested in talking about babies.

It was early evening. Two cards in the mailbox

reminded him that tomorrow was his 28th birthday. He had lived in Aunt Evelyn's apartment for six months and more had happened to him during those six months than during all of his previous seven married years. He started to write. It was a summary of his stay in Nice. His doubts and fears, successes and failures, and extraordinary good luck meeting people who helped him start up his business. Excluded were any mention of amorous alliances. Included was Romano, the problematic marriage visit from Rosemary, his empty house, and a quandary of what to do next. He attached it in an email to Ana. It was his first email to Ana in two weeks, and it was over two weeks since he had received anything from her.

Ana was surprised when the email landed in her inbox. It took nearly an hour to read it. There was nothing personal. The letter was something you would write to a friend when you needed advice.

Life for Ana was not good. She was overqualified for most vacant positions, and she worried that starting salaries were not sufficient to cover her expensive flat and car, nor the commitments to her family in Rovinj. Ana's only option was to continue concentrating on Multilingual Escorts and she was fed up to the teeth with travel.

After working Eastern Europe with McDonald, the machinery salesman, Ana had vowed 'never again', but then a lucrative offer tempted her to organize a Russian business meeting in Prague. She was just back. The head of the company, who thought he owned her, had cornered her after the meeting and come close to raping her. She was bruised, upset and frightened. And she realized that this was likely to happen again.

Time and travel had spoiled everything between her and Roger and though she still thought about him she had to be realistic. If they met again nothing would be the same. She had nothing to lose. She sat down and replied to Roger's long email.

Ana told him everything. How her and Kata started the escort agency for fun. How she met Jacub when she was only 20, had an affair, and went home to Croatia to have his child. Her sister adopted the baby, and Ana's heart broke in two each time she went home and saw her son, a son who would never know that she was his mother. To finish her degree at Manchester University and find money to send home, Ana had worked a seven-day week to cope with Brown's Garage and handle translation work with Multilingual. Both jobs were a success. But the escort agency grew beyond all expectations. When she met Roger he had changed everything for her. It was the first time in four years she felt serious about anyone since her affair with Jacub, but her intentions to cut down on agency work had been ruined by Brown's son entering the business. That was the week Roger went to Nice. Her financial commitments now meant she had to travel wherever multilingual services were required. Finally, she didn't hold back telling the story of her frightening experience with the Russian businessman in Prague.

Life takes a strange path Roger. Who would have thought when you went on holiday you would want to stay there? And who would have thought that my own fortunes could change so rapidly? Whatever you decide I wish you lots of success and hope your marriage problems unravel for the best.

It seems I am compelled to travel, but if I am home when you visit Manchester then I would love to see you.

My love.

Ana

Roger read Ana's letter on his birthday. He was stunned. Her letter explained everything. He responded within minutes.

Ana,

Why on earth didn't you tell me all of this in the beginning? I would have understood. It wouldn't have made any difference.

Love Roger

11. The Enforcer

A 28th birthday tinged with regret. He had been overwhelmed by Ana yet he had let his feelings for her evaporate into nothing because of a misunderstanding.

He lay on the beach and sunbathed. He swam, and in the evening he dined at Nice Casino without risking a single euro at the gambling tables. It should have been a perfect day, instead it was the most bloody awful birthday he could ever remember.

During the week he was thrown into the thick of it. Eric was sick. Roger struggled to man the office using his wavering French, and Melvin was awkward and worse than useless. Romano visited in a bad mood. He was a man short. Bruce had left without giving notice to return home to Scotland and Monty was stuck in an empty garage near Carros where the manager had done a runner with some of the stock. Now Romano needed to go back to Marseilles and borrowed Roger to drive him there. Roger realized he was not only a driver but an acting body guard – and that didn't feature in his scheme of things one bit.

At night he bumped into Monty at the gym. After a session on the punch bags they adjourned to the side room and Roger had his first lesson in unarmed combat. Over a drink Monty revealed that he and Bruce had worked well together for three years but now he was going to be lumbered with the task of training someone new. He grinned at Roger.

'You might be the new man. I'll put in an application for you.'

'Count me out,' said Roger, 'not part of the Kelly remit.'

'You had better make yourself scarce then mate, because you are liable to be roped in for all sorts of jobs in the next few weeks.' Monty was a pal. Forewarned is forearmed. Back at the office a welcome telephone call from a ship's chandler in Antibes informed Roger of two clients requiring paintings of their yachts. Smiling Eric was back, and Roger was out of the office like a flash and heading for Antibes.

The ships chandler was a likeable man from Hove. Ex-Merchant Navy, with clipped side whiskers and a deep tan which looked suspiciously false. He closed the shop and walked Roger to the harbour pointing out two yachts both unoccupied. 'Dutch Courage' owned by a Belgium, and 'Northern Lass' owned by an Englishman who had noticed Roger's poster at Nice Yacht Club. Neither were luxury yachts but both involved a good deal of work if full colour paintings were required. The Belgium boat would be easy but 'Northern Lass' was coloured an uninspiring black and moored awkwardly so that it was half obscured between two other yachts. Clear photo shots were tricky, and it would be difficult creating an appealing background.

The chandler was an unusual character, sporty and masculine but too friendly. Roger negotiated 500 euros per painting and the chandler agreed so easily that Roger wished he had asked for more. The Belgium boat owner was a very good friend of the chandler (wink wink) so there was no rush. The chandler made no secret of his preferences and suggested he close the shop for the day and take Roger out for lunch and a grand tour of Antibes (wink wink). Roger thanked him and backed out of the shop making a mental note not to wear tight jeans on his return trip.

It took a few hours of careful photography before he was satisfied that he could make a good job of the paintings. His first time in Antibes and he fell for the place. The town was easily walkable and he visited the sea front castle to see the Picasso collection, walked the harbour and the old town, and chose a sea front hotel for lunch eating outside under the shade of a parasol. A white-coated waiter demonstrated the art of professionally filleting a couple of mackerel performed with a flourish which was a joy to watch. Where in England did a professional waiter fillet your fish for you? And come to think of it – who in England was going to pay him 1,000 euros for two pictures. He bought the previous day's Express. Manchester – fifteen degrees and raining. He breathed in the clear salty air and dismissed all concerns that had troubled him earlier in the week.

Satisfied with his day, Roger was late back into Nice. His space behind the agency was taken by the Citroen parked next to Eric's Mercedes. Eric lived in the town centre and never moved the Mercedes so Roger drove round to the apartment and parked beside his Alpha Romeo. In future he might as well keep the Range Rover in the safety of the apartment's security operated car park.

Just as he walked in the apartment, Helen rang. 'I think you are avoiding me young man. Whenever I ring you are out.' He wished she would stop calling him 'young man.' It spoiled his erotic fantasies about her.

'Helen, you know I don't want to avoid you? The trouble is – I want to see you too much. But I warn you – if you want to land yourself in a mess then count on me'.

'Don't be silly Roger. Are you having a 'downer' at the moment? Its Ruth's party on Saturday. It's her last one before she goes home and she asked me to invite you.'

'How do I get there?'

'It's easy – I will email directions. I look forward to seeing you. Her parties can be a bit wild so bring your swimming trunks and your toothbrush.'

He brought Helen's email up on the laptop remembering Ruth had mentioned that the owner was keen to sell the property. He checked out a picture of the house and the estate agent responsible for selling it. It looked like an immense, lonely, sprawling conglomerate of buildings. A good sea front position, but isolated apart from a few beach huts. He supposed Ruth and her friends rented it cheaply for the summer.

There was no time to check the property out with Eric. Next day Romano blew into the office like a thunder-bolt and asked Roger to take him to a hotel meeting in a seedy area north of the Gare SNCF. Again it dawned on Roger that he was filling in as a bodyguard.

Five unsavoury characters entered the hotel while Roger stood outside keeping an eye on the Citroen. He was joined by a couple of their minders – a tall Nigerian with dreadlocks, and a tough wiry little man from Heywood with his shaven head and neck covered in a mass of tattoos.

'Does the job take you into Manchester?' asked Roger.

'I'll spend ten years in the cooler old love the moment I set foot in Manchester' said the man from Heywood cheerfully. Across the street a third-floor window opened and three prostitutes shouted down a variety of ribald offers.

'I don't understand a fucking word they're saying,' said the man from Heywood.

'But I've had the one in the middle with dark hair, and I've had it away with the fat one on her right as well. The fat one's a real goer' he said smacking his lips. The Nigerian came to life and shouted something at the prostitutes, then unzipped his fly and stood wagging himself at them. This is what my father would call 'real class,' mused Roger. The culmination of my architectural career.

'If I'd got one like that, I could make my fortune in Manchester without risking my neck protecting this lot,' said the man from Heywood nodding towards the hotel.

The hotel entrance suddenly became busy with a number of undesirables leaving the meeting arguing aggressively with each other. The Nigerian attached himself to one of them, waving goodbye to his admirers on the third floor.

'Keep your pecker up,' shouted the man from Heywood as the Nigerian left. Romano followed looking worse tempered than ever and dumped himself on the back seat of the Citroen and let out a stream of Italian oaths.

'Why is it I have to do business with crooks?' he said.

'Isn't it possible Mr Kelly to conduct my affairs without having to include those shits?' Roger referred to his watch, 'Mr Romano – have you ever eaten at the Acchiardo?'

'The Acchiardo – no! Where's that?'

'A restaurant in the old town – on rue Droite. I would like to take you there. My turn to buy lunch'.

If Romano was surprised, he didn't show it. They had to share a large table in the restaurant, and Roger went ahead and again ordered 'octopus casserole' figuring that if everybody else had liked it why shouldn't Romano? They shared a carafe of house red and Romano relaxed. He couldn't talk business problems in the restaurant, but he made up for it after lunch when they picked up the Citroen.

At Roger's suggestion they took a run out to the rambling party house which was on the market. There were no signs of life in the house, but outside a golden-haired Scandinavian was coaching two middle aged ladies on the tennis courts. In spite of the isolated location Romano showed interest in the house and thought it had potential for development. They diverted to the outskirts of Villefranche where the footings were well under way for the hacienda, and then through the iron gates of Villa Romano to see how Monty was coping training two new security guards.

This was the first time Roger had entered the grounds and seen the villa closely and he hadn't realized that Romano's mistress was installed there. She was a plump pale woman about the same age as Romano and berated him in Italian the moment she emerged from the side door. Like a second Italian wife thought Roger. Why do men who take a mistress nearly always choose a woman who resembles their wife?

'Mr Kelly, I must stay,' said Romano. 'Monday morning we collect the two future residents of the Delondis Villa – two new Russians. Thank you – you have made my day. We will meet at the office.' Roger went straight back to the apartment and got changed for the gym. Romano had his problems. If you owned a gym, hotels, and ten villas it was inevitable that you made agreements with the less desirable business elements running the town. He had a lot of respect for Romano, and a strong bond was developing between them. Nevertheless, he wanted to remain as independent as possible from Romano's business problems, and he had no intention of becoming a part-time body guard.

Saturday's party was in full swing when he got there. Very loud and very young.

Cars were parked everywhere. On the drive, on the grass, on the road – at a rough guess at least a hundred. It looked like one of those free for all gatherings where you don't need an invitation you just turn up. Ruth must have a lot of money to throw around if she could afford to finance efforts like this.

A Caribbean steel band entertained on the lawn and shaded by a marquee were plates of sandwiches and cakes, whilst drifting from somewhere nearby came the distinct smell of burnt barbecued sausages. Roger helped himself to sandwiches and roved around meeting nobody. Wearing his designer shirt and jeans was a mistake. Most party goers had picked their tattiest shorts to wear, and sun-tanned limbs with neat French hips were in ample evidence swaying to the Caribbean beat.

He followed his nose to one of the disused stables where the drinking crowd were English and German. Crates of beer were stacked against the wall and barbecued chicken and sausages were being washed down by pints of lager amidst shouts of English laughter and deep 'ja-ja's' from the Germans. Definitely the surfing set with all over tans probably achieved by spending all summer on the beach. There were no signs of Ruth or Helen and he was able to wander round the house at will. Space downstairs was massive, and he counted eight bedrooms on the first floor, and another six dormer bedrooms above. He exited by another entrance with an adjoining patio and a busy built-in bar where he found Ruth standing draped around the golden-haired tennis coach, with two of her mature friends struggling hard to gain his attention. In the background, he spotted Helen gazing into the eyes of a very young olive-skinned French man whose hand was held close to her chest, allowing one finger to creep below the low-cut front of her sun dress. Roger stepped out of sight feeling stabs of jealousy. If Helen called Roger 'young man' then did she call her party companion 'young boy'? Having seen her he wanted her badly but he should have made up his mind when he had the chance.

Back on the lawn some of the drinking crowd had joined the dancers and a statuesque German girl smiled at him and joined him for a dance. Unusually for the Germans she couldn't speak English, but she made up for it by an acrobatic display of body movement and then left him in the middle of the lawn to dance with another statuesque German. More surfers left their beers to give it their all, gyrating on the lawn. Other surfers brought their beers with them and slopped it around while they danced, and as the rhythm got faster and their shouts grew louder a radio transmitted the strokes of midnight. With a chorus of 'hurrahs' there was a rush as the dancers stripped off everything, threw their tattered shorts to one side, and ran naked down to the beach and into the sea. Roger watched carefully but saw neither Helen nor Ruth among them. He chuckled to himself. What would Carrington Brown have thought if his wife had been amongst the naked bathers.

Disappointed, and tired of his own company he eased himself silently away from the party to where he had parked the Alpha Romeo.

'You aren't leaving without me, are you?'. Helen appeared out of the shadows next to his car.

'I thought you were spoken for,' said Roger. 'I thought I was too old for you.'

'I saw you out of the corner of my eye. I was making you jealous.'

She got into the car and kissed him and his hand slipped down the front of her sun dress and cupped her breast.

'I said there was no room for passion in your car didn't I Roger? We are near to a private place I have in mind which offers us a little more room.' Helen directed him through a village hamlet to a small terraced cottage.

'My secret hideaway,' she said as she got out the keys. Inside was very warm. The room had a faint dusty smell as though it hadn't been used recently, and Helen opened a window. She delved into a cupboard and pulled out a bottle of cognac and they clinked glasses.

'I shall miss you when I go back to live in Poole, and I don't even know you yet. Are you taking me to bed Roger so I can get to know you better?'

They carried their drinks upstairs and she drew back the bed covers and closed the bedroom curtains. As Roger unbuttoned her dress, he was startled to realize how very nervous she was and he put his hands on her shoulders and kissed her eyelids.

'You will never know Helen how much I have wanted you.' He unclipped her bra and let her sundress fall and bent and kissed her breasts. 'And you are beautiful. So beautiful. You will never understand how beautiful you are.'

As she lay on the bed he talked to her, caressed her, and kissed her. He sensed the deep hurt of her marriage and a desperate yearning for love. He wanted to be the one to mend the hurt. To take her high above – into the stars and onto another planet, but most of all he wanted to look after her.

Roger had fantasized so many times about making love to Helen. Making love to her was going to be wonderful and it was. The sweet taste of her lips, the thrust of her small breasts, and the pulsing wetness between her legs led him into another world as she clung to him and he slowly entered her. Afterwards she held him tightly as though he might get up and leave her, and he kissed tears from her cheeks and felt the warm satisfaction of her body closely wrapped in his arms. He hadn't planned for this. He had tried to avoid this. But it was so marvellous now it had happened.

Monday, he met Romano early. The Russians were expected on a mid-day flight. He hadn't realized that their unpleasant predecessors were sales agents who handled the finance and legalities of the Delondis property, whereas today's visitors were the final purchasers who planned to live on Cap Ferrat.

Romano, Roger and Eric sat round a table in the back office hammering out final details to make sure nothing went wrong. Roger was still in a state of euphoria; it was only two hours since he had left Helen in bed while he shot back to the apartment to get changed. As it happened the day went smoothly. The two Russians were a charming couple speaking both French and English. They stayed all day at the Delondis Villa and went back again the following day. Roger returned them to the airport late on Wednesday and the sale was in the bag. They insisted he stayed with them to celebrate with a bottle of Dom Perignon until their boarding time was called. Roger hadn't a clue how much they were paying for the Delondis Villa, but one thing was for sure: when the Russians settled their account, he would be due a sizeable commission cheque. His first major sales success.

Romano and Monty were away in Naples. Roger took stock. He had instigated a multimillion-euro property sale. He was painting two yachts for the sum of 1000 euros, and he was involved in an affair with a beautiful desirable woman. He was sailing along on a 'high' – his life was on track.

But he should have known better – his life was never on track. Within the next 24 hours his plans and aspirations would be turned upside down and shot to pieces. History does not repeat itself – people repeat history, and Roger had always been a master at landing himself in a mess and nothing had changed.

On his morning run a dog got tangled with his feet and bit his foot. That was the beginning. Smiling Eric was bad tempered and petulant after an argument with his partner, and Roger had to deal with a couple from Chelsea who returned their keys to the office and complained about disruptive goings on in their adjoining villa.

'Very upsetting,' said the Chelsea lady. 'Shouts and screams – it sounded as though someone was being murdered.'

Roger apologised, and as the couple left the office he said to Eric, 'They were complaining about one of Romano's special guests, weren't they? Shall I take the Citroen and check it out?' He was glad to be out of the office. Eric and his partner were getting on his nerves and while the dog bite hadn't drawn blood, his foot still throbbed after the bloody thing had tried to remove his shoe.

Once clear of Nice traffic the villas were only a 15-minute drive away. When he parked outside, he was relieved to see that all looked well, but when he pressed the doorbell and a woman answered, his stomach turned over. In Roger's early days of boxing lessons, together with lectures by his father, he had been taught that you never ever hit a woman. The woman standing in the villa doorway might have been attractive if she hadn't been so badly beaten up. There were huge bruises on her upper arm, and yellow marks from previous bruises. One side of her face was swollen beyond recognition and her eye was black and almost closed. Her lip was split and there was dried blood on the corner of her mouth.

'Who did that to you?' asked Roger, and the woman started to cry. 'Whoever it is will not be doing it again in this villa. Get your things together and pack a case, and let's get you out of here.' She started to shake, and cry so much he could hardly hear her reply.

'He won't let me leave,' she said. 'And he has my passport and credit cards.'

'Don't worry about that,' said Roger. 'Just get packed and we will look after you once you are out of here. And whether the bastard you are with is your husband or your partner I suggest you make sure you leave him permanently behind.'

He accompanied her into the villa and tried to be helpful. Her name was Sally and she was a barmaid in a pub on the South Bank in London. That was where she had first met Jason. She followed Roger as he wheeled her largest case outside alongside the pool, and then stopped with a cry of fright. There stood Jason waiting for them. Poker faced, square jawed, wearing a baseball cap, and ready for trouble.

Without a word he stepped in front of Sally and slapped her face. Like a bullet Roger shot forward putting his twelve and a half stone behind a soccer tackle which carried the man backwards, and he slipped and fell into

209

the pool. Sally cried out hysterically, and ran into the villa sobbing as the man Jason slowly pulled himself out of the water leaving his baseball cap floating in the pool. He grabbed a towel, walked to the gate, and stood on sentry duty while he leisurely towelled himself dry.

Roger had enough experience to recognise a professional when he saw one. This man was lethal and probably a psychopath as well. He was a nasty piece of work and Roger stood little or no chance against a man who made violence his profession, and would now take great pleasure in knocking Roger into oblivion. But there was no way out – neither for him nor the girl. Either he stopped this lunatic or both he and the girl would finish up in hospital – or worse.

Roger took a safe position in the middle of the lawn where there were no solid objects to fall upon, and watched Jason as he threw the towel to one side and walked purposely towards him. He was slightly shorter than Roger but a couple of stone heavier and every inch was solid muscle. His face was tight skinned with small features, and his pale eyes were well protected by a deep forehead with hair cut short and lying flat to his head. Dressed in shorts and moccasins he will be able to move around easily, and the wet clothes will make him slippery. Why in God's name did I choose to wear tight jeans and leather shoes today of all days Roger asked himself.

The man Jason approached without looking Roger in the eye. When he threw the first punch it came at lightning speed from nowhere and missed, narrowly grazing Roger's ear. Roger had anticipated it, but he failed to anticipate the knee that followed catching him full under the ribs and causing his legs to give way as the searing pain knocked the breath out of him. He covered his head with his arms and curled up on the grass protecting himself from the kick that would follow, but the kick never came. Instead, Jason took a step back and waited. It flashed through Roger's mind that this bastard who had floored him so easily was now going to enjoy taking him apart bit by bit. The pain in his chest acted like a drug. He had too much to lose to be beaten so easily, and as he regained his feet energy flowed back into his legs.

Jason moved forward and Roger swayed out of his way landing a kick hard on his shin. He followed up with two straight punches – left and right catching Jason full in the face. It was like hitting a brick wall and a sharp jolt ran up Roger's left arm.

Jason came forward again and Roger blocked the first punch, but the second caught him at the side of the head and his ear imploded as his head spun. He danced out of reach. He bobbed and weaved and peppered Jason's face with a barrage of straight punches, and this time added a right hook which landed full on the side of the jaw.

It was a hard punch perfectly delivered. Nine out of ten opponents would have been halted in their path, but Jason continued moving forward unaffected, altering his stance to a crouch with his hands held high. As Roger circled out of his way it occurred to him that this was the moment which fighters dread. The moment when they have given their best and know they are going to be beaten. And this wasn't a boxing ring. Nobody would ring a bell and shout 'time'. The slaughter would go on long after all the fight had gone out of him.

Jason was a deadly mover and didn't waste energy. With a dry mouth and thumping heart-beat Roger danced backwards and to the side. He delivered upper-cut after upper-cut under Jason's crouching stance, and only succeeded in hurting his hands more than he hurt his opponent. As he stepped back, he was caught off balance when a foot snared him around the ankle. Jason sprang forward like a tiger and his head smashed into Roger's face. Roger felt his nose crack from the double butt, and he was blinded as blood poured from his nose. Jason was behind him pinning both wrists together with an iron grip, and his right arm under Roger's chin choking him.

So – this was it. He was finished. In one desperate last move Roger stamped with all his remaining strength on Jason's foot. There was a grunt of agony as he felt the heel of his leather shoe catch the toe underneath the soft moccasins. For a brief moment the grip on Roger's arms slackened and Roger stamped hard again, broke loose, and blindly swung his pointed thumb back into the face behind him. He felt his thumb connect and suddenly both arms were free and he was lashing out wildly with kicks and punch after punch until Jason was stretched out on the ground helpless, with one hand covering his eye. Roger stumbled to the end of the pool and collected a towel which he held to his nose. He turned on the poolside shower and stuck his head under it until he could bear the cold water no longer. He dried himself off, and collected two towels and walked over to Romano's special guest who was struggling to sit up.

'This ends now,' said Roger throwing him a towel. 'Either I am going to kill you or you are going to kill me

212

– and either way that would be awkward for both of us. I want you out of here by tomorrow, and I want your lady friend's passport and credit cards now.' Carl's face didn't move and he indicated his shoulder bag hung on a chair.

Roger extracted Sally's passport and found her purse and credit cards. 'And keep away from her when you get back to London,' he said.

He went into the villa and said to Sally, 'Stop blubbering – I need a hand,' and hustled a shaking Sally and the rest of her luggage into the Citron.

'Can you pull yourself together and drive because I can hardly, see?' She looked at his face and said nothing and climbed into the driver's seat.

Roger went back into the villa and looked around. As far as he could see she had left nothing behind. Special guest Jason still sat stunned with his hand covering his eye. Roger walked over to him and said, 'Jason – you are a piece of shit. Win or lose you are still a piece of shit and you will always be a piece of shit.' There was no immediate reply. Then Jason spoke for the first time. 'You should have killed me,' he said 'because if there is another time, I will kill you.'

Sally drove the Citron to the apartment car park and left her heavy cases locked in the car. He could hardly find strength to climb the stairs and Sally had to help him.

The bottle of brandy Romano had sent his father was still unopened and Roger poured two glasses, phoned Eric and asked him to send a doctor urgently. All credit to smiling Eric he moved fast and brought a doctor to the apartment within forty minutes of Roger's call. Roger couldn't breathe through his nose which was steadily bleeding. His head pounded from the blows to his ear and stabs of pain from his ribs were circulating round the whole of his body. The doctor who came with Eric was the sort of doctor you would label 'Romano' – unconcerned by the injuries which were probably a daily occurrence, and no more important than treating a common cold. He was French with a working knowledge of English and he set about patching Roger together briskly and uncompromisingly. He set the broken nose, put stitches in his ear, and bandaged the left hand which was swollen and unusable. After a brief inspection of his ribs, he advised an x ray plus an x ray of his swollen hand to be on the safe side. When he had finished with Roger he turned to Sally, cleaned her face with anti-sceptic, and was noticeably more sympathetic. He produced anti-biotic pills for them both, gave Roger an injection, and prescribed rest in bed for the next few days and was adamant that Sally did the same, avoiding travel over the weekend.

The man was brilliant, and when Roger inquired about the cost smiling Eric emerged from the shadows and assured him that the doctors bill would be covered by the agency.

Roger was near to collapse. He felt as though he had survived the valley of death.

The doctor sanitised his instruments and prepared to leave.

'Monsieur I have done my best for you. The nose and the ear should heal without a problem, but I cannot promise your face will regenerate the same perspective to which you were accustomed prior to your entanglement in today's foray. C'est la vie monsieur. All we do demands a price.'

When Eric and the doctor had gone Roger pointed to the second bedroom.

'Sally, stay until you are ready to travel. There's food in the fridge and I am going to bed, and I won't be getting out of it in a hurry.'

Still aching all over, with his head thumping, his last thought before the drugs took effect was, 'What a laugh if I wake up and nobody recognises the new face of Roger Kelly.'

12. Departure

During the night Roger developed a fever. He sweat buckets. He switched from hot to cold, from fiery sweats to shivering chills, his muscles ached and his head pounded. During the next two days he had very little recollection of his surroundings nor memory of previous events. He vaguely remembered an angel with a bruised face bathing his forehead and plying him to drink water. Then the sound of the telephone and there were two angels looking after him – and a visit from another doctor.

Sunday evening, he recovered his senses after sleeping the whole of the day.

'Sir Galahad awakes,' said Helen. Behind her he recognised the bruised face of Sally smiling instead of crying, and the first thing Roger asked for was a mug of tea.

For the next week he didn't go anywhere. Sally stayed until Tuesday when Helen took her cases out of the Citron's boot and ran her to the Airport. Helen called to see him twice during the rest of the week and cooked a meal for the two of them. One day they sat talking until after midnight, but she didn't stay and somehow, he sensed that their relationship had altered.

The left hand was still bandaged but the right hand was useable and midweek he began work on the painting of 'Dutch Courage'. Romano and Monty were back from Naples and Monty paid him a visit.

'You're a right twat for getting involved with all of that,' he said. 'You could have waited for me to get back and I would have dealt with it.'

'Sounds simple but I didn't have any options,' said Roger.

'Anyway, my advice is stay where you are until you feel better mate. There's trouble brewing between Romano and his colleagues and you're best staying well out of it.'

Monty collected the Citron from the car park and departed to pick up Romano.

Roger did some straight thinking. 'Trouble brewing'. There would always be some sort of trouble brewing – it was the nature of Romano's business. He walked into the shower room and examined himself in the mirror. Romano was a gentleman; this was no fault of his. But long term he had to accept that he was going to be mixed up with some dodgy characters so long as he worked with Romano.

He tackled painting the yacht with renewed vigour. October in Nice was warm and sunny with a soft fresh quality in the air. Sitting painting on the balcony was pleasant as ever, and he quickly finished Dutch Courage ready for framing, and then had to consider what he was going to do with 'Northern Lass'. He closed his eyes and tried to imagine what better setting could enhance a black yacht currently moored amongst a harbour full of colourful sailing boats which were all light and bright. 'Northern Lass' made him think of Manchester and Leeds, with soot blackened warehouses on a grey rainy day. He relocated the boat in full sail, struggling against mighty waves on a rough sea. Dark storm clouds surrounded the boat and in the corner of his picture he added a flash of lightning which reflected streams of seawater running from the ships deck. The idea grew so that his inspired paintbrush mirrored the power of the ocean, and his spirits soared along with the scene he was painting. He worked on the picture on and off until the weekend. Whether it was what the owner had in mind was questionable. But to Roger's eye it was a masterpiece.

The sharp pain in his ribs had subsided, and his left hand was now moveable with all the bandages off. No need for an x ray. Roger stood on the balcony in the warmth of the evening watching and listening to the buzz below with a tinge of regret. He was going to have to go home. He owned an empty house which needed refurnishing, and he wanted some breathing space to consider how he could continue working with Romano.

Sally and Helen had carried out a brilliant nursing job over the weekend. He was sorry Sally left before he could thank her properly. He wanted to speak to Helen but the arrangement was that she always phoned him – but what the hell! He phoned her and was surprised when Edward answered.

'I thought you were away for a month,' said Roger.

'Back early old chum. Home to reclaim my wife. I hear you have been in the wars. Listen, we are on our way out and passing your place. I would like a special word with you. Suppose we pop in for five minutes?'

'Love to see you,' said Roger. 'Come when you are ready.' He couldn't guess what Edward's 'special word' might be. Helen was first up the stairs ringing his doorbell. She looked radiant. 'He's gone to park the car,' she said. 'There's a lot happening. I will tell you all about it later,' and she put her arms round his neck and kissed him.

Edward looked at Roger's face when he arrived.

'By hell that's a beauty. And from what the girl told Helen – you were the winner. What happens when you are the loser?' Roger poured them both a beer and a glass of wine for Helen.

'There aren't any winners,' he said 'Only losers. Either way it's not my game.'

'I'm glad you have come to that conclusion old chum. I came to tell you that the word is that the Romano consortium is in deep trouble. Tax avoidance and legal actions pending. Big break ups within the group, and John is convinced that the whole organization is about to go belly up'. Monty had warned him there was trouble. This piece of information worried Roger immediately.

'Edward – thanks! I am going home anyway. Let's see how things work out. I would still like to operate my business here in Nice.'

'That's going to be difficult in itself Roger. The consequences of BREXIT are only just starting to trickle through. Working from inside an EU country when the UK has chosen to leave presents any number of problems. Helen and I are going back to live in Poole, and my base will be in the UK. John and Jane are the same. None of us really want to leave the French sunshine but for the next few years making a living based here in France will be too bloody complicated.'

'Well before you disappear to Dorset – may I borrow Helen one more time? These pictures need delivering to Antibes, and I don't feel safe to drive there yet.'

Edward was looking closely at 'Northern Lass.'

'That's Roger Matthews boat,' he said. 'That's magnificent. You want to deliver that picture to him personally when you get home. Your lecture on 'playing it straight' stopped him in his tracks – especially when you charmed his daughter.'

'Sir Galahad again,' said Helen. 'This young man is wasted. How about Monday Roger? I can drive your Alpha Romeo again.'

He thought she looked very happy. Something had changed. He watched from the balcony as they left and although Roger couldn't see properly, they looked as though they were holding hands. He sat drinking another beer. How devious human nature could be. Rosemary had conducted a secret affair with little Jack; Elissa was unfaithful to 'man bastard'; and only a few weeks ago Edward had twice suggested that Roger take Helen out. Now Helen was walking away hand in hand with her husband only days after spending a complete weekend in bed with Roger. Was anyone honest? Romano said, 'it was all a game'. Come to think of it, Romano was about the only person who played it straight.

The news that Roger Mathews owned 'Northern Lass' was a surprising turn of events. He must have been aware who he had engaged to paint a picture of his boat because he had seen Roger's leaflet in the Yacht Club so this wasn't a coincidence. Was this a test, or was it an inducement to wheedle information out of him that he wouldn't divulge when they met in Monte Carlo?

Roger felt too self-conscious and wobbly to venture far afield. He walked to a quiet spot on the beach and after immersing himself in salt water he could breathe clearly. The water was cool and invigorating. After two or three swims he felt a lot better.

Amused by the thought of delivering 'Northern Lass' personally he tinkered about in the evening with another sketch of the boat in dry dock. He added a trim, lamps, and recoloured different sections, transforming 'Northern Lass' from a plain black nondescript sailing boat into a slick sporty little craft which would be admired by the most celebrated of wealthy yacht owners.

He felt in better shape when Helen arrived on Monday. They swapped cars in the car park and set off for Antibes with Helen confidently at the wheel of the Alpha Romeo. Roger accepted being called 'young man' again, and he was quite happy listening to Helen as she put their relationship back on a more formal footing.

The chandler paid for 'Dutch Courage' and accepted that Roger would be delivering the other picture personally. He made more fuss of Helen than he made of Roger, the conclusion being that perhaps he had a foot in both camps.

Roger took Helen to the Picasso Museum in Antibes Castle. Walking back, she stumbled on some rocks and he caught her and all at once the tingle of attraction was aroused by the unexpected bodily contact. But it wasn't until lunch at the hotel with the fish-filleting waiter that intimate feelings swept back into his life. Helen leaned over and spoke to him across the table, at the same time fingering Cyril's amulet.

'I have a present for you, and I would like you to give me a present in return.'

She unclipped the chain round his neck and slid off Cyril's lucky charm replacing it with a gold St Christopher pendent.

'That's better,' she said. 'A quality gold chain deserves a real gold pendant.'

'The charm is 18 carat gold Helen. I had it valued by a jeweller.'

'It's sprayed metal young man. Your chain is 18 carat – look at the difference. I bet your jeweller valued the sprayed amulet so he could sell you a gold chain.'

Taken for a ride – again! Barney Hoffman the sly old devil. He looked at Helen and they both laughed.

'I think I have been mizzled,' said Roger. 'I thought my boxing glove amulet brought me good luck. Why I should think that I don't know.' He touched his nose. 'Thank you, Helen. I rely on St Christopher to bring be better luck on my travels.'

'Don't worry,' replied Helen. 'Your face will recover. You are still the handsome man who attracts the ladies. I am attaching your amulet to my key ring and I shall think of you every time I turn the key.'

Fish on Mondays was never a good idea. Roger ordered Beef Stroganoff with rice for them both. The meal was every bit as good as his previous visit and as the sun highlighted the flaxen tones in Helen's hair, he sat across the table admiring her every movement, her smile, and the soft sad look in her eyes.

'You know Roger – Sally wasn't the only damsel in distress who you rescued. Edward has broken up with his secretary and suddenly his attitude towards me has changed. I love Edward – and I don't want our marriage to break up. But he forgets. He is now fifty-two and I am only thirty-nine. I am not hanging around while he blows hot and cold on me, and attractive man though he may be, he will find it difficult competing with younger men.'

'And I am a younger man?' said Roger. 'Or so you keep telling me.'

She took his hand and held it under the table. Lovely desirable Helen. She drove back to Nice with Roger reflecting on everything she had told him. In the car park she turned to him and took his hand again.

'I have loved being with you today Roger but one thing is missing – you haven't put your hand on my leg.' She kissed him and he felt her urgency as his hand dropped and moved along the soft smoothness of her thigh.

'Edward's away in London,' she said, and they kissed again and climbed the stairs to his apartment. It was early and they made love and relaxed and then made love again. Gone was the nervousness. This time Helen showed a new self-confidence. Every moment with her was exciting – even as he lay in her arms talking before eventually surrendering to sleep.

At 3.00 am his mobile rang and 20 minutes later it rang again. He got out of bed and switched it off, and back in his arms Helen stirred and he entered her, and half asleep they slowly made love all over again.

When the landline rang twice just after 6.00 Helen said, 'Don't answer it – I think I had better go.'

Roger pulled on his jeans and walked her down to the car not wanting her to leave. When he returned to the apartment the phone was still ringing. Roger picked it up and answered, and that was the beginning of a never-ending nightmare. The nightmare which would define his last days in Nice.

A voice on the other end of the phone gabbled incoherently in French with one recognisable word – police. Eventually someone else took over and spoke to him in pidgin English, 'Monsieur Kelly – you come to your offices immediately.'

Roger got dressed and walked down with a sinking feeling in his stomach. The sight that met his eyes was horrific. Two police cars and a fire engine were parked alongside the Agency to discourage voyeuristic observers and diverting early morning traffic into another street. The outer door had been pulled off the hinges and lay across the pavement. All windows were smashed, and his leaflet 'Roger Kelly – draughtsman and designer' hung limply by one corner from a jagged section of the window.

An Inspector from the Gendarmerie guided Roger through the wrecked offices and round to the back. Eric's Mercedes was broken up beyond recognition. Tyres and seats were slashed. All windows were broken, and the car bonnet was open to reveal an engine split and flattened by a heavy mallet, with oil draining fast from the engine making a steady stream into the rear office. The Citron was no different. Everything possible had been destroyed except this time the car bonnet remained closed, crushed on top of the engine which lay hanging between the Citron's slashed wheels.

'So, who is responsible for this? You tell me Mr Kelly. Where are you when we try to reach you?'

Roger's experience dealing with the Dublin police had been a picnic compared with what followed. Trying to make himself understood at the *poste de police* was like banging your head against a brick wall, and still not feeling one hundred per cent he developed the mother of all headaches. He spent 10 hours waiting around to be interviewed, and at 7.00 pm without having eaten or drunk anything all day he was released and told to return to the station next morning.

He phoned Romano, then Monty, then Eric – and all their lines were dead. He received a text message from John.

> *Roger – the shit has hit the fan. Don't worry your money is safely tied up in your independent account. I am here to help.*

Roger checked his bank balance after John's text and was amazed to see that the last two weekly payments had been increased from 600 euros to 1000 euros. Nobody had mentioned it to him or why.

A police car waited for Roger next morning. He was driven out to Romano's villa where the metal gates had been covered in graffiti. Paint and whitewash daubed all over the gates and fencing. Through gaps in the fence the villa looked to be well locked with all windows shuttered with no signs of life, and the black saloons had both disappeared from the driveway.

Eric's flat was empty with no forwarding address when the police checked. Roger tried again to reach both

Romano and Monty but their lines remained dead. They had been forewarned of the crisis in time to cover their tracks and disappear, but the police would not be convinced that Roger hadn't the faintest idea where to locate them.

He was questioned over and over again and worse was to come. Two special police investigators arrived from Paris, and Roger was seated at a table in a dingy smoke-filled room, eyed over by two very unpleasant little men.

'I wonder if you are aware of the trouble you are in Monsieur Kelly? You belong to an international organization known to be money laundering and participating in tax fraud. You work as one of their enforcers, you and the big man, and you tell us that you know nothing.'

Roger had enjoyed a good breakfast and a good night's sleep. He had surrendered his passport, and he was being put through any amount of inconvenience. But at the end of the day, he had done nothing wrong, and the police could not prove otherwise.

'I do not work as an enforcer. My work is design, and I accompanied Antonio Romano to a number of meetings. No more.'

'So how do you explain your action at Romano's rented villa?' asked interviewer number one. The deep pouches under his eyes were almost obliterated by smoke whenever he opened his mouth. 'And during that action you blinded your opponent in one eye.'

'I stopped a thug from attacking a woman,' said Roger 'And then he attacked me.'

'So where is the woman? Bring her to us. We would like to meet her.'

'Catch the plane to London. I can give you her address,' replied Roger. Number two collapsed into a fit of coughing and spat into a waste basket.

'Don't be clever with us Monsieur. And realize that since the UK chose to leave the EU, British influence here in France is very much reduced.'

'Would you mind opening a window please,' asked Roger. 'Just because the French have never recovered from Waterloo doesn't give you the right to choke me.'

'Answers like that will get you nowhere Monsieur Kelly.'

'Nor will trying to pin on me responsibility for crimes I am not involved with,' replied Roger, but the questions meandered on. Eventually Roger had had enough of providing the same repeated answers to the same repeated questions. He stood up and pushed back the chair, towering above the pair of them.

'I have told you all I know. If Antonio Romano was involved in the criminal activities you accuse him of, then I know nothing about it. To me he was a perfect gentleman. Straight with me and honest. Now – unless you have evidence to detain me any longer, I wish to be released, and my passport returned.'

'Very well Monsieur Kelly you may go. Do not leave Nice without informing us, and your passport will be returned when we are convinced there are no further questions for you to answer.'

Roger walked away from the offices exhausted. As he left, he pulled down the hanging leaflet of Roger Kelly, architect and designer, screwed it up into a ball, and deposited it in a nearby waste bin. Two young gendarmes on duty outside watched him pointedly and laughed.

Roger was now branded. He was a Romano man. It's amazing how quickly news circulates and the girl in *'le pressing'* ignored him completely, and even the proprietor of his favourite café was notably cool. What puzzled Roger was the speed with which Romano and Monty had disappeared. And why Eric? He didn't hear anything from Helen, his chances of continuing business here in Nice were nil, and the important thing now was to leave behind the whole mess before the French police found him guilty of something else.

He met John and Jane in a quiet café near their offices. John had rechecked the legality of his agreement and apart from his trips off with Romano he had rock solid proof that the letting agency operated independently from the property holdings.

Without being asked John made an appointment to take Roger's books to the police and verify his independence. But there was a question to which Roger had no answer. Why had his earnings suddenly been increased to 1000 euros per week?

Roger made preparations to pack. Before going home to Manchester, he would spend a couple of nights with his parents. There was a mountain of belongings to take with him and there was no way he could fit even half of them into the Alpha Romeo. A wander round the market produced a massive second-hand leather case with sturdy locks. He was sure his father would be delighted to receive it if despatched in advance by carrier. Sadly, he gathered together instruments, drawing boards and files, and included them in his advance luggage. He was sure he would spend many more holidays in Aunt Evelyn's flat, but prospects of designing villas and yachts for the rich and famous he could forget.

It was two weeks since Roger had been for a run or had a workout in the gym. Until his passport was released, he couldn't plan to go anywhere so he might as well concentrate on recovering his fitness. Perhaps it was all in the mind but people seemed to have become damned unfriendly, and it was a great relief when he walked into the gym and the first person he met was Amin. Promptly Roger had a group of his North African friends surrounding him, shaking his hand and patting him on the back. God, it felt good – it felt so good after what he had been through. This was Romano's gym and he supposed it was inevitable that Amin and his friends had followed the whole saga.

Football practice took place most evenings and Roger was invited. He joined them two evenings during the week and arranged to play again on Saturday morning. One more time he was required to return for a grilling at the police station, and was at last dismissed after submitting his home address in England, and agreeing to report to the British police in case he was needed to appear in court. Midweek he received a telephone call from Carrington Brown.

'Roger old chum – sorry how things have turned out for you. I don't know whether you are aware of it but you have a plain-clothes French copper keeping an eye on you. He is painfully obvious. We passed twice meaning to call and changed our minds'. Roger took the phone to the balcony and looked across the road. Sure enough, a tall man trying hard to look like Maigret was stood outside the café.

'Got him,' said Roger. 'Do you think I should go out and chin him?'

'I think you are in enough trouble,' replied Edward. 'Your safest bet old chum is to stay inside and watch television. Roger – we are closing the house down and going back to Dorset sooner than planned. I tried to get hold of another Alpha Romeo like yours and the model has been changed. Helen has fallen in love with your car. I don't like to ask but in present circumstances I thought you might want to drive something more practical when you return to Blighty. I don't suppose you would consider selling it?' Edward's offer solved a problem for him. After using the Range Rover regularly Roger knew that he needed a larger car no matter how much he liked the Alpha Romeo.

'I paid £29,000 for it, Edward. But you are right. It's not going to be practical.

'It's yours for £28,000 minus my personal number plate which you can take off and forward to me in Manchester. I won't feel so bad about losing the car if I can picture your wife driving it.'

'Deal done,' said Edward. 'I appreciate that old chum. I am tied up and Helen is travelling ahead of me. The money is best transferred directly into your branch bank account in England. I leave it to Helen to arrange when she collects the car.'

Within less than 10 minutes Helen came back to him.

'Edward is going to drop me off tomorrow morning Roger. Is that too soon to collect the car? I intend setting off back to England at the weekend.'

'It's never too soon to see you Helen, but it's much too soon to lose you.'

Selling the Alpha Romeo closed down an episode in Roger's life. The win. His first sports car, and all that had happened since. Roger walked down to the car and removed personal items from the glove compartment. Six months didn't count for long enjoying the thrill of your dream car.

The Maigret plain clothes man moved to check where Roger was heading. He looked hot and uncomfortable wearing a raincoat and hat and he moved back again to his shaded position when Roger re-entered the apartment. Roger found a large beer in the fridge and walked across the road to Maigret and pointed a finger it at him and said 'bang!' Maigret looked astounded but then acknowledged the cold beer with a grin. Roger's favourite café proprietor next door nearly dropped her tray watching the bad Englishman in the act of bribing the French police. However, she was back to normal when he popped in for a quick lunch, and in the evening his popularity was fully restored when she patted his cheek (murmuring sympathetic noises) and provided two free coffees following an extra-large portion of '*tourte au poisson*'.

There was no sign of Maigret when Helen arrived the following morning. She was wearing an old denim skirt and soiled white T-shirt. Edward, who looked much less

231

suave dressed in oil-stained overalls, sped off in a hurry with a wave of the hand.

'Your face has healed well,' she said giving him a kiss. 'But you have lost your boyish look. Anyone meeting you for the first time will judge you a man to be reckoned with.' They walked down to the empty car park where the Alpha Romeo was parked in the shade next to the Range Rover.

'I'm not sorry to leave,' said Helen. 'Nice is lovely but the Brits lead a false life here. Will you come back and set up business again once the trouble is over?'

'Who says my troubles will ever be over?' said Roger 'The police don't think so.'

They both got into the car and he handed Helen the keys.

'Will I see you again Roger? I know Poole is a long way from Manchester but we might find a half way point to rendezvous. She had obviously been in the middle of cleaning when she came to collect the car. There were marks of perspiration under her arms and her bodily odour even more potent in arousing him than the usual fresh smell of perfume he associated with Helen.

'We will keep in touch,' he said and took her hand off the steering wheel and placed it on his knee. She stretched over to kiss him, and that was fatal.

'One more time Roger. I know I am being ridiculous – but one more time.'

She reached down and removed her pants and he glimpsed the soft triangle of pubic hair between the smooth thighs he loved to caress. She straddled across him and pushed his shorts down to his knees. When he entered her there wasn't roof space in the car to move, and he gripped her buttocks and pulled her hard to slide against him. Her breathe was hot against his cheek, and the sweet taste of her mouth swamped his senses. Her buttocks and stomach muscles tightened. She bit his neck as she strained to reach a climax – then cried out as she reached organism collapsing on top of him, her lips pressed hard against his. Their love making was over inside ten minutes. But their satisfaction still left them with an empty feeling – the feeling of something unfinished, something that they wanted to last longer and deeper. It was lucky their destinations were far part because he would never be able resist seeing her if she lived close by.

'I am sorry Roger but I must go. I will be thinking about you every minute of my long journey.' She detached Big Cyril's amulet from a keyring in her hand bag and fitted it onto the car keys. As the security gates opened and she drove away Roger watched the Alpha Romeo disappear until it was a speck at the top of the boulevard. Carl Delondis had said – 'some you win and some you lose.'

Well win or lose Roger had given both Helen and his car a good send off, but he felt sad and empty thinking about it as he climbed the steps back into the apartment.

Back to business Roger packed and deposited the large leather case with the carriers. Without a car he would need to fly home, and that meant serious reorganization. At the weekend the police contacted him – he could retrieve his passport when ready.

Roger joined Amin and threw his energies into a Saturday game of football, scored two goals, received a cheer and a dish of couscous and tajine. But the game didn't match those previous Saturdays when a veiled lady called Elissa took his arm and guided him back to Aunt Evelyn's apartment for a lesson in Arabian culture. He chuckled thinking of her and those first Saturday matches.

Jet 2 Direct flights from Nice to Leeds/Bradford Airport were curtailed in October.

Roger would have to fly from Paris. He booked the Saturday flight then found a small hotel near le Sacre Coeur and reserved a room for Thursday and Friday. A couple of days wandering around Paris would end his stay in France on a high note, and prepare him for grey days in Manchester.

He had a long conversation with Mick who was in stitches at the other end of the phone. Then he emailed his father.

Dad,

Things have gone wrong here in Nice. Business has collapsed and I am packing up and coming home. Hope to stay with you for a couple of days. Arriving next Saturday PM on the Paris flight.

I have had an accident stepping in to prevent a woman being assaulted by a thug. Result – I got assaulted instead. Nothing serious but a noticeable change of appearance. Forewarn mother. I don't want her having a heart attack. Look forward to seeing you both.

Roger

With the prospect of a pretty tame Saturday evening ahead he wrote a long attachment to Ana. He related the fight. The collapse of business. The police, and what turned out to be one hell of a mess. For a laugh he embellished the worst parts blaming his demise on the rescue of a 'damsel in distress'. He concluded,

> *I am catching the Saturday flight from Paris to Leeds and Bradford Airport to stay with my parents for a couple of days. No Alpha Romeo – I had to sell it. I will then be home again living in Manchester so when you take a break from your travels let's have a few drinks together. Can't promise you will recognise me but you might like the change?*
>
> *Love Roger*

His father sent a silly reply to his email.

> *Did you have to rescue the woman **because** of you, or **for** you?*
>
> *See you Saturday.*

Ana's reply was just as brief.

*Look forward to having a drink with you –
providing you can stay out of prison.*

Love Ana

His long epistle had made her laugh. Thinking about
him she could imagine the mess he had got into. She knew
now that Roger would never grow up – perhaps that was
what made him so attractive. She read his email whilst
taking a break from planning a conference in Darlington.
A lot of work was attached and together with a steady
insurance executive who had recently entered Ana's life
both work and social life had taken a happy turn for the
better. Nevertheless – it would be fun having a drink with
Roger if only to satisfy her curiosity. But his latest
predicament – and having to get rid of his Alpha Romeo
– she wondered what next?

Sunday, with a rucksack on his back, Roger set off to
repeat the Villefranche walk, and take a last look at the
site of his planned 'Hacienda Romano'. After all his work
– would the villa ever transpire? Roger was surprised.
Work had stopped, but the outer walls were half built, and
at one end of the building beams were already in place to
support part of the roof. His time hadn't been wasted.
Someone would want to buy it.

Gratified, he completed his day's trek and walked
down to Quartier du Port in time to see John and Jane
sailing into the harbour. They adjourned from Sky Fly to
the Yacht Club and halfway through a round of drinks

Edward and Charles joined them.

'Damned fine thing you did protecting that girl. Damned fine thing!' said Charles.

No mention of 'batting with the wrong side' and although Roger's leaflet had vacated the notice board it seemed his reputation was intact. The gathering developed into a farewell party. Edward and Charles intended relocating their business to the UK but also spending as much time as possible in Nice. John and Jane weren't sure about living permanently in London, and Roger was damned unsure (in fact bloody unsure) about leaving Nice and finding employment in Manchester.

The Edward Carrington-Brown charm was missing when he mentioned that Helen arrived safely home in the Alpha Romeo. He couldn't look Roger in the eye and stopped calling him 'old chum'. He knows thought Roger when they shook hands at the end of the evening. With luggage packed and accountancy details arranged with John there wasn't much left to wind up – or so he thought. Football practice on Tuesday and Roger wanted one more game before taking the train to Paris.

It was a wonderful sunny evening, and the pitch was perfect – playing on a dry surface was so different to the wet muddy matches you encountered at home. At the end of play Roger gave his Nike Superfly Boots to Amin's son, and thought that was the reason Amin was so insistent that he accompanied them back for a meal.

'I have special surprise planned for you – please you come,' insisted Amin.

Amin's home was an old terrace dwelling in one of the better streets at the back of Gare SNCF. He had met

Amin's wife before. She was welcoming as ever, and the spicy smell of cooking assailed your senses the moment you walked through the door.

Two small children politely obeyed instructions and were dismissed upstairs and Roger guessed this was a special meal cooked in his honour. The small dining room was dark when he entered, and he didn't immediately see the other guest sat unobtrusively and almost hidden by a long-draped curtain.

'Mr Kelly, I hope my presence will not spoil your meal.' Roger wouldn't have recognised Romano – only the voice. Romano's head was completely shaven. Thick stubble around his face was almost verging on a beard, and he was dressed in a faded Caftan which reached down to bare feet clad in frayed sandals.

'We meet again and by the will of God we both look different.'

'Nothing to do with the will of God as far as I am concerned,' replied Roger. 'It had more to do with your special guest's hard head.'

'Animals! I am sorry Roger. I am hiding here today because I have been dealing with animals. Greedy animals. And I promise you Roger none of today's troubles are of my doing.' They sat down to feast on the delicious choice of aromatic dishes prepared by Amin's wife. While they ate Romano talked, and the more he talked the more Roger believed him.

'Eric first received the warning. When big business gets into trouble, they look for scapegoats – and in Nice and in Naples, they choose me. I knew what would happen.'

He stopped eating and drew a flat hand across depicting a cut throat. 'Bad business means many people do not get paid. Both good people and bad people, big people and small people. There were over 180,000 euros in the agency fund over which Eric had full charge. When pressurized to cover small local debts he panicked. Instead of paying to stall off trouble the fool vanished taking with him all 180,000 euros. Now I am not safe from debtors or police, but please, take my word: tax evasion and money laundering are out of my hands. Romano's business is buying and selling property backed by a vast assembly of wealth operating from high places. Unfortunately, 'high places' employ criminal accountants and criminal gangs to carry out much of their work, and now I am in the middle of their mistakes.'

This was the true Antonio Romano speaking. Perhaps a dangerous man to those who double crossed him, and perhaps a ruthless man in business, but a man of honour and straight dealing – a man Roger admired.

'And what happens now?' asked Roger.

'Eric – he is a fool. It is better for him if the police catch him. Monty and I cannot be seen together. He is in London with some of my men trying to absolve our part in the collapse of the organization. Tomorrow Amin and I go to Naples and then we part. There are places in Naples where I am safe.'

'And what happens to your hacienda, Mr Romano? I walked there on Sunday and the walls are half-built.'

'The new villa you designed for me will never be mine. I forfeit everything I own in Nice and I must start again in Naples, or perhaps Sicily. Who knows my friend, perhaps one day you may occupy the dream you dreamed for Antonio Romano.'

Amin's wife cleared the table and left the men alone. Roger knew that wherever Romano might hide he would never be safe from gangland or the police.

'Roger, I think it is wise for you to leave Nice soon. The sale of the Delondis villa went through smoothly but I am sorry, I cannot pay your commission. Instead, I give you the Range Rover car you drive for me. It is yours – I put it in your name, and it is worth more than the commission you would receive for the sale of the villa.'

Could Roger legally claim that the Rover belonged to him – perhaps not. It didn't really matter. It only mattered that this man who he had enjoyed working with was in deep trouble and there was no way that he could help.

'Mr Romano – I thank you. I want you to know that working with you has been a privilege. Our work together gave me opportunities I could never have imagined.

'You are a man I respect and admire. I am only sad that I cannot be of help.'

Romano rose from his chair and threw his arms around Roger kissing him on both cheeks.

'Mr Kelly, Roger, the pleasure has been mine. Maybe we will work together again someday. But I must tell you now – I have a son, a young son, but when he grows older may he grow up to be a man exactly like you are.'

It was an emotional moment. A moment Roger would never forget. It was dark when he said goodbye to Amin and Romano, and the walk back to the apartment seemed to take for ever. He didn't sleep all night. Over and over again Romano's words and his predicament haunted him.

The shaven head, the stubble, the faded Caftan, the man who was Antonio Romano who would be hunted by criminals and police and could never be the same man again.

13. Reunion

Paris. He got out of Nice fast. He paid his Liverpool cleaning lady, re-parked the Range Rover in an unobtrusive space, and arrived in Paris in time to spend his afternoon in the Musée d'Orsay. Wonderful, glorious Paris. The most beautiful city in Europe. Two days here gave him time to think.

There was a terrace café adjoining his hotel on *rue des Abbesses*, and after dining well his spirits began to lift. He took a walk along *rue Pigalle* and declined the offer when a large lady emerged from a doorway and said, 'You come with me English boy,' (how did she know he was English?) and seated inside a café watching the world go by he reflected on his parting with Antonio Romano. Romano knew the risks. He was dealing with crooks, and it had appealed to Roger to be part of it. Now it had developed into something deadly serious and he was part of that too.

A drizzly Friday didn't spoil a stroll around the *Marais* and along the banks of the *Seine*. He missed out the *Champs-Elysees* in favour of the quartier Latin and onward to St Germain, loitering in *Les Deux Magots* café famed for the writers and artists who once met there. At night he returned to the Latin quarter and *Le Caveau de la Huchette* – a haunt visited in his student days. Small, dark, and not very exciting, he never had much luck with either the music or the talent when he visited le Caveau in his teens, so why was he drawn to revisit the place?

No visit to Paris was complete without climbing the hill to the *Sacré Coeur*. Before leaving, he dumped his luggage in the hotel foyer, had an early breakfast, and reached the top of *Montmartre* before the artists had time to erect their easels. He sat inside the church allowing peace from the music to disperse his lingering turmoil. Romano, Ellisa, Helen, Ana. In his student days he spent hours in *Montmartre* perched on the steps of Sacré Coeur alongside crowds of other students – feasting on torn off chunks of baguette eaten with shared cheese and salami. Life was simpler then.

Negotiating luggage through Gare du Nord was bloody awful, and the packed train to Charles de Gaule Airport worse still. The lounge waiting area was crowded with standing passengers with their hand luggage and it puzzled Roger how some travellers managed to board the plane with masses of so-called cabin luggage, whilst others were stopped and compelled to store their cases in the hold. A group of four beery Northerners were making an exhibition of themselves, and one of them placed a case on the seat beside him. Roger walked over quietly and removed the case from the seat and sat down.

'Hey what the fuck do you think you're doing – that's my case.'

'Don't worry,' said Roger. 'I don't fucking want it,' and the man took one look at him and gave no reply.

All seats on the plane were full. Roger had an aisle seat next to an elderly lady who smiled at him, then buried herself in her book. The noisy group were split up with three at the back and one sat behind Roger. They were loud, up and down out of their seats, the heavy knees of the man behind him constantly grinding into Roger's back.

Roger turned around, 'Would you mind keeping your knees to yourself and cooling it? You and your pals are getting on my nerves.' The man opened his mouth to say something and then thought better of it and said nothing. The elderly lady looked up from her book,

'Are you a policeman?' she asked.

'No, not a policeman,' replied Roger. 'To be perfectly honest I don't really know what I am.'

'Oh well – in that case I do hope you find out soon,' said the lady sweetly, and returned to her book.

October weather at Leeds and Bradford Airport had turned cold and misty. The Paris plane was late, and waiting outside Jet 2 arrivals Roger's father wished he had put on a warm coat. He never managed to time it right when meeting someone off a plane, and it irritated him paying the extortionate parking fees with which he always seemed to get saddled.

He didn't know what to make of his son. First the arrival of a whacking great case, and then an email saying Roger's business had collapsed and he had been injured in a fight over a woman. Another mess. Why couldn't he have fathered a loving daughter who lightened his life with weekly visits and clean well-behaved grandchildren?

He looked around the hall. People-watching at airports was always interesting. A tall fair girl standing near him was absorbed by her mobile phone. Definitely a model by the way she was dressed. Long slim legs under a tailored skirt and jacket. Even in his youth when he was the proud owner of his Triumph TR2, he never managed to meet stunning looking girls like her. A woman with a mass of frizzy hair tried to pacify her screaming baby with a dummy, and two small noisy boys bumped into him as they chased round in circles and disappeared out of the door followed by an irate parent. Grandchildren – perhaps not! It would be just his luck to get saddled with a couple of little Rogers.

There was an announcement that the Paris plane had landed. Slowly people began to trickle through. He could recognise Roger's walk from a distance and stood back to ascertain any collateral damage to his appearance before they met. Roger wheeled a heavy case and cabin luggage through the door and then suddenly stopped dead in his tracks. The tall girl with the long legs took a step forward looking at Roger and stopped dead too. Her mobile clattered to the floor and the casing split. They ran towards each other, with tears streaming down the girl's face. They were in each other's arms with Roger's luggage abandoned, his cases left in the path of exiting passengers. They were kissing each other, clinging to each other, sobbing, oblivious of everything and everyone around them. Roger's father picked up the broken phone and quietly moved the cases onto one side. Then he waited.

His heart was thumping so hard he thought it might burst. The back of his throat burned. His arms, his whole body hurt with a pain too acute to describe and he crushed her into his arms so tightly as to never let her go. Her tears wet his cheeks, his neck, his collar, and they kissed and kissed all the time murmuring each other's names.

Ana was trembling, and her lips were sweet and cold as their mouths met.

'Roger, Roger,' she said. 'Oh Roger I have missed you so much.'

There was a tap on his shoulder and he turned, with his arms still wrapped tightly around her.

'Dad,' he said. 'This is Ana'.

PART TWO

14. The Homecoming

In his wildest dreams Roger could not have imagined such a happy homecoming.

He had intended staying with his parents for two nights but he and Ana stayed for three.

Ana got on like a house on fire with his father, and his mother was so pleased to see Roger back in the UK (safe from the clutch of wicked foreigners) that she fussed around Ana as though she were welcoming the return of a long-lost daughter.

With an old-fashioned sense of propriety his mother allocated them with separate bedrooms, but after creeping into Ana's bed on the first night Roger simply moved beside her for the remaining two. They were both emotionally exhausted from their meeting at the airport and their lovemaking was silent and restrained. They knew this attachment was to be deep and permanent, and they subdued their relationship until they were completely alone.

It was cold and frosty. Together they discovered Roundhay Park and Harewood House, and on Monday Roger's father showed off his new BMW and took them to York. They walked the City Walls and after visiting York Museum enjoyed lunch in the famous Betty's Café. His father amazed him. He talked travel, politics, and business with Ana and never once mentioned Nice to

247

Roger. No discussion about why his business had collapsed nor sarcastic comments about rescuing a damsel in distress. In fact, their stay reminded him of childhood stories, where the happy family always return home at Christmas, and an amiable father stands with his back to the log fire smoking a pipe. Swap the log fire for electric radiators, give him a pipe, and his father had walked straight out of one of those famous stories.

Life had been tough for Ana and she enjoyed the welcome.

'How did you know which plane to meet?' asked Roger.

'There is only one flight from Paris to Leeds on Saturdays. I was working in the North and I met you to satisfy my curiosity.'

'And what did you discover?'

'You know what I discovered,' she said. 'You are a mad, impossible, attractive man who has never grown up, and how could I ever have allowed events to separate us?'

This was a more conventional Ana. The green streaks in her hair had disappeared along with the nose piercing, and gone were the multiple rings adorning each finger.

'And so – how about you? What did you discover?' she asked.

'The most beautiful desirable woman I have ever met. All of the exciting women rolled into one.'

'We won't dwell on that. You told me you had experience with just one woman'.

'Blame the sun,' said Roger.

When Roger piled his luggage into Ana's car and collected the house keys from his father, he was sorry to be leaving. He had always been on good terms with his mother but something had happened between him and his father and it was thanks to Ana.

This wasn't a happy ending it was a happy beginning.

Mathews Building Investments was in Hunslet. A group of large dark sooty buildings located amongst groups of other large dark sooty buildings, all conveniently placed by the side of the M62. Roger tried contacting Phillipa before they left but finished up simply leaving a message. The pictures of Northern Lass weren't framed, and he had no idea whether they would please Roger Mathews or not, but he would leave them at his office.

Traffic in the area was horrific and legible street names scarce. It was a hell of a job figuring out where they were going and Ana drove round in circles (tailed by a truck belching diesel fumes) before they eventually spotted a sign leading to Mathews extensive car park, occupied by a fleet of Mathews trucks.

'This is a miserable looking dump,' said Roger. 'Imagine having to come to work here every day.' He left Ana in the car and presented himself at the reception. Exactly as he had imagined. Polished wood and brass everywhere and yellowing walls hung with stern, moustached icons of authority. The uniformed commissionaire sitting behind a massive oak desk followed Roger's gaze.

'Founded by Quakers in 1880, sir. What can I do for you?'

'Some sketches for Mr Mathews. Can I leave them with you?'

'One moment, sir.' He turned to an ancient contraption on his desk and pressed a button. 'And your name, sir, is....?'

'Roger Kelly. I haven't an appointment. All I want to do is leave the sketches.'

An office door opened and Roger Mathews suddenly appeared, followed by Phillipa.

'You want to go already and you've only just bloody got here? Come in for god's sake – come in! And Bill, order tea and a few rounds of toast, will you?'

'Just one problem. I left my partner in the car.'

'Well bring her in. Phillipa – go and find her will you or this lad will be back in France before we get a chance to have a word with him.'

The office Roger walked into, was spacious and fresh. A large window looked out onto the car park, and a modern desk with neatly stacked papers alongside the telephone gave the impression that everything had its place. Under the window a desktop computer, printer, and more telephones added to the picture of a working environment minus frills. Roger sat opposite on a hard upright chair while Roger Mathews examined the pictures of his boat. Dominating the side wall of the office a large, framed photograph depicted modern two storey buildings in a tree lined setting, with open fields behind. Underneath were various shots of a football team – in one photograph the team were brandishing a silver cup.

Roger Mathews was an unappealing character. His chin almost touched the pictures as he examined the 'Northern Lass'. Bushy eyebrows and tufts of hair sticking out of his ears framed a red determined face that would always be 'right'. He had a habit of sniffing and one finger kept disappearing up his nose.

'You know lad I don't need to tell you – this is talent. It's not just the pictures. Lots of artists can paint pictures. It's the imagination that has changed the setting, and in my book change for the better is what life is all about.'

He stood up and went to the window. 'Look out there. Old out of date buildings with rows of cramped houses which only recently got themselves an inside toilet.

'The aim of Mathews Building Investments is to change all that. There are areas up North where we have provided whole communities with well-designed affordable housing. Don't associate me with that charade in Monaco. I am only there because the big deals with those who want to flash it around contribute profit towards the real work that needs to be done here.'

Bill the commissionaire arrived with a tray of tea and toast.

'I don't know where the ladies have got to. We shall have to start without them. So, tell me – what are your plans now? Do you intend staying home for a while?'

He poured out two cups of tea and swallowed half a cup scalding hot. He must have a throat like a rhinoceros thought Roger.

'At the moment my plan is to get home. I own an empty house that I haven't lived in for nearly a year.'

'And what about after that lad – what are you going to do with yourself?'

Phillipa and Ana walked in. All Roger Matthews's attention immediately switched to Ana, and Roger's stomach turned over with a jolt as if he was seeing Ana

251

for the first time through someone else's eyes.

'Mr Mathews – may I introduce my partner Ana.' Previously unseen charm radiated its hidden light as he took Ana's hand.

'Ana – my pleasure. Now I know where Mr Kelly acquires his inspiration to produce works like this,' and he gestured towards Roger's paintings laid out on the desk. Ana looked at them and laughed.

'I wasn't with him when he painted those pictures so I can't claim to be the person who inspired him. But I can assure you of one thing. It will be me who inspires him for any pictures he may paint in the future.'

Extra chairs were found. Tea and toast were shared. Roger Mathews ruddy face was a picture of curiosity with his eyes gazing unwaveringly at Ana.

'Ana might be able to solve a problem for you father,' said Phillipa. 'She is fluent in Russian and German.'

'Is she by God. That would be handy. Tell us more Ana.'

Ana took over. She was relaxed, confident, and concise, and within minutes had given an account of foreign conventions, meetings arranged overseas for tax purposes, and how many British companies used her promotional services to help expand into Eastern Europe. Accurate understanding avoided costly mistakes, and working knowledge of a language was essential when negotiating contracts. Roger Mathews and his daughter sat mesmerized.

It was a masterly act of self-promotion. He remembered first introducing Ana at the Beechwood Hotel and the attention she generated when they walked into the busy restaurant. She is as seductive in business as she is in bed he thought. There was a knock on the office door and a man wearing overalls interrupted them.

'I've got Newcastle on the phone Matt. The beams haven't arrived from Skanda Timbers and Reg can't get any sense out of them.' Roger Mathews (why did they call him Matt?) complexion turned from red to purple.

'They've done this on us before. What the hell do they think they are playing at?' He turned to Roger, 'Excuse me – I have to deal with this. Phillipa will settle up with you for the pictures.' He abruptly shook hands and stormed out.

'Excuse my father,' said Phillipa. 'Patience is not one of his virtues. Storage, pre-construction, and most of our manufacturing are based here, and father deals with all of the hassle. Over 130 workers – and he likes to think they are all part of his family.

Come and look at our canteen.' Catering staff were preparing lunch and the selection on offer was impressive. Through a side window Roger noticed another room with a snooker table, table tennis, a running machine and a rowing machine. They returned to the office and Phillipa handed Roger a cheque.

'I run our offices and showrooms at West Park,' she pointed to the framed photograph on the wall. 'My father has something in mind, and next time you must visit our showrooms. And Ana – don't forget to bring your tennis racket.'

She kissed Ana on the cheek and Roger on the mouth. It was a nice kiss but her teeth got in the way. He remembered enjoying dancing with her on that fantastic night in Monte Carlo. But Leeds wasn't Nice, and Roger Mathews wasn't Antonio Romano.

As they walked to the car he said to Ana, 'Well I'm not carried away with the father but you can't help liking his daughter.'

'Be fair! They both seem to like you, and it's not a bad start to our first week back together. And compared with some of the unpleasant individuals I've been dealing with whilst you were being inspired in sunny Nice, the father seems like a saint to me.'

Traffic on the M62 couldn't have been worse, and halfway down the motorway Ana drew into a service station and parked in the quietest spot. She put her arms round him and kissed him letting her tongue flicker against his. Her hand dropped down to feel if he was hard.

'Roger you sexy beast – whatever furniture is missing when we get back to your place, I only hope your lounge carpet is still there.'

15. Utopia.

Home. The front garden a jungle. Leaflets stuffed through the letter box, and a pile of bills which stuck underneath the front door when he tried to open it. The burglar alarm went off as Roger unlocked the back door and a nosy neighbour hobbled across. 'Nice to see you back Mr Kelly.'

The house was freezing cold and the lounge devoid of all furniture. Even the battered armchair was missing. Gone was the new TV, the new lounge suite, the new carpet and the new matching curtains. Easy International Credit had done their job.

Ana put her arms around him. 'Welcome home darling. I can't wait for our night of passion but I don't fancy starting it off with a spell stuck in my bottom from your wooden floor.'

They carried some of his luggage upstairs. His bed still there but no sheets and no duvet. Roger opened the wardrobe door and found a white shirt hung on a wire hanger carefully buttoned to display extensive blood stains covering the collar and halfway down the shirt front. Size 15 collar – Jack's?

The sight of the blood-stained shirt hit Roger hard. There would be repercussions. He wouldn't have dealt with Romano's solicitor had he understood the kind of pressure that would be applied to Rosemary and Jack. He dumped the shirt and turned to Ana,

'I don't know what happened, but this was never intended.'

'Don't try and explain anything,' said Ana. 'Let's put

off until tomorrow what we can't solve today. I think it's time I invited you to stay with me.'

For the next two weeks he stayed with Ana. Being alone with her was like meeting her again for the very first time. They talked, they walked, they made love. Each time they arrived back at Ana's flat their eyes would meet and they were in each other's arms – sometimes fierce and demanding, sometimes slow and tender.

The novelty of Nice and his brief affairs had encompassed Roger's senses, and quelled the burning passion for Ana that lay buried inside him. Ana felt the same way, and she knew it the moment she saw him again. This was the man she wanted – the man she had desired ever since he first stepped into Brown's Garage and she sold him a car. Every minute in each other's company retrieved precious time lost. They woke each morning touching hands, dazed, hard to believe that they were together again.

After seven sizzling days they set about the practical task of refurnishing Roger's empty rooms, dealing with bills, clearing the jungle, and reorganizing the complete house. Ana was moving in with him. A new lounge carpet was chosen to match her Scandinavian furniture, and Ana's king-sized bed would fit perfectly into bedroom two. A call to Mick prompted a hilarious all-night party, after which it took only two trips in Mick's white van to transfer the bed, Scandinavian furniture, and most of Ana's belongings into Roger's empty house.

By mutual consent Ana and Kata closed their Manchester office and agreed to operate independently.

'Escorts Bilingual' now became 'Bilingual Promotions' and Ana's desktop computer and files found their way into Roger's bedroom/office squashed between his desk and his filing cabinets. Ana was sorry to leave her flat. She bought it when she was on a financial roller coaster and loved the spaciousness and feeling of independence. She put the flat up for sale and the first viewer purchased it without even haggling over the price. Life was moving forward at a break-neck pace.

Ana returned to work and she was busy – tied up until Christmas organizing year-end meetings, and travelling to conferences. Roger stepped out of his euphoria and realized he was back to square one – no job and no car, and no idea what he was going to do now he was back in Manchester.

He applied for planning permission to build the extension over the garage uncomfortably aware that legally Rosemary was still joint owner of the property.

He was thinking about it when his mobile 'pinged' and a text message brought him down to earth.

Roger – a warning. I'm back in the smoke trying to stay obscure. There's a lot of trouble circulating around. Keep your head down, watch your back, and don't trust anyone. No word from the Governor. He has disappeared. Monty.

Roger rang the number and it was invalid. A throw away phone. An unsettled feeling emerged. He thought he had left all of that behind in Nice, but the text message and the blood-stained shirt were proof that he had not.

Further proof arrived later in the shape of a police car. The officer checked his identity and insisted that Roger accompany him to police headquarters on Northampton Road. Dealing with Greater Manchester Police was different to Roger's experience with French police and the Irish mess-up in Dublin. He was politely interviewed by an Inspector who explained that his presence there was merely a formality, and Roger was asked to repeat the same story he had repeated many times before. The inspector listened intently.

'I believe everything you are telling me Mr Kelly. However there seems to be an intense search going on to locate your Mr Romano and it's our misfortune to have to cooperate with the 'frogs'. I suggest you keep your nose clean and if you hear anything, or experience any trouble, contact me immediately.'

Roger was in and out of the station within an hour, and the officer who collected him ran him back to base. The same nosy neighbour from across the road stood outside his door to witness his return, and the gardener renting the skip added a branch of rotting apples so he could crane his neck to discover whether Roger was wearing handcuffs.

Thinking of the stained shirt – what dramas had the neighbours observed when Rosemary and Jack took their leave? Ana was away until the weekend and he didn't intend involving her with today's events. Life can only be understood backwards but it must be lived forwards, nevertheless, the police visit and Monty's text worried him and the unsettled feeling persisted. There was no getting away from it – Nice and Romano were not a closed book.

The phone call from Roger Mathews came as a welcome relief. He didn't fancy being tied up with Mathews Building Investments but he would be a fool not to accept the invitation and find out what was on offer. Next day he took the early train to Leeds and walked to Mathews Offices in Hunslet. Walking was easier than driving – you could read street names better, and you avoided having a ten-ton truck breathing down your neck.

When Roger was shown into Roger Mathews's office, he was introduced to a tall military looking man, mid-forties, with a tanned, deeply-lined face and an iron-grey crew cut.

'Let me introduce you to my operations manager. Peter Campbell – Roger Kelly.

'You two should get on well together because you are both a couple of independent buggers.' When they shook hands Peter Campbell had a grip like steel and Roger respected him immediately.

'Now Roger – call me Matt, everyone else does. I've brought you over here to make you an offer. It's a trial post, in a sense it's a position that you can create all on your own. You will be working alongside Peter here: visiting sites, sussing out problems, and sketching improvements and adjustments. At the same time, we are competing to provide the government with a standard workable design which will be replicated nationally and used on social housing projects. A bit different to designing villas and yachts for the rich and famous, but Peter and I think it's a bloody sight more important, and we can use your talents.'

It was a concise clear picture. Roger liked the idea of it, he liked Peter Campbell, and he had no hesitation in accepting the offer of a one-year contract with a substantial pay packet linked to results. Serious work would begin in January. Before that he was expected to spend a week in Mathews new offices, learning office procedures, and getting to know the staff he would be dealing with.

Ana arrived home early Friday evening. She could tell he had news to tell her but she didn't ask – in her cool understanding way her eyes read his, and she waited.

They went to bed and when he told her about the job it excited her. Ana was as ambitious as ever and he knew she wanted him to match her own ambitions.

She whispered into his ear. 'Don't hold back on me Roger,' and she made love like a hungry animal, biting and scratching him as he turned her in different positions.

In the half-light Ana's eyes never closed as she watched his face buried between her thighs, and her legs encircled his neck as she rolled over and took him in her mouth. He didn't let her climax, but pulled away and thrust inside her so he could enjoy the full intensity of her orgasm. Afterwards she sat up, looking down on him, smiling.

'You will need another car. Isn't this where we first started?'

'Yes, but we have come a long way since then – and I need a different model.'

'As long as you don't choose a different model to drive it,' said Ana.

'Never ever,' Roger replied.

Ana introduced him to one of her garage contacts and he bought a bargain priced Volkswagen Camper Van. He collected it at the beginning of the following week and Mick came over in the afternoon. Between them they converted part of the van into a travelling office, still keeping the sleeping facility which folded neatly out of the way. Ana was working away more than she was home, and after a couple of trips up and down the M62, Roger decided to stay with his parents during his trial week at Mathews offices.

Howard had become a father, and he and Joan were staying at her mother's, in Somerset, while Malcolm and Ruth were on a trial work visit to a Kibbutz in Israel, so any pre-Christmas celebrations were going to be with Mick and Wendy. They made a return trip to the Beechwood Hotel and Ana's pale blue dress had the same effect on him as the dress she wore on their first visit. They danced round the floor to a Latin beat – he had forgotten how tall she was when they danced together, and the cool smoothness of her cheek brushed against his.

'How is my film star tonight,' he asked.

'More in love with the leading man than ever,' she said.

They were giving the new Volkswagen a trial run and on their way home Roger turned off to park by the derelict cornmill. The bats weren't circling tonight but a half-moon cast a silvery glow on the water. It was cold and frosty. Ana moved close to him and he kissed her. She tasted of wine and their tongues linked as he slid down her shoulder strap and gently cupped her breast.

'Will you be staying with me tonight?' he asked.

'I want to stay with you even more now than I did on our very first night,' she said.

'And you better get used to it, Mr Kelly. I think I will always be staying with you.'

'But not in the Camper Van?' he asked.

'No – whatever Mick and Wendy get up to tonight I draw the line on the Camper Van.'

He accompanied Ana to Croatia for Christmas. It was a Christmas like no other. The charm of Rovinj, the welcome from her family. And perhaps notably the way he empathised with Luke, kicking the ball around every day, and awakened each morning when Luke climbed the attic stairs and clambered onto the bed shouting 'Roger, football – play football.'

The coastal weather was mild and Ana was intensely happy. Her fears about explaining away her past vanished. Together with Petra and Luke she conducted Roger around the town – her old school, the cobbled streets, the fishing smacks in the harbour. It was easy to imagine Rovinj in the summer with sunshine lighting the cobbled streets, and cafés overflowing with holiday visitors. Roger fell in love with Rovinj and the simplicity of life led by most of its inhabitants.

On Christmas Eve he helped Petra's husband stow away the fishing nets on his boat with Luke happily trotting around on sea legs already accustomed to the sea swell rocking the boat. Luke believed Saint Nicholas had given him a second father for Christmas.

At night Roger and Ana ascended the steep steps of

St Euphemia and held hands during the midnight service. Like being a small boy again, with all the magic of the Christmas story told every year at Sunday School. Ana's mother couldn't speak English but even without verbal communication she and Roger developed a close relationship. His visit was a success, and it was a brilliant Christmas. Ana was staying for a second week, but Roger had to be back to start the new job. He left with flying colours, and there were hugs from everyone and tears from Luke.

When Ana saw him off at the airport her green eyes gazed steadily into his and he knew the trip had been a milestone. She said nothing but gripped his hand as though she couldn't let him go. Roger boarded the plane with a new perspective on life. A life partner to Ana and a second father to Luke. A fire burned inside him.

16. Trapped.

Water and grit splashed across the windscreen and the wipers moved twenty to the dozen. The road was pitch black and headlights from the wagon on his tail-end dazzled him so that each time the traffic halted he was almost up the backside of the wagon in front. Travelling the M62 was a nightmare, and he always hit the heavy traffic. As he removed his mud-caked boots on the doorstep, he pictured arriving back at Aunt Evelyn's apartment in Nice. Warm sunshine and a glass of wine on the balcony. Roger laughed at the thought of it. Ana was in London and he now had to summarize the day and sketch perceived improvements by tomorrow. You earned your money when you worked for Mathews Investments. He would be lucky to eat before 9 pm – and then it was bed and sleep.

Working alongside Peter Campbell was not a bed of roses. He was not the easiest guy to get along with, never discussed his own private life, and didn't want to know anything about yours. Peter was a surveyor, ex Warrant Officer in the Royal Armoured Corps, and very much his own man. He wouldn't change. Everything had to be done at the double, he didn't accept excuses, and he was dedicated to his work which never finished until the day's job was completed. Occasionally he showed a flash of humour.

During a break Roger asked, 'Why does Roger Mathews like people to call him Matt?'

Peter grinned at him. 'No disrespect to you but he doesn't like the name Roger. Says it rhymes with too many other words.'

'That's a joke! I can think of a lot more things which rhyme with Matt. I'll list them.'

'Don't bother! After 25 years in the army, I bet I can think of more words than you can. Second thoughts – make out the list and I will pass it on to Matt.'

They both laughed, then back to the grind. Typical English weather. The site was sloppy and wet, they arrived early and wouldn't leave until the light faded. All part of the job when operating with Peter at the spearhead of Mathews Building Investments. Roger enjoyed the challenge, but this wasn't quite what he had in mind when he accepted the contract.

Most of the sites were scattered around Northern England. In spite of the weather this suited Roger because he hated being stuck in an office. His purchase of the Volkswagen Camper Van turned out to be a blessing; on a couple of occasions when working on his own, the weather conditions became so bad that he didn't fancy the idea of driving home and then driving back again the following morning. He completed his paperwork in Mick's office conversion, parked up for the night in a convenient spot, bought fish and chips, and then slept very comfortably on the fold-away bed.

Twice weekly the design team pulled him into their new offices. Some of Roger's suggestions for social housing were submitted and incorporated into the blue print. When the team leader went down with flu no one in design liked the idea of dealing with the visiting Minister from the Government Housing Department and the task

265

was palmed off onto Roger. The Minister turned out to be an affable character who enjoyed talking about football whilst eating his smoked salmon sandwiches in Mathews executive canteen. He accepted the prime features of the social housing model and left promising that he would do everything possible to ensure Mathews Building Investments won the contract. Success breeds success. Suddenly Roger found he couldn't put a foot wrong.

Ana was flying high too, but her change of direction from escort work didn't prove easy. She set about reshaping her business with cool deliberation but accepted assignments she would like to have avoided – especially those which meant working away. Weekends with Roger were bliss and their honeymoon never seemed to end. Social life was lively and they enjoyed some good nights with Mick and Wendy, and when at last Howard emerged out of the woodwork, he held a christening party which lasted all Saturday, and most of the Sunday. Then Roger's parents came to stay the following weekend to celebrate the homecoming of Aunt Evelyn. She entertained them with 'way out' impressions of drunken Aussies, and hilarious tales of some grand old Romeo who tried to woo and win her during her five-week boat trip back to England. It was another enjoyable occasion into which Ana fitted perfectly. More and more she found herself welcomed among friends and family.

Roger didn't hear any more from Greater Manchester Constabulary, and nothing more from Monty. Antonio Romano's predicament never left Roger's thoughts but a sense of reality took over, and whilst he wanted to learn more information as to what was happening to Romano, he was wary of any involvement in the problems which Manchester police had warned him about. The only news from France came when John contacted him with an accounts query. He and Jane were continuing business based in Nice, but apparently the Carrington-Browns had settled in Poole with no intention of returning to the South of France except for holidays. John didn't mention Helen, and Roger didn't ask after her. It niggled him a bit. Not a word nor a text message since she seduced him on the passenger seat, and then drove off in his much-loved Alpha Romeo. So much for that magnetic allure which he thought he had acquired during his stay in Nice.

Weekends were one thing, but weekdays he was back to a bachelor existence because Ana was still working away so much. This week it was London again, and before getting into her car she performed her Monday morning tease, arms around him, and pushing hard against him as her tongue flickered fleetingly in his mouth. Whenever Ana went away, he was left with an aching groin and she was well aware of the effect she had on him. The problem with work is that it gets in the way of pleasure he thought.

With his usual ache, he drove into the city and fed an hour's parking into the meter whilst he bought a fresh supply of inks and sketching pads from the stationers.

When he came out of the shop a Volvo had parked so close that the rear bumper rested against the front bumper of the Camper Van. Two men got out of the Volvo and stood in front of him. A six-foot muscle man with short frizzy permed curls, and a thin faced hard man dressed in black with a pigtail. They split. The muscle man walked round to the Volkswagen, opened the door, and sat in the passenger seat.

The hard man held out his tattooed hand, 'Mr Kelly – someone would like to meet you.'

Roger ignored the hand. 'Tell curly locks to get the fuck out of my car or I will flatten you, flatten him, and then call the police.'

Hard man took a step back looking surprised. 'No please – my apologies. We only intended to invite you to meet someone who is very interested in meeting you.'

'Well tell that someone whoever he is that he is going about it the wrong way.'

Curly locks got out of the Camper Van and tried to outstare him. He was cumbersome, bulked up with steroids and Roger reckoned he could obliterate him in two minutes flat. Hard man apologised again, said they would be in touch, and the pair of them drove off. What the hell was all that about? Roger was working at home clearing outstanding reports and had plenty of time to worry about it.

When Ana phoned, he didn't mention the incident but for the next few days he was on edge waiting for something else to happen. He didn't have long to wait. In the middle of the week a letter arrived addressed to Roger Kelly Esquire – two tickets for a boxing dinner at Manchester Sporting Club, a black-tie job with reserved seats. No accompanying note, no indication of who sent the tickets.

'Somebody must have taken a fancy to you,' said Mick. 'It's the last big night of the boxing season for the Sporting Club. Those tickets include a slap-up meal and five or six top class fights. Each ticket will be worth over £100 at a guess.'

Nothing is for nothing! From previous experience Roger knew that this was the way dodgy organizations worked. If they wanted something from you – supply you first with a free gift then call in the debt later. He felt uneasy about accepting the tickets but his curiosity got the better of him. Somebody wanted something from him and what had he got to offer them?

Boxing dinners at the Sporting Club were 'men only' and always held on a Monday night. He collected Mick and they joined a table of twelve – all marked down as 'special guests', with two seats reserved in the name of Roger Kelly. Dinner and comedians came first, then an interval, then the boxing. By the amount of drink being consumed it was clear that most tables were more interested in the men's night out than they were in the boxing, and many of the guests behaved as though it was the first time in their lives that their wives had let them out of the house. One exuberant guest on the next table suddenly stood up, deathly white faced and swaying, and was sick all over his dinner suit. Further away a loud beery argument sprang up at another table where two glowering guests removed their dinner jackets and were restrained from offering pre fight entertainment before the main show.

'Black tie or not this crowd aren't a very classy lot once they get a few bevies inside them,' commented Mick. He got up to take a break and relieve himself of his lager intake. Mick held his drink very well providing there were conveniences close by.

269

A bearded man wearing a white tuxedo jacket plonked himself down next to Roger in Mick's empty seat.

'Sid Cohen,' he said shaking hands. 'I'm the match maker. Did you enjoy your dinner?' Without waiting for an answer, he opened the boxing programme.

'Right! Let's have a look at tonight's fights. We are down to five fights tonight because this laddie from Liverpool has pulled out. But there are two good lads to watch out for. Third bout – another fellow from Liverpool, and he is going places. Polished, a lovely boxer, and he has won all six of his professional fights. Moving on to the Cruiserweights – bout four, Proctor from North Shields. He's, our man. A real killer. Hungry, a hard hitter, takes a punch and never stays down. He's won five of his eight professional fights by clean knockouts, and the other three by stoppages. Put your money on him and you can't go wrong.' Mick returned and Sid relinquished his seat.

'You're a big lad,' he said. 'You could be useful.' Gave a nod and turned away ready to leave.

'Sid,' said Roger. 'Hang on! I don't understand. We are having a fantastic night and I very much appreciate the tickets – but why are we here, and why did two stiffs intercept me in town last Monday?'

'Ah my apologies,' said Sid. 'That was a mistake. You're the man connected to the Romano organization in France, aren't you? You did us a favour. You put Juggernaut Jason out of action. Any man who can do that – Paul wants to meet.'

'Paul Sebastian?' asked Roger.

'That's him. I work for him. He promoted tonight's Sporting Club event. If you want to meet him then give his secretary a ring,' and Sid handed Roger a business card and dashed off to another table.

'You are beginning to surprise me,' said Mick. 'Porno photos, rescuing women from psychopaths, and now Manchester's number one boxing promoter is wooing you with presents. Have I missed something?'

'Balls!' said Roger, and they sat back and enjoyed the boxing. The boxing finished at 11.00 and in high spirits they moved on to Grosvenor Casino. Mick won at blackjack and Roger did well on the roulette table. It had reached the early hours of the morning when he pulled a half-intoxicated Mick away from an aging lady of the night who had attached herself to Mick with a view to relieving him of his winnings. Fortunately, they exited the casino quietly without a repeat performance of Dublin.

Roger had an early morning meeting and by the time he got into bed it was time to get out of bed again. Traffic was minimal, and in spite of a late start he drove into his reserved spot in Mathews car park before any of his colleagues, and was first person to take his place in the meeting. His mind buzzed from the previous evening, but he managed to concentrate as a sun burned Roger Mathews presented the meeting with his latest concept of social housing.

Matt saw himself as a modern-day Titus of Saltaire fame, providing better housing for the working classes. Roger was enthusiastic but still liked the idea of designing sumptuous villas for the rich and famous. Wisely he kept those thoughts to himself when he bumped into Matt in the office corridor.

'Now then lad – how are you getting on? I believe congratulations are in order. Some of the modifications you put forward have been accepted and it looks as though we might have won the Government contract too.'

'Thanks Matt – any success is due to Peter's support, not to mention cakes and sandwiches in our excellent canteen.' Matt looked pleased.

'Well, I am glad you have settled in alright. After your French experiences I didn't know whether you would. Come into my office a minute I want a word.'

The new office was a carbon copy of the traditional office in Hunslet: polished wood, stern moustached icons on the wall, and another set of photographs of the Mathews football team.

'We are just back from Antibes. Took a trip through to Nice and was surprised to see the activity going on around the Romano properties. All his villas in apple pie order, and the town centre letting-office up and running again. Didn't you have something to do with that new villa of his outside Villefranche?'

'I designed it,' said Roger. 'Whether it ever gets built or not is any one's guess.'

'Well, you're wrong there, lad. It's finished, and its occupied. But there's no way we can find out who owns it and there's no way we can find out who has taken over the villa business. It's like bloody well tapping into M15. I was going to ask you – have you any ideas?'

'Search me,' said Roger. 'I haven't seen or heard anything since I left Nice. What does the new villa look like Matt?'

'Oh marvellous! Bloody marvellous! If you're responsible for designing that lad you've done a job to be proud of. In fact, I wouldn't mind the design plans if you can lay your hands on them.'

'Sorry Matt – no such luck! The master plan was destroyed along with everything else when gangland set fire to the offices. Best I can do is let you have the plan of my own dream hacienda from which the Romano villa was copied'.

Matt's finger disappeared up his nose and Roger didn't know whether his answer was believed or not. The plans belonged to Romano. He had paid Roger for them, and there was no way anyone else would ever get their hands on them. But his talk with Matt re-awakened lingering thoughts of Romano, the image of their final meeting stamped into his mind. He owed it to both of them. He had to go back to Nice and see the villa and he had to show it to Ana.

Ana's car was parked on the driveway when he arrived home. She looked tired and dejected.

'So why home so early?' asked Roger.

'Company mismanagement,' she said. 'Meetings cancelled halfway through due to disagreement with the Russians. It means I will have to go back to London again.'

'Ana – why are we working so hard? We travel all over the place and hardly see each other.'

She thought about it before answering.

'It's not just ambition Roger. We are working flat out because we have to. I have a family to keep in Croatia and you can expect a pending settlement with your wife in the near future. Let's earn money while we can, because just as life is sailing along nicely bad times pop up and knock you off your feet.'

In Roger's head loomed the picture of a sunlit apartment with flowers on the balcony, and the sight of the villa he helped create sat on a cliff top with the silver tipped waves of the Mediterranean calling him from below.

'You need a holiday,' said Roger. He drove Ana into Manchester to the best Italian restaurant he knew, and she relaxed over a couple of dry Martinis, scallops, and a meat pasta. As they sat in the side lounge finishing coffee a flower seller came to the door and he bought Ana a bunch of roses. Each time Ana worked away their relationship seemed to become more intense than ever when she arrived back home.

'You know what I am going to do to you tonight don't you?' said Roger.

Ana's eyes met his and her hand dropped to his knee. 'No. But I want you to tell me'.

The thrill of being together remained as exciting and erotic as ever.

Planning permission for their house extension was granted and he discussed it with Ana who always discovered an angle he had overlooked.

'Before going ahead with the alterations why not have the house valued? The extension will bump up your resale price and if some smart arsed solicitor spots it you may find that half the added increase will be included in any settlement you make with Rosemary.' She smiled at him. 'You didn't think of that did you?'

There was a lot Roger didn't think about – but he was learning. Ana contacted Hunters Estate Agents who came out and valued the house. Roger topped up his wine stocks at Zorba's and Alex recommended three Greek brothers to build the extension.

'Make sure you pay them on the dot Roger. They have been working for months for a slick bastard who is keeping them hanging on.'

Two of the brothers presented themselves the very next day and Roger was impressed. This was a good bunch of guys who he could work well with, so he engaged them to start work immediately.

'Full payment as soon as the job is finished,' promised Roger. 'Alex tells me you are having trouble – have you been paid yet?'

'The Sebastian boys – no chance. They want us for other jobs, so they make us wait. Perhaps we have job working somewhere else and we have to drop it to please them. Then they pay us. Big mistake doing any work for them.'

That figures, thought Roger. It tied in perfectly with his own calculations of how the Sebastian brothers might do business, and he was still mystified by the free boxing tickets when he and Mick met for a late evening drink.

'What's the aftermath of last Monday's boxing? Have you met the big boy yet?'

'I'm postponing the pleasure. Keeping the big boy hanging on until he sends some more free tickets.'

'That's a let-down,' said Mick. 'I thought by now you

would have accepted a beneficial inducement towards pugilistic stardom.'

Roger hadn't intended following up on Sid Cohen's invitation, and the Greek brothers' description of their dealings with the Sebastian brothers wasn't encouraging. But the boxing night had got under his skin. Something in Roger relished the challenge of meeting the man who controlled Manchester's boxing world, and he wasn't going to rest until he knew why he had been singled out for attention. Roger chuckled to himself. Ana definitely wouldn't be impressed, and his father would say he was a damned fool – did he want to get mixed up with another crowd of rogues?

Ana was back in London. He rang Sebastian Promotions on a day when he was supposed to be working from home. The builders had started work on the extension, and the house was upside down as though a bomb had hit it. There was no hesitation when he made the phone call.

'Come over and see us,' replied an oily voice.

His Sat Nav guided him to the address on Sid's business card and he was surprised to find himself on a barren stretch of wasteland in an area of back-to-back houses awaiting demolition. The single word 'Sebastian's' adorned the side of a ramshackle building which extended to a scruffy yard piled high with bricks and plasterboards with two disused petrol pumps completing the picture. He drove round to the front. A Rolls Royce and an assortment of cars were parked on a muddy patch, overlooked by a tower block of dilapidated council flats. Roger got out of the Volkswagen and stood in an oily puddle. Paul Sebastian would not win a prize for his parking facilities. Whatever they wanted from him it would be a bit of fun to start the relationship by offering them a discount on a new office design and car park to match. He laughed to himself as he picked his way through the mud. Nothing like implied criticism to cement new bonds of friendship.

There were no signs of life as he entered reception even though bangs and thumps came from somewhere within the building. The girl behind the desk ignored him and continued filing her nails but adjusted her sweater to give him a bird's eye view of two super-sized implants. She sneaked a glance to see if he was looking.

'What do you want?'

'I'm here to see Paul Sebastian.'

'He's out!' she said. 'I'll get someone.'

The someone was an intimidating hunch backed man who was deaf and dumb but looked powerful enough to lift a ten-ton truck. He arrived within minutes and guided Roger across the wasteland to the tower block of council flats. From the moment Roger stepped inside he knew he had made a serious mistake accepting the invitation. He should have been warned by the town centre kidnapping fiasco. This was a dangerous set-up. In the foyer a muscle-bound tattoo artist stood on sentry duty next to a lift marked 'out of order'. Up the hazardous cracked concrete steps to the first floor of the flats where another sixteen stone shaven headed guard was posted. Paint peeled off ceilings, the walls were plastered with graffiti, and Roger noticed signs of damp and subsidence as they ascended to the second floor. A bored Arnold

Schwarzenegger look-alike waved them upwards and onwards to the third, where two equally impressive custodians barred their entry before thoroughly frisking Roger from head to toe.

The hunch-backed guide disappeared, and one of the custodians took Roger's arm and conducted him through the door into a corridor of offices which came as a shock after ascending the creepy broken-down staircase.

The corridor he entered would not have looked out of place on one of Monaco's most luxurious yachts. Silver chandeliers ran the full length of the passage and thick wine-coloured carpeting added lustre to white office doors encrusted with gold paint.

It was like stepping into a palace. It dazzled Roger's eyes. No expense had been spared to create an impression of pure grandeur. How did Paul Sebastian manage to get away with a set-up like this? The police must know about it, and it confirmed Roger's theory that sometimes the police closed their eyes to certain members of the criminal fraternity when it suited them to do so.

The office into which Roger was escorted gave the impression of two flats knocked together to create one grandiose space. The floor was covered in white carpet, and a white piano with open keyboard stood next to the panoramic window. Two white leather sofas were placed beside a bar and cocktail cabinet at the far end of the room, with a set of desks and filing cabinets placed midway facing a second window.

Dominating the surroundings sat a massive fat man behind an equally massive mahogany table and looking at the wide shouldered silhouette from the back his appearance reminded Roger of a preying manta. Roger's escort stepped promptly to one side and stood behind the fat man who remained motionless staring at Roger. Nothing moved. The small red rosebud mouth and blue eyes were like buttons on the heavy jowled face, and his short wavy brown hair looked out of place on the huge domed head.

He continued to study Roger then leaned forward and pressed an intercom button. 'Morris – he's here,' he said.

This was a game. Roger turned round, selected a chair, and sat cross legged staring back at the fat man. The bodyguard didn't like it – he moved forward but a raised hand detained him just as a tall thin man wearing glasses hurried through the door and joined the fat man behind the mahogany table. He opened a brief case and took out a sheaf of papers. His face was a blank mask.

'So?' said the fat man 'You were invited here because you wanted to meet us.'

'No,' said Roger. 'Paul Sebastian wanted to meet me.'

'I'm not Paul,' said the fat man.

'Let's get to the point Leslie. Tell the boy why he's here.' He stood up and held out his hand. 'I'm Morris Brooks, and this is Leslie Sebastian – Paul's brother. We handle all of Paul's business. Mr Kelly – you have had a working relationship with Antonio Romano. Our company has been financially involved with the Romano consortium for many years until legal problems recently effected their business and we had to dissociate ourselves from that partnership. Last year our solicitor got rid of unwelcome occupants in your house. Now we need a favour in return. Mr Romano has disappeared off the map completely, he has gone underground but he must be somewhere because we understand his properties in France and Naples are up and running again.'

The thick lenses of the glasses focused on Roger. 'We need your assistance – you must know something, and we want you to help us find your friend Antonio Romano.'

This explained everything. This was the reason why he was here, and whatever his reply he wouldn't be believed. Behind the thick-lensed glasses Morris Brooks was inscrutable and Roger marked him down as very dangerous. Romano's words resonated in his head, 'play the game – it's all a game,' but he couldn't afford to get the game wrong with these people, even though he had no intention of helping them.

'Tell me Mr Brooks – how do you think I can do that?' asked Roger. 'The police can't find Romano, and his creditors can't find him. Nobody can find Romano, but I will be pleased to tell you what I told the police many times over. I designed a villa for Romano, and worked with him on some of his properties. I never knew his other business, but I respect the man. To me he was a friend, and I don't believe he was involved in the crimes he was accused of. He hasn't contacted me and he hasn't contacted his right-hand man. I wish I could help you and I wish I could help him.'

Leslie snorted. His little mouth and face twisted as he half rose out of his chair.

'You're not coming straight with us. You were a man he trusted. Let's make this clear. Romano's organization is in debt to Sebastian Promotions – and only Romano can make sure we get back what they owe us. We don't play games, we want the truth, so don't mess with us boy.'

His stare changed to a glare and the twisted smooth face warned Roger that this man was psychologically unbalanced. Roger relaxed and let a minute pass before he replied.

'That's not going to be an issue, Mr Sebastian. I only mess with the people who mess with me.' Leslie's bodyguard took another threatening step forward. Morris Brooks quickly interrupted and took over.

'Mr Kelly we are already aware of your reputation. You are the man who put down Juggernaut Jason. He was our best man in London before you blacked out his eye and made him unemployable. We have every respect for you because Jason caused us a lot of trouble. But you must understand that Leslie means business because the search has gone on long enough. We must find Romano before someone else finds him.'

'Then have respect for what I am telling you Mr Brooks. I'm sorry! I cannot supply you with the information you require because I haven't got the information to give you. But tell me – did you need to employ a psychopath like Jason?'

'That's our business,' said Leslie. 'But now we need someone to replace him.'

'That is your business too Mr Sebastian and I can't help you with that either. But while we are talking, I appreciate your assistance persuading my ex-wife and her partner to leave my property, but I would have preferred things done differently.'

The ogre glared at Roger. Morris gave a glassy smile.

The thick impenetrable glasses and the large false teeth lent a bite-like impact to the gesture. A shark!

'I came here to meet Paul Sebastian,' said Roger, 'but obviously I made a mistake.

'I am an architect. In the next few weeks, I intend visiting Nice. Anything I find out while I am there will be passed on to you and I trust this will clear any debt you believe I owe you.'

Morris produced another show of teeth.

'I knew we would understand each other, Mr Kelly. You now have a new career and new employers, and I am sure you value your new career sufficiently not to allow any trouble from your past to leak out and interfere with your current standing. Give us the information we want and you can be sure all details of your previous occupation will remain private between us.' It was an obvious threat – cloaked but undisguised.

'In the meantime,' continued Morris, 'allow us to show good faith and offer you the benefits of our hospitality. Club membership, exclusive tickets, perhaps even the right selection of women. You only have to ask.'

There was another snort as Leslie Sebastian heaved himself noisily out of his chair and made for the door closely followed by his minder.

'Hospitality depends on results boy,' he called over his shoulder. He was surprisingly light on his feet. At least 20 stone and he moved fast like an athlete of half his weight. Never mind the bodyguard – dealing with someone as heavy as Leslie would be dealing with the unstoppable. Morris adjusted his glasses and got up, gathering his papers together. The glassy smile was gone.

'I think we have an agreement Mr Kelly. Contact us when you get back from Nice.'

He left as hurriedly as he arrived. Part of the power game – it was intentionally abrupt to leave Roger in no doubt of what was expected of him.

Left alone in the empty room, Roger's self-confidence wavered. This hadn't gone well, and he knew it. There was never an intention of introducing him to the boxing promoter. Instead, he had been purposely compromised into something he would find difficult to get out of.

Roger descended the worn stairs, past the security, and stepped out into the freedom of Manchester's polluted air. It was like breathing nectar. What a set of bastards. He got to the car and a leaflet lay folded underneath the windscreen wipers – 'Paul Sebastian's Boxing Gym'. He screwed it up, started the car, and set off in the direction of home. How was he going to extract himself from this bodge-up?

A black cloud threatened to interfere with everything Roger was trying to achieve. Roger spent three long troubled days working on site with Peter before Ana arrived home. The Greeks had finished for the day, but she still had trouble finding a place to park her car between the skip and the rubble. One look at Roger told her there was something wrong. She studied his face and took his hand.

'Do I have to wait until later or are you going to tell me now what has gone wrong with your week?'

'Let's leave it until later. Whatever is wrong is down

to me.'

Roger hadn't meant to tell her anything, but his problems were difficult to hide. For the fourth night running he was chased by dreams of a blood-stained shirt and he awoke drenched in sweat. Ana got out of bed and brought him a towel.

They sat together, propped against the pillows, drinking green tea in silence until Ana said, 'Don't you think it would help if you tell me what this is all about?'

At three in the morning, he told her everything. From the dodgy solicitor and how Rosemary and Jack had been pressurised into leaving the house, to the kidnap attempt and boxing tickets, to his visit to Sebastian's offices and their subsequent claim that he owed them a favour to reveal Romano's whereabouts.

'And if I knew,' concluded Roger, 'it's the last thing I would ever divulge to that evil bunch. The trouble is – I am constantly going to have them on my back still believing I know something which they don't.'

'I have met the Sebastians,' said Ana. 'You can't blame yourself for accepting their boxing tickets because if the Sebastians wanted to see you they would see you no matter what. It's going to be uncomfortable Roger, but you are going to have to play along with them until they get tired.'

He hadn't realised Ana was familiar with the Sebastians, but he knew she was right. Had she had dealings with them through her escort agency? He didn't ask. They talked for over an hour before sleep claimed them both and the blood-stained shirt was banished from further dreams.

Disturbed night or not Roger was out of bed by seven. He put on his trainers and ran twice round the village. Spring daffodils lined the hedges and cherry blossom covered the trees. He had previously noticed a Goldfinch's nest in a beech tree at the corner of the cricket field. The nest was now concealed by leaves, but the fledglings had hatched out already and there were flashes of colour from their parents, in and out, feeding their young ones. To hell with it! He had stood his ground with the Sebastians. Today was Saturday. Ana had completed her London contract and she was home for the week. On Friday they were on their way to France, and he could take another look at the villa he designed which he never believed would be built. Thoughts of Nice calmed his troubled mind.

Ana had breakfast ready when he returned. She sat at the table looking radiant wearing a denim shirt and pale blue jeans. He showered and changed, and while he drank his coffee her green eyes probed his eyes, searching, investigative, and always understanding.

'I really think it's time to settle with Rosemary, then you can forget the bullying incident and put it behind you Roger.'

Ana was reiterating his own conclusions. The payment would eat into his savings, but the settlement had to be made – and the sooner the better.

He phoned his father and they set up a meeting with his father's solicitor during the week. The sum of money suggested by the solicitor was far in excess of the £50,000 Rosemary had tried to squeeze out of him. It was now exactly one year since he and Rosemary split up and he made his first trip to stay in Aunt Evelyn's apartment, and it was also the anniversary of his first meeting with Ana.

For the rest of the week Roger couldn't think clearly about anything. It wasn't until their plane was cleared for take-off and he and Ana were flying high above the Manchester clouds that the old Roger came flooding back. When Ana asked him what he was laughing about he squeezed her hand and told her she would find out soon enough, and apart from spilling half a glass of red wine over her white chinos the flight passed without any other mishaps.

17. Escaping the Debt.

He was back. Nice. Sunshine. Aunt Evelyn's apartment. His morning runs. He opened the balcony window and looked across at the little café – God how he'd missed those leisurely breakfasts of croissants, apricot jam, and real coffee.

Ana was enchanted. She loved the apartment. He couldn't wait to show her Quartier du Port, and the run out to Villefranche and Hacienda Romano. Months of work designing a project which he hadn't believed would ever come to fruition, but it had come to fruition in spite of the circumstances surrounding it. Memories of Romano and Monty flooded back.

Jet 2 had landed them in Nice Airport at 11.25 am. They were straight through customs and onto the Airport Bus. They dumped their cases in the flat and Roger took Ana across to the café for a welcome hug, kisses on both cheeks, and free coffee on the house. Over *steak-frites*, Ana's green eyes scrutinized him with a slight smile playing on her lips.

'I'm surprised that after your French welcome and the liaisons which inspired your art, you had anything left for me.'

'Don't mention it,' said Roger. 'After sleepless nights imagining you on one-to-one escort duties I would gladly have stayed in Nice if the police hadn't chased me out.'

All of a sudden it struck him – it would be a real mess if Elissa had parted from 'man bastard' to resume cleaning the apartments, and lay waiting for him amidst a room full of red roses. He chuckled at the thought of it.

On the way back up to the apartment he checked the mailbox. A card from Aunt Evelyn sent before Christmas plus a plain envelope marked R. Kelly. Inside the envelope a polite note written in perfect English asking if he would please contact the writer who planned to commission a villa on the side of Lake Geneva. It was a Swiss address – the letter dated late November.

He said to Ana, 'Given time I could make a success of Nice. You and I could be living a less stressful life here in the sunshine.'

They left cases unpacked and he led Ana down to the car park. The Range Rover needed a wash but started first time. Roger let the engine run while he cleaned the windows and then they were off, smooth as a bird – along Promenade des Anglais, down through the lovely old port, passing yachts and villas sparkling in the sunshine until they reached the outskirts of Villefranche and the very first sight of his dream – standing proudly, and immaculate in all its glory. Gardeners were busy laying out the borders. This should have been Romano's. His dream belonged to Romano.

They got out of the Rover and stood watching as rows of plants were dug into the flower beds. It was all there. The wrap around wooden porch. Panoramic views from every corner window. Unexpected touches of colour – a follow up on early sketches he made of the Marigold yacht.

'Ana – I had never done anything like this before. I wasn't qualified. But I was given the chance to create something meaningful, and I succeeded.'

Ana didn't speak. She slipped her arm in his and

gently compressed it. Ana understood. She didn't have to speak. Ana always understood.

They drove back through Nice centre and sorted cases out in the apartment. He had travelled light and so had Ana. He didn't need much for a seven-day holiday break, and Ana was only staying for five days then travelling onwards to Rovinj where she kept plenty of clothes.

He took her to Chez Acchiardo in the evening to sample the '*plat du jour*'. No other restaurant meant quite the same to him.

When they returned to the apartment Roger said, 'Today is Good Friday. When I am with you, I can't promise to be good,' and Ana watched him through half closed eyes as he pulled her T shirt over her head and knelt down to slowly remove her jeans and pants. Any sense of the past was forgotten – elapsed, melted away to a million long years ago. Two bodies and minds lost in the thrill of passion as though making love for the very first time. They stayed locked in each other's arms all night without moving, never stirring, until rays of sun infiltrating through the slats compelled them to get out of bed and enjoy the day.

It was six months since Roger left Nice in a hurry. At the back of his mind was a concern that the police would know he was back and haul him in again. But everything went smoothly and he made sure past events stayed in the past by relegating his unpleasant meeting with the Sebastian Brothers onto the back burner.

Brexit or not, John and Jane were still enjoying excellent business in Nice. Roger contacted them and they met at the Yacht Club for a lobster and champagne evening serenaded by a very English band. The evening was a success. So was Sunday's visit to the SkyFly when April sunshine turned to showers, and Jane served wine and sandwiches in the confines of the cabin.

It was Ana's first visit to the Cote d'Azur. After a weekend walking Nice, he took her to Antibes, and then for a day in Cannes. Five days flew by and it seemed like Ana was on her way to Croatia before she had even had time to unpack her bag. But they were used to separations. On their way to the airport Ana examined the logbook.

'This Range Rover is a beautiful car, Roger. It's a top spec. and it seems a shame to leave it here to rust.'

'One problem – its left-hand drive,' said Roger.

'Have you and I ever avoided doing things differently?' asked Ana. She kissed him. 'Think about me – and don't get yourself into trouble.'

Roger laughed to himself as he watched her make her way through customs. Five fabulous days – five scorching days with her – a honeymoon all over again and how could he ever stop thinking about Ana? Nevertheless, he was disappointed. Why on earth couldn't she have stayed for the full week instead of dashing off to see her family in Rovinj?

Taking the Range Rover back with him made sense. But before motoring home there was a lot Roger wanted to check out, and he gave himself a couple of days to do it. Driving alongside Romano's rental villas he saw Matt's judgement was correct. The villas looked in pristine condition and were all fully occupied. The newly painted central office had been renovated to look pretty much the same as before except that rentals advertised in the window were plainly available to the general public as opposed to only letting villas to strictly selected tenants.

A trip out to Romano's villa revealed it to be still locked and shuttered with graffiti plastered all over the iron gates, and when Roger drove the car over to take a last proud look at his Hacienda, he tried unsuccessfully to engage the gardeners in conversation only to learn absolutely nothing. So, had the business in Nice been re-started by the consortium under a different name? Was it possible that Romano still controlled it from some remote castle hidden away on a faraway island? At the end of the day Roger was no wiser, but whatever the answer he wished Romano good luck.

He had trouble finding Amin's house and there was no answer when he knocked on the door, then realized that the house was no longer occupied. No signs of Amin or his football friends at the gym. And on Roger's second visit to the gym he tried to describe Amin to the receptionist who was too amused by his attempts to speak French to offer much help. Eventually Roger left his mobile number with her, and asked her to pass it on to any gym member called Amin.

He watched the street life from the apartment balcony. Did he really want to leave? The apartment's Liverpool lady arrived with mop and bucket as he was packing.

'Are you here for long luv?' she asked.

'Just going,' he replied. 'But back again very soon – you can count on it.'

291

As a final thought, Roger contacted the letter writer from Bern and was lucky enough to catch him with his first telephone call. Roger explained that he was now based in England hence the late reply. Liam from Bern politely dismissed all apologies.

'Are you in Nice now Mr Kelly?' he asked. 'I will be delighted to cover your expenses if you could meet me in Geneva?' Was this the fulfilment of his ambitions? Romano had painted the picture – *Potential clients will admire your design Mr Kelly and seek to discover the name of the architect. Your name becomes important.*

It meant a snap decision. 'I can be in Geneva by Saturday,' replied Roger.

Starting out from Monaco it took Roger a steady eight-hour drive via Grenoble before he reached Geneva and booked into the Beau Rivage Hotel. Hang the cost! If he was going to drive all this way for a business meeting, he was going to do it in style and stay in a classy hotel. Besides, he wasn't paying the bill.

He didn't eat in the hotel but wandered out to find a suitable restaurant for dinner. Roger always imagined Switzerland as very clean and pure, with thatched cottages, cow-bells, and mountain guides yodelling from the mountain tops.

After wandering through a few streets at the back of the hotel, he was surprised to find himself in the middle of the roughest red-light district imaginable. Time only 7 pm and there must have been more prostitutes touting for business on this one street than you could find in the whole of London and Manchester joined together. What's more, most of the prostitutes looked frightening – who were their customers?

This wasn't a night to get himself into trouble so Roger back tracked and found a pleasant little restaurant overlooking the '*Jet d'eau*'. He would have far preferred to sit watching the comings and goings of the naughty ladies, but sometimes one has to adjust one's taste in entertainment to a higher plane. Geneva – the centre of international diplomacy. He wondered – did many of the diplomats hold meetings on *Rue de Berne* with the naughty ladies?

Liam met Roger for breakfast in the Beau Rivage. He turned out to be an intriguing man. Banking took him all over the world and apart from his yacht in Nice he owned houses in Frankfurt, Hong Kong, and London. Whilst eating a plateful of sausages and eggs he described the piece of land he had bought overlooking the lake at Vevey. His eyes never left the wiggly bottom of the waitress as he described his vision of a comparatively modest villa where his wife would feel safe when he travelled away on business. The waitress with the wiggly bottom was rewarded with a ten-euro tip, and since money seemed to be no object Roger pondered on what Liam might consider to be a modest sized villa.

A chauffeur driving a vintage Bentley collected them from the hotel, and during their drive along the lakeside Liam expanded his views on finance and banking. He was such an agreeable, modest man that Roger couldn't picture him in the cutthroat world of high finance. But for anyone wishing to escape the strains and pressures of modern living Liam had chosen the right place for a villa.

Vevey had to be perfect – it was beautiful! One glance at where Liam's piece of land was situated told Roger that this was the ideal spot to accommodate his original sketch of a waterside villa. His own 'hacienda' – unchanged, unadulterated, unspoiled. If they could reach an agreement the job would be a cinch.

They ate lunch in Vevey's main square, and in the afternoon Roger completed his measurements and took photographs whilst Liam spent most of the time on his mobile phone holding a long conversation with his wife. Whatever they discussed added to the mood of conviviality, and by the time they made the return journey to the hotel Liam sizzled with enthusiasm. He insisted on paying for another night in the hotel so they could meet again next morning, and when later Roger set about sketching a rough plan of the villa (a plan which he knew by heart) he looked out over the calm waters and flickering lights of Lake Geneva thinking to himself – 'this is too damned good to be true'.

Casting his mind back – he had given up on his ambitions too easily. He had set out to make a name for himself and succeeded. His leaflet in the Yacht Club had resulted in three contracts from Yacht owners, and now the undertaking to design a Swiss villa was as good as in the bag. As far as he was concerned his connections with Romano were forgotten and need not affect future business. Roger was pleased with himself and slept well.

Can it be experience, or some inwardly-born sixth sense that suddenly provides us with premonitions? In the morning Roger was struck by an uneasy feeling – something felt as though it was wrong. Liam was late and when he arrived, he was not alone. The woman with him certainly wasn't his wife, nor was her companion a banker, and the tall swarthy man with a crew cut walking behind them definitely wasn't a banker either. Liam didn't look at Roger. His face wore the frightened expression of a man under duress, he made no attempt to sit down, but was dismissed and left immediately.

Everything happened so quickly – too quickly for Roger to do anything. The man and woman settled at Roger's table uninvited, and the man raised his arm to beckon a waitress revealing a brief glimpse of a black automatic strapped underneath his jacket.

Roger stood up and exploded. 'Who the hell do you think you are?'

'Sit down Mr Kelly,' said the woman. 'You won't achieve anything by making a scene.'

The dark suited minder placed himself within hearing distance – watching.

'And what do you think you two are going to achieve?' demanded Roger.

There was very little to choose between them; they might have been born twins. The woman's iron-grey hair was cut short and mirrored the same style as the man. They were dressed in charcoal grey suits, with the same grey lined faces covered by the same grey horn-rimmed glasses, and the only thing differentiating one from the other was the woman's skirt. She slid a business card across the table and tapped it with an ebony painted fingernail.

'My colleague and I represent an international inquiry agency given the task of investigating the collapse of the Romano business consortium. You have been identified as a significant employee, and you have been watched ever since you arrived back in Nice.'

'I don't give a fuck who you are,' said Roger. 'You have no right to watch me and no right to interfere with my client. This is Switzerland – not Chicago. Let's include the police, shall we?' As Roger moved out of his chair the man gripped his arm.

'The police can't protect you – we can. Before complicating matters my colleague has something to show you.' There was no attempt to make introductions. Tight lipped the woman opened her handbag and took out a handful of photographs.

'Roger – I'm sure you remember Eric? These are photographs of him when he was found dead in his hotel bedroom.'

The horrific nature of the photographs could not disguise who it was. There was no mistaking him. Eric hung by a cord – naked. Tongue bloody and protruding, with his eyes screwed up in agony.

'And here is a photograph of his partner – dragged out of the harbour in Marseilles only three weeks ago.'

Roger went into shock. He couldn't move. The waitress came to the table and the man ordered three coffees and a double brandy. Roger's hand shook as he sipped the brandy and he slopped half of it onto the table. The woman said nothing more but watched him intently as she returned the photographs to her bag.

'Mr Kelly,' said the man, 'the disappearance of Antonio Romano has implications worldwide. True – Romano was a mere puppet handling properties for an organization operating only in France and Italy. But his property consortium was tied to other consortiums run by people in very high places, and the people in high places believe Romano can provide a link to the organization's financial collapse.'

Both the grey people were English. The brandy took effect and Roger calculated he was dealing with two professionals who made investigation their full-time mission.

'Our employers are not responsible for what we have just shown you, but it is their duty to warn you,' said the woman. She adjusted her glasses and glanced at some papers while waiting for his response. Her grey eyes seemed to penetrate his head and bore into his thoughts.

'So where do I fit into this?'

'Oh, come on Roger. Don't play us for a couple of fools.' She gave a dismissive laugh – a silly laugh. She might have been questioning a friend's party piece. 'You have been carrying out a detailed inspection of the Romano rental villas and offices. You drove out to check on Romano's home and newly built villa. And you spent time looking for his North African friends who we believe were closely involved in his disappearance. You must be reporting to someone.'

He felt himself boiling over. The ruination of a brilliant holiday and the destruction of his business plans. Gun or not he had nothing to lose.

'Tell me,' Roger asked, 'do you two get well paid for this job?' The question came as a surprise to them both. The man moved his chair back slightly puzzled. 'If you two are not fools then your employers are. I have been interviewed by police in Nice and Manchester, pressured by the northern boxing fraternity, and now still, you people imagine I know something which you don't. What do you think you are doing interfering with my life? I worked with Romano. I was curious to see the property I designed, and I tried to meet with North African friends in Nice who I used to play football with. Romano employed Italians. The North Africans have nothing to do with Romano. They won't know where he disappeared to and nor do I.'

The grey man looked at the woman and then placed a bulky envelope on the table. His stubby fingers were covered in hair, and it struck Roger that wearing three rings on his right hand was unusual. Nearby the tall swarthy looking man continued to watch them.

'I am going to ignore what you have just said. There is a lot of money in that envelope Mr Kelly. The choice is yours. Describe your African football playing friend who is closest to Romano and give us his name. And also – what about the big man? The bodyguard? Perhaps you can tell us where he disappeared to?'

'You aren't listening,' said Roger. 'I don't know, and your disgusting photographs don't scare me. Take your money and your gun and go to hell. Tell your employers to go to hell too. I don't deal with the world's shit.' He got up and walked out of the room to the hotel reception.

The man followed and called after him but Roger ignored him. The Range Rover was brought round to the side of the hotel entrance and Roger was handed his car keys – together with a bill for 920 euros. Liam hadn't lived up to his promise. The hotel invoice even included

Liam's sausage and egg breakfast.

Roger paid the bill and walked round to his car sick to the teeth. The grey couple's swarthy minder had followed and stood in his way.

'You aren't going anywhere. They haven't finished with you yet.'

'Get out of my way,' said Roger.

'You need a fucking lesson son,' and the man swung a haymaker. It was meant to be a warning, rather than a punch, but Roger's reaction was automatic. He ducked, bent both knees, and put power into a left to the man's paunch followed by a right which connected somewhere on his temple. He kicked the man's legs from under him, jumped into the car, and drove out of Geneva as fast as he could, his mind a blank without any idea which route he was taking nor where he was heading.

The Geneva experience screwed up Roger's mind all the way to Calais. The images of Eric, the shock, and the knowledge he was a marked man. On his first night's stop in a Reims motel, he vomited. Half the night he was up and down with a bilious attack. He realized that when he first moved the Range Rover out of the apartment's car park someone must have spotted it. It meant he and Ana had been followed wherever they went in Nice and the aspect of being closely watched made his blood run cold. Roger remembered nothing about his long journey home.

On the final leg of the trip, he discovered that driving on a three lane British motorway in a left-hand drive vehicle wasn't as easy as he thought. Tired, with senses dulled, the final blow came when he arrived home at dusk and scraped the side of the Range Rover against the concrete gatepost as he backed into his driveway. And he wasn't insured. Why hadn't he left the bloody car in Nice where it belonged? Inside the house he switched his mobile on to receive a text message from Liam.

I am sorry Mr Kelly but we cannot do business together. In my position I dare not risk being involved in your problems.

His problems weren't going to disappear. Roger retired – despondent and vanquished.

By morning Roger concluded that he wasn't accepting any more aggro from anybody.

He phoned Peter Campbell and asked for the rest of the week off. Work was busy and Peter grudgingly barked his consent. Next Roger checked with his father. Initial negotiations with Rosemary's solicitor were at a sticking point. Rosemary's solicitor was holding out for an increase on their original offer, and it could become a long-term headache said his father. A long-term headache – another one. He couldn't do anything about Rosemary's solicitor, but he would draw a line under another headache right now.

He phoned Sebastian Promotions and received a call back from Morris Brooks the same morning. Roger was on his way to meet him when the Greeks' van arrived loaded with paints and plaster boards. The extension was nearly finished. A bit of good news to balance out his diabolical week.

'Did the Sebastian boys pay you?' asked Roger as he was about to leave.

'The Sebastian boys pay nothing until they have to,' replied the senior brother.

'Zay is a set of cunz.'

A set of 'cunz'. That described them perfectly. It was the first laugh Roger had had for days.

The car park wasn't as muddy as when he made his first visit to Sebastian's ramshackle offices. As Roger stepped out of the car the residing Rolls Royce drew up beside him and a big man got out who had the distinct look of Leslie, but different.

'I see you have been reconfiguring your Range Rover?' he said, and ran his hand over the dented side. 'Ask Sid and he will introduce you to our garage who will fix it for next to nothing.' He extended his hand. 'Paul Sebastian. And you are the infamous Roger Kelly I presume? Come on in – let's get to know each other.'

Into the offices and past the sulky receptionist, the room they entered was the total opposite to his brother's vast deluxe showroom in the high-rise flats. Papers were strewn everywhere in disorganized chaos and wastepaper baskets overflowed. Stained deep pile sofas took up most of the space, and the only desk and office chair available was piled high with files and trays containing even more papers. Paul picked up the phone and made himself comfortable in the nearest armchair.

'Send in the usual and ask Morris to come over,' he said. Framed photographs of boxers old and new eyed them from every wall. Every boxer who ever won a title must be here in this room. Overlooking the desk Mike

Tyson hung at a precarious angle smiling at them through cracked glass, and Roger walked over and straightened the picture.

'That was your man,' said Paul. 'At his peak he would have crucified his current namesake, and obliterated our other shining star in the first round.'

The receptionist wheeled a trolley into the room. On top were two plates heaped with hot bacon sandwiches. On the bottom a selection of mugs and a large pot of steaming tea. This was the last thing Roger expected and he found it completely disarming.

'Help yourself,' said Paul. He nodded in the direction of the departed receptionist. 'Just look at what our bacon sandwiches can do for you. She was only size 32" when she first started working here.'

Morris Brooks marched through the door like a hurricane. He ignored the bacon sandwiches, cleared the office chair, and sat grim faced and unfathomable, eyes down behind his thick glasses. He took no notice of Paul.

'Tell me, what have you got for me today, Mr Kelly?'

'Absolutely nothing,' said Roger. 'But we need to talk. I am putting an end to any further cross questioning. Last week I was in Nice. First, I was shadowed, then followed to Geneva where two investigators frightened away my client and then thought they could terrorise me into supplying information I don't possess. Enough is enough! Romano's assistant and his partner have been murdered – we are moving into a different ball game, and I am out of it.'

'We know about the murder of his assistants,' said Morris. 'But let's be quite clear Mr Kelly – we may require information, but we don't murder people. So, tell me – who were these investigators?' Roger handed him the business card. Morris examined it and passed it to Paul.

'Falcon International,' said Morris. 'Serious profession-als. We have had unpleasant dealings with them.' Paul offered no comment. He continued eating bacon sandwiches as though he was watching his favourite TV soap.

'And what was the outcome of this interview Mr Kelly?' Roger briefly outlined his tour of Nice where he discovered nothing. He described the traumatic interview in Geneva and concluded with his rejection of the investigation agency and their uninvited bribe.

'The two grey haired interviewers you describe are renowned for their tenacity,' said Morris. 'They are dangerous people. I am surprised they allowed you to walk away so easily.'

'They didn't,' said Roger. 'Their minder tried to stop me.'

'And...??'

'I knocked him out,' replied Roger.

Paul laughed like the rat-a-tat-tat of a machine gun. He got up and slapped Roger on the back.

'Unbelievable!' he said. 'Fucking unbelievable! Falcon Internationals' two prized grey buzzards, and you knock out their pistoleer. I must tell Sid this one.'

He brushed away an accumulation of sandwich crumbs and disappeared through a side door. Morris showed no signs of amusement.

'Do you realize that knocking out their man was

asking for trouble? You are unlikely to hear the last of it. I think, Mr Kelly, that you are turning out to be more of a liability than an asset. Unless there is anything else, we can safely say that business between us can be concluded.' Ana had said he would have to play along with them but why should he?

'There is one thing Mr Brooks before we conclude our business. I am working with three Greek brothers who completed building work for you and are waiting to be paid. Their payment is now well overdue – I would appreciate it if you will settle their bill please.' Morris Brooks remained impassive. His face never flickered behind his thick lensed spectacles.

'You are your own worst enemy, Mr Kelly,' he said, and walked out of the room without further acknowledgement. So that was the end of that. The Sebastians lived by their own rules. Paul's face appeared round the side door.

'Come through Roger. Renew your acquaintance with Sid.'

Continuing his acquaintance wasn't on the cards. Roger had made his point and couldn't wait to get out of the place. You couldn't dislike Paul Sebastian but you certainly couldn't trust him.

Madison Square Gardens, Rocky Marciano, Ali versus Frazier, all flashed through Roger's mind as he stepped into the vast area of training space. A superb professional boxing gym different to anything he had ever seen before. The professional secret behind the facade of ramshackle offices.

Standing side by side like a couple of benevolent

well-wishers Paul Sebastian and Sid Cohen were a class act. Out of his dinner suit wearing track suit bottoms Sid Cohen looked much smaller, and beside him the fully suited Paul looked even bigger and even more imposing. Paul put his arm round Roger's shoulder.

'You know I had nothing to do with what went on between you and Morris. Leslie conducts his own affairs. We operate the two businesses separately and we don't get involved in Leslie's duff investments.

'Boxing and only boxing,' interrupted Sid.

'You will be interested to hear that we had trouble with Falcon International ten months ago. An employee who we sacked blew the whistle on us. Accountants were sent to examine our books and Falcon investigators accompanied them.'

'Plus, Falcon's troublesome ex-army pistolero,' added Sid. 'You did well not to get yourself shot,' and they both laughed. With his dapper beard and quick movements, Sid was the perfect foil to complement Paul's relaxed approach. The pair of them are as tricky as a box of monkeys, thought Roger.

'What do you think?' Paul gestured towards the ring where two heavies sparred, watched over by their trainer. 'Could you give either of those two a run for their money?' His mobile rang. He patted Roger on the shoulder and walked out of earshot. Sid shouted instructions to the boxers in the ring and climbed through the ropes to brief their trainer. The place was alive. The smell of sweat and the sight of boxing gloves always awakened a strange sense of compulsion in Roger. It was similar to the same force that had propelled him to risk an

305

affair with Helen.

Four boxers were using the bags and a fifth hard hitter left to join a fellow boxer on the skipping ropes. The rhythm of feet and ropes added to thuds from the punch bags, and from the other side of the gym came the loud distinctive patter of someone using the speed ball. The atmosphere was electric. Bearing in mind the trouble that brought him here Roger was annoyed to find himself drawn to the place, and he yearned to be inside the ring battling it out with one of the fighters.

'There isn't another gym like this anywhere in Manchester,' said Sid. 'It's quiet now, but by 5.00 o'clock this place will be heaving.' Paul finished his telephone call and re-joined them.

'That was Solly on the phone,' he said to Sid. 'Our boy must have delivered a hell of a knockout punch on Saturday. Solly's boy has only just recovered.'

He turned to Roger. 'Listen Roger I won't beat about the bush. Boxing is a hard game and it's our job to find hard men who want to box. Having heard about you I wanted to meet you but you aren't a man who wants to become a prize fighter so I am leaving you with Sid – he will show you around. What I want to say is this – boxing promotion doesn't just involve finding men to fight in the ring. We can always use a man like you. So come down and see us any time and if you fancy a training session with the professionals Sid will look after you. And don't forget – we pay good money. Who knows what we might be able to put your way?' He grinned at Roger and gave him another pat on the back then with a nod to Sid he left the gym followed by two hefty minders.

Paul Sebastian had turned out to be a convincing talker and a likeable liar. The separation of boxing from what went on in Leslie's high rise deluxe offices was pure bullshit. Each brother would be well aware of any dodgy deal the other might be doing and no surprise that both brothers needed bodyguards.

The rest of the morning turned out to be an unforeseen pleasure. If you wanted to talk boxing then Sid Cohen was your man. He pointed out different training techniques, showed Roger how to vary a routine on the speed ball, and told tales of the old days when he fought for £50 every week.

Roger liked him. He would be a tricky character to cross but he was more trustworthy than the Sebastians. They stopped to watch as two young Asian boys climbed into the ring.

'Keeping these lads on the right road is no easy task. Drink, drugs, women and family can all interfere with training. And when we shared a promotion with the London crowd, we came across that psychopathic bugger Jason, and he was our worst nightmare. You did Paul a valuable favour there.'

'Jason didn't do me any favours,' said Roger, running a finger along the bone of his nose.

'That's nothing in the fight game. Look at this.' The nasal bone was missing from the bridge, and Sid could flatten his nose to his face like a piece of jelly.

'Remember Marciano?' said Sid. 'He fought Ezzard Charles with his nose split down the middle and still beat Charles. Knocked him out in the eighth round.'

If Paul Sebastian was a good talker, so was Sid

Cohen. It was fascinating listening to him. He lived for boxing. All the old boxers – their fights, the number of times they fought. His stories and memories steered Roger completely away from his reason for being in the gym in the first place, and by the time he shook hands with Sid and thanked him for the morning he felt more like moving into the gym than walking away from it. He walked through reception with his mind buzzing.

'Mr Kelly – Mr Brooks left an envelope for you,' and the sulky receptionist actually smiled at him. The envelope was addressed to the Greeks. Roger's dented Range Rover literally flew back to his house without the wheels touching the ground. He might have lost his contract with Liam, but he reckoned he had come out on top in his first round engaging with the Sebastian Brothers.

18. Sweet Smell of Success.

To the Greeks, Roger was a hero. When he handed them the Sebastian brothers' cheque, he became a star – the vanquisher, their champion. Bottles of wine followed – and then they worked like fury and finished the extension well ahead of schedule.

By the time he collected Ana from Manchester Airport the extension had become his new office with relocated desks and tables leaving room for Ana to spread out in their previously shared workspace. He told her nothing about Geneva, and told the brothers not to mention anything about their cheque. He didn't feel a bit like a hero. He had lost money on the Geneva escapade and although he didn't expect the Sebastians to bother him again he knew that the episode was not a closed book.

Ana had extended her stay in Rovinj by two weeks. She exploded into his arms at the airport, and driving home the sun shone more brightly, and the leaves on the trees seemed greener now she was back. This summer was going to be a very special summer. Roger would make it a summer to look back on. He couldn't know, no one could have known, that summer was the lull before the storm.

Clearing up after the extension was a full-time job which business affairs didn't allow time to complete. On Roger's second day back at work Peter Campbell twisted his foot down a drainage channel and broke his leg in two places. He was rushed off to the LGI and it was two days before the surgeon was available to operate on him. Roger was trained to take over, but in addition to the usual tasks he needed to make regular visits to the hospital and confer with Peter on anything he wasn't sure about. Add that to catching Matt between offices to deliver an end of week progress report followed by traffic problems on the M62, and by the time he arrived home it felt as though half the weekend was over before it had even begun.

Peter's accident meant their relationship developed on a more personal level. The same applied with Matt who relied on Roger for all up to date information. Expansion into new projects had been temporarily put on hold so that full priority could be focussed on the government's social housing scheme. Progress was slow, the most recent delay being caused by a row of houses awaiting demolition and two senior residents determined not to move out of their long-established homes.

Roger found himself in the thick of it. Dreamy days were over. Employment with Mathews Enterprises took priority over everything else and was made even more important when settlement with Rosemary's solicitor happened quicker than forecast. By the time Roger had completed the settlement, and paid the Greek brothers for the extension, his lottery winnings shrank down to nothing. Roger joined the ranks of the needy. Earning money was a necessity and became a serious business.

Ana settled into his old office and was mainly engaged with translations. Requests to host business meetings were suddenly few and far between and she started to feel the effect of a drop in her earnings. Thinking back how amicably Phillipa and Ana got along at their first meeting it puzzled Roger that Ana had never received an inquiry to use her services. Then out of the blue Phillipa telephoned and invited Ana to meet her in their new offices.

The result was an agreement for her to coach Mathews top executives in German and Russian three days per week, with the offer of a very generous pay package attached. The offer came just at the right time, but the downside was that any illusions of independence were now demoted to zero – both of them were fully reliant on earning their living with Mathews Building Investments.

Ana had the Range Rover repaired by one of her old contacts, and since she was used to left hand drive, she adopted the Rover and left her Mercedes parked on the driveway. She was straight into her new work routine. Teaching sales executives turned out to be absorbing and stimulating. Ana was happy – very happy, happier than she could ever remember. Globetrotting assignments had finally come to an end and at last. She could spend time with the man she yearned to be with, and for whom her feelings became stronger and stronger the more she saw of him.

May turned out to be a glorious month. They were both very busy during the week but that did not stop them enjoying some wonderful weekends together. She had said Roger would never seduce her in the Camper Van, but he did. They enjoyed two consecutive warm weekends walking the Dales, and at night parked by a peacefully flowing stream where they barbecued steak and sausages before making love on a blanket, and then again inside the Volkswagen. Ana slept in the roof space while Roger slept below. When her long legs descended in the morning it was a contest to catch her and remove her track suit bottoms before her feet touched the ground – and she always let him win.

Summer moved on. They were invited to dinner with Howard and Joan, and any Saturday night spent with Mick and Wendy turned out to be uproarious. But with so much of their business based in Leeds it was inevitable that when Ana started playing tennis with Phillipa Mathews their friendship would extend to social occasions. Ana's language coaching lessons lasted late into Friday evenings, and she began staying over so she could play tennis with Phillipa on Saturday mornings. Some Friday nights Roger met Ana after work and they both stayed with his parents. Other times she made use of the company flat, which was always free at the weekend. Friday nights weren't a problem to Roger, but the trouble was that Saturday morning tennis tended to direct their afternoon social activities to the wrong side of the Pennines which interfered with any other plans he had in mind.

Training at home became more convenient than driving down to the gym. Roger added a punch bag and rowing machine to the furnishings in his home extension and managed thirty minutes training most nights. A free Friday night gave him the additional opportunity for a run and a leisurely work out, and so he included the purchase of a barbell, dumbbells and bench which meant he could perform a session with the weights after using the bag. If he had stuck to training instead of a Friday night out on the town with Mick, then he might never have bumped into Paddy O'Ryan. And if he hadn't bumped into Paddy O'Ryan and watched him box at the Irish Centre it's unlikely Roger would ever have returned to box at Paul Sebastian's Boxing Gym.

But life is full of 'ifs'. A famous golfer once said, 'give me two 'ifs' in any one round of golf and I will beat my opponent.'

It was years since they had seen Paddy. He used to join them on their Friday 'boys' night out' and compete with Mick as to who could discover the seediest drinking joint in which to finish the evening. He shouted to them as they walked into a bar in the Northern Quarter and gave them a big Paddy welcome.

As ever, he was semi-inebriated and standing holding court with three flashy party goers who were drinking his cocktails and applauding his jokes. Mick sailed straight in. Within minutes he was part of the circle and attached to a bright young girl from Trinidad who draped herself round his neck and stood on tiptoe to speak into his ear. The youngest girl wearing the shortest skirt and the most make-up attached herself to an unprepared Roger.

She was Tracy from Ballymena and told him that even if a man was hung in diamonds, she would never ever marry a fuckin' Irish man. Roger told her his name was Kelly, but he wasn't Irish and didn't want to get married. This seemed to please her. She offered him a sip of her cocktail and hitched her skirt up another inch and said, 'You's is alright Roger, you's is my sort of man.' Paddy was oblivious of his own blonde companion, delighted to meet Mick and Roger again, and ready to

313

move on to the next bar.

It was a warm night and Manchester's Northern Quarter was throbbing. Crowds of drinkers were outside every bar, inside the bars, and occupying every brightly lit space available. The six of them pushed their way through to Paddy's next chosen watering place and descended the stairs in the direction of the music. Tracy tripped, and broke her heel, dropped six inches in height and clung on to Roger. In bare feet on the dance floor, she wrapped her arms around his seat, squeezing his buttocks and rubbing her powdered face against his stomach with one little leg between his as she swayed to the music.

'Roger you's is tempting me,' she said. Without shoes she didn't top five feet and if she dropped any lower Roger feared he might finish the evening missing something. There was a tap on his shoulder and an Irish voice said, 'excuse me' and a tall curly headed man relieved him of a willing Tracy who seemed happy to be tempted afresh, Irish man, and marriage material or not. They obviously knew each other, and after a five-minute smooch Tracy and her new partner left the floor and came to join Paddy's little group standing on the edge of the dance floor.

Paddy's reactions were astonishing. He threw his arms round the man and hugged him exuberantly again and again. Two long lost friends – separated for the endless duration of one week (albeit an Irish week), and more hugs followed.

'Roger,' said Paddy, 'dis is Conner, and you's is looking at de best pound for pound fighter ever to step outside of Dublin.' Conner turned his attention to Roger and hugged him just as exuberantly.

'And don't forget,' continued Paddy shifting back to Conner, 'if you's is wanting a bit of sparring practice then Roger's the man, and he's also the man to have around if you's gets into a rough-house.'

Roger gave a smile and a nod but didn't reply. The music was so loud he could hardly make out a word anyone was saying, apart from which he didn't relish the description of being 'a good man to have around in a rough-house'. Roger remembered many years previously punching the bags alongside Paddy at the gym, and also having to rescue him from trouble one Friday night when he was stoned and legless. As far as he knew Paddy was a bit of a hard case who only fought when he was drunk, but from what he could make out he and Conner had recently turned professional.

Music and chatter became faster and louder, and faster and louder still on their visits to the next two bars. Cocktails had a befuddling effect on Roger so that he dropped any attempt at trying to follow the various scraps of gossip and was more than happy to take a step back. Mick was besotted with the girl from Trinidad, and Tracy was wrapped around Conner. Paddy suddenly separated from his blonde bombshell and barged into the middle of the dancers. Loudly shouting something in Gaelic (which sounded like a war-cry) he swung into action with a whirlwind performance on the dance floor.

From past experience this was a danger signal, especially when he attempted an Irish jig which seemed to bring out his patriotic anti English sentiments. The girls must have recognised the danger signals as well.

'Two o'clock,' said the blonde bombshell – who Paddy had neglected all night.

'Two o'clock,' echoed the rest of the girls, and as one they disengaged from Mick and Conner, said 'Good night', and headed by the blonde bombshell marched off out of the club to get a taxi. Mick looked astounded.

'Has de girls gone?' said Paddy when he finished his jig.

'Not a problem,' said Conner.

'Not worth the cocktails,' agreed Mick.

'No worry,' said Paddy. 'I 'tink dat Mick and I have another wee spot which will suit us all very well wit' a few friendly ladies to entertain us.'

'Pass,' said Roger. 'I leave the friendly ladies to you three,' and to a chorus of dissent he unsteadily exited the dance club and joined the girls in the taxi queue. He was out of practice. It had been a good night but it was a long time since he had enjoyed one of Mick's boozy night's out. When the taxi landed him home, he dived straight into bed and was still there when Ana arrived home after lunch on Saturday. She picked his shirt up from the floor, examined the powder stains, and smiled at him.

'I'm pleased you aren't losing your touch. It's important to keep in training so you can look after me.' Ana's reactions always surprised him. What would Rosemary have said?

'A mistake following a mistake,' replied Roger. 'I'm glad you approve.'

Ana was dressed in her tennis gear and had never looked more attractive. Tanned and fit with her bronzed legs enhanced by a white skirt, tennis was to Ana what football had meant to him. He would join the Mathews team next Autumn. That would fit in with Ana who could play indoors at David Lloyds if the weather was dodgy.

'No chance of you making the same mistake next Friday night,' said Ana. 'We are going to a rugby club barbecue. Go and clean your teeth lover boy and I will make you a coffee.' When he came out of the bathroom, she was sitting up in bed waiting for him. The pale skin of her breasts contrasted with the golden tan of her chest and Roger forgot all about the coffee. As he gently caressed her, Ana's thumb explored the bead of excitement that formed on the end of his erection.

Whenever they made love on an afternoon the rest of the day was lost. Roger could not imagine life without Ana.

Peter Campbell's leg was still in plaster and Roger had to drive him everywhere. The broken leg had taken more out of Peter than he realized, and by 4.00 o'clock he was tired and ready to pack up work and return home. It was a bad time to be out of action. Suddenly work on the housing estate outside Halifax ground to a complete halt. The two senior residents who refused to vacate their properties were kicking up a fuss, and the local Labour MP was holding a protest meeting regarding pensioners being forced to abandon their lifelong homes.

Matt called Peter and Roger into his office. Matt wanted someone to represent the company at the MP's meeting, prior to which he suggested it would be a good idea to visit the two pensioners and find out if there was anything that might persuade them to move. The pot leg made visiting awkward for Peter. Roger made it plain that he didn't rate himself as a diplomat so trying to influence two awkward senior citizens wasn't a task which held any appeal. He voiced his self-doubts.

'As it happens, I agree with you,' said Matt. 'I definitely wouldn't pick you out to be a diplomat, but some bugger has got to do it and on this occasion it's you.' Peter slapped Roger on the back and they laughed.

Friday night was barbecue night. They joined Phillipa and her boyfriend at the rugby club then stayed the night with his parents. He spent a gruelling morning with his father discussing his recently diminished finances before collecting Ana from tennis and setting off to Halifax on their diplomatic mission.

Revisiting the estate, Roger's first impression was of a row of very old black terrace houses which looked completely forlorn on the edge of the empty building site.

The first resident was an eighty-year-old man with a wicked sense of humour. The man was no trouble. He was pleased to have a chat and offered them both a cheese and pickled onion sandwich. He confided that he didn't know why the MP had called a meeting because he was going to live with his daughter and the only reason that he had kicked up a fuss was for the fun of it.

The old lady in the end house was a different matter. She was very upset. She had lived in the same house with her husband for forty-eight years. She was now on her own, hadn't any relatives, had nowhere else to go and nobody to help her. Over a cup of PG tips Roger explained that Mathews would reserve a new home for her on the site and temporarily accommodate her until the new house was built and fully ready for occupation. She was deaf and cantankerous, and he had to shout, apart from which conversation was made awkward because it was plain to see that she didn't trust him.

'I have never had to move before,' she said. 'Tell me – what do you think I am supposed to do now, and how can your company assist?' she addressed the question to Ana.

'Mrs Ramsden,' said Ana, 'please don't worry. We will help you pack and get you moved next weekend. I will make sure you are safely installed in your new home, and I won't leave you until I am absolutely certain that you are happy and comfortable.' Ana's smiling green eyes rested reassuringly on Mrs Ramsden, and without further objection the old lady suddenly sat bolt upright, straight as a ramrod ready for battle.

'Alright then – that's agreed! But just make sure you keep to your promise. I will move next weekend and I shall expect to see you both before then.'

Full marks to Ana. Roger was certain he wouldn't have had the least chance of making an agreement without her.

'That was a promise above the call of duty,' remarked Roger as they left.

'I was thinking of you,' said Ana. 'It will keep you in Matt's good books for when you make a Roger bodge-up of something.' She squeezed his hand on the steering wheel. As he took the motorway, he considered what Ana had just said. Loss of a client like Liam in Geneva was a bodge-up but hardly his fault. At the moment he was on a roller – he was a success, even if today was largely thanks to Ana.

At the beginning of the week Ana wasn't working. She went straight to Halifax and spent two days helping Mrs Ramsden pack. They were both back in Halifax the following Saturday afternoon and shared transportation of all of the old lady's personal belongings between the Range Rover and the Camper Van. Temporary accommodation had been arranged in one of Mathews modern terrace houses less than five minutes away, and after a couple of trips most items were in place and ready to unpack.

Roger and Ana worked in harmony all day Saturday and most of Sunday. When Mathews removal van arrived, they had planned exactly where the furniture was best positioned, and on Sunday evening they had tea with a happy Mrs Ramsden. Roger phoned Matt on Monday morning.

'How did you get on?' he asked.

'Send in the demolition squad,' said Roger, and he could tell Matt was impressed. Matt didn't believe in wasting time. When Peter and Roger visited the site midweek half the row of houses has been transformed into piles of rubble, with bulldozers hard at work demolishing what remained.

Peter accompanied Roger to Thursday's meeting. The MP and the trade union official eyed them both warily. Rodger's suit was getting a bit tight around the shoulders and biceps, but he didn't believe he and Peter (with his leg still in plaster) made much of a daunting pair. The junior reporter from the Yorkshire Post didn't seem to think so either. She took the end seat next to Roger, never stopped talking, and played footsie with him all evening.

In addition to the officials, Roger counted another twenty-seven people attending the meeting. It was very political. The union official spoke first about the Conservative Government's appalling record providing affordable housing for the working man, and the MP followed by highlighting the callous way elderly people were being removed from their homes in order to build prestigious four bedroomed properties designated for sale to wealthy purchasers.

The MP was a pleasant looking guy and a good speaker, but uncomfortable when handling belligerent interruptions. A woman chimed in that she was a single parent with seven children, and nobody had done anything for her, what would Labour do? From the middle row of seats, a rough voice kept shouting something unintelligible. Then an old man stood up waving a stick and shouted, 'What is Labour going to do to combat the Conservative Government's ruthless building programme in Halifax?'

'Thank you for your question,' replied the MP. 'Tonight, we are fortunate in having present a representative from Mathews Building Investments who work in partnership with the government to carry out government housing plans. Perhaps he might like to answer that question.'

Roger had prepared a copy of Matt's plans for the social housing village but he never got a chance to present them. From the back came Mrs Ramsden's voice – loud, no nonsense, and aggressive. He hadn't noticed her.

'What has Labour ever done?' she shouted. 'What do they know about old people's problems? Do they really care about anything other than waving the red flag and wriggling themselves back into power?' The young MP tried to reply but Mrs Ramsden was too deaf to hear him, and each time he tried to speak her voice cut in with another thrusting comment. Next to Roger the young reporter was in stitches.

'Excuse me!' she said 'I'm going for a pee or I will wet my knickers.' Mrs Ramsden was not a woman to be silenced.

'And Mathews Builders are wonderful,' she shouted. 'They build beautiful houses for older people. They have moved me into a new house and sent a girl who is a saint to look after me. If political parties copied Mathews Builders, then England would be a better place.' The meeting never really got off the ground. Interruptions were followed by more interruptions, and you couldn't help but feel sorry for the young MP.

At the end of the meeting Roger had to make excuses when Mrs Ramsden marched over to him to ask why Ana hadn't come to the meeting. The young reporter was an attractive chirpy character. Full of fun and good company. She took photographs of the platform, photographs of Roger with Mrs Ramsden, and photographs of Peter who was busy talking to some of the meeting's attendees. When the meeting broke up the reporter looked at her watch.

'Nice meeting you both. I must dash. I have a bus to catch. Hope to see you again sometime'.

'We are going back to Leeds,' said Peter. 'Can we

offer you a lift?'

'I never turn down the chance of a car ride with two handsome men,' she replied. 'My newspaper doesn't think I'm worth a car yet, and I can't afford to buy one'. Peter was still having trouble moving his leg and the reporter took his arm as they made their way to the Camper Van.

'Whether our long-winded tenant furthered Mathews reputation or not is debatable,' said Peter as he struggled into the car. 'I know one thing – I badly need a drink after listening to that little packet, so if anyone knows of a good pub near here speak up.'

'The Shibden Mill Inn,' said the reporter. 'Just off the main road on our way back to Leeds. And by the way I'm Linda.'

Peter was obviously charmed – especially when Linda told him that her boyfriend was in the army and serving in Afghanistan. They sat on the outside terrace of the Shibden Mill and Peter talked as he had never talked to Roger during their many hours driving around together. He saw another side to Peter. When they dropped him off at his home Roger thought – he's fallen for her. He's fallen for the reporter, and it looks as though she's impressed with him too. Linda lived on the other side of Leeds.

'You haven't told me much about yourself,' she said as they drove across town.

'I don't want the Yorkshire Post giving away all my secrets, do I?'

'Perhaps next time,' she said as they drew up to her house. 'I still live with my parents so I won't invite you in.'

Roger laughed as he handed over her camera.

'Next time,' he replied. 'When you've graduated to your own place.'

'Next time,' she laughed. 'I'll take a note of that. Meantime I had better let you get back to your saint.'

He watched her until she reached her door. Linda was certainly a sparkler. With her laughter and dark curly hair, she reminded him of his early days with Rosemary and if it wasn't for Ana, he could fall for her himself. He turned the idea over in his mind. Tonight, he had missed Ana like he always missed Ana. He sometimes wondered if he was his own man anymore.

'So how did it go?' asked Ana. She was translating a manuscript from German to English when he walked into his old office and threw his jacket on the spare bed. She got up from her chair and kissed him, picked up his jacket, found a clothes hanger, and hung it on the back of the door.

'One problem,' said Roger. 'It went well but you should have been there with me. You were missed – and you may be interested to hear that you have now acquired the reputation of a saint. It's a new one on me. I always thought of you as a sinner.'

'Suddenly you have taken my mind off this translation,' said Ana. 'I think I would rather be a sinner than a saint. You look tired. Let's go to bed and sin first, then you can tell me about your day afterwards.'

He didn't see Peter until Tuesday when he was taking him to the LGI.

324

'I saved this for you,' he said. Splashed across the third page of Saturday's Yorkshire Post was a picture of Roger and Mrs Ramsden under the heading…

REPRESENTATIVE FROM MATHEWS BUILDING INVESTMENTS MAKES GENEROUS OFFER TO RESIDENTS MADE HOMELESS BY GOVERNMENT EVICTION ORDER.

'A good outcome, don't you think? A complimentary article like that won't do Matt any harm. So how did you get on with our friend Linda – did you er…?'

'No, I didn't,' interrupted Roger.

'Don't get touchy old man. Only asking. I just wondered how it is that you got your photograph in the paper and not me?'

'I've wondered that myself,' said Roger. 'You sailed away and stole the show. I had you both down for a secret trip to Gretna Green.'

'Now that shows the value of experience. She fancied you but you didn't tumble to it. Given half your chances I would have swept her away to an exotic island of sunshine and Palm trees.'

'Wait until you get your plaster off before you try that,' said Roger. He cruised around the LGI looking for a parking space. With luck this would be his last hospital trip and Peter could get back to driving his own car. Peter was a great guy who he got on well with, but at the end of the day he was still the chief, and Roger wanted to keep his personal affairs separate from business. With that thought in mind he cursed inwardly when they entered the

325

hospital waiting room and he saw Paddy. Typical Paddy, he threw his arms around Roger then turned and looked at Peter's leg.

'Ah now – here's another young fella who t'inks he can take up skiing wit'out first getting his body into shape.'

Apart from his pot leg Peter's body was in perfect shape but he was amused and didn't raise an eyebrow. A strong-looking woman with the distinctive Paddy jaw emerged from the treatment room and hobbled towards them.

'And this is me muther who practices skiing down the cellar steps.' His mother gave Paddy a make belief clout on the back of the head.

'Who'd have a son like this?' she asked 'I wanted him to be a priest, but he reckons he's a boxer. If he couldn't get out of the way of that one, he'd be better off becoming a priest.' Laughter rippled around the waiting room. There were a lot of people waiting and Paddy was keeping them entertained.

'Are you's coming to see me fight on Friday?' asked Paddy. 'The Irish Centre here in Leeds?' A nurse came out of the treatment room and called for Peter Campbell.

'One minute,' said Paddy. 'I'll bring you the luck of the Irish.' Without any objections from Peter, he bent down and scrawled his name on the plastered leg. 'There now – dat leg will be as good as new when dey take's off de plaster.'

'Mr Campbell,' repeated the nurse. A highly amused Peter hurriedly said goodbye and limped off into the treatment room as Paddy and his mother departed.

Someone in the waiting room clapped, and laughter ran through the room again.

'Those two are a good turn' said the man in the next chair. 'Can't you call them back – we can all do with a laugh waiting around in this place.'

Roger hung about for two hours before Peter walked out smiling, minus the plaster.

They got into the car and drove round town to the Hunslet factory where Matt had set up an afternoon meeting.

'Actually, I did a lot of skiing in the army,' said Peter grinning, 'and I did a good bit of boxing too. Your pal is a character – I wouldn't mind seeing him fight.' As Roger steered his way round rows of Mathews wagons Peter added 'And by the way you can expect to be confined to barracks after today. This is the big project Matt has dreamed about for years. The perfectly planned self-sufficient village – it's going to be all hands-on deck for the design team for quite a few weeks.'

Roger digested that news with a sinking feeling. After taxiing Peter around for a month, he had been looking forward to a spell travelling the area as a free spirit.

The weather was warm and sunny. His first day back in front of the computer was hard work even though he knew he would be breaking off at regular intervals to rendezvous with Peter. Matt congratulated him on his handling of the tenant problem, and now expected him to join the team of architects and come up with inspirational ideas.

Peter phoned him at home.

'Roger I'd like to go to the boxing on Friday night. What do you think?'

'Yes – only one thing Peter – sometimes a rendezvous with Paddy can turn out to be a bit rough.'

'Rough?' said Peter. 'Who do you think you are kidding? You don't know what rough is. See you there.'

They met outside. Roger had never been to the Irish Centre before but although it was situated in a rundown area the inside was pleasant and well organised. Unsure what time the programme started they arrived early and got ringside seats. It never occurred to him that the Sebastians would be involved with promotions in Leeds but the sight of Sid Cohen told him otherwise and a glance through the programme told him why. Paddy was fighting an eight-round bout placed number five fight on the bill. Out of a total of six contests that was a high rating and when Roger looked at Paddy's opponent he recognised the name of the Sebastian cruiser-weight protegé from the Sporting Club evening – Proctor from North Shields.

'These sods are using Paddy as a chopping block,' he said to Peter. 'He's in with a brilliant boxer who hasn't lost a fight'.

'Do you think he knows what sort of fighter he's up against?' asked Peter.

'Paddy doesn't know much about anything,' said Roger. 'He works on the roads as a casual labourer. He's a tough lad with a big punch but he isn't a thinker.'

The first four fights were good fights with plenty of support for contestants with an Irish name. Peter knew his stuff. He picked the winners of all four fights before any contestant had thrown a punch. Number fight five was called and Paddy entered the ring and sat smilingly on his stool as though he was expecting a pint of Guinness. Their seats were within spitting distance of Paddy's corner and he spotted them and gave them a cheery wave.

Proctor from North Shields entered the ring with Sid Cohen and a few others fussing around him. He had acquired a Mohican haircut since Roger watched him at the Sporting Club, and the haircut combined with the tattoos generated the desired impression of a blood-thirsty warrior.

For the first two rounds Proctor avoided Paddy's swings and peppered him with straight punches and Paddy's face was beginning to look like he had spread strawberry jam on it. The boy from North Shields had a habit of sticking his left out like a marker before following with a big right. Roger had noticed the same move when he had watched him fighting previously in Manchester. He walked over to the corner while Paddy was being soused with water.

'Paddy – stop fucking about. You are going to lose. Listen – when he sticks his left out like a marker and waves his glove in front of you knock his arm to one side as though you were using a road mallet, then step to the right and left hook him under the heart with your best punch'. As he sat back down in his seat, he noticed for the first time that Leslie Sebastian was sat in the seat opposite and glaring at him.

Round three progressed much the same as round two and Roger gave up hope for Paddy. Then Proctor stuck his left out stiff as a rapier and circled his glove like a drill before using a hammer. Paddy crashed his right down at the point of his opponent's elbow, stepped right, and dug in with a left hook that sunk so deep that it seemed to disappear under the ribcage. Proctor gasped and Paddy sunk in another, followed by two wild haymakers which both caught Proctor clean on the jaw and his Mohican haircut hit the deck with some heck of a wham which didn't need the obligatory count.

A doctor and the seconds moved quickly into the ring and the Sebastian protegé was propped in his corner to receive medical attention. Leslie Sebastian and Sid Cohen both had their heads together looking across at Roger with what looked like a death wish. His advice had been noticed.

'I don't think I'm too popular with the dodgy crowd who train Proctor,' said Roger. 'It might be an idea to sneak out of here without watching the last fight.'

'You have to be joking,' said Peter. 'This looks like being the most fun I have had for ages. We will wait for Paddy, and all leave together.' Paddy joined them at the end of the final contest and the three went into Leeds to enjoy a late-night pizza.

'I told you's,' said Paddy, 'Roger's is your man.' Peter looked at Roger.

'Yes – I do believe he is. We shall make sure he is in our football team next season.'

Roger wasn't so sure he was anybody's man tonight. After assisting Paddy to beat their potential champion he wondered what debt the Sebastian brothers might try to exact from him this time.

19. Rainbow's End

The dye was cast. Roger's association with the Sebastians wasn't going to disappear. A week after watching Paddy at Leeds Irish Centre he was thrown into the company of Sid Cohen at a kosher restaurant on Cheatham Hill.

Wednesday was an awkward night. Howard couldn't find a babysitter, Mick didn't like kosher food, and Roger was the only member of the lottery winners to accept an invitation to attend Ruth and Malcolm's welcome home party. Reading between the lines the trip hadn't been a great success and neither of them found living on a kibbutz matched up to their expectations. Later Malcolm intimated that whilst his parents were delighted to see them both back home Ruth's parents were disappointed that he and Ruth hadn't stayed in Israel, and a certain coolness now pervaded the relationship between the two families. Be as it may, Max organized an extravagant celebration to coincide with his own wife's birthday and the first guest Roger recognised (dwarfed by Claire and her mother's coiffured hair styles) was Sid Cohen in a seat of honour next to Max on the top table.

It turned out to be a brilliant night! An all-Jewish occasion with Jewish humour and traditions in abundance, and Max, sailing along in excellent form with snippets of wisdom, and frequent toasts from a wide variety of friends. Ruth looked as though she was pregnant and glowed with each toast. Max and his wife were besieged with cries of 'mazel tov'. And to a round of foot stamping and applause Malcolm came out of his shell to sing a Jewish song learned whilst living on the kibbutz. But it wasn't until Sidney came to pay his respects to the elderly lady sitting next to Ana that he acknowledged Roger's presence and even then, he wasn't very friendly.

'You didn't do us any favours when you advised your Irish pal how to knock-out our boy did you?' asked Sid as he straightened his tie in the men's room. 'Anyway – we have got your boy on board. He will take a bit of handling, but I want you to come down and see him training. You might do us a bit of good and him too. We have two months before the serious boxing season starts and, in that time, we have to straighten out his punches and straighten out his head'. Difficult, thought Roger. But further chance of discussion was cut short by another round of clapping and cheering from the crowd surrounding Max. So, Paddy had been taken over by the Sebastians. Was that good or bad? It might be good for the Sebastians but would it be good for Paddy? Would they look after him?

Ana enjoyed meeting everybody. She was a good mixer and a good listener. By the end of the evening, she had become an expert in Jewish traditions, learned a few Yiddish words, and copied down a recipe for how to bake the best kugels. When they got into the car she said, 'What a friendly crowd. But how come you are so popular with your interrogators all of a sudden. Isn't Sid Cohen on the Sebastian pay-roll?'

'I made it plain I had nothing to offer,' said Roger.

'It didn't look like that to me,' said Ana. 'Are you sure you haven't offered to take part in some of their strong-arm stuff?'

'I am not offering anything,' said Roger. 'I'm going

to watch a mad Irish man box while you play tennis.'

The following Friday evening he left the office and drove straight to Sebastian's Gym. He had guessed right. Trying to get some sense out of Paddy was an entertainment in itself and was likely to drive his trainer and Sid Cohen mad. If Paddy was supposed to deliver a right hook it was likely to become a straight left, and if he was required to try a straight left then he threw a right uppercut. Roger climbed into the ring and sparred with Paddy for four rounds watched by Sid Cohen. Apart from the sparring Roger put in his best night's training for months and spent time afterwards learning some of the modern routines used by the professionals. When he got home, he sat outside with a whisky as the light faded. It had been a good night, he needed it. After a week stuck in the office, he had to find a let out somewhere, and whether Sid Cohen and the Sebastians were a dodgy crowd or not, he couldn't wait to get back into the boxing ring again.

It was on his way to meet Ana from tennis next day that he first noticed the house. Whenever possible he visited his parents on Saturday morning then cut through from Moortown to Adel. Today he had wandered off course. The house stood on its own backed by woodland at the very edge of the village only fifteen minutes' walk from Mathews new offices. On first sight it was a wreck in the middle of a jungle, with gardens so overgrown that it was impossible to draw a dividing line between where the garden ended and the woods began. Ivy had gone rampant covering the entire house and most of the windows as well. But what a beautiful property this must have been, and what a beautiful property it could be if the right people got hold of it.

Roger was early. He got out of the Camper Van and looked over the padlocked gates. The original owner must have had aspirations to give the property the appearance of a mill because a large wooden wheel had been added to the side of the house and the residence named 'The Old Wheelhouse'. A couple of stables converted into garages looked to be in good condition, and a solid little concrete gatehouse was just right to be made into a compact office. Ideas flowed. What tremendous potential! Roger never lost his urge to create another hacienda even if it overlooked wild woodland instead of the Mediterranean.

He consulted his watch and got back into the car. He and Ana were driving out to some distant country restaurant with Phillipa and her boyfriend later this afternoon. Phillipa was lovely but he wasn't so sure about her boyfriends. He hoped this latest one didn't turn out to be one of the 'hooray henrys' he had been landed with on previous occasions.

In spite of the never-ending debate over the merits of Brexit, the UK building trade was booming. Houses were selling fast, and everywhere you looked householders were investing in property extensions and house alterations, with scaffolding and builders' skips dominating the best residential areas. Mathews Investments were no exception. They were experiencing one of their busiest years ever. All departments were under pressure, and the detail and design work surrounding the new model housing village was driving the design team into depths of despair.

Ana moved from strength to strength and seemed to be making herself invaluable.

Twice she was called away from teaching to host business meetings, and on one occasion he was able to watch her entertaining foreign visitors and admire the woman he loved moving gracefully from group to group showing off her rose tattoo wearing a long wine-coloured backless dress. Across the room Ana saw him watching her. Their eyes met and she held his eyes prisoner for seconds and her lips parted as she suggestively bit her lower lip. That weekend they spent two tranquil days of sheer bliss camped by Ullswater Lake, and eating their evening meals in a charming little pub on the outskirts of Penrith.

They took a ten-day holiday. After his brief visit to Italy when he crossed the French border into San Remo, Roger wanted to travel further down the coast. They landed in Genoa, and after two days moved on to Santa Margherita where they based themselves in a traditional old hotel with a spacious bedroom overlooking the town's roof tops and ancient church. They visited Portofino, and another time took a train to the farthest village on the Cinque Terre. They marvelled at the century's old seaside villages and breath-taking views of the rugged Italian coastline, and stopped to eat in cafés perched precariously on the cliff edge. The weather was too hot. It took two days to complete the walk around the five villages and by the end of each day it demanded all their remaining strength to climb into the enormous enamel bath in their bedroom. The hotel food was so good that searching for other restaurants was pointless. After dinner they concluded their meal with an evening stroll round Santa Margherita harbour, then returned to the hotel bedroom with a bottle of wine and spent hours making love cooled by a creaking fan which whirred continuously throughout the night.

Ana's language skills were constantly in demand as an influx of overseas suppliers visited Mathew's offices to negotiate and bid for contracts. Roger hadn't been keen on the idea of him and Ana working for the same company but the arrangement worked perfectly. They travelled to and from Leeds together and didn't see each other for the rest of the day until their journey home. On a weekend they developed a different routine. Sometimes Ana took the Range Rover and drove back after tennis, other times Roger took her and collected her if they had plans to stay within the Leeds area. The ivy covered 'Wheelhouse' stayed on Roger's mind and one afternoon he diverted to show the house to Ana. He climbed over the fence and took photographs front and back while she stood watching.

'I sketch how it looks now,' he said, 'then I imagine the house how it once looked in days of glory and I sketch it again.'

Typical of Ana she saw the potential straight away and formed her own picture of how the property could be developed.

'And then what?' she asked.

'I will buy it for you. You can have your own tennis courts.'

'Roger the dreamer,' said Ana. 'Thanks, darling but I already have what I want.'

336

'Not quite,' said Roger. 'And don't forget – I built my hacienda for someone else, and I still have to build one for myself,' and he knew Ana would keep thinking about it long after seeing the Wheelhouse.

Their social calendar became more crowded. George at Zorba's Store served a girl a packet of Kleenex Tissues and fell in love with her over the hardware counter, then threw an engagement party. They joined Mick and Wendy for frequent visits to Ana's favourite restaurant in Chinatown, and Aunt Evelyn had a habit of popping over unexpectedly and not always conveniently.

Roger found it difficulty keeping social life separate from work. Phillipa frequently arranged nights out after Saturday's tennis – usually in the company of one of her boyfriends who she changed as often as she changed her underwear. The latest – Tristan, she met through the Young Conservatives, and Roger considered him to be an out and out twit. His laugh would ascend to a high falsetto at the least provocation, and when Phillipa brought him with her to Manchester for a weekend it took Roger all his time to remain vaguely civil. He enjoyed Phillipa's company, but what the hell was she playing at bringing along an idiot like Tristan?

Phillipa's Manchester visit preceded Matt calling every member of the design team into his office separately for a progress report. When it was Roger's turn Matt appeared absorbed with his head down studying the plan on his desk. Suddenly he raised his head and glared at Roger from under his bushy eyebrows.

'What did you think of this Tristan fellow then?' The unexpected question took Roger aback. Not the progress report he was prepared for.

'I don't know him Matt. He seems alright.'

'You're a bloody liar,' said Matt. 'I bet you think the man's an absolute pillack, the same as I do. What's my daughter doing with a ninny like him?'

Roger felt uncomfortable. Any attempt to interfere with Phillipa's private life wouldn't go down well.

'If it's any consolation Matt, her boyfriends never last for long. Tristan isn't worth worrying about.'

'Tristan,' said Matt. 'What's the world coming to? The trouble is that everyone she chooses is the bloody same.'

Then unexpectedly he sat back and laughed. Ten thirty on a Monday morning and Matt fished around in his desk, brought out two glasses and a bottle of Bells and poured them both a large double. He clicked glasses.

'You're doing alright lad. I've every faith in you. Knock that back then off you go and solve my building problems for me.' Roger returned to his office bewildered.

'Matt's one on his own,' he said to Ana as they sat on the veranda after dinner. Ana thought about it before making any comment.

'Matt's great to work for but he is old fashioned. Phillipa is only twenty-two and she doesn't take her partners seriously. As for these plans of Matt's to create a self-sufficient complex in the middle of his new model village – I think he is wrong.'

'In what way?' asked Roger.

'Well cinema, church, shopping mall, village green.

The cinemas we go to in Manchester centre are always half empty, and even with the massive estate Matt plans to build, will there be sufficient shoppers to make the complex profitable?' Roger topped up her drink. Ana could be relied upon for practical opinions.

'Matt is determined to press ahead. Good ideas would be welcome.'

'They aren't my ideas. It's just that in Croatia and Italy they do things differently.

'Even the smallest village has its own sports centre with football pitch, tennis and squash courts. They become a central meeting point for parents and children whether they play sport or not. Add two or three essential shops and I think you would be more likely to achieve what Matt is looking for.'

Ana had had a long day translating a novel for a German publishing company. They retired to bed and she was asleep the moment her head hit the pillow. Roger couldn't drift off. He respected Matt and supposed it was a compliment being taken into his confidence, but figuring out the ramifications attached to this social housing estate wasn't fun and other ideas started to take shape and make a circular tour of his brain. He wasn't going to sleep, and careful not to disturb Ana, got out of bed.

He put on a track suit and walked through to his new office. The spacious lay-out beckoned him back where he wanted to be. Independent and creating his own visions. The office was warm and stuffy. He could even imagine the late summer sun had a touch of Nice about it. He opened the side window to let in some air and his shoulder brushed against the punch bag which began to sway keeping him company with a satisfying creak. His swivel chair was comfortable and the drawing board set up waiting for him. He began to sketch and there was no stopping him.

Travelling across the paper his pen had trouble keeping pace with his ideas and his ideas had trouble keeping pace with his pen. At 6.00 am Ana awoke and found him missing. She came into the office with a coffee and sat down beside him wearing his dressing gown. Wasn't that where their love story began? She admired his work, pointed out a few of her own suggestions, and then dragged him back to bed where he slept until 10.00 am. He let the team manager know what he was doing, ate a big boy breakfast, and then worked solidly throughout the day until he had a viable plan to present to Matt.

Ana was close at hand working on her translation. They had a coffee together and she added her own interpretation of what was required. When he put away his pens, she was jubilant but said nothing although her eyes said everything. But when he turned off the light again his mind wouldn't settle, and he had his second sleepless night tossing and turning in all directions, with his imagination working over-time.

Wednesday was Ana's teaching day. She took charge and drove the Range Rover to Mathews offices. He had never worked closely with the design team but Simon the team leader was a good man, and Roger didn't want to override his authority. When the blueprint outlining his ideas was rolled out, followed by an illustration of how the plan might look, the whole team gathered round. Within minutes they were sold on the whole concept and Simon contacted Matt to say they had come up with a new prototype. At the other end of the phone a sceptical Matt wasn't encouraging.

'Right! 9.30 am prompt at the factory – and God help you if you waste my time.'

'God help us if we do,' remarked Simon as he put the phone down.

Roger had made a good job of the design work, nevertheless it was an interpretation of Ana's ideas, and he wanted her with him when they met Matt. They arrived at the office at the same time as Simon, but Peter and Matt had beaten them to it and the atmosphere wasn't good. Anything delaying Peter wouldn't be well received.

Roger laid out his drawings explaining that Ana's ideas had instigated his work and from thereon Ana took over. First, she painted a picture of villages she had visited on her travels and the unifying effect of sport experienced by village residents both old and young. She pointed out Roger's layout of the sports centre offering swimming, indoor tennis courts, and squash. Coupled with outdoor tennis courts and a football pitch, a large cafeteria attached to the sports centre could be built to seat customers inside and out, offering a view of most sporting activities. A medical centre on the other side of the building and, completing the semi-circle a group of three shops, a general store, a pharmacy, and most importantly a bakery which could provide additional café facilities. A school, separate nursery and safe play area (equipped with swings and slides) was positioned on the far side of the football field – and all sections were linked by a maze of tree lined avenues and flower beds.

Roger had gone to town with vivid colours on the intersecting avenues and made a glorious feature of the flowerbeds. Emphasis was placed on the area being 'car free' and a separate fold-over page re-illustrated a plan of the surrounding village where road links included a cycle path, with safe pavements separating pedestrians from cars.

Ana's whole theme was built around health and community – bringing people together with sufficient shopping facilities, a good school, and the possibility of taking part in creative activities within a convenient area.

Matt sat expressionless throughout the presentation, and Peter gave the impression that he would listen politely before he knocked it.

'And what about a pub?' he asked. 'Surely that would bring the community together and achieve more than the whole of Roger's elaborate plan?' Ana had anticipated the question of a pub long before Peter asked it. She smiled and her eyes rested on Peter.

'Why do the British believe the English pub is the answer to everything? A pub is the last thing you want in a village. Sale of alcohol encourages youths to hang about, drink and cause trouble. And if the general store has a licence to sell wine and spirits it becomes a target for break-ins, and together with your proposed shopping mall the area degenerates into a scruffy spot with troublemakers hanging around the empty vandalised shops. There's plenty of pubs and struggling shopping malls around Halifax, Peter. Matt is looking to provide a model social environment. It's something you are passionate about isn't it, Matt? What I am passing on to you is simply a picture of what I see elsewhere. And what happens in some other countries seems to me a lot better than what happens on our own big housing estates here.'

Ana sat down. She had pitched the whole plan perfectly. Brilliantly. And everyone in the room knew the plan was brilliant.

Simon polished his glasses and said nothing. Matt's finger investigated his nose while he thought about it. Peter turned to Ana and complimented her.

'That is a superb detailed piece of work you have achieved between you, and I want to congratulate both of you.' Then turning to Matt, 'But before we consider this, may I point out that any change of direction will take months to turn around, mean fresh planning applications, and involve the long process of obtaining an agreement from the government.'

'But it will create a unique forward-looking flagship for Mathews Building Investments,' interrupted Roger. 'And Peter – if it costs less than building a shopping mall, a church, and a cinema, won't that make it more appealing to government?'

'We will retire to the canteen,' said Matt. 'You buggers have given me a headache.'.

Matt didn't decide to adopt the plans that day. It was over a week before he got in touch with Peter and asked if they could all meet again in the new offices. Phillipa was there, and the whole design team attended. Roger's plan was adopted to a round of applause, and Ana was brought into the meeting with equal acclaim. For the first time it struck Roger – he and Ana were madly attracted to each other but in addition they had now become a team, and that was how they were perceived in the workplace.

The rest of the month was a roller-coaster. There was a holiday break from language tuition and the executives took Ana out to dinner and bought her an engraved silver bracelet. Matt called Roger into his office, extended his contract, and offered him a substantial pay rise. Detailed work on the Halifax social housing site started all over again and Roger was outside working with Peter – this time in much better weather, and only a forty-minute drive away from home. Peter accepted the change in direction without animosity, but barked out instructions as though Roger was his new apprentice.

In a more affable moment, he said to Roger, 'You're a damned nuisance you know. I agree with your proposals – a superb piece of work. But you have landed us right in the fertilizer. Now I have to re-allocate planning space, you will be re-sketching it, and I have to monitor your results. If you aren't at football practice next Saturday, you're sacked.'

Managing the Mathews football team was Peter's second love in life. Roger bought a new pair of boots and was in top form when he played. Half the players were builders he had met on site, and they gelled together well. At the end of the game, he was voted captain – and once again found himself pushed into the limelight.

It was bank holiday and he and Ana drove up to Northumberland for a few days. Everywhere was busy – schools were still on holiday and most places were fully booked. However, as luck would have it, he stepped into a room cancellation in a hotel overlooking Bamburgh Castle, and although the weather was changeable and the sunshine spasmodic, they managed to enjoy two mornings and an afternoon lying out on the smooth stretch of sands between Bamburgh and Seahouses.

'It's not the South of France,' said Roger. 'But something about this weekend seems very special.'

'I know what you mean – all our weekends are special, but there's something different about this trip that is perfect.'

They would be lying on the beach, and one time walking on Holy Island, and Ana's eyes would meet his. Whatever the time of day, they both knew they had to get back to their hotel room. 'Do not disturb' notice was hung outside on the door handle and the latch dropped. Ana would tremble with excitement as he kissed every inch of her body, and she gasped when he entered her and her eyes took in his every movement as she willed him on. Their desire never waned. It continued to be a deep feeling for each other which had to be satisfied, and the slightest touch triggered it off.

The merry-go-round continued to turn. A new role at Mathews was offered to Ana. She was asked to create her own language and business hospitality department, with a full-time salary and the authority to engage assistants and run her own section. For the first time since leaving university, Ana had found an interesting job which challenged her and also offered her security. She was delighted.

September still felt like summer. The weekends dawned brightly, and the months stretched ahead with euphoric certainty. Roger turned down the offer of a company car in favour of a monthly fuel allowance which helped run the Volkswagen. Peter was taking regular trips to London to take part in the 'Green Energy in Your Home' conferences, and selected Roger to accompany him. Between Ana's new wage package and his own improved contract, the money began to flow back into the Kelly coffers, and he hardly missed the expensive pay-out which came when he settled his divorce bill.

The weekend was all planned out. It was his mother's birthday and his father had organized a theatre trip on Saturday evening, then lunch at his parent's house on Sunday to include Aunt Evelyn and six of his parents' golfing friends. Roger had just collected Ana from tennis when she received the first call on her mobile. The call was from Croatia, and when Ana answered her phone, their perfect day came to an abrupt end.

Suddenly summer was over, and the cold grey of autumn descended on them like a cloak. The roller coaster had travelled its distance.

20. Without Hope

Ana's unexpected departure spoiled the weekend. Roger consoled himself with the fact that she hadn't been home to Croatia since their trip to Nice, and even if her sister was ill, he expected Ana back within a few weeks. He had a heavy workload to cope with. Matt couldn't make up his mind whether he wanted Roger supporting Peter on the building sites, or else involved in the ever-changing design problems in planning department. Keeping both camps happy didn't leave Roger much time to worry. Ana kept in touch and by the sound of it her sister was on the mend.

Two weekends passed pleasantly. He enjoyed a couple of Saturday morning football matches, and twice drifted down to Sebastian's gym to train with Paddy. Manchester Sporting Club was holding its first boxing dinner of the autumn season. Roger bought two tickets, Peter came over to Manchester, and they watched a much-improved Paddy box six rounds and win on points.

When Ana hadn't appeared home after two weeks Roger started to get worried. Peter sensed the change and reverted to Warrant Officer Campbell again. Short sharp commands erased any possibility of lethargy, but Roger remained uneasy until three weeks later when Ana was on her way back and touched down at Manchester Airport.

The moment he met her he could tell it had been a bad trip. Over the phone she had explained that Petra was in and out of hospital, but he hadn't expected Ana to come back looking so tired and physically worn out. She was glad to see him. She kissed him, and hugged him, and told him how much she had missed him. But this wasn't Ana – she went straight to bed and all she wanted to do was to sleep the day away.

What happened in Rovinj wasn't going to interfere with their lives. Roger set out to put things right. He couldn't take time off work, but he made sure he finished early, took over shopping and cooking, and moved into the spare bedroom so she could sleep without being disturbed. Every day he bought her a fresh bunch of flowers so that the house started to look like a greenhouse. As he deposited fading bunches on the compost heap it struck him that he hadn't touched their back garden for months.

He dragged Ana out to walk around the village. They walked and talked, and she told him how Petra was undergoing chemotherapy, and how ill she was after each session. During this period, Luke developed asthma and she and Petra's husband got up most nights to deal with Luke's asthma attacks. Ana had completely lost her appetite. He cooked small carefully presented portions of food, trying to make them appealing in order not to outface her. He set the table and dressed it with roses and called her when the meal was ready.

She watched him and quietly smiled, 'This is a Roger I haven't seen before. He is new to me. Not the dragon slayer.'

'This is an Ana I haven't seen before either, and wherever the dragon may be lurking you and I are going to slay it together.'

But Ana made no attempt to resume her new post with Mathews – she wouldn't even discuss it. Roger made excuses for her when he visited the office, and shared his troubles with Peter whilst working on site.

'She's suffering from depression,' said Peter. 'I know what it's like. My wife had depression for months after a miscarriage. Ana's a fighter – carry on as normal. Just give her time and she will snap out of it.'

Snapping out of it didn't happen. She insisted he left the spare bedroom and slept with her in their king-sized bed but nothing else changed. She would put her arms round him and hold him tight – but Roger sensed she did not want to make love, and he didn't try.

One evening he arrived home to find Phillipa sat with Ana in the lounge. Phillipa stayed for dinner and didn't leave until late. She was the perfect guest. By now, her and Ana were close friends, and she made it clear that Matt would keep Ana's job open as long as was necessary until Ana felt well enough to return to work. Over dinner she made them laugh with stories of Matt's reactions to various boyfriends (especially a new bearded cook called Basil) and Ana so enjoyed her company that Roger left them alone for an hour while he worked in his office. His spirits soared. As Phillipa left he thanked her and received his usual kiss. But the moment she was gone Ana seemed drained and depressed again, and he was disappointed to see how she slipped right back down to rock bottom.

He wasn't going to be beaten. He made jokes, made mistakes, made a mess. He was Roger-the-bodger all over again and kept things going, never letting Ana see he was finding it hard to cope. He would catch her looking at him and then she would quickly look away – as though he had caught her thinking some secret thought she didn't want

349

to share. At work his concentration went haywire.

October brought with it cooler weather. The autumn leaves changed colour and the surrounding trees in the village were turning into a mass of contrasting gold. When he and Ana walked round the village early on an evening, they both appreciated the beautiful tapestry of vibrant shades, and walking with her arm tucked in his, Roger felt a sense of peace which radiated from that closeness between them. The feeling was always there – laid like a warm sleeping butterfly across the pit of his stomach. Things were improving – Ana was coming round, and at last she made a move and began work translating through her contacts made over the internet. They started to make love again, her appetite improved, and normality very slowly edged its way back into their lives.

When the second telephone call came it was late in the month. Suddenly Ana was Ana again. She sprung into life. Clear cut decisions – cool, decisive, and authoritative, worried he might try to change her mind.

'I'm sorry Roger – but I have to go. You do know that I have to go darling, don't you? No matter how much I want to stay with you, I have to go. I can't live with myself if I don't.'

There was nothing Roger could say. It was fate, circumstances. Perhaps they had been living a dream that was too good to be true. That night they made love, and it was need rather than passion; love making which drew him into her as though Ana wanted to absorb him, take him away with her, and keep him there forever.

He ran her to the airport the following day. There

were no reassurances, no last-minute promises, they parted in an unnatural silence, numbed with very little to say to each other. Roger drove home from the airport empty of all emotions, with ice cold feet like the beginnings of flu. Ana's red Mercedes and the left-hand drive Range Rover sat forlornly on the house driveway awaiting him.

There was a text message from Ana when her plane landed, then another text the same night. If Petra had been rushed into hospital, she must be very ill, and Roger understood that. But it was a hell of a jolt losing Ana when they had so much to look forward to, and he had no idea how he was going to handle life until she came back.

He had booked two weeks in Cyprus at the end of October and he cancelled it. Rain rattled down in buckets as he sat at his desk in the evening overlooking the wet garden trying to come to terms with the latest turn of events. His thoughts went out to the family – he had loved being with Luke the last Christmas, with the little boy climbing on his bed and shouting 'football'. And Ana's sister Petra. So happy to feel well again – and now the same problem all over again and the misery of hospital treatment. A splash of water alerted him to a leak above the window frame. He mopped up the water (thinking of sunny Cyprus) then left a message asking the Greeks to call round and take a look at the leak when they had time.

On site, Roger was working alone for a few days. He had to push himself to make any headway, with legs heavy as lead and an overwhelming desire to down tools, leave everything, and hide away in some far-flung corner of the earth. The Greek brothers rescued him from the whisky bottle – two of them were waiting for him when he reached home. The leak had been mended and could they have a word with him?

'We have bought two houses Mr Kelly,' said the senior Greek. 'These are investments and we turn them into flats. We are here to ask if you could plan this work for us?'

'Where are the houses?' asked Roger.

'Near Leeds cricket grounds. And we must obtain permission from the council before we begin, and we would ask for you to do this for us.'

Headingley Stadium was within easy reach of Mathews football pitch, and it struck Roger that taking a look at the properties might solve the prospect of a bleak Saturday afternoon on his own.

The decision snapped him out of his despondency and kept him busy both days. He played football Saturday morning, looked at the houses in the afternoon, and spent most of Sunday discussing with the Greeks how best to re-structure the floor space to turn it into flats. Monday morning was the start of another week working in Leeds office.

After dealing with the houses in Headingley, he set off to stay the night with his parents taking the road through Adel and passing 'The Old Wheelhouse'. Light was just beginning to fade, and pink clouds and half of a crimson sun cast a rosy glow on the ivy-covered house as the sun began to set behind the property.

Roger stopped the car and backed up to sit watching the grey slates on the roof merge with the dark greens of the ivy. Tall trees on sentry duty still displayed foliage of lighter greens and autumnal gold, and a carpet of rust-coloured leaves spread out across the lawn extending as far as the studded oak door. If he could capture even a fraction of this aura on canvas what a picture it would make. It would be something uplifting to occupy him. Ana was away for the long haul.

Both parents were diplomatic and didn't press him for details when they didn't see Ana. In the office the design team knew Ana had resigned without giving any indication of when she might resume work, and Matt gave Roger a consoling pat on the shoulder as he passed through the department. Later Peter called on his way home and suggested they finish the day with a drink at the Lawnswood Arms.

'Its bad luck,' said Peter. 'But it's worse luck for Ana and a hell of a lot worse for her sister. That said it's not going to help you or anybody else if you retreat into your shell and make a big deal out of it. You're back on site with me after this week. We have a lot to do and I want you backing me up. Live your life man, and keep your fingers crossed that everything with Ana turns out for the best.'

It sounded like a lecture from his father. Another lecture – that was all he needed.

But a surprise was in store. Except for a card and a present from his parents, his twenty ninth birthday might have passed uncelebrated. But it was company policy to keep tags on employees and Peter came into the department on Friday lunchtime and announced Roger's birthday. To a round of applause he was presented with a new laptop, followed by Phillipa with a tray of coffee and cakes. It was hard to be miserable.

Roger made his way back to Manchester remembering his first meetings with Roger Mathews and his first meeting with Phillipa on the dance floor in Monte Carlo. He hadn't planned it this way but his immediate future rested with the Mathews set-up, and personal problems could not be allowed to interfere with gains made over the last year. Easier said than done – but he had to get on with life.

He didn't see Ana until November. During the intervening weeks he set about working with Peter coordinating all aspects of the revised social housing plan. There were numerous companies to consult, and he accompanied Peter on most of his visits.

Afterwards they weighed up the possibilities on site, then Roger mapped out their findings before discussing the results with Matt, and sometimes Phillipa, in the privacy of the Holbeck office. Roger worked all hours. When he got home the empty house seemed soulless. He got into the habit of working late and missing eating so he could wrap up business for the day and shoot off back to Manchester for a training session at Sebastian's Gym. He was operating on overdrive.

Training at Sebastian's was one thing, but playing football again was the highlight of Roger's weekend. After Saturday's match he sat with Peter in the changing rooms discussing how best to re-position some of the players.

'You've rearranged my building programme so you

might just as well rearrange my football team,' said Peter. 'Are you sure you won't be giving me more surprises?'

'Not that I know of. Perhaps a 'bordello' added to the sports centre.'

'Good idea. But Matt definitely wouldn't approve. Anyway, from what he tells me your speciality is designing stunning mansions for the well-heeled.' They were packing their sports bags and he could tell Peter wasn't in a hurry.

'If you have got half an hour to spare Peter, I have come across a place ten minutes from here. It isn't a stunning mansion – but it could be. I was going to ask if you would come and have a look at it sometime.'

'That sounds interesting. Come on then. Let's take a look now.'

Roger drove them both to the edge of the village, took a wrong direction, and had to turn around and back track before he found the right road. Mid-day was the perfect time to see the Old Wheelhouse. Wood Pigeons sat cooing on an overhead branch, and Crows and Jackdaws circled the trees fooled by the trickle of sun into believing it was early Spring. What he most admired about Peter was the fact that he didn't mess about. He was a man of action who always got on with the job.

'That's definitely my kind of pad,' he said, and climbed over the fence to take a closer look. He walked round the property and prodded around, pulling ivy away from the wall at intervals, and examining another area in a bad state of repair.

'This must have been the kitchen and there's obviously been a fire. The fire damaged plaster and window frames but apart from that structurally it still looks sound. Strip all this ivy away, and replace a few slates on the roof, and this place could be turned into a very saleable property.'

'So why do you think it hasn't sold?' asked Roger.

'It could be many reasons. Usually, the owner is asking too much money. And a lot depends on the Estate Agent being close by and on the job. There you see –.' He picked up the sale notice lying on the ground. 'A London Agent. That tells you everything.' Two white rabbits shot in front of them as they crossed the lawn.

'So, what has my unpredictable friend got in mind? Unless Matt gives you a super salary boost, I can't see you earning the cash to renovate that little beauty.'

'I have a few unmentionable ideas,' said Roger, 'but otherwise I plan sketching a before and after scenario, to fill in the lonely hours of my new bachelor existence.'

'Treasure those hours. I have to take my wife and two kids to a school party now. I must have been mad leaving the army. See you Monday.' Peter got better for knowing.

Roger led the life of a nomad. Backwards and forwards to Leeds. Some nights staying with his parents, some nights at home. The Greek brothers needed more help than he had bargained for. Once or twice during the week he worked evenings helping them, then it was a quick snack in Headingley before driving home, often with unfinished diagrams needing completion. Frequently he caught himself nodding off on the motorway, and one evening was forced to draw into the nearest service station where he slept the night in the Camper van and woke up frozen stiff.

He started missing out on sparring sessions. Sid Cohen phoned him. Paul had three boxers, including Paddy, taking part in a shared promotion at York Hall in London and wanted Roger to join the group.

'Paddy will be more confident with you in his corner. We pay overnight expenses and I promise you a good night's boxing,' Sid assured him. Roger didn't need to be asked twice. Paul Sebastian had hired a minibus to transport the team down to London and Roger cancelled football to travel down with them.

From start to finish it was a wild weekend. All three boxers won their fights, and Roger's influence saved Paddy and another young boxer from taking more punches than was good for them. Working as a second in the fighter's corner was a new experience and he took the job seriously.

Tables in a West End restaurant had been booked for when the boxing finished, and Paul Sebastian was a brilliant host providing only the very best for all members of his party. The Chinese meal was a sumptuous occasion, and no expense had been spared in providing the very best hotel rooms. And that was only the beginning. Entertaining his party of boxers and trainers then progressed to an amazing jazz club, followed by an hour in the casino joined by the four models who had toted the placard numbers around the ring at York Hall.

Paul beamed and gave him a nudge, 'Everything OK? If you fancy one of the girls, it's on the house.'

Roger didn't, but knew there was more to come when the party gathered expectantly in Paul's palatial bedroom suite. More drinks all round, two bottles of champagne, then Paul the perfect English gentleman, ushered the models into the room as though they were Royalty. One by one they performed a strip tease and the only man watching who was stone cold sober was Sid Cohen.

The noise must have been heard across the hotel when Paddy joined the last strip tease artist and discarded items of clothing in concert with her, starting with his socks. It was ridiculous but hilarious. Roger clapped and shouted with the rest of them but was clear headed enough to notice that Sid didn't look too comfortable with the way events were heading, and used his glasses to glance at a message on his mobile phone.

To a round of applause the model finished her strip tease by taking off her briefs, and Paddy fell onto the floor whilst struggling out of his under pants. The model planted a foot on his bare bottom, then danced across to Sid and removed his glasses, cocked up one leg and 'hey-presto' – the glasses disappeared.

That had to be the finale. Sid wasn't amused and refused the invitation to recover his glasses. The model made a great display of retrieving them herself, and handed the glasses back to Sid after polishing them. The party broke up, but what amazed Roger was the complete spirit of abandon that Paul displayed at what looked like a standard occurrence whenever the boxing team came to London.

Three of the models left after having been tipped £300 apiece, and the fourth model remained with Paul. The expense of the trip could be multiplied by thousands. How did this kind of spending equate with the Sebastian's ruthless reputation, and how did brother Leslie and hatchet man Morris Brooks fit into these sorts of arrangements?

Not the sort of night approved by posterity, but the only night in weeks Roger had enjoyed a good laugh and slept without having nightmares. Their bus left London at midday. Paddy sang Irish songs and Paul and Sid joined in the chorus. Totally out of context, the whole weekend was an eye opener from start to finish. He had left his mobile at home – a slip of the memory dating back to the days when he wanted to remain out of sight and unreachable. With cheery wishes and thanks for the weekend the bus dropped him off home.

When he stepped into the house and saw his answerphone flashing his heart sank. Ana's recorded voice was muffled and difficult to understand. She had left two messages. Petra's husband had been caught in a storm at sea and swept overboard. Petra was home from hospital and had collapsed when she heard the news. She had been rushed back into hospital by ambulance with a suspected stroke.

Roger phoned and texted Ana again and again without getting any reply. His fun boxing weekend was shattered. What did this mean for Petra and what would it mean to Luke. He knew the consequences. Ana would stay in Croatia and look after both her sister and Luke, and what chance was there of her returning to England in those circumstances? The reality of the situation hit him like a ton of bricks.

He wanted to fly over to see Ana in Croatia, and she replied 'No! Please don't come Roger.' He insisted, and the reply came back immediately 'Please! No Roger. Do not come it will only make things worse.'

From then on communications between them almost came to a halt. If Ana telephoned it was very late and always the same story. Petra remained seriously ill in Bolnica Hospital, and Ana was by her side as much as she was possibly allowed. Roger felt helpless. But what could he do?

It had been a foggy miserable day. He had spent most of the evening playing about with sketches of the Wheelhouse – wasting his time because right now he couldn't care less about the place. When his mobile pinged with a text message he was surprised to see it was from Monty and he called Monty straight back. Monty had stopped using disposable phones because this time Roger's call connected.

> *'I am working at a casino in Brighton mate – and still keeping a low profile. I've thought about you a lot because we aren't out of trouble yet. Sorry I haven't kept in touch. I change my address every six weeks. I've grown a moustache, and I wear a wig. You wouldn't recognise me. But I know from underworld gossip that those bastards who are trying to nail Antonio are still looking for me as well, and I thought it was a good idea to bring you up to date.'*

Nearly a year since the breakup of Romano's business and still no signs of the troubles being resolved.

Roger described his encounters with the boxing fraternity and gave a narrative of dealing with Falcon International. Monty knew Eric had been murdered but hadn't seen the photographs and persisted with his warning.

'Always remember we are dealing with a complex bunch of evil devils who don't forget. Eric was a bent little bugger for making off with the cash but he didn't deserve to be murdered. Keep your ears open and your eyes skimmed – nothing is settled yet.'

It was a short conversation, but it was bad news. If Monty and Romano were still covering up their identity then nothing had moved on, and the last thing Roger wanted was any further involvement with the whole messy business.

Rain, fog, training, work, the M62 – time sped by too quickly. On the occasions he managed to speak to Ana he was upset for her. She was going through a terrible time and her voice would break when she described her sister's condition.

The Greek brothers were taking a risk and altered the inside of their houses before planning permission was granted. Further work on Matt's estate awaited the final go ahead from London and Roger found he wasn't needed on site, and became desk bound with a hum drum set of tasks to perform. At lunchtime Phillipa joined him regularly.

She asked after Ana and understood how bad he was

feeling. She smiled a lot and laughed a lot, and he always felt much better after they had enjoyed a coffee together.

He hadn't given much thought to the 'before and after' aspects of the Wheelhouse, but Phillipa caught him one lunch break doodling in his scrap book and outlining the house in its present ivy-covered state.

'That's the Old Wheelhouse isn't it, Roger? It's been like that as far back as I can remember. Dad was once interested in buying it, but I don't think he knew what he would do with it once he bought it, and the idea fell through.'

'There's plenty I could suggest,' said Roger, 'but it would cost someone a packet of money and at least a year's work to knock it into shape.'

'Sketch out some ideas Roger. I know you got Peter interested because he mentioned it to my father. You took a look at the house together, didn't you?'

Phillipa gave him one of her fresh-faced smiles. She had recently had her teeth straightened and she looked every bit the English rose who you would take home and introduce to mother. The usual kiss followed and she returned to her office.

He bought himself a steak, chopped up some salad, and baked a potato in the microwave when he got home. After dinner he set up his sketching board and began considering what he would do if the house belonged to him. He rang Ana but she wasn't answering, then Mick wasn't answering either, and with nothing to distract him he put in a useful couple of hours letting his imagination play games with his pencils.

Next day he slid his work under Phillipa's office door

and thought no more about it. He was very surprised when he got a call from Matt two days later.

'Get your coat on lad and come and meet me at the Wheelhouse. I've got the keys and Peter is meeting me there in an hour. And bring Phillipa along if you can find her. I've been trying to get hold of her all morning.'

Roger was amused. If Phillipa didn't want disturbing, she hid away in a quiet corner of the canteen with her laptop. Roger found her, bought two coffees, and after finishing them they made their way to his car.

'What is it that has made Matt so interested in The Old Wheelhouse?' he asked.

'Your sketches, I think. And the company is always on the look-out to develop smaller projects which can be made profitable with a quicker turn round. Besides, he has got a lot of faith in you.'

'If he wants me to turn the grounds into another sports centre there's no shortage of space. But to do that you can forget tennis – we will all be chopping trees down every Saturday and Sunday for the next five years.'

They arrived early and sat in the car looking through the fence. The house appeared dark and foreboding in the wet, a complete contrast to the sunny day when he brought Peter. And without the harsh calls of circling crows, it was deadly quiet.

'You never told me how you re-modelled your face after I met you in Monte Carlo?' said Phillipa 'What happened to you?'

'Remodelled? I didn't think it was that bad Phillipa. But I got my nose broken rescuing a damsel in distress.'

'Have you rescued many damsels in distress?'

He laughed. 'Quite the opposite. Usually, it's me who needs rescuing from them.'

Matt's car drew up followed by Peter, and they both exited their cars in unison. Matt stopped at the fence and stood with feet apart looking grumpy.

'It doesn't look very appealing today,' were his first words as they unlocked the gate. 'Myself, I'd rather live in the gatehouse.'

'If Roger has any more expensive ideas about altering our plans for the village, we might all finish up living in the gatehouse,' said Peter. Matt grunted. Roger looked through the windows as they passed. The concrete bungalow looked in better nick than the main house. Somebody had lived in it more recently.

'It's a bloody cold day,' said Matt. 'I think we will all have a little tot of whisky before we look around.'

Through the studded door and into the hallway – and a large fat rat squealed and streaked out of a corner and ran the full length of the corridor before disappearing at the other end. Roger looked at Phillipa – she didn't bat an eyelid.

'Well nice to know something is attached to the old place,' said Matt. They walked into the nearest room where old chairs and an abandoned settee littered the floor.

Matt opened his case and brought out his bottle of Bells and four plastic cups. He poured out four double shots and the first person to drain her whisky in one go was Phillipa. Roger began to see her in a different light.

'Let's get cracking!' said Peter and they started an inspection of the downstairs rooms.

Five rooms in all – reception, lounge, small room (probably an office space) and large dining room and kitchen which had both borne the brunt of the fire. All rooms had cracked ceilings and damaged wall plaster and were in need of new window frames. In the lounge Peter crossed into the dining area and put his foot through a rotten floorboard. Some of the floorboards on the staircase were rotten, but the five bedrooms were if anything in better condition than the rooms downstairs.

'This house will have been built before the nineteen hundreds,' said Matt. 'You can tell by the size of these rooms. The original occupants of this place must have each owned their own jerry, because there's only one toilet in the whole of the house.'

It was a very high old-fashioned toilet with a wooden seat and pull-down string. Roger thought of the expression 'sitting on the throne' and Phillipa viewed the toilet and scraped enamel bath with distaste. Upstairs or downstairs, with or without lights, the whole house was dark as a result of the overgrowing ivy and surrounding trees, and when they walked outside and round the back of the house the state of the huge gardens facing them looked to pose more of a problem than the repairs needed to make the house habitable.

'I'd have that silly wheel removed for a start,' said Phillipa. 'It's situated in the best spot to build a patio and conservatory.'

Peter had come straight from one of the sites and was dressed in strong boots and carried a walking stick. He hacked his way through the shrubs and overgrowth following the remains of a footpath leading to the back of the garden which eventually merged with unploughed fields and woodland. Almost completely covered by a fallen tree and dead branches was what looked like the surface of a tennis court, with straggles of broken netting lying underneath the brambles.

'There you are Phillipa. Tennis courts as well. A decent loo to sit on and this could be your dream house,' said Matt. 'Get that kitchen in order and Basil can cook us a meal and we will all come to visit you.'

'Is there any need to be sarcastic dad?'

'Sarcastic – what's sarcastic about that?' asked Matt. 'Right! That's it for today. There's a good warm pub five minutes from here where we can take stock of our findings.' They passed the stables and gatehouse without bothering to look inside. Phillipa got into Roger's car, and they followed Matt and Peter.

'Working with my father isn't all whisky and roses,' commented Phillipa. 'Nor is it easy still living at home. When the day comes that I take home a boyfriend he likes, it will be cause for celebration.'

Roger laughed but didn't comment. He guessed it was a day when her and her father were at cross purposes. Sometimes when he talked to Phillipa she seemed very young.

The pub was better from the outside than it was inside, although the place seemed to be a favourite with Matt. They gathered round a table and a sloppy looking waitress came to take their order. Hot dish of the day was her home-made steak and kidney pie, otherwise it was sandwiches and Auntie Mary's Apple Pie. Matt and Peter both chose the steak and kidney pie. Roger didn't like steak and kidney pie and he didn't fancy Auntie Mary, nor her apple pie, so he opted for sandwiches. Phillipa said she didn't want to eat anything, and settled for a coffee made with hot milk and another whisky in it.

'What's the verdict?' asked Matt. 'What do we think of the place?'

'On a cold miserable day when we are greeted by a rat it's easy to dismiss a house that has been left empty for years,' said Peter. 'What impresses me is that, in spite of the need for internal renovation, there are no signs of damp anywhere. It's a very well-built property and, providing council doc-umentation confirms that the whole of the garden belongs to the house, then there is easily room to halve the garden and build another couple of properties with space to spare.'

'And you Roger? What do you think?'

'I can't put a value on it, Matt – that's Peter's field. I pass the house regularly in the car, and each time I imagine what a magnificent house it has been, and how it could be magnificent again with a few alterations. The setting is superb with the woodland in the background. What I can't imagine is the time and cost involved in restoring a place like that to its former glory.'

Matt turned to Peter, 'You've taught this lad well Peter. He isn't just a dreamer of sports centres, he actually considers my costs.'

'I was thinking of your costs when I plumbed for sandwiches,' said Roger as Auntie Mary arrived with a round of ham and cheese on a small plate.

'Those don't look bad,' said Phillipa, and pinched one from him. The steak pie followed, accompanied by a side dish of vegetables and a jug of gravy. Roger admitted to himself that he was wrong – the hot meal looked good, and Matt and Peter tucked into it as though they were starving. He looked around. The four of them were the only clients in the pub.

'This place used to be humming when I was a young fellow,' commented Matt. 'I used to bring your mother here' he said turning to Phillipa. 'In fact – on the other side of the road there's a narrow lane where I used to park the car. For all I know you could have been conceived there.'

Roger choked on his sandwich. Peter knocked his fork on the floor, and Matt sat chuckling with a malicious expression on his face.

'You can quite see why my father doesn't approve of my boyfriends can't you?' asked Phillipa. 'None of them are crude enough for him.'

A fencing game between father and daughter. The atmosphere between them reminded him of the cut and thrust he used to experience with his own father.

After the meal they separated into their own cars and Phillipa left with Matt for his Holbeck office. Peter looked at Roger and raised an eyebrow, 'When you work with Mathews it's a family business. Take no notice of that little drama. Matt thinks the sun shines out of her backside, but they are both strong minded and they clash. Let's see what comes of today. It wouldn't surprise me if Matt hasn't got that house in mind for Phillipa.'

On the way to the office Roger contemplated how Matt ran his business. He could understand the success of Mathews Building Investments with Matt at the helm. He was a character with something very likeable about him. He made you feel part of the business and he was tickled by Matt's sense of humour. Roger stayed late to catch up on outstanding reports, then decided to visit Leeds centre and try a meal in one of the restaurants on Greek Street. After eating he took a walk round town, popped into a pub for a drink, and by the time he pointed the car towards Manchester the grey day had changed into a frosty star lit night.

When he arrived back at the house the Range Rover was parked outside on the kerb edge, and Ana's red Mercedes was missing. He went into the house. Ana's cabin luggage lay open on the bedroom floor with sweaters and underwear spilling out of it but no signs of Ana. Surely, she could have let him know she was coming. He went outside and moved the Camper Van, then backed the Range Rover onto the driveway. Inside the house he sat down with a thousand heartaches and questions that he had felt so many times before during the course of his chequered love life.

He didn't make any effort to contact her – if Ana couldn't text or phone him then he wasn't going to text or phone her either. He stayed up waiting until well after midnight then went to bed and slept surprisingly well. Still no signs of Ana next morning.

In the work's canteen Phillipa joined him for coffee and she knew something was wrong. Roger left the office early and broke all safety rules weaving in and out of traffic on the M62. He walked into the house to find the table laid with a bottle of wine and Ana's sea food mezze to greet him. Ana stood cool and graceful waiting for him.

His stomach turned over as always when he had missed her, and she stepped forward and her soft sweet kiss lingered on his lips as no other kiss but Ana's would ever linger.

'I am sorry Roger – I didn't want to let you know I was coming in case I didn't make it. I can't stay for long. I must get back as soon as I can.'

They sat and ate almost in silence. Eventually Ana said, 'Roger – I have sold my car. I sold it for £20,000 which is a lot less than it is worth and I want to ask you if I can buy the Range Rover from you. I need it to take as many of my belongings back with me as possible, and I need it in Rovinj for taxiing between hospitals and taking Luke to school'.

'You don't have to buy the car from me Ana. It's a great car but left-hand drive is no use to me over here.' They looked at each other and Ana took his hand.

'We have always been honest with each other, and I want to be honest with you now. I don't know when I will be back Roger, that's if I ever get back. I left Luke with my sister years ago and I can't leave him with her again. Petra will be lucky if she survives her present treatment, in fact she will be lucky if she survives at all. I paid £20,000 into your bank account this morning, and I pray for a miracle which will bring us together. But I cannot leave my mother with the responsibility of my sick sister and Luke.'

How do you feel when someone you love dies? It was the same feeling. How could it end this way? He wouldn't let it end this way. They stayed wrapped in each other's arms all night and awoke very early in the morning.

Ana said to him, 'Don't cancel football Roger. I want to come with you to see Phillipa.'

Neither of them ate breakfast. Ana made arrangements over the phone while Roger sorted out a clean football shirt and gathered his kit together. Phillipa was there to meet them on the football field.

During brief lulls in play, he could see Phillipa and Ana walking round the field together. Ana had so much to lose – nothing made sense. When the whistle blew Phillipa had gone, and Ana was walking round the field on her own, head down and coat collar turned up, both hands thrust deep into her coat pockets. She looked so alone, and for the first time he was struck by the magnitude of the sacrifice Ana was making, and he had no idea how he could save their relationship.

He took her for late lunch on the outskirts of Manchester then they returned home and tried to sort out Ana's personal belongings without becoming emotional. Roger made a meal, and they ate in the kitchen, reminding him of the first time Ana stayed before he went on holiday to Nice.

At night their love making was a slow subdued exercise of being close together, and when he awoke to pay an early morning toilet visit, Ana's head had moved to share his pillow – and the pillow was wet with her tears.

All day Sunday he helped her pack. Cases and small items of furniture were carefully slotted into the Range Rover. With the doors open, cold seeped into the house as they carried items to the car, and they were both frozen and in need of a hot shower when they had finished. He would not have believed the car could hold so much.

When the last item of Ana's clothing had been cleared from her wardrobe and squeezed into the available space, it was early evening, and they finished with a sense of achievement mixed with the sense of an ending. As Roger locked the car door and handed Ana the keys, she turned away from him and broke down.

'Oh God – please tell me why Roger? Please tell me why – why does it have to be like this?'

'Ana – it doesn't have to be like this. There must be another way.' She sobbed uncontrollably and pushed him away.

'I've tried – God I've tried so hard. But there isn't another way, Roger. You don't understand. There's is no other way. I have to go back and you would never settle in Rovinj.'

They talked and talked until they were exhausted. They retired and talked some more between tears and more tears. This wasn't the end. There was no way it could be the end. When their emotions were totally drained, pacified, without discovering a solution, they made love convinced that there must be an answer.

Manchester to Croatia was quite a trek and Ana was making the journey in winter, not spring. In the morning he pleaded with her to stay. Then he pleaded to accompany her down to Dover and he would catch the train back. She gripped his arms and he would remember her with tears rolling down her cheeks.

'No, go Roger, please go. Don't wait to see me leave. Don't make it any harder. Please go now.'

That morning's passage down the motorway was the longest, and the worst journey of Roger's life. When he

372

returned home in the evening, he harboured the impossible hope she might still be there. But she wasn't – Ana had gone.

21. No Solution

Weeks passed by and Roger didn't know what to do with himself. Nothing worked.

Empty of Ana's clothes and possessions his home was like a morgue, it wasn't a home anymore. Something would change. He tried telling himself there was no way he was going to lose Ana, but their parting scene played over and over again in his mind.

At the office colleagues were noticeably tactful. In his present mood he wasn't an easy guy to get along with and tucked away at his corner desk it was a relief not to talk to anyone. He had no idea what he wanted out of life but after twice being held up on the motorway, and twice arriving home so late that he didn't bother to eat, he knew there was one thing he could change. His house had lost its charm forever.

Two women in his life had walked out of this house and there wasn't going to be another. Hunters sent an assessor round who revalued the property complete with new extension at nearly double the price he paid for it five years ago. That made up his mind – the house went up for sale.

He had a lot to think about. Phillipa joined him in the canteen and as they watched staff decorating a Christmas tree, she diplomatically asked him what he intended doing over Christmas.

What would he be doing over Christmas? He didn't know and he didn't give a damn. Sometimes there was something charmingly naïve about Phillipa, and he didn't

374

like telling her that he needed the bonhomie of English Christmas like he needed a hole in the head.

But there was no dismissing it. Christmas was four weeks away, and in December he was roped into the Yorkshire Variety Club's Annual Charity Dinner held at the Queens Hotel. It was always an important event on Matt's calendar and Matt had booked a table for twenty. Peter phoned and sounded pleased as though he had done Roger a favour.

'You are honoured. I've got you a ticket and we will be mixing with the bigwigs. Matt likes to think we contribute something towards charity at Christmas, so we pay for our own tickets. £75 when I see you. It's worth it. The dinner's crap but the list of guest speakers is impressive, and it won't harm your career to be seen hobnobbing with the big hitters.'

It was the last thing Roger wanted. Putting on a social face to improve his career prospects never featured highly on his list of priorities and right now it featured well below zero.

Sebastian's Boxing Gym had become the only place Roger could lose himself. Not exactly a men's club but he knew most of the boxers who trained there and felt comfortable with the professionals. After five days sitting at a desk his body yearned for a good work out. A hard session made him feel better – a form of self-punishment. Relief from contemplating the future.

On the Friday before Saturday night's charity dinner something told Roger it was the wrong time, and he was in the wrong frame of mind to stick on a pair of boxing gloves. But Paddy was leaving to join Conner in Ireland, and Roger wanted to wish him good luck before he went.

'Too late,' said Sid. 'Paddy abandoned ship for Dublin yesterday. We've knocked the mad bugger into shape and now he is leaving us to fight across the water. But listen – that's gratitude for you! It's all you expect from the boxing game.' Sid took his elbow, 'Come and see what you think to our new lad. A new sparring partner for you. You can help us show him the ropes.'

The new lad in question was far too handsome to be a boxer. Dark wavy hair, the perfect aquiline nose, soulful brown eyes, and a creamy pearl coloured skin most women would die for. Definitely a boy who would attract a host of admirers and a generous dowry if he picked the right girl. Mothers would be falling over themselves encouraging their daughters to compete.

'My wife's sister's boy,' said Sid as he introduced him. 'Now watch yourself here Laurie. Roger is a hard man, and he eats lads like you for breakfast.'

Laurie shook hands with a flash of charm and a dazzling white smile. He couldn't be above eighteen or nineteen years old at the most. What was Sid doing bringing a young lad like this to a place like Sebastian's?

They both climbed into the ring with Sid in attendance. Laurie would be a couple of inches smaller than Roger and weighing at least two stone lighter. He smiled as they squared up. The boy was nicely built but Roger noticed there wasn't any sign of a single muscle on him. It would make a pleasant change to enjoy a few rounds of boxing instead of having to dodge Paddy's head shattering swings.

Roger relaxed and measured his distance with a long probing left. Like lightning Laurie stepped underneath and shot out a straight left and right. Both landed with pinpointed accuracy on Roger's left eye, jolting his head back and sending his brain spinning. Laurie danced away, smiled, and said, 'sorry.' Then like a ballet dancer he moved forward, in and out, attacking with straight punches and hooks delivered at speed from all angles.

Roger was taken by surprise. Over three rounds he boxed on the defensive with a rapidly closing eye and a fuzzy head. He managed to survive without further injury but didn't land a single punch on the elusive Laurie.

Sparring is different to fighting – it's acknowledged to be a learning process. This boy was a star prospect probably coached for years by Uncle Sidney. Roger had been used as a fall guy to test the boy out, and Sidney had known very well what he was doing.

A group of boxers had stopped training to watch, and when Laurie climbed out of the ring there were shouts of approval. Trustworthy Sid patted Roger on the back but didn't look at him. No complaints thought Roger – 'it's all in the boxing game.' But looking back, first impressions had been correct. Sid Cohen might be a likeable guy who could mesmerize you with his boxing stories but never forget he is employed by the Sebastian's and he is quite prepared to use you.

As Roger collected his sports bag from the changing rooms Sid was still fussing around Laurie with a couple of the regular professionals patting Laurie on the back. Roger picked up his bag and nobody even noticed he was leaving as he quietly walked out of the gym.

It was a beauty. Roger examined his eye in the mirror. He could wear a pair of dark glasses, but they wouldn't disguise the eye. A perfect image for tonight's charity dinner providing Matt and Peter with solid proof that he already hobnobbed with the 'big hitters'.

Roger sat down and considered the situation. He had better change his mind about staying with his parents tonight. It would trigger off a month's lectures from his father, and the return of his mother's worried expression.

Sidney had pulled a fast one on him. Amused by his own gullibility Roger brushed and examined his dinner suit. It was the first occasion he had had a chance to wear it since buying the suit for Monaco Yachting Week. He sorted out a pair of poser style sun glasses to hide behind, and examined the overall picture in the mirror. It wasn't right. Dress was optional, and on second thoughts the Havana style cream suit which he bought on his shopping trip with Elissa would look better with dark glasses. Probably not cricket but he wasn't a cricketer.

He tried again to speak with Ana on her phone. It was no use – she wasn't answering and he guessed she avoided having a conversation because it upset her. They exchanged text messages daily but that wasn't the same. He longed just to hear her voice and the tight band around his chest grew tighter.

Football was cancelled until after Christmas, so he half-heartedly started clearing the back garden when a call from Hunters informed him that his first prospective buyers were on their way to view the house. They wasted his afternoon. A local couple who pretended to be interested, but really came to nosy around and discover the asking price. The back garden remained untouched, and he got washed and changed in good time wishing he was going any place other than Matt's charity dinner.

And the Camper Van wouldn't start. He had left the courtesy light on all night and the battery was flat as a pancake. He fiddled around for ages, cursing his luck as the night air started to freeze, but he couldn't get a flicker out of the engine. Saturday night, and the village garage closed early. He rang the RAC (Roger was insured for home-start) but he sat around waiting for well over an hour before the RAC arrived to get him started and on his way.

He was late into Leeds and finding a place to park in Leeds centre made him even later. When Roger walked into the Queens function room the Master of Ceremonies was in the middle of his welcoming speech and the surprise entry of a man wearing a cream suit and sunglasses seemed to upset him. Mid-sentence the speaker paused, and all eyes were on Roger. With a half-closed eye, and glasses too dark to see through,

Matt's table was a nightmare to find amongst the sea of black dinner suits.

He floundered around, apologised for knocking into a table, and was lost until Matt stood up and waved at him. Roger collapsed into the vacant seat next to Peter's wife with a sensation of relief. A bead of sweat trickled down the back of his collar. This was the kind of Roger bodger entrance of old that often tormented him in his dreams. The speaker cleared his throat and resumed where he left off. Out of the side of his mouth Peter exclaimed, 'Bloody hell Roger,' and from the far end of the table Matt's wife Rene glared at him with looks which would kill.

Roger wet his napkin, took off his glasses and dabbed his eye. Matt appeared amused, and Phillipa sitting next to bearded Basil sat with a puzzled look on her face.

Apart from a few department managers the remaining guests at the table were complete strangers to Roger, and happily no one paid him any more attention. There was a lull. The speaker stepped down to make way for a comedian. Simon, Head of Design, whispered something about Roger into his wife's ear and she turned to take a better look at him, whilst Matt's wife continued glaring intently as though she believed she might make Roger vanish.

Roger hadn't set eyes on Rene Mathews since she explained that, 'we don't want the wrong type of people occupying the villas on Cape Ferrat.' In Monaco she was dressed like a Christmas tree tonight she looked like a French Poodle. It was hard to imagine her in Matt's parked car doing anything which might have once led to the conception of Phillipa.

Dinner was served. Susan poured the wine. She was exactly the kind of women you would expect Peter to marry – attractive, intelligent, and with a good sense of humour.

Thanks to many weeks collecting Peter from home when he had a pot leg, the Campbell family were no strangers to Rodger, and their tete-a-tete together over tonight's dinner was the best part of the evening. Roger looked around. On the table directly in front, one of the guests was the Lord Mayor of Leeds dressed in her full chains of office.

Peter pointed out one or two politicians and TV personalities who Roger hadn't spotted, but when he turned to the left his first thought was 'what rotten luck!' The whole of the Sebastian entourage was sitting on a side table – with Paul and Leslie Sebastian, Sid Cohen, and hatchet man Morris Brooks deep in conversation with an imposing character who appeared to be their special guest.

Paul saw him and raised a friendly hand in acknowledgement. Then Sidney said something to rest of the group and they all looked across at Roger and laughed. Tricky Sidney.

'That's the chief constable of Leeds,' said Peter.

'No – that's the Sebastian brothers. Boxing promoters,' said Roger.

'Yes, but their guest is the Chief Constable of Police. He is supposed to prevent careless blokes like you from receiving a black eye.'

Roger put his glasses back on. He wondered whether the chief constable of Leeds had ever visited Leslie's block of creepy Manchester flats with bodyguards posted on every floor?

'I don't envy the chief constable. You haven't lived until you have been in the company of fat Leslie and his poker-faced side kick. The chief constable might finish the night in a cellar, bound and gagged and held to ransom.'

'Tell me more,' said Peter. 'Better still – save it! One of your admirers will be round in a minute to take a photograph of you.' Roger followed Peter's gaze.

The curly head of Linda from the Yorkshire Post was working her way round the tables assisted by an offbeat young boy whose hair stood up in bleached spikes. Guests started to move about. Phillipa came over and introduced Basil who turned out to be a very likeable guy. As Phillipa returned to her seat she whispered, 'Have you been rescuing damsels in distress again?'

Without warning, the imposing figure of Paul Sebastian left his party and walked across and stood in front of Roger. There was an immediate silence at the Mathews table.

Until he was actually standing in front of you it was easy to forget that his height and bulk were as big as his personality, and Paul Sebastian wasn't going to go anywhere without commanding the moment. He looked round the table as though he owned it, nodded in the direction of Matt, then put his hand on Roger's shoulder, 'I hear your eye has been sparring with one of Sid's relatives. I should have warned you. You will disappoint me if you don't avenge that eye.'

There was a camera flash. Linda had arrived. Paul laughed, then gave Roger's hand a shake as the camera flashed again, and with another nod to Matt he returned to his seat at the Sebastian table. All eyes were on Roger again, and this time Matt didn't look amused.

'So, what's with the Roy Orbison glasses?' asked Linda. Rene and some of the guests were still watching. Linda raised Roger's dark glasses then turned to Peter.

'Look what happens when he stays with me for the night. I have to fight him off.'

'You mean when I stayed at your mother's?' asked Roger. He felt uneasy.

'No – you're behind the times. I've moved into my own place now, but no car yet and I still rely on handsome men like you for transport.' Oblivious of her audience she took another photograph then moved on with her spiky haired companion.

'I'm afraid that little lot isn't going to go down well with the other end of the table,' remarked Peter. 'Let's hope the photographs are good.'

'I don't know about Roger's boxing promoter friend,' said Susan, 'but the photographer is very attractive, and she couldn't have made her interest in Roger more obvious if she tried.'

'What about her soldier boyfriend in Afghanistan?' commented Peter. 'He might come home and shoot Roger, and that's providing Matt doesn't shoot him first.'

A different photographer circulated the room and there were more camera flashes. The evening was drawing to a close. A final speech asking for charity support during the coming year and the parties began to break up. Peter and his wife drifted round to see Matt whose attention was focused on departing customers. Roger had had no luck from start to finish. Now was a good time to leave and call it a day.

The cloakroom attendant mislaid his coat and took ages trying to find it. Then he was delayed by a pompous man who insisted they had met before, and Roger had to convince him that he had never set eyes on the man in his life. Outside it had turned foggy and frosty. Standing at the wrong end of the Saturday night taxi queue and struggling with two heavy canvass bags was Linda, scantily dressed in a flimsy spring coat in which she looked frozen.

'If you trust me driving with one eye, I can offer you a lift,' said Roger.

'I don't trust you at all,' said Linda, 'but thank you – yes!'

He had parked near Park Square. He took Linda's bags from her and prayed the car would start. It started perfectly and that felt like the only good thing that had happened to him all evening. Linda told him she was renting a furnished flat in Headingley. It was near one of the houses being renovated by the Greeks, so even in the fog he had no problem finding it. He took charge of her equipment bags and carried them onto the first floor.

'I only moved in last week,' said Linda. 'You will have to take me as you find me.'

The flat was very small. Joint lounge and kitchenette, with one bedroom and a shared bathroom and toilet at the end of the corridor. It brought back memories of his student days. That first tatty flat with a toilet which didn't always flush and a bath which took half an hour to empty. He remembered his mother's look of horror when she first visited, and his father's delight at getting rid of him.

'How do you go on with your bathroom arrangements Linda?'

'If I want to pee during the night, I use the bucket under the sink,' she said, 'and when I want a poo, I sometimes have to wait my turn at the end of the corridor.' There was one thing about Linda – she was refreshingly candid.

They sat drinking herbal tea and looking through her scrapbook of newspaper cuttings. Most things she told him he had heard before when he and Peter gave her a lift, and most of her conversation was still concerned with her soldier boyfriend stationed in Afghanistan – now keeping watch on them from a safe position on the sideboard.

'Tell me about the saint,' she said. 'Did she give you the black eye?'

'I wish!' said Roger, but instead of answering he changed the subject. Linda sat close to him on the settee, friendly but no games of footsie like on their first meeting. She got up and looked out.

'It's very late and I'm ready for bed,' she said. 'Its foggy out there and you don't have to drive back to Manchester at this time of the night. You are welcome to stay as long as you understand – you will be sleeping on the settee, and I will be sleeping in the bedroom.' The way she said it started them both laughing. There was no mistaking the ground rules.

'Thank you, Linda, – your settee is fine. I wasn't looking forward to the drive back.'

Linda opened up the bed settee and found him a couple of blankets and a pillow. Laughingly she put her arms around him and kissed him.

'Don't think of waking me with coffee before ten, will you?' and she left him to sort out the bed. It was a while before he managed to doze off. The settee smelt of stale cigarettes and every way he turned an upholstery button stuck into his back.

Linda amused him. After weeks living amongst storm clouds, she was a breath of fresh air. He had made a fool of himself at dinner. He thought of Ana. Circumstances beyond his control and he couldn't blame himself for that either. But he was losing her. The empty drag in his stomach and the sour ache at the back of his throat returned to torment him, as it did every night.

Neither Roger nor Linda slept until ten. The catch on the door woke her on his early morning trip to the bathroom, and when he came back, she was sat at the breakfast table. Linda hadn't acquired much in the way of crockery and cutlery yet. Spooning corn flakes out of a tea mug was a bit awkward and he could see she was embarrassed. She washed the remains of the flakes out of the mugs, switched on the kettle and made coffee.

'Efforts to prove my independence haven't gone down well with my father. He believes the less he helps, the sooner I will abandon the idea. I brought towels and sheets from home but very little else.'

'I have a wholesaler friend who supplies hotels and restaurants,' said Roger. 'When items get broken, he splits the remains of the set, and you can choose what you want. He is open today. I will take you on a shopping trip if you like.'

'Can't afford it,' said Linda. 'After paying my deposit I'm broke until the end of the month.'

'Well, if you entertain your soldier boyfriend at Christmas he won't expect to live on cornflakes out of a mug. I can easily arrange a month's credit with the wholesaler and I promise – payment won't be a problem.'

'OK, but no charity,' said Linda. 'I pay my way.'

Yesterday's episode with the flat battery had prompted Roger to pack a sweater, jeans, and a warm jacket. He collected his spare clothes from the Camper Van and changed, and with the cream Havana suit safely stowed away they set off in ample time to catch Sunday's early morning opening. The wholesaler was situated in Batley and had originally started business on the outskirts of Manchester. The owner and staff were all from Bangladesh and they remembered Roger from his days in Town Planning when he helped them complete a planning application.

Linda was given five-star treatment and she came away with an assortment of dinner plates, side plates, and dishes, with cups and saucers to match. Ashan then found her half a dozen each of knives, forks and spoons, and a couple of pans thrown in for good measure – all at ridiculously low prices with payment when money was available. Roger and Linda were bowed out of the warehouse like a king and queen. IKEA was on the doorstep and Roger suggested a few bright modern lamps to brighten up the flat. Linda was ecstatic, and he was surprised at how much he enjoyed helping her – it took his mind off other things.

Returning through Leeds he parked on exactly the same meter he used the previous evening and took Linda for lunch on Greek Street. When they carried their purchases up to Linda's flat, he watched as she arranged everything in her limited space. Now was the right time for him to leave – it had been a good day. His mobile buzzed. Hunters had another prospective client who wanted to look round his house. Let's hope the client was an improvement on the last.

'I must go Linda,' he said. 'Have a really good

Christmas – and tell me all about it in the New Year.'

This time she didn't kiss him fleetingly, and a familiar feeling invaded his groin. He kissed her back and left before he got carried away. There was over an hour to gather his thoughts together on his homeward journey. What was happening to him? A virtual schoolboy half his size had given him a black eye in the boxing ring, and now he was acting like a father to a sexy little thing who had taken a shine to him.

Monday was a strange day. He was late and walked into a curiously alien kind of atmosphere in the office. Simon, normally friendly, acted distant and vague and didn't mention whether he had enjoyed Saturday night's dinner or not. The whole design team kept their heads down and didn't look up from their computers. Roger felt like an unwelcome part-timer to whom everyone had to be polite but who wasn't recognised as belonging to the overall scheme of things. He had definitely been the subject of conversation long before he arrived.

Office life can be funny. He had past experience of it when working for Town Planning. Roger took his sore eye to his corner station and buried himself in graphs and valuations only stopping to buy a lunchtime sandwich which he ate at his desk. When the five o'clock bell went everyone left but Roger, who was still there when the cleaners showed up with buckets and brushes. Peter rang from his car phone, back late from surveying a prospective tourist centre near Windermere.

'Roger – pick up a copy of the Evening Post and have a look at the photographs. Matt is going to blow his top tomorrow. Don't go into the office. There is a farmer in Ripon wanting to convert a barn and outer buildings into bed and breakfast. Take down his address and go and see him. That should keep you occupied for a couple of days – meantime I will have a word with Matt.'

Before getting on the motorway Roger stopped at a newsagent's and bought the Evening Post. He spotted the problem immediately. Pages four and five were covered with shots of every table at the Charity Dinner. At the top of page five was a full picture of the Sebastian entourage showing everyone at their table. On the adjoining picture Roger was prominent in his cream suit and dark glasses shaking hands with Paul Sebastian whose large frame blotted out Matt and everyone else. Underneath it read 'Paul Sebastian boxing promoter meets Roger Kelly of Mathews Investments' and the photograph of them conferring together made it look like a couple of gangland bosses straight out of the 1920's.

Worst of all that one picture was the only picture featuring the Mathews table and the brief underlying print gave the impression Roger was top man at Mathews Building Investments.

Absolutely hilarious. Mick and Howard would love it. Linda wasn't to blame; it would be the newspaper who chose which photographs they wanted to print but for Roger, he knew it spelled trouble.

For the next two days Roger stayed busy organizing building plans for the farmer's B & B conversion in Ripon. He slept in the Camper Van overnight and both breakfast and lunch times joined the family at their large kitchen table where he ate eggs. Eggs with beans, eggs with ham, eggs with everything.

The farmer was a bulky, ruddy-faced man whose head sank deep into his chest, and whose mouth was lost between puffy cheeks. He sat suspiciously watching Roger through narrowed eyes. He didn't agree with any suggestions put forward. Everything was too costly, and no matter how low the final building quote he was certain to launch a bargaining match to try for less.

Roger was only there to draw up an overall plan because costing was Peter's side of the business. By Wednesday afternoon Roger had completed everything he could do and he left before dark – complete with two dozen fresh eggs.

At home there were three messages. Hunters were bringing two more prospective buyers to view his house at the weekend. Next – Mick had been trying to catch Roger for two days and had departed that afternoon to Australia to spend Christmas with his brother and sample life 'down under'. This sudden decision had to have been influenced by Wendy who shocked Mick by giving him the 'Heave Ho' and transferring her affections to the police sergeant with whom she worked. Roger had heard that men far outnumbered women in Australia and that wouldn't suit Mick.

The last message was the inevitable – would Roger phone Matt as soon as possible. He waited until morning and then contacted him at the Leeds factory. He guessed some of the heat would have been taken out of Matt if Peter had already spoken to him. Nevertheless, Matt exploded down the phone, blaming Roger for a picture that made Mathews Investments look like they were controlled by the London Mafia. Roger wanted to laugh but gripped the phone tightly and bit his lip.

'I thought you finished with all that when you left Nice. What the hell do you think you are doing getting involved with another bloody mobster?'

'Matt – I box, and I got hit. This could have happened playing for the Mathews football team and I didn't ask the owner of the boxing gym to come over and offer his commiserations.'

'But what about that photographer woman of yours? She took the photograph.'

'It's only the second time I have met her in my life. Ask Peter. Besides – she can't be blamed. She took plenty of snaps of our table, but the newspaper would pick which ones they wanted to print.' Matt wasn't pacified.

'We will have a word when I see you in the office,' he said. And it dawned on Roger – Matt imagined he was having an affair with Linda. He thought back to his black eye and flat battery. When was life ever fair? Sod it! Everyone could think what they wanted. Any more worries and he would join Mick in Australia.

At his office desk he worked steadily through until lunch break – and as he made his way to the canteen Phillipa joined him.

'Dad's cut up about Saturday night,' she said. 'Roger – tell me truthfully, are you going out with that girl who took the photographs?'

'I wish I was, but I'm not, and Ana is so upset with herself that I can't get her to even speak with me'.

Phillipa looked surprised, but didn't comment. She was a wonderful listener. Grouped together at another table the design team were eating the canteen's Christmas lunch and watched him as he took coffee with Phillipa. A touch of envy surrounds any loner who occupies an important position too quickly especially if he is singled out to take coffee with the boss's daughter. Human nature being as it is, Simon and staff wouldn't shed any tears if Roger fell from grace.

Two weeks to go before Christmas. December wasn't the best time to put a house on the market but top marks to Hunters for supplying him with prospective buyers so quickly. Selling a house is never easy. Saturday's clients messed around all morning and left saying they would think about it, and Sunday's couple turned up late accompanied by Hunter's agent and were gone within twenty minutes saying they had another appointment.

At the last minute, a solicitor from London came alone and she was very positive. She and her husband both had to move to Manchester and were staying until January to conduct a thorough search of the area. She was smart, attractive and tough. Charm was wasted on her, and Roger sold the advantages of living in the village as clearly and truthfully as possible.

The next few weeks were uneventful. No further contacts came from Hunters Estate Agents, and it appeared that Roger's sales pitch to the solicitor hadn't born fruit. There were no further recriminations from Matt (nor Peter) regarding the charity dinner, and at the last minute Phillipa caught him as he was packing up for the holiday and invited him to her New Year's Eve party.

Christmas day was on a Wednesday. Roger and

Evelyn were staying with his parents over Christmas, and he collected his aunt on Christmas Eve and they set off for Leeds in the afternoon. She had bought a dog from the rescue centre. It was a small, yappy dog of an indeterminate breed, but he could see that his aunt was very attached to it. Roger chuckled. His father wasn't a lover of dogs nor cats and Roger pictured the dog confined to a cardboard box in the outdoor porch.

Three days staying with his parents passed uneventfully, but Roger was very unhappy and everyone could see it. His aunt kept the party going, and his mother was at her best when entertaining. The weather stayed fine enough for some good walks, and Roger was out of bed early to stretch his legs and used his aunt's dog as an excuse whenever he wanted to get out of the house.

On Boxing Day, his father took him out for a quiet drink on his own. He too was upset over Ana and he thoroughly cross-questioned Roger before he would actually believe that her disappearance wasn't due to a quarrel. Ana and his father had been very close. Her family crisis in Croatia upset both his parents but no call from her, no card, she had stopped replying to Roger's texts and emails – all of this was beyond explanation.

Roger was going through hell, and he tried to hide it. He was more open with Aunt Evelyn as they travelled home. He had always been able to talk to her and he took notice when she gave him advice.

'No matter how much she thinks about you Roger she has made a decision to cut herself off. There isn't an answer. It's a terrible situation but Ana is fighting with herself to do what is right – and she is doing what is right, she has to think of her son.' Evelyn was very worldly and didn't beat about the bush. When he dropped her off, she made it clear that he was going to have to rethink his life.

Alone again in his empty house common sense advice didn't offer any consolation. Nobody could advise him – he knew what he had to do. A quick check on the internet told him there were direct flights to Pula from Stansted – one flight per day Saturday and Sunday. He had noticed a small hotel by the harbour in Rovinj and had no trouble booking it for two nights. He packed a bag and took the car to Manchester Airport and then caught an overnight train to Stansted.

The flight to Pula was scheduled for take-off at 10.00 am. It was delayed, then delayed again with engine trouble, and finally the flight departure time was postponed until 4.30 p.m. with free use of the complimentary airport lounge. He slept most of the day away in an armchair, remembering his previous Christmas in Rovinj when he stayed with Ana's family. What a wonderful Christmas with Ana – what a wonderful family. How different this visit was going to be.

Eventually he flew out of Stansted an hour later than the re-scheduled departure time and landed late in the evening to a wet wintry night. Pula Airport was quiet and a taxi whisked him to Rovinj inside fifty minutes. He had been right about the hotel; it was a good choice. A family-owned hotel which did everything possible to make sure you were comfortable, and ideally situated a short walk along cobbled streets from where Ana lived. The hotel provided him with a specially cooked late meal and a tall, uniformed waitress stood curiously watching him while he ate.

As he finished his meal the hotel owner came to his table with two glasses and a bottle of liqueur. He filled the glasses and sat down uninvited. He was a jovial character who spoke good English, and by the time Roger retired he knew all about the man's wife, children, and separate electrical business and in turn the hotel owner knew more than Roger wanted to tell him about his own personal business in Rovinj. To hell with it – what did it matter? Tomorrow was another day.

Breakfast at 8 a.m. then he telephoned Ana but got no reply. He texted her telling her he was in Rovinj, let an hour's breathing space elapse, and climbed the cobbled streets leading to her mother's house. Her mother greeted him and invited him into the main room. The one room which was used for everything. He remembered it so well from the previous Christmas. The large scrubbed wooden table, a television in the corner, and two worn easy chairs complimenting the chairs underneath the table. There were no signs of Ana, and over a cup of rakija her mother tried hard to tell him where Ana was but he couldn't understand what she was trying to say. Ana's mother looked older and more care-worn than a year ago.

Roger gave her a hug and left after an hour to stroll round the harbour, then up and down some of the narrow streets he had once walked with Ana, Petra, and Luke.

A year ago, the weather had been cold and sunny and bright. Today it was dull, wet, and miserable which did nothing to ease his apprehension as to why he had made the journey. At lunch time he went back to the house and the door was opened by Luke who turned and said, 'Is Roger'.

The man standing behind Luke had very broad shoulders, startling blue eyes and a deep tan. With his coloured headband and gold earrings he looked like a pirate but was obviously a fisherman, and Luke clung onto him adoringly. A lot of questions and answers clicked into place.

The man invited Roger into the house and shook him by the hand. He was a very handsome man, charming, and very likeable. While Luke jumped all around him, playfully climbing on and off his knee, the man attempted to explain with gestures and limited English that Ana was attending church and then going to visit her sister in hospital. But he didn't need to explain anything. The man belonged to Rovinj and he had entered Ana's life when she desperately needing someone. He didn't blame her but his heart felt like bursting.

Ana's mother made coffee and looked worried and upset while the three of them sat round the table. Roger tried to act normally but had trouble keeping his hand steady without spilling his coffee. When he left, he ruffled Luke's hair, hugged Ana's mother again, and clasped the warm, iron grip of the pirate wishing him safe sailing and good fishing as the man walked him to the door. Ana had chosen well.

It started to rain heavily. Roger returned to the hotel and texted Ana again to tell her he would be waiting in the hotel for the rest of the day. He waited and waited.

He had dinner and a long drink with the hotel owner before he received a reply from Ana.

*I am sorry Roger, I can't see you. If I do it
will spoil everything. Please Roger don't stay
– go home. I am so sorry. Love to you. Ana*

The next day Roger left the hotel for Pula Airport and
had to re-arrange his flight to travel back via Italy to
Manchester. There was no room for doubt. His trip had
achieved nothing except to reinforce what he already
knew. Nothing in his power could change anything – it
was the sad end of an affair.

Roger returned disorientated and needing breathing
space. A few days to come to terms with reality, but there
wasn't a cat in hell's chance of that. The London solicitor
and her husband urgently wanted to take another look at
his house and after spending all morning in and out of
rooms, they left only to return once more on New Year's
Eve, this time accompanied by a Hunter's representative,
and repeat exactly the same procedure all over again.
When they had gone Roger was more disorientated than
ever. He hadn't planned to go to Phillipa's party but he
would go if only to prove to himself that he could survive
without behaving like a manic depressive.

Matt's house was an old property which looked as
though it had been extended, and extended again. It was
Roger's first visit and when Phillipa greeted him the party
had already spilled over into the house, besides occupying
most of the space inside a large marquee. She steered him
into the marquee and briefly introduced him to a small
group of beer drinkers he vaguely remembered from

rugby club barbecues. High pitched shrieks told him some of Phillipa's regular admirers were present, including Tristan out-laughing a New Year fairy whose musical tinkle punctuated her every word.

Talk amongst the rugby group centred around business, in particular there were concerns about a virus running rife in China. Between sucking and blowing his pipe an older rather self-important man wisely pronounced the seriousness of the virus and warned it would spread throughout Europe and drastically effect business. Scrum-half George in the group agreed. He imported electrical goods from 'the Chinks' and hadn't damned well been able to get hold of a single kettle in time for Christmas.

'If George couldn't produce steam from his kettle before Christmas, then it's no use him counting on steam from his kettle in the New Year,' drawled scrum-half number two. 'Particularly if he persists trying to create steam with the iron lady.' Everyone in the group laughed apart from George the kettle importer.

'Who's the iron lady?' asked Roger.

'I can see you're a newcomer around here,' drawled scrum-half two. He was the tallest person in sight and towered over everyone else. His slow, affected speech travelled down from above and his words were like a proclamation from God.

'Our hostess is the Iron Lady. Famed for her purity amongst the Knights of the Round-hay Rugby table.' Another laugh. 'And our friend George here is the much-frustrated Sir Lancelot. An ardent suitor with a dead lance.' The slow, superior drawl produced more guffaws of laughter. Roger didn't like their references to Phillipa. He excused himself and went into the house to find the bar.

Most guests were in couples – part of a young crowd. Matt's older guests had congregated in the lounge (with no signs of Matt or Rene) talking and drinking with acquaintances they obviously knew. A tall woman in a full-length gown bumped into him, and nearly knocked his glass out of his hand. She apologised and dabbed splashes of Heineken from the front of his jacket with a paper handkerchief. She was showing so much cleavage that if he looked down, he would be able to see the colour of her shoes.

He walked back into the marquee. Tristan's laughing fairy was circling the floor alone. She introduced herself as Erica, kissed his cheek and laughed.

'It's like New Year is so exciting, isn't it? It's like we don't know what the next twelve months has in store for us, and it's like you never know who you may meet.' Erica tinkled with laughter. Roger's jaw ached wearing a set smile.

'Let's make the most of life while we can,' he replied – and laughed. 'It's like a Chinese virus is coming in 2020, and it's like it's so deadly that it's like some people believe it may kill us all off.'

Erica looked startled. She didn't laugh, and moved away from him as fast as she could. Now why did I say that Roger asked himself?

Out of the corner of his eye he saw Matt arrive on the scene with a distinct look of resignation on his face and they both saw each other at the same time. He had expected a cool reception instead Matt came straight towards him literally beaming.

'Good to see you lad. Glad you could make it but I'm sorry to see you are on your own. Any news? It's a bad lot for the lass,' said Matt shaking his head. 'It really is a bad lot. Do you think there is any likely-hood of Ana coming back in the near future?'

Phillipa appeared like magic at his shoulder, 'You have decided to honour us with your presence have you father?'

Matt looked uneasy. 'Oh, you know me love. These sorts of occasions are a bit false. They aren't really my cup of tea. I was just asking Roger about Ana.' It wasn't a subject Roger wanted to be reminded of but he had to answer.

'Ana hasn't answered any of my calls, and not a word from her over Christmas.'

'You have to go over there, lad and see what's happening. You won't rest until you do. If you can bring her back, you will be doing us all a favour as well as yourself.' The empty feeling dragged at Roger's stomach and he changed the subject. He hadn't the heart to tell them he had already been to see Ana and failed.

'Where's Basil tonight?' he asked.

'Working,' said Phillipa. 'Chefs are very valuable on New Year's Eve.'

Matt snorted and put his arm round Roger's shoulder. He turned to Phillipa, 'I'll check with you later love. There's something I want to show the lad.'

Looking back, he realized Matt had used him as an excuse to absent himself from the celebrations. He took

Roger into a room converted into an office, brought out the obligatory whisky bottle, and proudly showed photos of the charity dinner as featured in January's new Yorkshire Life. Two photographs did full justice to Matt's table, and although Roger's cream suit and dark glasses were very apparent fortunately, they weren't obtrusive. There was no mention of the controversial photographs in the Evening Post.

Matt was oblivious to the party outside. He talked about years of struggle trying to change the family business, and his aspirations to be a power for good, building new affordable homes. They discussed the model village and the sports centre, and Matt had ideas about how to market the village and replicate the design in other parts of the country. He talked sense, and sitting discussing a project which they had spent so much time planning was more enjoyable than taking part in social chit-chat.

By the time Roger re-joined the party Phillipa was organizing Auld Lang Syne, and as everyone formed circles Rene Mathews suddenly appeared for the first time all evening. Roger found himself holding the sweaty hand of a big perspiring man on his left side, and by accident Rene Mathews hand on his right, whilst at the same time she completely ignored him. He hadn't expected a kiss from either of them, but he was surprised when Rene dropped his hand at the stroke of midnight and kissed the sweaty man.

It was late enough. He was well over the limit and hoped he would be able to negotiate the keyhole without waking his parents when he got to their house. More importantly – he hoped the police wouldn't pull him up along the way. He found Phillipa and thanked her for the evening. She held his hand for a long time before she kissed him, and then kissed him again.

'I really am sorry Roger,' she said, and he knew she meant Ana. Quite by accident he had grown to be part of something – and, excluding Rene Mathews, he was treated as part of the Mathews family. To be friends with Roger Mathews and his daughter, and be pals with a guy like Peter Campbell meant a lot. Not all of life was a disaster.

Roger spent New Year's Day with his parents then set off back to Manchester. Linda had sent a charming message wishing him 'a Happy New Year', and Mick texted to say he was lying on the sands of Coogee Beach surrounded by a gorgeous array of sun-tanned, 'Sheilas'. Both messages were food for thought.

The day began with a boost to his moral. Hunters phoned with an offer made by the solicitors of £10,000 below Roger's asking price. He refused it. Next day his lie-in was disturbed by another call from Hunters – this time the offer was £8,000 below market valuation. Roger was half asleep when he took the call.

'Tell them no chance,' he said. 'I will drop my price by £3,000 and that's final. I am in no mood for haggling and its early days.' Within thirty minutes Hunter's came back to him – Roger's final price was accepted with the provision that he vacated the property by the end of February. Roger agreed.

Only the second day of 2020 and he was on the move

– but where? There was nothing and nobody to stop him from going anywhere he wanted, and did he intend hanging about? But what was he going to do with himself if he moved on, and where did he want to go?

22. Il Funerale

Any plans Roger had envisaged were halted and decisions temporarily shelved. After months of delay government backing was confirmed and at last the company could press ahead with Matt's model village and sports centre. There was a surge of activity to make up for lost time. All available building workers were mustered, and all stops were pulled out to urgently complete the footings and ensure foundations of the village were swiftly put into place.

January wasn't normally a busy month but the number of meetings between Matt and his suppliers gave Roger the impression that trouble was afoot. Alarm bells were ringing throughout the UK as the radio, the newspapers, and television warned of the spread of the new flu virus, coupled with further warnings regarding the serious implications of changed EU rules coming into force. If you weren't struggling with your own crisis, then the media created one for you.

Peter pulled Roger out of the office to deal with inquiries and help tie up contracts. In effect Roger was switched from design to company representative and the change of responsibility suited Roger down to the ground. Travelling the country gave him time to think and time to plan, and he was pretty much his own boss. He hadn't come to any conclusions about what he wanted to do. In the meantime, he had better find somewhere to live before the end of February, or he might finish up lodging with the Salvation Army – or worse still, with his parents.

Visits to estate agents based within striking distance

of the office produced nothing. He didn't view a single property he wanted to rent, let alone anywhere he wanted to buy. Linda was helpful. Twice she accompanied him on his Saturday afternoon tour of estate agents in North Leeds, and twice he took her for an evening meal and then surprised her by leaving early with the excuse that he had to catch up on some work.

Linda's soldier boyfriend was called back to Aldershot to await a new posting. Previously Linda hadn't seen him for a whole year, and it might be another year before she saw him again. She told Roger she wasn't going to wait around and live the life of a nun, but Roger's trip to see Ana lay like a black hole at the back of his mind, and although he was tempted, he didn't rise to the hint.

Three weeks after his visit to Croatia, a manilla envelope came through the post marked with a Croatian postage stamp. Two booklets fell out. One ten-page brochure detailing a sports centre on the outskirts of Rovinj, and the second brochure little more than a pamphlet but clearly illustrating what looked like a superbly appointed centre in Slovenia. Nothing accompanied the booklets, not even a sticky post-it note. Crazy. It was inexplicable that Ana could end their relationship this way.

Roger passed the factory early the following morning on his way heading north. He knew the information would prove valuable and expected to leave both booklets at the reception desk. He hadn't seen Matt since New Year and he badly wanted to avoid a post mortem on his Croatian fiasco but Matt was already in the building and instructed the commissionaire to ask Roger to wait. Matt looked bad tempered and worried when Roger walked into the office, but ordered a pot of tea and became completely absorbed leafing through the brochures.

'This material is just what we need,' he said. 'Brilliant photography. It gives us a bit more idea of what we are aiming for.' Matt walked over to the window and gazed out over his favourite view. Streets of old houses that one day he had ambitions to knock down and re-build. 'So, what happens now lad? I gather she isn't coming back.'

'What can happen?' asked Roger.

'Well Peter tells me you are making a fresh start. You have sold your house. And if you choose to live on this side of the Pennines that will certainly suit us – but have you found anywhere to live yet?'

'Not yet,' said Roger. 'I want somewhere temporary, but finding it isn't easy.'

'So I understand. Peter and I have been discussing it. We might be able to offer a solution. Give him a ring and then let me know what you think.' Matt concluded their discussion by getting up and walking Roger to the door.

'Meantime lad, get out there and bring in as much business as you can. The shit is going to hit the fan anytime soon, and Mathews Investments want to stay ahead of it.'

He didn't ring Peter until a couple of days after his talk with Matt and he had no idea what to expect.

'Matt has bought The Olde Wheelhouse,' said Peter. 'I think he wishes he hadn't bought it because he believes now is the wrong time to buy anything. We looked inside the bungalow last weekend and it's quite habitable. It could act as a stopgap until you find what you want. Get the keys from Phillipa and take a walk round it.'

Roger would like to have inspected the gatehouse on his own but Phillipa insisted on meeting him there. Saturday football was postponed due to the soggy pitch and heavy rain, but the weather didn't appear to effect Phillipa who arrived dressed in full riding regalia ready to brave the wind and rain so long as she could trot around the countryside on her favourite horse. It would be a mistake to underestimate Phillipa. She was her father's daughter.

They walked around the bungalow together and Phillipa wasn't impressed. In fact, she couldn't understand why her father, nor Peter, had even suggested the idea.

'It's not very comfortable and you are going to be really isolated Roger. And you might be here longer than you imagine. Finding a place to buy takes time.'

She didn't stay long and left the keys so he could make a detailed circuit on his own.

The gatehouse had been built as a residential property but more recently used as an office. Two adjoining rooms were a mass of wall cupboards with power points everywhere. There was a tiny kitchen with a cooking ring and pantry, and a combined toilet and bathroom too small to swing a cat, with a bath used for rubbish judging by the state of it. One other small room overlooking the gardens might have been a lounge before becoming an office rest room, and the warmth of the fading décor was a welcome change from the austere bleakness of the rest of the bungalow. It was the only room with any appeal at all.

Roger had brought a flask. He propped himself up against a window ledge to drink his coffee whilst considering his options. Outside the rain turned to sleet, and gusts of wind blew wet snow against the window panes. His mind travelled back to Nice and Aunt Evelyn's apartment with the sun kissed balcony and Elissa paying him a visit in her tight transparent tee shirt. His mobile pinged. Saturday morning and Peter was still working at the village site, up to his neck in problems.

Peter's text simply said,

> *Take a look at the stables Roger when you get there. Room inside for a killer Kelly boxing gym.*

Roger buried himself in his anorak and walked the length of the drive around the side of the Wheelhouse to the two stables. Both stables were heavily padlocked and with sleet blowing in his face he had difficulty locating which key unlocked which doors amongst the heavy bunch of keys. Peter was right. The interiors were vast. Very dry and without signs of oil marks anywhere.

In just one of the stables there was space to store a houseful of furniture with room to spare, and that alone solved a major problem. But was it the solution to another problem – without Ana did he want to settle any place here in this bloody awful climate? What was the point of it? Why not join Mick and the two of them work their way round Australia. Or make a trip in the Camper Van and spend a year travelling the continent on the proceeds from selling the house?

He took a last disinterested look around the bungalow and made a mental note of the size of each room. What the hell was he doing even considering living in this bleak little hole?

In an awkward place above the bath, he noticed a trapdoor which must lead to a loft, and by standing on the edge of the bath he was able to reach up and push open the door and pull himself into the loft. His hand caught on a light switch which illuminated another very large storage space, totally clear apart from the water tank propping up a number of boards, each board wrapped in sacking. He lowered two of the smaller boards into the bath but had to exit the loft and balance on the bath edge to struggle with the third one which although very light in weight only just cleared the door with half an inch to spare on either side.

All three packages were obviously pictures. Roger carried them into the little room at the back of the bungalow then collected his Stanley Knife and a folding seat from the Volkswagen. The two small pictures were old prints, badly faded, and framed in glass. But when he cut away the sacking from the largest picture it was taped and professionally covered in a thick brown paper which was difficult to remove.

Whoever had packed and taped this picture hadn't intended it to ever see the light of day. Roger cut carefully round the frame and tore away sheet after sheet of wrapping. The picture would measure approximately three by two feet and he propped it up against the wall facing the door and gazed at it spellbound. Matt had to see this. He didn't expect Matt to be home, but he phoned him just the same. Matt answered.

'Matt I'm in the bungalow at the Wheelhouse. There's something you ought to see.'

'It had better be good,' said Matt. 'I'll be round in 20 minutes.'

Roger fetched his toolbox from the car, found some hooks, and hung the picture.

As you walked into the room the picture was the first thing you saw enhanced by the light from the adjacent window. Matt arrived and Roger guided him to the backroom where Matt stopped dead the moment he stepped through the doorway. They stood together in silence – captivated. The artist must have stood in exactly the same position one hundred years ago. Exactly the same position where they were now standing when the picture was painted, long before the gatehouse was ever built.

Looking through the bungalow window to the right you caught the corner view of the ivy-covered Wheelhouse, with its driveway leading to the front door. Hanging on the wall the picture replicated exactly the same view of the house ivy free, in its days of stunning grandeur. Three tall chimneys towering majestically above the sloping roof, and subtle greys in the brickwork complemented blue painted woodwork and brightly curtained windows mirroring the light. On either side of the long driveway the rows of pink cherry blossom were in full bloom, and behind the house the pine trees and silver birch shimmered under a blue cloudless sky. First impressions were breath taking.

A pony and trap were parked by the main door, and a top hatted man offered his hand to a woman wearing a bonnet and long white dress as she stepped down from her seat. Waiting behind stood a shining black and gold coach with the coachman holding the reins of two white stallions, and a man dressed in black tails with a red waistcoat stood at the house door in an attitude of welcome with an Irish Setter beside him.

The first break in the weather made way for a shaft of sunlight which shone directly into the back room. It was a strange feeling – the room seemed to float. The picture of the Wheelhouse dominated the room and at the same time transferred itself to the view of the house outside. The two merged so well you couldn't look at one without looking at the other. The back room of the bungalow transcended into a moment of time gone by – a magical place. Roger broke the silence.

'I think it's my turn to buy Auntie Mary's meat pie at your favourite pub.'

'I think you are right lad – it is,' Matt agreed. His car led the way to the pub and Roger followed. Neither of them had much to say as they ate lunch. Two people who were passionate about beautiful buildings. Both knew that restoring the Wheelhouse to its former glory could result in something special.

'Ring me on Monday,' said Matt. 'Give me time to mull it over.'

There were no second thoughts. Roger stayed the night with his parents and took his father to look at the bungalow the following morning. They swept floors, cleaned out office cupboards, and assessed how many tins of emulsion were needed to make the place habitable. Occupying the gatehouse became a reality.

Roger checked with Matt on Monday before doing anything else. He could tell Matt had spent the weekend thinking about what he was going to do.

'I haven't got the spare labour to do anything with the Wheelhouse until the end of summer, but stay in the bungalow with my compliments,' said Matt. 'We have got six months before we decide how to tackle the Wheelhouse. Bring Phillipa on board and get together with Peter. We have a mission for the future lad – and that house is part of our mission. I can tell you I'm looking forward to it.'

A mission! Roger worked steadily all week covering half of Northern England on his travels. He called the Greek brothers. They met at the bungalow and arranged to replace the cracked bath with a shower. The younger brother confirmed he wasn't busy and could emulsion all rooms, and have the paintwork finished within a week. Roger gave him the job.

Wasting time wasn't an option. Carpets were not included in the sale of his house and since one colour ran throughout the living room, hall, and bedrooms this could easily be re-cut to cover the concrete floors of the bungalow. To prepare for the removal van red labels were attached to the king-sized bed and all other bulky furniture which would have to be stored; white labels were stuck on furniture and essential items which he should be able to squeeze into the bungalow's limited

412

space.

He turned down a trip to London to act as corner man for the Sebastian's next boxing promotion, and made an excuse when Linda offered him a free ticket to partner her at a Yorkshire Post staff function. He was one hundred per cent focused. His plans were nicely in place.

On 7th February, Matt startled everybody by calling a full staff meeting in the canteen. Friday afternoon work stopped, chairs were carried out of offices, and everyone took their seats worried about what might follow. Matt launched the meeting with the news that in January two Chinese girls staying in Yorkshire had been taken ill with the Coronavirus and it had already spread. He emphasised that the virus was reported to be so serious in parts of China that all shops and public buildings had been closed, and the general population were confined to their homes. Matt was ahead of the game.

'If the virus spreads here as quickly as I believe it will then I shall temporarily close both our factory and our offices. What I want to say to you all is simply this. Make preparations to work from home. Most of us work from computers and I regularly communicate with overseas customers on the internet. I don't like doing business that way but there's a lot of things I don't like doing in today's world. If I can keep our business on track, and I can keep you and your families safe, then I have done my job and there is no reason why we cannot succeed by adapting and doing things differently and all stay fully employed.'

Matt had made a rousing speech, and everyone recognised that he had the good of his workforce at heart. In unison the whole canteen stood up and clapped and

413

cheered him. You could not fail to be moved. Matt grunted, gave a nod to Peter, and moved out of the canteen to his office.

This wasn't the time to be wandering off on some hair-brained adventure. The meeting lent new impetus to Roger's sense of urgency. The bath was to be replaced next week, and internal decorations to the gatehouse were complete with rooms ready for carpeting as soon as the Greeks brought along their carpet fitter. Roger took the week off work and began filling the Camper Van with pots, pans, clothing and personal items that he wanted to have in place before making the final move.

He made three trips from Manchester to Leeds. The middle office at the gatehouse became a bedroom, and the old-fashioned cupboards and shelves receptacles for shirts and folded garments without having to take up space with chests of drawers. He bought a small free-standing wardrobe from IKEA, and purchased a neat little fridge which fitted under the marble slab in the pantry. The pantry had a small, frosted window and shelves on either side of the marble slab. Roger stacked one side with tinned food, pastas and dried goods, and the other side with pans, plates, and dishes, with his cutlery tray neatly placed underneath. He stood back pleased with the result. Only halfway through the month of February and he had turned a concrete block into a liveable residence.

On St Valentine's Day, 14th February, Antonio Romano was murdered in Naples. Roger was unloading rolls of carpet when the text message from Monty flashed through on his mobile.

They have killed him. The bastards have found Antonio and murdered him. They garrotted him and left his body in an alley.

Roger sat down heavily in the middle of the concrete floor. Without being asked, one of the Greek brothers went to the pantry, opened a bottle of whisky, and poured out a double. It was a shock. He had come to believe Romano too illusive to get caught by the police or his enemies. He phoned Monty but the connection went dead. Roger couldn't explain to himself how he was affected by Romano's death, but he had to stop himself from crying and nothing seemed to matter anymore.

He worked the next week with Armageddon hanging over him. His father saved a copy of the Telegraph where two columns on page seven reported the murder of an Italian gang leader thought to be connected with the money laundering scandal. Roger felt sick when he read the report and sick whenever he thought of Romano lying dead in an alleyway.

Late the same evening he received a telephone call and the sarcastic voice of Morris Brooks greeted him from the other end of the phone.

'Mr Kelly, you will have heard the news. What we have wanted to avoid has now happened, and there is no possibility of our friend Romano ever revealing where our money has been hidden. But perhaps you can still help us.'

'I can't help anybody Mr Brooks. I am moving house.'

'We are fully aware of your move Mr Kelly. We are

also aware of where you are moving to, and the breakup between you and your Croatian girlfriend which is unfortunate. But there is still one last service we would like you to perform.

'Romano's funeral takes place on the last day of February. We are sending you flight tickets and details of the church where the funeral takes place, and we want you to report back on what and who you see at the funeral.'

'I don't promise,' said Roger, 'but I will try to make it possible.' God they were a formidable creepy bunch. Once mixed up with people like the Sebastians you were never free of them, and worst still they made it their business to know everything about you. But the idea grew on him. It was the last mark of respect he could offer the man who had first helped him. A man who treated him like a son, and this was all Roger could offer in return.

He rang Morris Brooks and confirmed he would make the trip. Travelling on a Thursday he could attend the funeral on Friday 28th and be back in time to deal with the removal van planned for Saturday 29th. It was a tight schedule but if it went wrong, he couldn't care less. Everything was wrong.

Twice Phillipa came to see him whilst he was working in the bungalow. On the first occasion she brought bearded Basil with her, and the second time George the Chinese kettle importer who stood apart as though he was dealing with a bad smell. When Roger's mother called to see him, he was fitting a two-seater settee into the small lounge.

The settee was positioned perfectly so he could look at the painting whilst looking outside at the house and driveway. She completely ignored the painting and her only comment was that the bungalow felt damp. Funnily enough it was something he hadn't noticed. A fan heater and a portable oil heater had survived his student days and were good enough for use in the office and bedroom. His tiny lounge displaying the painting deserved something better and he invested in a white oil filled radiator with timer control. Now that carpeting was down and furnishings were in place, he couldn't care less what anybody thought of his new abode.

Linda's company offered a brief respite from the deep hurt surrounding Ana and Romano. He collected Linda from Headingley, showed her the bungalow, and then took her for a drink in one of Headingley's student filled pubs. She was intrigued by the house and bungalow but he could tell she believed it was a lonely spot. She studied him over a glass of lager.

'Roger – do you like me?' she asked.

'What makes you ask that?'

'You haven't tried once to get me into bed.'

'That's not always proof of how much you like someone,' said Roger. 'But I promise you – there is nothing I would like more, but now isn't the right time.'

'I think you are a wounded soldier,' she said. 'You are frightened of being wounded again.'

They said goodnight in the car and he could easily have changed his mind as she made sure the taste of her mouth lingered on his lips long after she left him.

There were daily updates on infection rates and deaths from coronavirus. Radio and television couldn't find anything else to broadcast, and it was the subject of every conversation. Older people worried about catching the flu while the younger end dismissed it as another media scare. Peter was one of the chief doubters.

'Bloody ridiculous,' he said. 'A Chinese mobilised scamdemic.'

Scamdemic or not, a cruise ship off the coast of Japan was quarantined with over six hundred cases identified on board, and deaths and serious outbreaks were spreading fast in Northern Italy and France. When Roger ascended the steps of the plane to Naples, he had kept his trip a secret. Somehow his father had guessed he might attend the funeral and had rung specially to warn him that he was a bloody fool if he even considered the idea. He was unsure whether his father was more concerned about his son catching covid or finishing up with a knife in his back.

A street map of Naples located the position of the church in the Mercato district, and a quick search on the internet recommended a small pensione within easy reach of the church. He found the pensione down a scruffy street situated on the second floor above a delicatessen. Entry was by way of a narrow door squashed between the delicatessen and a gift shop, and expecting the worst he was amazed to step out of the creaking lift into a reception worthy of a five-star hotel. His bedroom was little short of luxurious, and the Italian breakfast deserved a Michelin commendation. A good start to a traumatic assignment.

The walk through the Mercato district of Naples was uncomfortable. Yesterday's taxi from the airport was driven by a Hungarian who spoke excellent English and

Roger played safe and booked him to wait outside the hotel from 2.00 pm onwards.

'You like me earlier you text me,' assured the driver, but wending his way through this maze of narrow shabby streets gave Roger the jitters and he wished he had arranged for the taxi to transport him to and from the church before and after the funeral.

The service began at 11 a.m. As he exited the narrow alleys, he found the church set back on a wide busy thoroughfare, reminding him of a Methodist church in a Lancashire mill town, round windows placed under roof tiles, and one entrance at the top of a steep flight of steps. No signs of a Godfather style ceremony. Mourners dressed in black ascended the church steps, and two police cars and a group of Carabiniers kept a low profile further along the street.

Getting into church presented a different problem. Two black suited guards were going to bar his way, and one of them grabbed his arm and declared 'privato'. Roger tensed every muscle and held his ground. He hadn't travelled all this way to allow a couple of stiffs to push him around, and if the stiff holding his arm wasn't careful, he might finish up at the bottom of the church steps.

Intervention arrived just in time. The man who intervened was as wide as he was tall, and Roger recognised the London connection with the scar covered by the black Fedora. He waved the guards aside and conducted Roger into the church.

'Your presence is not welcome here,' he said. 'Leave after the service finishes.'

'What makes you think I want to stay?' Roger replied. The man gave him a look of hate and went to stand on the other side of the church.

Inside, the church was dark and ornate, and a sickly smell pervaded the atmosphere.

The only light came from somewhere underneath the roof from where an unearthly blue glow illuminated the alter, and joined the shadows cast by the flickering candles.

Roger joined the procession of mourners who slowly walked past the open coffin, each making the sign of the cross as they passed. The sight was revolting.

Antonio Romano's body was unrecognisable. He lay on a coloured fabric with arms crossed and hands encased in white gloves, immaculately dressed in a suit, white shirt and tie. But there was nothing the mortician could do to mend Romano's face. His face had been eaten away and both eyelids and part of one ear were missing. It took a terrifying moment before he realized that the eyes staring up at you from the remains of the face were made of glass.

A wave of dizziness impelled Roger to clutch onto the back of a church pew to steady himself, before stumbling to a seat at the back of the church. Nothing could have prepared him for a sight like this. Romano had been strangled. His body thrown on one side and left in a rat-infested yard to rot like some useless piece of garbage. Antonio Romano – the man Roger admired. The man who had treated him like a son. What foul bastard could be responsible for this? Roger pressed his knees tightly together to stop his legs shaking from the shock.

The church was still half empty. Occupied pews in front were a slowly expanding sea of black. Then, one by one, leaders of the mob trickled in to take their reserved places in the front rows of the church. Men who knew each other – men who came without their wives and used the church as a meeting place with little respect for the man lying yards away dead in his coffin. Little hawk-faced men proudly protected by their tight suited minders. The large self-important big timers, overweight and vastly overconfident, flashing gold teeth and gold watches. Smiles, hugs, and handshakes, and waves across the aisles as they acknowledged each other's presence. When the deals went wrong the greetings and the handshakes amounted to nothing. Each would plot to blame the other, and if they couldn't wipe one another out legally they would do it illegally.

There was a hush and standing mourners stood back in respect as the veiled figure of Romano's wife together with his son walked slowly to the front of the church. One step behind them was a woman who Roger met once at Romano's villa. Did his wife know this woman had been Antonio's mistress, and did she accept it?

The voice interrupting his thoughts was the only thing that gave away the identity of the man who pressed in front of him and sat down at the other end of the pew.

'I can't risk sitting with you,' whispered Monty. 'I'll be in touch later.'

Nothing about Monty looked the same. His drooping moustache, the wig, his long shabby raincoat and high heeled boots. Roger followed his progress to the end of the row. He looked up to find the owner of the Fedora watching him intently from across the other side of the church, and the man standing beside him wearing the black eye patch was Jason.

The service progressed. The heavy music passed over Roger like a stifling blanket as he sat with his head bowed remembering the man who had played such an important role in his life. He looked at his watch – half past midday, and Jason was now stood alone with his one eye still fixed on Roger. Jason had vowed to kill him if they ever met again, and the way Roger felt he almost wished that the nasty piece of shit would try. But that would be stupid. He might have Jason's sidekicks to contend with as well as Jason, and that would be a different ball game.

Keeping his mobile hidden he texted his taxi driver, and instructed him to come to the church immediately and park outside. When the ceremony ended Roger ignored all protocol, he was first out of the church and straight into the taxi. He collected his case from the hotel and the taxi deposited him at the airport in record time to catch the afternoon flight to Manchester.

He hadn't had time to think and only when he fastened his seat belt did the full reality of what he had seen hit him. The whole sickening experience. Romano defiled– the horrific end to the life of a man who had been his mentor.

He tackled Saturday's removal with a mental black-out. By Sunday evening he was fully installed in the gatehouse with kitchen cupboards and pantry shelves over stocked in answer to the media scare of pending shortages. Reporting to Morris Brooks didn't go well. He had no idea what Morris wanted but judging by his sarcastic tone Morris conveyed the impression that he expected a lot more. Too bad! Roger didn't ask the Sebastians to send him the airline tickets.

In bed early, Roger awoke sweating with a throat that felt like he had swallowed a packet of razor blades. By Tuesday morning he knew he had caught Covid, and by the time he showed signs of recovery, Matt had temporarily closed all offices and the UK was ready to enter a national lockdown.

EPILOGUE

Lockdown – Another Story

The Corona virus changed the world. The cure for love sickness and an excuse for doing nothing about nothing. Into my second week of the damned virus, I would gladly have sacrificed anything to be rid of it.

I saw no one. I hadn't registered with a doctor, so none came. My parents drove over twice and left three litres of milk and groceries on my doorstep, and after his dismissive comments about a 'spam-demic', I was surprised when Peter visited me and resorted to shouting through the letter box. And if the world had to stop visiting then the world discovered texting, and every hour my mobile 'pinged' with some useless piece of information.

Four days after speaking to Morris Brooks I received a follow-up call from Sid Cohen. 'Leslie wants to see you,' he said. His call came at the worst time – I was in bed feeling deadly.

'Tell Leslie I have caught the virus, but if he wants to share it he is welcome to come over here and see me. Ask him to bring Morris along too.' There was silence at the other end of the phone. 'I'll pass on your message,' said Sid and rang off.

One month after his call, Sid was compelled to close down Sebastian's gym and Paul cancelled all further bookings of boxing promotions. Via the grapevine I later learned that both Paul and Leslie left Manchester to start business afresh in America. I never heard from the Sebastians again, and I never found out what became of Sid Cohen.

Back on my feet after three torturous weeks, I took stock of the situation. Wi-Fi connection in the front office was perfect but there was no way I could get a clear signal from my television, and nobody was prepared to come out and fix it. That didn't really bother me. The news via the radio bombarded me with Covid statistics so why watch it all over again on TV? Nevertheless, without a television I was going to be even more stranded.

A few days prior to government restrictions coming into force, I was startled to hear the unwelcome voice of Rosemary when I answered the phone. What the hell did she want?

'I have just spoken with your mother,' she said. 'I have been made headmistress at St Mary's so I am going back to live in Manchester. But I can't cope with the new job and handle Scott as well. Would you like to look after him?'

Scott would be three years old now. Did I want to be tied down with a dog? Then it struck me – why not? This place is perfect for a dog, and I am tied down anyway.

The following day Rosemary's satnav guided her to the Wheelhouse and when she dumped the dog basket at my gate, Scott trotted out of her car without any hesitation. I don't know whether the dog remembered me or not, but he came straight over and wagged his tail, gave me a lick, then shot through the gate to chase a squirrel.

'You two will be able to play until your hearts content in these gardens' said Rosemary. 'In fact, you have enough space to recruit your own little battalion of dodgy friends and run a protection racket.' And without a smile or another word my ex-wife drove away. Over the next five months it was Scott who kept me sane.

Days became routine. Evenings a nightmare. National lockdown dictated that only essential services remained open. Shops, restaurants, sports facilities and all forms of entertainment were closed, and the public were asked to remain inside their homes apart from taking one hour's daily exercise. I queued weekly at the nearby supermarket and played dodgems with mask-attired shoppers who changed sides of the road to avoid passing each other.
Work generated from Mathews' Zoom meetings became so spasmodic that days lost their meaning, whilst long dreary evenings extended into nights that seemed to last forever. It was a challenging, brutal time to be stranded on my own.

After nights of brooding with Scott at my feet listening to my complaints, I made a choice. If this deadly virus meant living the life of a hermit, then I would make the most of it. My best pal was back by my side, Spring was round the corner, and what better place to become a pioneering recluse.

I began clearing the overgrown mass of shrubs around the bungalow and house.

B & Q continued trading and I topped up my toolbox to start building a summer house on a concrete patch behind the bungalow. Every morning before breakfast I took Scott for our first walk. Raucous cries from crows and jackdaws heralded the first twinkle of morning light, and competing songs from a robin and blackbird nesting outside the bungalow window ensured we both woke early.

It was good to walk with Scott. He darted around freely, chasing everything that moved, then he would bark and come back to make sure I was still with him. Clumps of daffodils were cropping up all over the gardens, and early Spring hastened varying colours of green amongst the random variety of trees. A flock of goldfinches displayed stunning colours whenever we disturbed their section of the hedge-groves, and I noted that the jackdaws had adopted the ivy-covered wheel as their own territory. Suddenly this new life wasn't so bad – I felt free. The sun was shining, and I was no longer making those bloody awful journeys down traffic clogged motorways. Shakespeare summarized it perfectly. 'It is not in the stars to hold our destiny but in ourselves'. I was all set to survive.

Summer 2020 turned out to be glorious. As the days grew longer, I worked longer, and became a champion odd job man. Muscles turned into steel bands and my hands toughened up like old leather. The summer house was finished, and I would sit outside until the light faded reading a book or planning next day's set of tasks. The blackbird and robin were now so tame that they almost ate out of my hand, and Scott got used to Kelly the bird man, and lay watching me with tail twitching as I crumbled up one of his dog biscuits.

I spoke regularly with Peter and Phillipa and occasionally risked police reprisals by driving over to see my parents, talking to them while keeping my distance. Messages from Mick told me he was stranded in Australia, and frequent texts from Linda kept me amused with her idea of 'social distancing' which involved two guys resident on the same corridor. But I could not understand why I hadn't heard from Monty. Why hadn't he phoned? I couldn't initiate a call to him because his number was again obsolete. Surely, he could have made contact with me.

I was adding finishing touches to the newly built summer house when the Greek brothers called me.

'Mr Kelly – we are a family bubble, so we work. You ask your boss if he likes we start on his house.'

I immediately phoned Matt and he was delighted. He put the whole job of renovating the Wheelhouse into my hands with instructions to delegate the work and check the quality. Within a week the house was shorn of ivy and the brothers were on the roof replacing loose slates and guttering, and rebuilding the broken chimneys. Their idea of scaffolding was unlikely to meet health and safety standards, but it worked well for them, and none of the brothers fell off the roof.

Out came old window frames, floorboards were replaced, and re-plastering commenced room by room. I texted photographs to Matt and made sure I consulted him before pressing ahead with re-plumbing and re-wiring. Every day developed a sense of purpose and by night-time I was tired out and pleased to roll into bed.

Twice I met with Phillipa outside Sainsbury's and

brought her up-to-date over a take-away coffee. On each occasion she met me looking fresh-faced and sparklingly attractive, and I returned to the bungalow aching for the company of a woman. And that was when I received Ana's email, her first communication with me for over six months.

My Dearest Roger,

I have been lying in bed thinking about you as I do so many nights. You will never understand why I couldn't see you – but perhaps now you will try.

My sister died after Christmas, and I got married last month. You met my husband. He is a lovely man and he will make a wonderful father for Luke.

If I hadn't met you before I met him, then I would be perfectly happy. As it is I am happy, but he will never mean the same to me as you do Roger, and I will never love anyone as much as I have loved you.

You may know – I have opened my own office in Rovinj and while this dreadful virus is around, I am helping Matt with our project which somehow means that there is something of you still with me as I work.

One day you will appreciate that we have been blessed. Our love will stay the same

429

*forever. A passionate love which will not be dulled by time and events, because you will always be with me as you are **now** – my wonderful Roger. God bless you and keep you, my darling.*

Please forgive me if you can.

My love. Ana

Her email was heart rending. It shattered the shield I had built around myself. I lay down on the bed with my agonizing love and broken dreams for Ana tearing me apart, and I simply wanted to hide away from the world. Then the inexplicable happened. Scott followed me into the bedroom and started to whine. He jumped onto the bed and tried to lick my face, and when I pushed him away, he jumped back and barked at me and wouldn't stay down. Scott had been disciplined to stay off beds and sofas from being a pup and rarely broke the golden rule. Did the dog understand me? Explain it how you will, what mattered was that I got off the bed, pulled myself together, and fought off the weakness that filled my head.

'You are right, you hairy hound,' and I scratched him behind the ears. 'This is no time to give up on life. You and I are not going to be beaten.' Nothing had changed, but I learned to live with the truth, and accepted the pain.

During Zoom meetings neither Peter nor Matt had mentioned they were working with Ana. They spared my feelings, but it felt like a betrayal. It solved a problem.

430

This lockdown couldn't last for ever, and as soon as the Wheelhouse was finished then I was finished too. I needed to put all of this behind me and tackle something new.

Minus the ivy, and thanks to the Greek brothers, the Wheelhouse had taken on the appearance of the magnificent property that Matt and I first visualized and replanning it would be a waste of time. External alterations would spoil the character of the whole building, and it gave me a kick to sit looking out of the window and see how closely the house now resembled the painted picture hanging on my wall.

I was acting as a glorified caretaker. Unless I had serious work to do the oncoming winter months would drive me mad and I made this clear when I spoke with Matt. Neither he nor Rene had ventured outside their door since the pandemic began although to be fair Matt kept his finger on the pulse, and never missed a trick.

'Hang on in there, lad,' he said. 'I won't leave you stranded. By the way,' he added gruffly, 'I ought to mention it – Ana has been in touch with us. Things in Croatia can't be as bloody awful as they are here. She has opened an office in Rovinj and offered to help us communicate with a couple of sports centres who can provide equipment for the village.'

'Thanks Matt!' I replied. 'I knew that – but thanks for telling me.'

Our conversation didn't alter anything. For some reason the mundane work landing on my laptop wasn't even vaguely connected with the sports centre which I had proudly planned. If that's how it was going to be –

good luck to them. Living rent free in the Gatehouse bungalow I wasn't going to grumble, but it strengthened my resolve to move on if this government ever allowed us to get back to normal.

A few weeks after talking to Matt I returned from my morning run to find a silver-grey Range Rover parked outside the gate. My pulse rate shot up to over 200. Ana? Then I remembered – half the local population own a silver-grey Range Rover, and the model I bequeathed Ana operated on left hand drive.

When Phillipa struggled out of the Rover with a large suitcase, closely followed by a cocker spaniel (the double of Scott), my first reaction was disbelief.

'I hope you don't mind but I've come to join you for a while. You have lived here on your own long enough, and it is high time I took a hand in planning the Wheelhouse.'

The idea wasn't feasible. Two dogs and the pair of us trying to work and live together in the confines of the concrete bungalow.

'Phillipa – I would love to have you here. But what's Matt going to say about it?'

'He doesn't know,' laughed Phillipa. 'We are all getting on each other's nerves at home, and he and I aren't on speaking terms,' and with a smile she wheeled her case into the bungalow.

Phillipa and I were close friends, but anything else was off limits. I had no idea what her intentions were, but I couldn't imagine our relationship staying 'off-limits' if she stayed with me for long, and Matt and Rene weren't going to like that situation one little bit.

Yet fate weaves its irreversible spell. After months alone I wasn't going to object to a radiant Phillipa keeping me company. So, the scene was set. On that same morning the reception office became Phillipa's domain. Worktable and chairs were pushed to one side with the dog baskets stowed underneath. Phillipa wouldn't let me vacate my bedroom, and fetched a camp bed from her car and squeezed it into a draughty spot underneath the reception window.

'You won't be comfortable sleeping there,' I said.

'Don't worry Roger – it's going to be fine with me,' and she took my arm and we walked over to the Wheelhouse and I introduced her to the Greek brothers.

What followed was inevitable. Phillipa took over. I didn't object. It was her father's house and Peter had been right – Matt probably bought it for Phillipa in the first place. Within a week, one of Matt's men broke the rules to come over and fixed the television in the bungalow. He then toured the Wheelhouse with Phillipa as she planned a new bathroom and toilet, an extended dining kitchen, and the present dining room changed into a temporary bedroom until upstairs was ready for occupation. She was now the woman in charge.

Amazingly we got along fine without getting in each other's way. But the situation was unreal. I vacated the office in favour of working from a table in the tiny lounge, meantime Phillipa worked nonstop answering phone calls and dealing with a mountain of briefs operating exactly as she had done throughout lockdown. At night we sat apart observing a strict protocol watching some banal television series or else piecing together the parts of one of the jigsaw puzzles Phillipa had brought with her. I had never attempted a jigsaw puzzle in my life. It made me laugh – if Mick could see me, he would be in stitches. Killer Kelly alone with an attractive English rose, sitting putting a jigsaw puzzle together.

But neither of us were fools. We both knew there was an unspoken attraction lurking between us. And I waited, and Phillipa waited, for what we both knew must surely happen. There was no awkwardness. We took turns making trips to the supermarket and shared some rollicking disasters preparing meals in the cramped little kitchen. Twice a day we walked the dogs, and I maintained my daily run before the light disappeared. There was never a hint of romance, but circumstantial needs eventually won the day. In the middle of a programme neither of us wanted to watch Phillipa suddenly stood up.

'Roger, this is ridiculous. I don't like my camp bed and I'm taking a shower.'

By the time I turned off the TV and sorted out the dogs she was in my bed waiting for me. She was fresh and slim and lovely in my arms, and the sheer joy of sex after such a long abstinence was overpowering. Phillipa wasn't a virgin, but she had never experienced a climax. It took a few nights, but when we got there her response drove me on like a man demented. To hell with everything! Why should I be the one to worry about upsetting the apple cart?

A lot happened during the following months. Christmas was spent in an even stricter lockdown with only the dogs for company. I took a crash course over the internet to complete the architecture qualifications which I should have finished whilst studying at college, and all the while cooped up alone under virtual house arrest, we were blessed by some mystic force, even though most of it was sex. Phillipa was fun. We shared the same sense of humour, and our relationship remained happy and delightfully uncomplicated.

There were ground rules. Lovemaking with Phillipa was a predictable affair and it was taboo to stray from the chosen path. The first time I tried she nearly jumped out of her skin, and on the second occasion she shot straight out of bed and said, 'That is absolutely disgusting Roger.'

The rules were plain enough. A simple enjoyable relationship, minus vows or any commitments, and much as I liked Phillipa that was exactly the way I wanted things to stay.

Strangely enough Phillipa believed that when the Wheelhouse was finished, we could both move into the house and live together, still leading our own independent lives. For me that was a nonstarter. I couldn't imagine sharing space with George the Chinese kettle man, and I didn't think Phillipa would welcome Linda from the Yorkshire Post. And that wasn't accounting for Matt either. I think he was still persuading himself that his daughter and I lived together at the bungalow in some sort of brother and sister scenario.

As restrictions extended into March, we all got edgy. Relations with Matt degenerated into cool exchanges, and outside working hours Phillipa's social circle of friends increased their never-ending telephone calls, so that I spent more and more time with the dogs, and punching the punchbag, than I spent with Phillipa.

The lockdown ended without warning. In April, hotels, pubs, and restaurants were allowed to re-open, and at last the whole of the UK rejoiced in a moderate degree of freedom. We wasted no time shedding our shackles.

I took Phillipa and the dogs for a massive boozy pub lunch, and returned to base travelling at ten miles per hour after drinking more wine and beer than I care to remember. Following that I lost Phillipa completely. She blew a fuse. Business took second place, and she was away visiting her horsey friends, or acting as a tour guide joyfully showing them around the Wheelhouse one by one.

Matt came out of hiding to take a look at the house and made his views very plain. When he asked what we planned I could see where the conversation was leading.

'There's no reason why we can't stay the same,' said Phillipa. 'But I don't want to marry Roger and he doesn't want to marry me, so you will have to get used to that idea father.' Matt was Matt – he remained cool and didn't blink an eyelid.

'Please yourselves,' he said, 'that's none of my business. But make up your minds what you want to do, because you are not occupying the Wheelhouse and living together over the brush.'

I never did figure out what Matt expected of me. Although he sometimes treated me like a family member, he would have thrown a fit at the thoughts of me as his future son in law, and his wife would have had a heart attack too.

Peter opened the North Leeds offices with a skeleton staff and pointed out I was damned lucky that co-habiting with the boss's daughter had worked out so well.

I couldn't stomach any more office work. We paid for a few adverts in 'Farmers Weekly' and based on previous experience with the Ripon farmer I was directed to travel the North to test out whether there was a market for barn conversions. Wearing mud splashed boots and faded chinos I took Scott with me, and we spent more time tramping the fields in search of illusive farm owners than we spent trying to persuade them to venture into the bed and breakfast business. I didn't make a single sale, but it was wonderful to be roving free again, and sleeping nights in the camper van.

Arriving back from the Dales, I bumped into Matt, Peter, and Phillipa taking a studied stroll around the Wheelhouse.

'We are turning the house into flats,' said Matt. 'Phillipa will take the ground floor, then we will alter upstairs and divide it into three luxury flats to rent out.'

Phillipa flashed me a smile – I could see she had got from Matt exactly what she wanted.

'And the Gatehouse bungalow will revert back into just one office,' concluded Matt.

'That means you are going to have to find somewhere else to live.'

You could rely on Matt never to beat about the bush. Our trusted relationship and tête-à-tête discussions had faded into obscurity along with the tots of whisky, and any further alliances with his daughter. I was sorry. I liked Matt, but there was no doubting our changed circumstances. My trusted position had reverted to zero.

When they had gone, Phillipa took my arm. 'I think we will go back to being just good friends Roger.'

We understood each other perfectly and neither of us suffered regrets or hard feelings. Two days later Matt returned to transfer Phillipa and her belongings back to the family home until the Wheelhouse was ready for occupation, and I returned from my travels to find Scott lying outside brooding over the loss of his companion.

I gave it six months. Until Australia opened its borders there was no chance of getting to see Mick and until then I wasn't going anywhere. Meantime I needed temporary accommodation and my first thought was to check property advertisements with Linda who still worked for the Yorkshire Post.

We had kept in touch with silly text messages throughout the year, but I got a shock when I saw her. She was now part of the Headingley student scene, had turned 'punk' and had done everything she could possibly do to make herself look sexless. We met in the New Inn, and if I was looking for post pandemic entertainment then Linda fitted the bill – she kept me laughing all night while I tried to match her capacity for alcohol.

The pub was near her flat and with a head swimming from pints of cider, and Linda falling over her combat boots, we ended the evening in her freezing cold bedroom.

Space in the narrow bed was cramped and Linda's spiky haircut got up my nose. After a few pathetic attempts I failed to consummate our bedtime union and gave it up as a bad job. Linda didn't seem very worried. She passed out and snored like a trooper all night. Prompt at 7 a.m. Linda awoke in sparkling form, and she was so pleased at having eventually got me into bed that I wondered if she had been too inebriated to have the faintest recollection of what never happened.

I dropped her off at the Yorkshire Post and waited while she looked through back numbers of the paper's advertising section. Thanks to a reduced student population there were plenty of vacant properties to choose from and Linda pointed me in the direction of a couple of beauties. I left pondering why I hadn't snapped her up before she joined the beatnik set, and I became 'not cool enough' for her?

After a brief search round, I settled for an unfurnished red brick house in Lawnswood, with four roomy bedrooms and a sitting tenant. I took full charge of the rent, and was put in touch with another prospective tenant looking to share a house – a likeable bearded guy who worked for a charity group. The uncultivated garden suited Scott, and the leaky garage accommodated my punch bag and weights. I cleared the Gatehouse and stables and found that most of my possessions fitted perfectly into the empty bedrooms, with the exception of the bedroom belonging to my sitting tenant whose room overflowed with a motley collection of his own furniture. It was a good mix. Robin was studying accountancy and spent most evenings at his girlfriend's flat. Alan had ambitions to be a songwriter, and when he wasn't in his bedroom struggling to write his next lyric, he would sit in the lounge strumming his guitar, good for a lively song or a serious political debate over a pint of beer.

At work Peter had me in and out of the offices constantly switching jobs. I sketched a rough plan of the Wheelhouse apartments, and turned two new farm inquiries into contracts. Whenever we met in the canteen, Phillipa and I had coffee together and our relationship was as good as ever. She made an excuse that she wanted to visit my new house out of curiosity, and I reckoned George the kettle man was still missing out when Phillipa twice stayed with me overnight in the king-sized bed.

But there was no going back – things had changed. I was excluded from the urgent action surrounding Matt's model village, and when Simon informed me with a jubilant smirk that the sports complex was to be named the 'Ana Petrovic Health Centre' I got my first taste of company politics. A newly appointed manager arrived and took the whole project out of Peter's hands, while Simon as head of design was the man chosen to work alongside him. Somebody did me a favour. The new manager turned out to be an arrogant sod who knew it all, and Simon's jubilation was short lived.

Over a beer Peter assured me plenty of important work would be coming my way, but I remained side-lined from the village project until unexpectedly the new manager got the sack and I was thrown back in at the deep end.

I had lost interest. I was insulted to have been left out for so long, and many of my original ideas had been watered down. Matt could do what he liked with the whole project because I wouldn't be around to see it completed. But one good thing came out of my renewed involvement. I found that I was exchanging information with Ana in Rovinj, receiving and replying to her emails. Just knowing she was well and the exchange of news helped soothe a deep hurt and if I was soft enough to occasionally shed tears on my pillow nobody knew about it.

Months passed pleasantly but uneventfully. Gyms and night clubs remained closed, and masks were compulsory on public transport. The general population stayed cautious and there were staff shortages everywhere as the country edged back into a kind of constrained normality. I saw more of my parents, took a couple of trips to Manchester to see my aunt, and called upon Howard who had become a complete family man (much to Joan's delight) but to me he seemed like a lost friend.

Linda was running around in an old Ford Fiesta and called to see us regularly. She immediately took a shine to Alan, de-spiked her hair, and judging by the number of mornings she monopolised the bathroom their get together was proving a great success.

I was happy to let life take its course, and would have steered clear of trouble if Aunt Evelyn hadn't asked me to take her on a visit to our apartment in Nice.

My Aunt had had a rough ride during lockdown. Stuck in her house alone she had avoided Covid but suffered nearly every other complaint under the sun. Travel was still prone to disruption and airlines hadn't sorted themselves out yet. I thought it was a bad time to travel anywhere but Aunt Evelyn was very insistent – she was determined to visit Nice while the weather was good, seeing it as a cure for all her recent ills. I couldn't let her down.

I booked two tickets flying out of Manchester on a Thursday, returning midweek. The moment the tickets arrived I knew the trip was a mistake. Matt picked the beginning of the following week to hold a two-day conference based around progressing the sports centre, and after months of exclusion my input was suddenly regarded as essential. The meeting was an ego trip for Matt – two days of hot air, the first of its kind since pre-pandemic. Peter labelled the meeting a waste of time, nevertheless this was Matt's latest big obsession, a showpiece to launch the new village and sports centre, and God help anybody who didn't play their part.

Timing would be a gamble – but when isn't life worth a gamble? I would have a few days to fine tune everything outstanding providing I was back in the office by midweek, and having suffered Covid statistics, the politicians, and BBC news for over a year I was happy to get away from it all, if only for a five-day break.

I left Scott with my parents and sped down to Manchester with joy in my heart. Arriving at my aunt's house I was shocked to find her looking ghastly, and being injected for food poisoning after eating a seafood lunch with her friends.

It was the night before we were due to leave, and Aunt Evelyn was in no fit state to travel. The masked doctor grounded her for 48 hours, and when we left her house, she was dead to the world having been subscribed a couple of strong sleeping tablets. I was sorry. I thought a lot about my aunt, and in hindsight I should have postponed the trip. But to blazes with it. Five days at our apartment in Nice felt like winning the lottery all over again, and the chance was too good to miss.

Looking back is easy. When I boarded the aircraft, I experienced a strange feeling of excitement mixed with a warning sense of something pending. But even if I had heeded that warning it wouldn't have persuaded me to cancel the trip.

My allocated seat was on the same row as a man wearing a bright yellow zipper with the adjacent seat between us deliberately left vacant. Conversing through masks is an arduous task, particularly across an empty seat, but my fellow traveller was determined to talk. Even at the best of times, my knowledge of French makes conversation difficult. But while wearing a mask – I hadn't the vaguest clue as to what the man was talking about.

When the stewardess reached our seats with her hospitality tray, he insisted on buying me a drink, then turned singles into doubles before discovering he had mislaid his bank card. The man was charmingly apologetic when I settled the bill, but after that I took a complete dislike to the sly bugger and pretended to be asleep.

We disembarked together and suffered another hour of anti-covid delays. When we were through customs the man thanked me, and still wearing his mask suddenly threw both arms around me, gave me a parting hug, and disappeared.

I always split travel money into two pockets. On the airport bus I returned my passport and wallet to a zipped safety pocket in my jacket, then checked the other pocket for my note case. The pocket was unbuttoned and the notecase missing – taken, I suspect, when my little shit of a travelling companion gave me a hug. The bus was halfway to Nice. I had lost about 200 euros but what could I do about it? Reporting the theft to the police would be a long thankless task, and apart from a yellow anorak and a large nose sticking out above his mask, I had absolutely no idea what the thieving little bugger looked like.

It was a bad start and didn't get better. The apartment hadn't been cleaned for over a year. *Monsieur le directeur* said cleaners weren't available and the Liverpool lady had returned to Beatle country prior to Covid. I borrowed cleaning materials and set about sprucing the place up and when I took a break, I was disappointed to look across and see that my favourite café opposite was closed and boarded up. The buzzing atmosphere of the café was missing, as it was in other places too. Nice would never lose its charm, and there was plenty of outside café life, but mandatory social distancing and mask wearing dampened down the whole experience, and whilst the French were as captivating as ever the virus had definitely spoilt their tourist trade.

Restaurant la Baie d'Amalfi had packed up and gone out of business, and Acchiardo on Rue Droite had altered beyond all recognition. Spaced out dining replacing the fun and intimacy of shared tables, and every day pizzas and spaghetti replacing their signature *plat de jour*. And where was *Poulpe et seiche à la Niçoise*? Perhaps the octopus around Nice had caught the virus. I gave Restaurant Acchiardo a miss.

John and Jane had wisely chosen to continue business

from their villa outside Nice throughout the epidemic. They sounded pleased to hear from me, and as I walked down to meet them at the yacht club a flight of butterflies hit me in the stomach. Parked next to John's BMW was my white Alfa Romeo sporting a new number plate with the initials HCB. Helen was here.

Sat around a table on the club veranda any disappointment with my trip soon vanished. It was not a celebratory meeting – rather more of a subdued occasion, with a wealth of catch-up stories and news. Life for John and Jane in France had been much the same as life for Helen and Edward in England. Edward lost money on the stock exchange, and Helen's estate agency in Poole never got off the ground. But afternoon sunshine lit the facades of the white, pink, and yellow harbour buildings surrounding us, and yachts bobbed up and down on the water to the sounds of the sea. Totally and utterly enchanting. It would take more than a virus to ever alter this.

And Helen – just sitting looking at Helen was wonderful. She hadn't altered one bit. Still the same classy Helen, beautiful as ever wearing one of her summer dresses in soft muted colours, and still that same touch of vulnerability that attracted me to her the first time we danced together. Memories of making love gripped my imagination like a vice, and each time I caught her looking at me I knew she felt the same way.

Saturday afternoon and evening disappeared in a euphoria of drinks, dinner, and stories. We laughed a lot, and exaggerating the worst events of the past without dwelling too much on their outcome. I was asked about

445

Ana and skipped the detail saying she had family problems in Croatia. Jane eyed me dubiously, and John wasn't slow in noticing the way Helen and I looked at each other. Helen had just spent a week staying with them at their villa while she re-opened the Carrington-Brown house with a view to selling it as soon as the market recovered.

A tall American woman with her tiny husband joined us at the table for a short time. Listening to them talk I realized that apart from my spell of loneliness I had been lucky to lead a charmed life, rent free and tucked away in the grounds of the Wheelhouse while much of the world had been turned upside down. Sometimes when we enjoy a stroke of good fortune, we tend to ignore just how lucky we are.

Helen was leaving for England next morning and when our little gathering broke up at the end of the evening, I knew she would offer me a lift back to my apartment. We walked outside together, and Helen handed me the car keys.

'A chance to drive your Alfa Romeo again,' she said with a smile. I opened the door for her, and she stepped into the car.

'I had expected at least one email from you,' I said.

'Why?' she asked. 'You never contacted me.'

Helen was like a magnet. I parked behind the apartment and she walked inside with me. We stood facing each other and I started to unbutton her dress. She very rarely wore a bra and as I unclipped it her breasts seemed fuller than I remembered.

'I don't think I can call you young man any more,'

she said. It was a more confident Helen, a woman who was two years older. Her nipple grew hard against the palm of my hand and as our mouths met her hand dropped down to unzip me and gripped hold of my erection. We half stumbled into the bedroom and her tongue never left my mouth. Nothing had changed between us but this was a different Helen. Surer of herself and her love making much more uninhibited. Never once did I feel that I was in charge, and it was Helen who dictated the pace of our lovemaking and brought it to its climax. She held up her hand.

'Enough! My young man has matured since I last saw him, and he is going to make me a drink and tell me all about it before we make love again.' We talked until three in the morning. I think Helen heard most of my story without telling me very much of her own, but two years disappeared between us just as though it was only yesterday when we lay together ignoring the telephone calls.

When Helen was ready for sleep, she moved away to the other side of the bed and slept soundly. Next day she returned to the Carrington villa, then came back to me in the middle of the afternoon and stayed overnight. We made love several times and each time was better than the last. I hadn't felt like this since making love with Ana, but once again it was love on borrowed time – and do I ever learn by my mistakes?

Helen wasn't in a hurry to leave. We sat on the balcony leisurely eating fresh brioche and plum jam bought from the bakery round the corner. She noticed I was quiet.

'Roger, you look shocked. Did you believe our feelings would change?'

'I never thought about it, Helen. But I never thought I would meet you again.'

Helen sat looking at me deep in thought. Her eyes and brow were debating a question. She reached for her handbag and took out a wallet.

'I have something to show you Roger. Something I would like you to see.'

She carefully spread across the table a batch of coloured photographs showing a beautiful little girl who looked a lot like Helen. There were photographs of the girl with Helen, some of the little girl on her own, and some sitting on a swing with a smiling Edward supporting her.

'This is Helen junior. Her name is Lucette and she is almost two years old. But if you look closely at her you will find that there is a little bit of Roger in her. She is your daughter Roger.'

How do you feel when you suddenly discover you are a father? There was no mistaking it. Helen junior looked a lot like me and not the faintest bit like Edward. Hearing about fatherhood is one thing, but looking at photographs of your own flesh and blood awakens something entirely different – especially when the child is exquisite and perfect. I sat stupefied – too shocked to digest what Helen was showing me. Helen moved closer and held my hand.

'Does Edward believe that Lucette is his?' I asked.

'Edward was going to leave me when he found out I was pregnant. He knows you are the father. But his ego got the better of him. None of his friends would be any

448

the wiser, and when Lucette was born, he became so devoted to her that it no longer mattered.' We sat together in silence for a long time. She broke the silence and laughed.

'You remember that 'one last time' in the car before I drove away? That did it.'

'I remember,' I said. 'It felt like unfinished business. But if yesterday is a repeat performance, then you are likely to be the mother of triplets this time.'

We both relaxed and laughed. There was such a strong feeling between Helen and I from the very beginning. She stayed with me for the rest of the day. It was a strange day after the news she had given me, and when she left me, I knew I wouldn't stop thinking about her, and this was not going to be the end of our affair. I didn't feel good. I felt like a cheat although I wasn't sure who I was cheating. Then thinking again about the pictures of my beautiful daughter I realized – perhaps I was cheating myself.

When the airport taxi arrived on Tuesday, I was relieved to be going home. I picked up a brown envelope that someone had slid under the door and stuck it between the pages of GQ Magazine which I dropped down the side pocket of my cabin luggage, then ran down the apartment steps straight into the taxi. This was a visit tinged with regret, and for now I wanted to leave the memory behind.

Generally, I leave myself plenty of time when I travel, and even allowing for extended health checks I was early for the flight. I drank a coffee and watched a group of Manchester lads noisily enjoying themselves – masks or not. Nice Airport was quieter than usual but with an increased police presence. Most airport shops were closed, but the top-end retailers had done a terrific job of artfully dressing their windows in anticipation of resuming normal business once the airport became busier.

And then I spotted him looking in one of the windows. The little sod who relieved me of my note-case – no mistaking him, wearing the same yellow zip jacket and the same tee shirt underneath. I dropped my case on a spare chair next to the Manchester lads.

'Can you guys keep an eye on this case please? I want a word with that little shit who stole some money from me.'

'Go to it mate. If you need any help, give us a shout.'

My crooked little French friend turned around and saw me. He moved like lightening but bumped into a lady with a pram and I caught him by the back of his collar. I hauled him off his feet and shook him like a rat.

'Either I get my money back now, or I break your neck.'

A whistle blew and within seconds an airport gendarme was pointing a revolver at me. Three others joined him in quick succession and gripped both arms from behind and slipped on a pair of hand-cuffs. The little man pointed accusingly at a tear in his jacket, then said something to the police. I recognised one of the gendarmes at the same time as he recognised me. He had been on duty when the police first interviewed me two years ago during their hunt to locate Romano, and from there on I didn't stand a chance of explaining anything. Support from my Manchester friends didn't help me either. They laughed and cheered and banged their glasses on the table, and as I retrieved my case from them, they jeered at the gendarmes and made catcalls as I was led away.

What happened to the slimy French man I will never know. Apparently, he told the police I mistook him for someone else, so he wouldn't press charges. The police didn't believe my story (if they understood it) and I remained in police custody for two days until a senior officer could be found to interview me. I was fined for affray, and it was sods law that there wasn't enough money in my current account to pay the fine, and sods law that when the police finally allowed me to use my mobile, the battery was flat, and I had forgotten to pack my charger. A Hungarian born policewoman came to my rescue and recharged the phone overnight, but it was well into the weekend before I had negotiated some sense out of my Bank Manager and paid the fine. I exited Commissariat de Police with as much dignity as I could muster after spending three nights in their cell.

It was pretty obvious that my re-valued input in the office had been missed. Matt wouldn't accept calls to explain my absence. Peter texted back 'Sorry mate, nothing I can do – it's out of my hands'. Phillipa ignored my texts completely, and my return ticket was wasted since flights back were unavailable. I made the five-hour train journey to Paris where I got caught up in a twenty-four-hour strike before connecting with Eurostar after yet another long-protracted wait.

From leaving Nice it took me three full days before boarding a train from Euston to Piccadilly, by which time Matts big showcase meeting must have been well over and done with. It wasn't until Eurostar crossed into England that he left a voice message on my phone.

'When you get back don't bother coming into the office. At the end of the month, I am paying you three months' salary. I don't want to see you again at Mathews Investments. You and I are finished for good.'

If you were going to get fired it couldn't be made much plainer than that. One slip of judgement, one stroke of bad luck, and future options and all my hard work wiped out in a flash. The rest of the train journey provided me with plenty of time to think about it.

Time rolled back as I drifted in and out of consciousness. Rosemary, Ana, Nice. Sex lessons with Ellise, working with Romano, Covid, the consequences of my affair with Helen – all came to visit me. I didn't remember the brown envelope until I was well on my way to Manchester, and opened GQ Magazine to find it sandwiched between the pages, untouched, after the police had rummaged around in my case. Large hand-written print addressed the envelope to Roger Kelly, and when I slit open the envelope the two photographs which fell out made a complete mockery of all my naïve beliefs, and the trouble taken to defend them.

The first photograph showed a foreign newspaper – probably Argentinian, with a close up of the date which was ringed, and I interpreted it as 10th of June 2021.

The second photograph was of Antonio Romano and Monty, arms around each other's shoulders, standing in front of rows of grape vines illuminated by the glaring sun, with a smiling Monty holding the newspaper and pointing to the ringed date.

Romano was the Romano I first met. His hair had regrown perfectly, and he stood confident, sun tanned, and immaculate in one of his pale grey linen suits with his sparkling white smile proclaiming he was alive and well. And when I looked closely at Monty, he had never looked happier. Gone were the wig and false moustache. He was back to his old fighting weight and his shaven head had turned to a glowing golden brown like a second sun. I turned the photograph over.

Greetings Mr Kelly. Thankfully I am not dead. Will you please destroy both of these photographs.

How had they staged it? How had they been able to substitute another body for the supposed dead body of Romano? It didn't seem possible – and then I remembered the unrecognisable rat bitten face, the missing eyes, and the white gloves which covered the missing finger. If someone in the Naples police force had been paid to cooperate, then the body in the open coffin could have belonged to anyone.

Apart from the shock, I felt cheated. Swindled. Double crossed. When I received the news that Romano was dead it had killed everything. I was upset over Ana. The news of Anthonio's death had seemed like the end of the world, and I had made the risky trip to Naples only to make a blasted fool of myself.

But then with each half hour of the train journey I started to think again. My special friend Antonio Romano was still alive and so was my special pal Monty. Good luck to them both – they deserved it. Romano had fooled the crooks who wanted him dead, and fooled the police who would have planted blame on him. He was too clever for all of the bent buggers, and the dishonest consortiums who were so determined to nail him. And God, how I wished I was somewhere in the sunshine, working alongside him and Monty right now.

I started to laugh as I thought about it. A little boy on the opposite seat stood in the isle and gaped at me. His mother looked at me warily – then hastily pulled the boy safely onto her knee. Via Piccadilly I arrived at Manchester Airport having been away seven days longer than my planned five-day break. And let's face it – I had nothing to laugh about. The trip had been an unmitigated disaster. My employer had sacked me long before I was ready to move on. I carried a dangerous secret which I would have to live with for the rest of my life. And then to crown it all, I was a secret father – and who knows what long-term repercussions that might lead to.

Before collecting the Camper Van, I wandered into the airport bar and sat contemplating my homecoming over a double whisky. I wondered if there would ever a be a level path for me to walk on. Whenever life was going well, it turned out I had overlooked something. I had now acquired a police record, and whether it was wise or not to defend a woman from a maniac, or whether it was my fault when I arrived late to Matt's charity dinner sporting a black eye – none of these deeds are considered a recipe for success, especially three nights spent in a police cell. But if it happens to anybody, you can bet your life it happens to me. I was still Roger-the-bodger, after making all that effort trying hard to leave the old Roger behind.

The warmth of the whisky began to circulate, and I took another view. How often have we said, 'Life is a journey not a destination'? Who can know anything about life unless you make mistakes and learn to roll with the punches? If I hadn't met Ana, would I really understand how it felt to lose someone who I loved so intensely with all my heart? And if I had never worked for a man like Romano, how would I know what it was like to have to defend myself against a maniac like Juggernaut Jason – when all the chips were down, and stacked against me? And what would I have learned about anything if I had stayed in a deadbeat job, and was still married to Rosemary?

As I left the bar, I noticed the back of a pin striped figure which I thought I knew, sitting beside a buxom blonde in the adjoining restaurant. The same large head, the same jutting square jaw, the same cheesy complexion. It had to be Big Cyril – and I can't possibly tell you why, but at that moment I was absolutely delighted to see him.

He recognised me immediately and gave a big grin. He had replaced the two missing front teeth with two gold teeth which, alongside his designer suit, added to a new aura of prosperity.

'Don't let me interrupt your meal,' I said. 'I just came over to say hello.' He didn't get up but crushed my hand with his mighty paw and carried on grinning at me. Then he touched his nose and pointed a finger, 'You forgot to duck,' he said.

'Cyril,' I replied, 'that's the story of my life. I always

forget to duck.'

I collected the Camper Van from the airport car park, and set off back home. I had travelled full circle – I was back where I began three years ago. But what of it?

All of us have to start somewhere, and there are plenty who remain where they started. In the last three years I had lived the life of ten men, and nothing could beat that experience.

I switched on the radio. A nostalgic recording of some old swinger called Fred Astair was being played – 'Let's Face the Music and Dance.'

I hummed and tapped out the song over and over again all the way down the motorway.

Acknowledgements

A special mention to my cover designer - the talented Simon Cryer of Northbank Design (www.northbankdesign.co.uk), whose expert eye for colour and creative options made my choice of cover an easy task.

Also, thanks to Sara my editor, whose suggestions and focused scrutiny obviated frequent grammatical short comings.